North to the Baltic Sea

Also by Michael Oliver

North by Polaris

> It may be helpful for those unfamiliar with sailing ships during the Napoleonic War to visit https://apianus.wixsite.com/michaeloliverfiction where you will find some useful information.

North to the Baltic Sea

Book Two

The Michael North Series

Michael Oliver

Copyright © 2017 Michael Oliver

ISBN 978-1508970200

ISBN 1508970203

All rights reserved. No part of this publication may be reproduced or transmitted in any form or by any means, electronic or mechanical, including photocopying, recording, or any information storage system without permission in writing from the author.

The right of Michael Oliver to be identified as the author of this work has been asserted by him in accordance with the Copyright, Designs and Patents Act, 1983.

This is a work of fiction.

Edited by Catherine Hanley
www.catherinehanley.co.uk

Cover design by Good Wives and Warriors
www.goodwivesandwarriors.co.uk

*I dedicate this book to my wife, Sue.
She is truly wonderful.*

Chapter 1

<u>New Year's Day, 1802</u>

The four months between the beginning of negotiations and the signing of the Peace of Amiens were filled with ambiguity. Was Britain still at war with France or not? It transpired that this little non-war of 130 days was about to lead to a bigger non-peace of 420 days, though nobody knew that at the time, of course.

For the weather-battered jacks of the Royal Navy the winter of 1801 was simply a period of grinding labour, chilblains, coughs and colds, aching hernias and the usual monotonous mixture of drudgery, dismal food, sleeping in a hammock that was rarely dry and a precious few moments of the warmth of friendship and faint laughter.

For the 46-man crew of His Majesty's Cutter No. 3, the New Year had dawned half a mile off the coast of France watching a fishing smack tacking towards them. Cutter No. 3 was a strange hybrid of a galley and a very slim sailing ship. It was less than seven feet wide but almost 40 feet long and equipped with two masts and two banks of oars. Tom Johnstone the smuggler had designed it, based on the Deal cutter, to be able to sail swiftly but also to be rowed against the wind and therefore to escape the conventional sailing cutters of the Revenue.

The Admiralty had approved the construction of six of these little ships and, led by the frigate *Fisgard* of 38 guns, they were under the command of Captain Sir Michael North. *Fisgard* herself had been built in France and named *La Resistance*. She had been captured by *Nymphe* and *San Fiorenzo* in March, 1797, and her new name was a nod towards history: a few weeks earlier there had been a farcical attempt at invasion by the French near the town of Fisgard in Wales, and *La Resistance* had been captured attempting to reach home.

North watched through his glass from the quarterdeck of *Fisgard*, which was a mile further from the shore in deeper water, as the fishing smack touched the side of Cutter No. 3 and a figure jumped from the boat into the cutter.

The little fishing boat with her rust-red sail turned nimbly and, catching the gathering breeze, made her way back to the low lines of sand dunes of France.

Twenty minutes later the cutter, her crew rowing hard, came alongside *Fisgard* and the tall, lean Henry Gillespie, by profession gentleman and spy, climbed swiftly to the frigate's deck and removed his old-fashioned tricorne hat to the ensign.

North's flotilla had been charged with two duties. She was to augment the Revenue service by acting against smugglers and she was to support and assist the agents of William Wickham's clandestine Home Office department as well as the more irregular intelligencers under the leadership of Magistrate Patrick Colquhoun, Michael Bryan the art dealer and spy, and the Duke of Bridgwater.

Fisgard, followed by Cutter No. 3, turned towards Guernsey as

Chapter 1

<u>New Year's Day, 1802</u>

The four months between the beginning of negotiations and the signing of the Peace of Amiens were filled with ambiguity. Was Britain still at war with France or not? It transpired that this little non-war of 130 days was about to lead to a bigger non-peace of 420 days, though nobody knew that at the time, of course.

For the weather-battered jacks of the Royal Navy the winter of 1801 was simply a period of grinding labour, chilblains, coughs and colds, aching hernias and the usual monotonous mixture of drudgery, dismal food, sleeping in a hammock that was rarely dry and a precious few moments of the warmth of friendship and faint laughter.

For the 46-man crew of His Majesty's Cutter No. 3, the New Year had dawned half a mile off the coast of France watching a fishing smack tacking towards them. Cutter No. 3 was a strange hybrid of a galley and a very slim sailing ship. It was less than seven feet wide but almost 40 feet long and equipped with two masts and two banks of oars. Tom Johnstone the smuggler had designed it, based on the Deal cutter, to be able to sail swiftly but also to be rowed against the wind and therefore to escape the conventional sailing cutters of the Revenue.

The Admiralty had approved the construction of six of these little ships and, led by the frigate *Fisgard* of 38 guns, they were under the command of Captain Sir Michael North. *Fisgard* herself had been built in France and named *La Resistance*. She had been captured by *Nymphe* and *San Fiorenzo* in March, 1797, and her new name was a nod towards history: a few weeks earlier there had been a farcical attempt at invasion by the French near the town of Fisgard in Wales, and *La Resistance* had been captured attempting to reach home.

North watched through his glass from the quarterdeck of *Fisgard*, which was a mile further from the shore in deeper water, as the fishing smack touched the side of Cutter No. 3 and a figure jumped from the boat into the cutter.

The little fishing boat with her rust-red sail turned nimbly and, catching the gathering breeze, made her way back to the low lines of sand dunes of France.

Twenty minutes later the cutter, her crew rowing hard, came alongside *Fisgard* and the tall, lean Henry Gillespie, by profession gentleman and spy, climbed swiftly to the frigate's deck and removed his old-fashioned tricorne hat to the ensign.

North's flotilla had been charged with two duties. She was to augment the Revenue service by acting against smugglers and she was to support and assist the agents of William Wickham's clandestine Home Office department as well as the more irregular intelligencers under the leadership of Magistrate Patrick Colquhoun, Michael Bryan the art dealer and spy, and the Duke of Bridgwater.

Fisgard, followed by Cutter No. 3, turned towards Guernsey as

Gillespie made his way aft to the quarterdeck. He was about to follow North to the cabin when there was a hail from the mainmast tops. 'Deck there! Sail aft of the larboard beam!'

North turned and snapped open his glass. He called to Lieutenant James Lang to bring the ship about to face the newcomer. Gillespie clicked his tongue in annoyance. 'I fear I am the cause of this, Sir Michael. If I do not miss my guess that is the French privateer ship *Gaulois* of 44 guns. She was in the harbour at St Malo a few days ago. My hasty departure from France was because it seems I was recognised and betrayed by her captain, an Irish turncoat.'

North smiled. 'Well, it would appear that this is a testing moment, Harry. Are we at peace or at war? Until the Treaty is actually signed nobody is quite certain. I suppose I shall have to allow the gentleman the first shot if there is to be a duel! Mr Peach, signal to Cutter No. 3 to make her way back to Shoreham, she has no place here if there is to be a fight.'

The question was answered after a fashion as the two ships came closer. *Fisgard's* crew had been at action stations since the first rose-pink moments of the cold dawn, and it seemed that *Gaulois'* captain had also sent his men to the guns. Framed in the open gun ports, men of traditionally enemy nations stared silently at each other across 50 yards of grey-green water. The ships were now moving slowly on a parallel course. The ocean was almost as still as the expressions on those faces. The wind, a wide-eyed spectator, had dropped to a whisper. Which was the cat and which the mouse?

Not one hand on either ship moved a linstock to a touch-hole or took up the slack on the lanyard of a flintlock trigger. It was an agonising moment for many men on either ship. There had been nearly ten years of open warfare between the two countries before the Peace. It was a peace that few people believed in. Here in the open sea, well away from land, it seemed to many that any small difference between war and peace was irrelevant. In any case, the final defining moment of peace did not exist until a treaty was signed. War – provisional peace – peace – war? That same enmity that had France and England at each other's throats on and off for hundreds of years was almost bred into their bones.

The tense silence was broken by a hoarse Irish voice, amplified by a speaking trumpet, from *Gaulois*'s quarterdeck.

'Now would that be you, Michael Orrick North, you fecky Tan?'

North was staring at a short, broad-shouldered man on the other ship who was dressed in a green tailcoat and yellow breeches. He was well known to North from long ago. North had left Ireland behind at the age of thirteen and come to London with his elder brother and the rest of the family after the death of his father, a cash-poor landowning English baronet in County Clare.

His childhood had been as Irish as English but his Protestant background in a Catholic County Clare had limited his dealings with many of the local people. His memory of

Benedict Smythe was one of a hulking bully who had turned coward the moment North had finally snapped and split his nose with a sharp jab of his fist.

'Oh, it is you, then, Benedict Smythe, is it? I see you still dress like a colour-blind popinjay. You look like a fat little leprechaun in that rig. Here you are then, just where I would expect to see a treacherous blackguard like you. Well, what do you want? Come along, I haven't got all day!'

Smythe lowered the speaking trumpet and shouted, 'Heave to and stand by to be boarded, you fecking English gob-shite!'

'Now, now,' shouted North, 'just because you've turned your coat and become a French poodle it doesn't mean you need to ape their appalling manners, Benedict. If you haven't got anything useful to say I suggest you scuttle back to St Malo and hide in the harbour with the rest of the pirate scum.'

Several men were standing around Smythe, pulling at his coat and speaking urgently to him. It seemed the privateer's crew were at least reluctant if not completely against a sea-fight. Smythe was gesticulating and began to shout in at them in atrocious French.

'Cowards! Shit-faced weasels! Can you not see the blather-mouth is bluffing?'

He turned again to shout into the speaking trumpet, 'North, you no-good son of an English bastard! Hand over that dirty little spy and I'll let you go on your way!'

North grinned. Turning to his crew he called out, 'what do you think, lads, shall we hand over an Englishman to a stinking traitor who licks Boney's boots and wipes his arse?'

The chorus of obscene and detailed suggestions as to Smythe's ancestry, physical features and sex life from 270 British seamen left no doubt that his impertinence offended them.

In any case it seemed that the wiser of the French privateersmen would prevail. It was not their business to fight against odds that were of little difference. They may outgun the Royal Navy ship but they were only too aware that this was not an undermanned slovenly merchantman. In any case calling *Fisgard* a 38-gun ship was only due to classification. Apart from her twenty-eight 18-pounders and ten 9-pounders, she carried a further eight 32-pounder carronades and her crew were very good at using them. Technically there was a greater advantage of weight of shot to the French but that was of little comfort. The privateers were businessmen first and patriots second, and besides, the equivocal state of the so-called provisional peace or truce meant they could not rely on keeping the prize even if they could capture her.

Unfortunately the distance between the quarterdeck and the guns was not enough to lessen the impact of Smythe's shout of 'Fire!' and four of *Gaulois*'s 18-pounder guns thundered out before the rest of the gunners could stop their nervous comrades.

North staggered back as a ball slammed into the binnacle

sending fragments of the compass flying in all directions. Lieutenant Lang shouted, 'Hold your fire!', but it was too late. A perfectly timed and executed broadside from *Fisgard*'s larboard battery screamed across the intervening space and hammered the side of *Gaulois*'s hull. Every British gun was fired seconds after the gun next forward along the side – a rolling broadside that was less harmful than a simultaneous discharge which could have risked the ship's timbers.

In less than half a minute the weight of shot from *Fisgard*'s long-gun broadside inflicted serious damage and casualties but it was her four larboard 32-pounder stubby carronades which utterly destroyed the aft end of *Gaulois*'s quarterdeck and killed or maimed every man standing upon it.

Officers on both ships were screaming, 'Hold your fire! Hold your fire!'

North watched with no satisfaction as Benedict Smythe staggered to the side, his clothes soaked in scarlet blood. He raised the stump of his arm as if unaware that it was severed below the elbow and gushing his life-blood away. He pitched over the rail into the sea, sinking below the waves watched in silence by both crews.

North was conflicted. The privateer had fired the first shots. The two countries were technically still at war even if an unofficial armistice existed. He would be within his rights to take the privateer as a prize and argue the case later in the prize court. She was severely wounded and as he watched her

colours were struck.

His mind was made up by a shout from Midshipman Grey at the stern. 'Sir! There's a 74 approaching, about a league to the north. I'm not sure if she's British or French!'

North levelled his glass at the distant ship. She appeared to be in excellent condition, except for a large tan-coloured patch amounting to a quarter of the main foresail. There was a flick of crosswind which caused the flag on her mizzen to snap out and display the blue, white and red vertical bands for a second or two. He picked up his hat from the deck. 'Very well, Mr Lang, we will withdraw. Make all sail and set a course for home. I am going to speak to the surgeon; please bring me a report as to casualties and damage as soon as possible.'

Despite the proximity of the privateer's guns the damage was moderate and the casualties light. On the orlop deck half a dozen men needed more than just a few stitches and bandages. One man had lost so much blood he expired before Dr Levy could save him. Another would need to have his left leg amputated above the ankle and there were several with broken bones. In all three men died and eight were wounded. Any casualties were a cause for deep regret but in this period before an anticipated peace the unnecessary conflict was particularly unfortunate.

Fisgard's upper works were filled with men, clattering and heaving, fixing the damage and scrubbing away the stains and smoke of the pseudo-battle. Among them were John Grimes, a

sending fragments of the compass flying in all directions. Lieutenant Lang shouted, 'Hold your fire!', but it was too late. A perfectly timed and executed broadside from *Fisgard*'s larboard battery screamed across the intervening space and hammered the side of *Gaulois*'s hull. Every British gun was fired seconds after the gun next forward along the side – a rolling broadside that was less harmful than a simultaneous discharge which could have risked the ship's timbers.

In less than half a minute the weight of shot from *Fisgard*'s long-gun broadside inflicted serious damage and casualties but it was her four larboard 32-pounder stubby carronades which utterly destroyed the aft end of *Gaulois*'s quarterdeck and killed or maimed every man standing upon it.

Officers on both ships were screaming, 'Hold your fire! Hold your fire!'

North watched with no satisfaction as Benedict Smythe staggered to the side, his clothes soaked in scarlet blood. He raised the stump of his arm as if unaware that it was severed below the elbow and gushing his life-blood away. He pitched over the rail into the sea, sinking below the waves watched in silence by both crews.

North was conflicted. The privateer had fired the first shots. The two countries were technically still at war even if an unofficial armistice existed. He would be within his rights to take the privateer as a prize and argue the case later in the prize court. She was severely wounded and as he watched her

colours were struck.

His mind was made up by a shout from Midshipman Grey at the stern. 'Sir! There's a 74 approaching, about a league to the north. I'm not sure if she's British or French!'

North levelled his glass at the distant ship. She appeared to be in excellent condition, except for a large tan-coloured patch amounting to a quarter of the main foresail. There was a flick of crosswind which caused the flag on her mizzen to snap out and display the blue, white and red vertical bands for a second or two. He picked up his hat from the deck. 'Very well, Mr Lang, we will withdraw. Make all sail and set a course for home. I am going to speak to the surgeon; please bring me a report as to casualties and damage as soon as possible.'

Despite the proximity of the privateer's guns the damage was moderate and the casualties light. On the orlop deck half a dozen men needed more than just a few stitches and bandages. One man had lost so much blood he expired before Dr Levy could save him. Another would need to have his left leg amputated above the ankle and there were several with broken bones. In all three men died and eight were wounded. Any casualties were a cause for deep regret but in this period before an anticipated peace the unnecessary conflict was particularly unfortunate.

Fisgard's upper works were filled with men, clattering and heaving, fixing the damage and scrubbing away the stains and smoke of the pseudo-battle. Among them were John Grimes, a

sending fragments of the compass flying in all directions. Lieutenant Lang shouted, 'Hold your fire!', but it was too late. A perfectly timed and executed broadside from *Fisgard*'s larboard battery screamed across the intervening space and hammered the side of *Gaulois*'s hull. Every British gun was fired seconds after the gun next forward along the side – a rolling broadside that was less harmful than a simultaneous discharge which could have risked the ship's timbers.

In less than half a minute the weight of shot from *Fisgard*'s long-gun broadside inflicted serious damage and casualties but it was her four larboard 32-pounder stubby carronades which utterly destroyed the aft end of *Gaulois*'s quarterdeck and killed or maimed every man standing upon it.

Officers on both ships were screaming, 'Hold your fire! Hold your fire!'

North watched with no satisfaction as Benedict Smythe staggered to the side, his clothes soaked in scarlet blood. He raised the stump of his arm as if unaware that it was severed below the elbow and gushing his life-blood away. He pitched over the rail into the sea, sinking below the waves watched in silence by both crews.

North was conflicted. The privateer had fired the first shots. The two countries were technically still at war even if an unofficial armistice existed. He would be within his rights to take the privateer as a prize and argue the case later in the prize court. She was severely wounded and as he watched her

colours were struck.

His mind was made up by a shout from Midshipman Grey at the stern. 'Sir! There's a 74 approaching, about a league to the north. I'm not sure if she's British or French!'

North levelled his glass at the distant ship. She appeared to be in excellent condition, except for a large tan-coloured patch amounting to a quarter of the main foresail. There was a flick of crosswind which caused the flag on her mizzen to snap out and display the blue, white and red vertical bands for a second or two. He picked up his hat from the deck. 'Very well, Mr Lang, we will withdraw. Make all sail and set a course for home. I am going to speak to the surgeon; please bring me a report as to casualties and damage as soon as possible.'

Despite the proximity of the privateer's guns the damage was moderate and the casualties light. On the orlop deck half a dozen men needed more than just a few stitches and bandages. One man had lost so much blood he expired before Dr Levy could save him. Another would need to have his left leg amputated above the ankle and there were several with broken bones. In all three men died and eight were wounded. Any casualties were a cause for deep regret but in this period before an anticipated peace the unnecessary conflict was particularly unfortunate.

Fisgard's upper works were filled with men, clattering and heaving, fixing the damage and scrubbing away the stains and smoke of the pseudo-battle. Among them were John Grimes, a

newcomer to the ship, and William Talbot, an old hand who had sailed on North's ships since the winter of 1799.

Grimes, on his knees, paused for a moment as he scoured the bloodstained deck with brick-dust. He caught his breath. 'These blasted rheumatics is killing me. No prize money and poor old Ben'll have a peg leg as his re-ward. Tain't right, Billy.'

Talbot muttered, 'Stop your gab, Jack! Time'll come for prize money. Sir Michael has allus done right by us. I got sixty pound prize money saved up.'

'Sixty pound? I ain't even got a tester!'

Billy poked a finger into his waistcoat pocket and drew out a sixpenny piece. He tossed it to Jack. 'Here you is cully, you wanna a tester, have this one on me. Now shut yer moanin' and get scrubbing.'

....

As he prepared to write his journal entry, Michael North looked down at his hands. Was there a tremor in them? He knew and reluctantly accepted that people thought him a hero, but if only they knew! Every battle and every blast of the cannon had left its mark on his nerves. Was it heroism to have to screw up his courage every time he shouldered the responsibility of leading his crew into battle? Some captains filled themselves with alcohol to cope with the loneliness of command and the fear of death or perhaps worse the fear of being maimed. He knew that he could not use that resource.

He enjoyed his wine but knew his limitations.

On the one occasion he had been hopelessly drunk, many years ago, it had been pure luck and the loyalty of a common sailor that had averted disaster to his ship. Only that man knew that Midshipman North had fallen into a drunken sleep on watch and that the ship was almost lost in the turbulent seas off the Mull of Kintyre.

That experience had taught him never to drop his guard. But it was still hard to resist just one more glass.

He picked up his pen again and thought back to the day he had made his first inspection of his flotilla.

It had been a little over a month ago on 24th November and the complete though miniature flotilla was anchored off Shoreham. The schooner *Juniper*, which he had had with him from the time when she was tender to his last command, the 74-gun HMS *Prince Rupert*, was at one end of the line, at the head of six of the graceful galleys, though barely half of the necessary 270 men to crew them had arrived.

A draft of 50 sailors to man the cutters came from *Prince Rupert*. They had been the first to arrive followed by 80 volunteers who would have been discharged from *Thunderer* and *Victory*. There were 42 men from Nelson's *Medusa* who should arrive by the end of the day and the marines were settling down in the barracks huts in Shoreham harbour.

Only three of North's promised extra lieutenants to command

the cutter-galleys had arrived, including the only one North knew, Lieutenant the Honourable James Lang, late of *Prince Rupert.* North possessed sufficient prestige and influence to be able to gather as many of his followers around him as he could and James Lang was one he greatly valued. For the past seven years, from midshipman to lieutenant and lately 3rd lieutenant on a 74 captained by North, Lang had proved himself time and again in competence in the daily round as well as in the fire of battle.

Captain Gustavus Spicker, another stalwart friend and follower, had brought *Fisgard* to anchor offshore earlier that morning. North had stood on *Fisgard*'s quarterdeck beside Spicker watching as the ship glided along the line of anchored boats. The galleys had simple and clean lines. They were longer and narrower than the usual ship's cutters, being 40 feet in length but only six feet nine inches wide, giving them the appearance of greyhounds beside their more conventional cousins. Each was fitted with a single 24-pound carronade in the bows and eight swivel guns as well as being provided with a number of muskatoons. Carrying two 18-foot masts with lateen sails, each would be commanded by a lieutenant supported by a midshipman, master's mate and marine corporal. Each crew of 30 seamen would be supplemented by a dozen marines. North had arranged for the marines to be issued with Baker rifles rather than sea-issue muskets, having been impressed by what he had seen of the use of them made by French soldiers serving as marines on the various ships he had fought. North and Spicker had looked over the flotilla.

North said, 'Not exactly what we're used to, Gustavus, but fit for purpose. With the Peace coming we are fortunate in having employment and we must make the best of our mission. People seem to admire smugglers but smuggling is against the law and compliance with the law is what makes the difference between a civilised nation and barbarism.

'I am the first to declare that a liking for fine wine has sometimes made me passively complicit in the smuggling of the past few years but now with trade opening up again between this country and the Continent there is no need for illegal importation. On the other hand I admit I will be making the most of the Peace to fill a cellar with legitimately imported good French wine to span the period of the next war.'

Spicker grinned, 'speaking of which, Sir Michael, I have a fine white wine which was produced in Alsace from a grape called Pinot Blanc, very much like the Klevner of my own country. The locals called it the *blanc vrai* and I would value your opinion of it. It is legally imported, of course. It is chilled and waiting for us in the cabin.'

The two friends sat at the small oak desk and drank their wine. Spicker said, contemplatively, 'this smuggling business. You know there are some who believe that these men are heroes – fighting the system of government, providing some things that cannot be otherwise obtained and so forth.'

North replied, 'I believe Dr Samuel Johnson sums up the

official view, he called them wretched men who defy justice and the law when they bring goods into the country. Then again, the opposite opinion has been held by prominent men believing, perhaps, that it is unnatural to blame men who would otherwise be good merchants if the state did not impose such harsh taxes as to make evasion so attractive.'

Spicker nodded in agreement. 'In the recent conflict where open trade between France and this country has been denied, the view of some is that this is simply a way of sustaining an importation that might otherwise have continued open and above board, don't you think?'

North drank more of the excellent wine. 'If we were talking about a gentle group of benevolent traders perhaps I would not be so comfortable about hunting them down but in many cases these men are violent and without restraint. You may have heard of the Hawkhurst Gang?'

Spicker shook his head. 'Only vaguely. They were obviously based in Sussex?'

North went on to recount the story of the gang of smugglers that had thrived between 1730 and 1750. They had become so powerful and murderous that even the local people had turned against them. One of the triggers had been that they had buried a Customs Officer alive and thrown a witness down a well and buried him with stones. The people in that corner of Sussex along the Kent border formed a militia to oppose them and the affair culminated in 1747 when they did battle with the smugglers who were bent on destroying the nearby Kent village of Goudhurst. The last two ringleaders, Arthur Grey and Thomas Kingsmill, were caught a year or two later and executed, bringing to an end twenty years of mayhem.

Spicker said, 'In many cases the Revenue officers themselves are hardly examples of honesty and diligence though, are they? It doesn't help that the low pay only seems to attract older men who might not be able to find a berth on a warship.'

'True, but there are some excellent and honest men too, men who believe as I do that the smugglers give comfort and revenue to Bonaparte and his gang by buying the goods in France. On the other hand, unfortunately some of the cutters' captains are less than eager in confronting suspected ships way out at sea.

'However, Gustavus, it is my opinion that these miscreants will have quite a shock when tackled by naval men. Our jacks may shrug their shoulders at the trade and say it is none of their business but when they see the way the smugglers live, with their fine clothes and quality horses, they are less likely to sympathise.'

Spicker nodded. 'It is not only the trade from France and the French, is it; what about tobacco? I believe even the East India company ships regularly smuggle huge amounts of contraband into the country. There are many clever tricks, even working tobacco into hempen ropes!'

North reached over for a glass that Spicker had refilled. 'One of the most cunning ways of evading duty is to dry the leaf and pack it into tubs, for which purpose special drying rooms heated very high have been built in Jersey and Guernsey. It is reckoned that 40lbs weight of water can be expelled from 100lb of tobacco allowing the importer to pay duty on just 60lb. It is illegal of course but a tangled nightmare for the Revenue collectors.'

Chapter 2

In February Lieutenant Cornelius, in command of Cutter No. 4, had reported the flotilla's first clash with smugglers further along the coast to the west.

The smugglers had chosen the western part of the Solent between the Lymington and Beaulieu rivers – known as Thorns Beach – and had sunk forty barrels of brandy a few hundred yards from the coast tethered to rocks ready to be retrieved from the shore.

In the stygian darkness of night, four small boats were rowed out and the smuggler gang began to lift the barrels into their boats. Just as they were fully encumbered in this exercise Cutter No. 4 swooped in under muffled oars. At the same time the cutter's marines ran down on to the beach and held half a dozen people including two women at gunpoint. They had been loading the first of the barrels on to donkeys to carry the brandy away to nearby Park Farm.

Lieutenant Jan Cornelius, the son of a Dutch smuggler himself, had obtained the use of a paid informer of the Lymington customs house. Cornelius had the advantage of being married to the sister of one of the officers; the brother-in-law was being carried on the cutter as they ambushed the smugglers.

Under the threat of swivel guns the smugglers were forced to retrieve the remaining barrels and were then carried into

Lymington.

North had no sooner congratulated Cornelius than a more disturbing report arrived, carried by Lieutenant Black of Cutter No. 2.

Cutters No. 1 and No. 2 had been sent to patrol the French coast off Cherbourg. Cutter No. 3 was also in the area, having been despatched to lie off Barfleur ready to take off another of Colquhoun's agents who would be leaving France within the next 48 hours.

Cutters No. 1 and No. 2 were under sail in the area of sea between Alderney and the French coast when they saw a pair of luggers approaching from the south. There was a *de facto* peace between the two countries, therefore the British cutters' declared intention was to stop and board the luggers to search for contraband regardless of nationality. At first it seemed that the captains of the luggers would give no trouble as they were hailed and heaved to.

Lieutenant Lang, having taken temporary command of Cutter No. 1, had come alongside Lieutenant Black's cutter and as senior officer told him to remain in a covering position while he took four seamen and six marines in the cutter's gig over to the luggers to rummage.

The larger of the two ships was named *Angela of Sark*. No sooner was the boarding party on board than shots rang out; the cutters prepared to fire on the luggers. A white flag was swiftly run up on the *Angela* and the cutter's gig set off back to the cutter under another white flag.

In the stern-sheets of the gig was a squat, shabbily dressed man wearing enormous thigh boots and sporting a long drooping moustache. The boat stood away from the cutter and the man shouted across to Lieutenant Black. 'We've got your Lieutenant Lang and if you don't give us clear passage we'll hang him from the mast, now what have you got to say to that, mister?'

Black was furious. 'What I have to say to you, sir, is that now I have you under my guns and unless Mr Lang is released unharmed with his party, I will shoot you dead this instant!'

'Will you now? Will you now? Well look here, what is better? You allow us to go on our way and we will set Mr Lang and his men down on one of the islands in the Havre de Flicmare. They will be unharmed as long as you are not in sight when we do it. If that doesn't please you, then shoot me and have the blood of your mate on your hands. Come on now, what is it to be?'

Black looked him directly in the eye. 'I agree with your terms with one exception, but remember this: each night you will wake from your sleep knowing that I will never stop until you are hanging on a gibbet at Execution Dock.'

The man smirked. 'And what is your exception?'

'The other lugger, the *Marigold*, remains here under the guns of Mr Lang's cutter. When I have retrieved the hostages I will

Lymington.

North had no sooner congratulated Cornelius than a more disturbing report arrived, carried by Lieutenant Black of Cutter No. 2.

Cutters No. 1 and No. 2 had been sent to patrol the French coast off Cherbourg. Cutter No. 3 was also in the area, having been despatched to lie off Barfleur ready to take off another of Colquhoun's agents who would be leaving France within the next 48 hours.

Cutters No. 1 and No. 2 were under sail in the area of sea between Alderney and the French coast when they saw a pair of luggers approaching from the south. There was a *de facto* peace between the two countries, therefore the British cutters' declared intention was to stop and board the luggers to search for contraband regardless of nationality. At first it seemed that the captains of the luggers would give no trouble as they were hailed and heaved to.

Lieutenant Lang, having taken temporary command of Cutter No. 1, had come alongside Lieutenant Black's cutter and as senior officer told him to remain in a covering position while he took four seamen and six marines in the cutter's gig over to the luggers to rummage.

The larger of the two ships was named *Angela of Sark*. No sooner was the boarding party on board than shots rang out; the cutters prepared to fire on the luggers. A white flag was swiftly run up on the *Angela* and the cutter's gig set off back to the cutter under another white flag.

In the stern-sheets of the gig was a squat, shabbily dressed man wearing enormous thigh boots and sporting a long drooping moustache. The boat stood away from the cutter and the man shouted across to Lieutenant Black. 'We've got your Lieutenant Lang and if you don't give us clear passage we'll hang him from the mast, now what have you got to say to that, mister?'

Black was furious. 'What I have to say to you, sir, is that now I have you under my guns and unless Mr Lang is released unharmed with his party, I will shoot you dead this instant!'

'Will you now? Will you now? Well look here, what is better? You allow us to go on our way and we will set Mr Lang and his men down on one of the islands in the Havre de Flicmare. They will be unharmed as long as you are not in sight when we do it. If that doesn't please you, then shoot me and have the blood of your mate on your hands. Come on now, what is it to be?'

Black looked him directly in the eye. 'I agree with your terms with one exception, but remember this: each night you will wake from your sleep knowing that I will never stop until you are hanging on a gibbet at Execution Dock.'

The man smirked. 'And what is your exception?'

'The other lugger, the *Marigold*, remains here under the guns of Mr Lang's cutter. When I have retrieved the hostages I will return here and the *Marigold* will be allowed to go on its way, you have my word.'

The man paused; this wasn't quite what he had planned. 'Your word as an officer and a gentleman?'

'You have my word!'

'Very well then but cross me in this and you'll regret it.'

'Oh no, mister, the regrets will be yours. You may have won this round but the fury of the entire Royal Navy will be set upon you by this dastardly act. Now get out of my sight. You have thirty minutes.'

Once the *Angela* had reached the horizon to the north, Black had his cutter brought alongside the *Marigold.* There were nine men on board, six having been taken off by the *Angela* before she left. They all raised empty hands in surrender.

'Who is in charge here?' asked Black.

After a few moments hesitation a stocky, fair-haired man shuffled forward and knuckled his forehead. 'That's me, sir, Pascoe, I be the mate.'

'I intend to search this ship, Pascoe. Now, you can either tell me what you are hiding or stand aside. If I find contraband without your help I will certainly take you off with me before I release the lugger. If, on the other hand, you co-operate I might feel differently.'

Pascoe shrugged his shoulders, 'Captain Rees left us here to face the music while he and his sons went off with Captain Potter, so what do I care about his profits. Follow me.'

The hull of the ship was a treasure trove of illicit cargo. Hidden in barrels of flour were cotton bags of tobacco. More tobacco had been stuffed into hollowed-out hiding places in the half dozen spars lying on the deck. Lifting the decking up exposed three coffin-like boxes each containing 180lb of tobacco. But the more interesting find was not revealed by Pascoe. It was hidden behind a false partition at the stern. Three young black women were tightly packed into a space three feet high, less than six feet across and eighteen inches wide. One of them was unconscious and the others clearly dehydrated and sick. Vomit and excreta covered their legs and the floor of the tiny chamber.

They were lifted out and carried to the deck of the cutter where they were washed and wrapped in blankets. They revived a little after being given water and Black ordered one of the men to make up some gruel in the galley space below.

He turned to Pascoe, fury in his dark blue eyes. 'Slaves! My God, I should have you cast into the sea with a round-shot chained about your ankles, you devil!' The sailors and marines around him were equally incensed.

Slave ownership might not be illegal but it was certainly repugnant to many of the population. Slave trafficking was not against the law either, so why hide them in a secret compartment? There was a mystery here.

The cutter's marines and sailors were all volunteers, though not kept in the most salubrious of environments. But even with their poor pay and living conditions they could feel disgust for the way the women had been treated. There were several black sailors amongst the cutters' crews, some of them had 'run' from plantations on the American mainland; one had swum out to *Prince Rupert* earlier in the year from the coast of Brazil to gain his freedom.

There were also some like Reuben Hibbert who had been made free men and had chosen to volunteer for the navy. Whether runaway slaves or freed, all of these men had become part of an undiscriminating crew. With their own Spartan existence it was not surprising that sailors probably had more real understanding of slaves and ex-slaves than those living on land.

Black asked Pascoe, 'If these people and these goods were so well hidden that your captain felt he could leave you behind without you being arrested, why did he and Palmer resist when we wanted to search your ships?'

Pascoe replied, 'There's much more goods on the *Angela*, sir, and not well hidden. Sixty barrels of brandy and half a ton of tobacco. Palmer and Rees invested all their money in these cargoes and if they was seized they would even lose their boats if not their lives.'

'Are they carrying slaves on *Angela*?'

Pascoe shook his head. 'No sir, the women on this boat were

being taken to a man in Sussex, I don't know his name. They've been paid for and the man what bought them came on board in Bordeaux to make sure they was well hidden. I think he's some sort of servant for one of the gentry and he don't want it known that they're being brought into the country.'

'Where were you supposed to land your cargo?'

Pascoe said nothing.

'Come on, man! You'll be lucky if you get transported to the other side of the world for life. If you want less then you need to co-operate.'

'But Rees said we would be let go, you gave your word.'

'I said I would let the ship go, I said nothing about the cargo and crew. Now, where were you headed?'

Pascoe's shoulders slumped; he knew that he had to protect his own skin.

'Rees and Potter live in France, they think they're safer there but their partners – Rees's brother and another man called Ibsen, have a business in Bridport. We run the cargoes into Eype-mouth or East Ebb Cove, west of the town. Ibsen has a hideout in a farmhouse the other side of the hill behind Thornecombe Beacon called Doghouse Farm.'

Pascoe was taken off with the slaves before Cutter No. 2 went to the bay to the north of Barfleur where they picked up

Lieutenant Lang and his men. One of the marines had been killed on the *Angela of Sark*, and two others wounded – another charge against the smugglers. On their return to Cutter No. 1, the *Marigold* was released and sent on her way, minus her mate and her cargo.

After Black had reported, North asked, 'Where is Mr Lang now, Frederick?'

'He took the other cutter to the coast near Bridport hoping to intercept the smugglers again, sir.'

North immediately gave orders for *Fisgard* and Cutter No. 6 to get under way with Cutter No. 2 and went on board the frigate to take command. He had the slave women transferred to *Fisgard's* sickbay and asked one of his Barbadian seamen to find out what he could from them. It transpired they had been landed in Marseilles from a Guinea slaver by a French trader and brought to Bordeaux overland.

Chapter 3

James Lang was as angry with himself as he was for the fact that he had been kidnapped by the smugglers. He had not given in without a fight in which three of his men had been wounded and two of the smugglers killed. Ten against forty, he had stood little chance; beaten to the deck and pinioned he had watched impotently as the *Angela of Sark* moved away from his cutters and an hour later into the Havre de Flicmare. He and his men were hustled from the ship on to a barren, muddy islet two miles off the coast. Marine Private Dick Jarrold, one of the wounded men, was in a bad way. His breathing was laboured and as Lang put his head to the man's chest he could tell that his lungs were filling with blood. There was pink foam on his lips and he struggled to speak.

'My ... wife ... my little boys ... sir. What will ... happen to them?'

'I swear to you Jarrold, I will make sure they are taken to my father's estate, housed and fed for as long as they need.'

Jarrold forced a smile. 'Don't worry ... about me ... sir ...' He never finished what he was saying. Lang gently reached down to cover his head with his coat. The men with him watched as he got to his feet and waved a fist as the distant smuggler as she neared the horizon. He did not raise his voice but his words were clear to all. 'I swear I will never rest until this infamy is punished!'

Lieutenant Black arrived with his cutter a little later and as soon as he was back on board his own boat Lang ordered Black to return to Shoreham to report. To his own crew he appeared a man possessed. Shouting at them to strain every muscle and nerve he set off towards the English coast. While feigning unconsciousness on the *Angela* he had heard clearly that Bridport was the smugglers' destination and Black's information had confirmed it.

....

It took less than three hours for *Fisgard* to reach Bridport but there was no sign of either lugger. Cutter No. 1 made her number as *Fisgard* approached from the east. Lieutenant Lang came on board the frigate looking furious and determined. He was only suffering a black eye and wounded pride but the death of Marine Jarrold had appalled him.

North handed him a cup of tea. 'Well, James, a bit of a mess but not your fault. I am as determined as you are that Jarrold will be avenged and to that end we will leave no stone unturned. What have you to report since you arrived?'

'I believe I missed the luggers by less than half an hour, sir. They could not have even had time to unload the *Angela of Sark's* cargo. My guess is that they landed somebody to warn their associates and then sheared off. When I was on the lugger I pretended to be unconscious and learned that the smugglers' headquarters is a farm west of the town called Doghouse Farm, off the hill of the same name.

'As soon as I got here I immediately sent Sergeant Jobbings

and nine marines who are fit enough to move quickly, with my bosun and six men on to the shore. I gave them instructions to move inland to Doghouse Farm and surround it, covertly. When you arrived I was about to go into Bridport and if they are there, arrest the smugglers' partners.'

North said, 'Very well, James, take your cutter and Black's and do that. Give my compliments to the customs house and they are to assist you to search the premises of Ibsen and Rees's brother in the town. I want two Revenue officers to join me at the foot of Doghouse Hill within the hour.'

The farmhouse was situated on elevated land about a quarter of a mile inland from Doghouse Hill along a muddy track. The owner had planted a horseshoe-shaped copse of pine trees around the back of the farmhouse, imitating that other smuggler Isaac Gulliver – now reformed – in providing a landmark for his ships. North had taken with him Lieutenant Compton of the marines with 20 of his men. Leaving them to set up a roadblock and await the arrival of the Revenue officers, North walked along the farm-track with his coxswain, Cluney Ryan, and three men following.

Sergeant Jobbings and Gregory, the cutter's bosun, met him about halfway along the path. Fifteen minutes ago a man riding a heavy farm horse had come along the track in a hurry and entered the house. There was smoke coming from the chimney of the farmhouse but no other sign of life.

'Sergeant, wait here. Mr Compton will bring the Revenue

officers along the track. When they join you bring them to the farmhouse. Ryan, gather up half of the marines from around the house. We will go in there in five minutes.'

Ryan and five marines met North in the cobbled yard at the side of the house which bore no windows. With a wave of his arm they moved forward, Ryan and Seaman John Grimes producing pistols as North drew his. North hammered on the door and called for the occupants to open it. The response was a loud explosion and the thud of a pistol ball as it splintered its way through the door but harmed nobody – a pointless gesture. There was a shouted argument between several men inside.

North signalled to the marines who came forward and started to batter the door with their rifle butts.

A voice bawled, 'All right, all right, we surrender. Let me open the door!'

As soon as the door was open a crack the marines thrust it forward and charged into the room. Two men were standing with hands raised and another was lying on the floor having been thrown there by the opening door. A fourth man was partially hidden as he stood on a staircase, pistol in hand. As North entered he fired the pistol. There was a gasp beside North and one of the marines fell, clutching his chest. Half a dozen muskets roared almost as one as the marines fired at the man on the stairs. He fell forward, his hands pressed to his stomach, and tumbled down the steps to fall on his side on the floor.

'Stand fast!' shouted North. He bent to the wounded marine. He was pale and his tunic bloody but he gasped, 'I'm all right, sir.'

'No, you are not all right, Grimes. Ryan, get him on to that settle and take care of him. Corporal, take one man upstairs and make sure nobody is there. Private Richards, you take another man and search the rest of the rooms and the cellar. At this point I am only interested in making sure there is nobody else loose in the house.'

He walked over to the three men who were now quaking in the midst of the threat of muskets.

North looked at one of the men. He was the only one wearing a coat and his knees and thighs were smothered in grey horse hairs. It did not need the fresh mud on his boots for North to be able to identify him as the man who had recently arrived.

'You, man! You have just come from Bridport – who sent you?'

The man was sullen but obviously nervous.

'Come on, speak up or I will have you seized up and flogged!'

Shaking with fear, the man gasped out, 'Mr Frank Ibsen, sir, my employer – I work as a clerk in his counting house.'

'Whose house is this?'

'Mr Ibsen's, sir.'

'What message did you bring?' The man handed him a folded piece of paper which was addressed to John Rees. The message was that Potter and Rees were returning to France without unloading the *Angela of Sark* having encountered Revenue cutters and lost *Marigold's* cargo and her mate. It was possible that the Revenue or the navy would be here within the hour. They must conceal any suspicious items and if questioned insist on their own innocence.

North folded the letter and thrust it into his tailcoat pocket. It would add to the evidence against Ibsen.

The man lying at the foot of the stairs was John Rees. There was a sharp intake of breath from one of the men as North walked over to the body and turned it over with his foot. Rees groaned out a death rattle and his eyes, which had been staring at the ceiling, closed slowly.

North turned to the messenger. 'You know this house – show me the hidden places and I will try to have your life spared.'

The man was trembling badly as he led them around the house though much of the contraband silk, tea and spirits they found was openly stacked in the cellars. There was a hidden brick-lined passageway from the rear of the cellar which ran two hundred yards underground north to a cow-barn which ostensibly belonged to the neighbouring Ebbsview Farm. Two dozen barrels of brandy were hidden under hay-bales there. Naturally the farmer denied all knowledge and there was no direct evidence against him. Nevertheless, convinced that he was involved, North was tempted to circulate that he had 'co-operated' with the Revenue in exchange for immunity.

Leaving the two Revenue officers with half a dozen marines and four seamen to help them carry away the contraband and prisoners on two farm-carts North rejoined the *Fisgard* and took her into Bridport harbour. There was an angry crowd of around 250 citizens in the streets being held back by about 80 seamen and marines of the two cutters.

At the sight of a naval captain the crowd surged forward angrily. North raised his hand above his head and in a voice used to being heard above the strongest gale shouted, 'Stand still or be shot!' This brought some calm but clearly the mob was on the verge of violence.

North, conscious that people in the coastal towns were frequently resentful to the point of open aggression when it came to smuggling, had a solution always in reserve for moments like this. He drew a square of parchment from his tailcoat pocket and, standing on a nearby mounting block, began to read.

> *Our Sovereign Lord the King chargeth and commandeth all persons, being assembled, immediately to disperse themselves, and peaceably to depart to their habitations, or to their lawful business, upon the pains contained in the act made in the first year of King George, for preventing*

tumults and riotous assemblies. God save the King!

The crowd was suddenly silent. The Proclamation of Riotous Assembly in accordance with the Riot Act had been read out to them. A lone voice from the crowd called out, 'Let me pass!' A rotund man, red-faced with anger, pushed his way to the front of the crowd. He pointed at North.

'You, sir! How dare you, sir! I am Magistrate Lauder; you have no power to read the Riot Act!'

North replied, 'I am Captain Sir Michael North, and I am the Member of Parliament for the Borough of Steyning. As a Member of Parliament I am *ex officio* a justice of the peace. Now you, sir, will come forward and advise your fellow citizens as to their conduct. If this is typical of your town, then those charged with its administration are a damned disgrace, sir!'

Lauder was lost for words for a moment but then came forward and held up his hands to the crowd. 'Go home, all of you, and stay there. The law must be obeyed.'

The crowd shuffled their feet, still reluctant to leave.

North drew his sword and raised his voice. 'Mr Lauder, the law requires me to wait for one hour before firing on the crowd but my men are angered by the actions of some of your citizens on certain smuggling ships and I may find it difficult to control them, is that clear!'

He had said this loudly enough for feet to start moving away from the harbour square far more quickly than they arrived. The inhabitants had also passed amongst them the news that the frigate in the offing had just run out its guns and that the guns were pointing directly at the town.

'Now, Mr Lauder, you will wait here while I speak to my lieutenant.' He beckoned to a marine corporal to stand next to Lauder with his rifle at the ready.

James Lang reported that they had gone to Ibsen's offices and warehouse on the far side of the square where Ibsen was hurriedly emptying the contents of a strongbox into two large chests which were about to be loaded on to a carriage waiting at the side of the building. He arrested Ibsen and two other men who appeared to be clerks. As he started to search the building he became aware of angry voices outside the building and realised a mob was forming. He decided to move the prisoners to Nicholas Bowles's shipyard for safety while leaving a corporal and six marines to keep the building secure.

In the event they had not reached the shipyard. Ibsen was now being held inside the Salt House while Lang threw up a cordon to keep the crowd back.

After ordering Lang to transfer the prisoners to the *Fisgard* North turned to Lauder.

'Now, sir. There is a den of smugglers in this town that I intend to root out. At this moment I am unsure of the flag you sail under but it would be as well for you to make up your mind whether you intend to support His Majesty's laws. You will join me in extirpating this scandalous trade being carried on under your nose or join Mr Ibsen in irons on my ship. Is anything I have said just now making sense to you?'

Lauder swallowed, 'Sir, I am a magistrate bound to uphold and enforce the law but my resources are limited.' He paused as if mentally changing a course he had followed for many years. 'I and my office are at your disposal, sir.'

'I am pleased to hear it. I would venture to say that your future health and longevity depend upon it. Can I be clearer?'

Thoroughly terrified and brought to heel, Lauder, murmured something.

'Speak up man!'

'I understand completely, Sir Michael.'

'Good. Now, you will return to your office with my lieutenant of marines and prepare delivery notices to the Dorchester Assize for three men who were found with contraband in Ibsen's farmhouse. I will have word sent when I need you next.'

He turned away and spoke to Captain Spicker, who had landed with more marines from *Fisgard*. 'Gustavus, take charge here. Mr Lang will apprise you of all the information you need. I am sending all your marines on shore with the master-at-arms and twenty seamen. You will cause a thorough search to be made of the town and arrest any persons found in possession of contraband goods. It is a matter for you to assess whether there is sufficient evidence for each arrest but I intend this to be a hard lesson for these people. I do not want to see minor players dangling from a rope but the more atrocious perpetrators must be sent to the Assize. All goods seized will be carefully listed and stored in the Revenue House under guard. There will be no repetition of the scandalous behaviour of those in this town that broke in some years ago and stole back their smuggled goods.'

Chapter 4

James Lang came on board *Fisgard* with his report. Bridport was in turmoil. More than 150 armed seamen and marines were breaking down doors, throwing the inhabitants on to the street to be held under menacing muskets as their houses were scoured for contraband. The searches had been progressing for less than two hours but already four men and a woman were chained to the railings in front of the customs house and awaiting transport to the cells at Winchester. The town seemed to have so much illicit wine, spirits and tobacco squirreled away that there were scarcely enough carts and wagons to haul it away.

Lang sat with tea in hand, listening to his captain.

Their backgrounds were dissimilar in many respects – North that of an impoverished Protestant Irish baronet, Lang the son of a lord whose line stretched back to the Conquest – but as mentor and follower the two men were as close as elder and younger brother.

Lang had the privilege of Eton and had he not left there at the age of sixteen to join the navy, would no doubt have entered Oxford and the same college where his father had studied. Lang had been carried on the books of Collingwood's ships since the age of 12, but he had never set foot on a ship until the day when, dressed in his best clothes with a trunk full of cambric and linen, he had taken that first step of destiny. Early promise then blossomed into an outstanding ability.

North had also joined his first ship at 16 but for two years previously had finished his education at the Naval Academy at Portsmouth and, thus qualified when he was 20, took his examination for lieutenant and was promoted almost immediately. As a child he had briefly attended the Royal School at Dungannon but his main childhood education had been in the hands of his father's impoverished cousin. That worthy had taken to the life of a professional tutor after many years as an academic in Trinity College, Dublin. It was doubtful that a more complete and wide-ranging education could have been visited on the young North in the hallowed halls of Eton College.

Lang was conscious that North had helped him become the competent young lieutenant that he was and his loyalty to his captain was second to none. He had also been pleasantly surprised at North's erudition during evenings spent discussing the classics and literature. The greatest gift Dungannon College had given to North was its focus on literature.

North broke into his thoughts. 'A day that began badly seems to have ended satisfactorily, James. I shall return with *Fisgard* to Shoreham leaving the marines with you and the three cutters and crews. You will have temporary command. Continue the good work.'

The mystery of the three slave girls was still unsolved. North had Ibsen brought up from the hold. He stood in shackles in front of the desk in the cabin.

'Mr Ibsen, let me just remind you of the trouble you are in. Your farmhouse was found to contain contraband silk, tobacco and brandy worth more than £2,000 and other things besides. In your warehouse we found a hidden cellar with enough wine and spirits to drown the entire population of Bridport. If it had been customed there would have been no need to conceal it so secretly. The 700 bottles of Hollander gin are in stone bottles imprinted with the names of the producers and could only have been conveyed here from the Low Countries. On that scale it would be difficult to see how you can avoid having your neck stretched.'

To North it seemed ironically fitting that the hangman's rope was nicknamed a Bridport Dagger.

Ibsen was clearly shaken by his arrest. He had taken great pains to make sure that the local dignitaries were as deeply involved, terrified of his thugs or as well bribed as he could make them. North watched him carefully, assessing him. As Ibsen swayed against the movement of the ship he still appeared arrogant

Ibsen knew that getting out of this mess was going to cost him a small fortune; he needed to find out how much it would take.

First he tried to point out to his captor what to him seemed obvious. 'You will never get me convicted, Captain. The

Assize is lukewarm towards fighting the trade and besides I can find others prepared to swear that I knew nothing of these things. As gentlemen I am sure we can settle this matter in some way?'

North said, 'what makes you think I am going to allow you to be tried in Dorchester? You are on your way to London. Conspiracy to Murder is triable at the Old Bailey and I can assure you the smuggling offences will only add weight to the evidence.'

'*Conspiracy? Murder?* What the hell do you mean?'

'A conspiracy is defined as two or more people entering into an agreement to commit an unlawful act – ample evidence being found to relate that to smuggling. Far worse, your associates on the *Angela of Sark* have murdered one of my men.'

'But I knew nothing of this.'

'You and your friends set out to play a dangerous game. Any reasonable man can see that if you contemplate a venture of this kind the likelihood of violence is very high. If such violence results in murder all those who have been part of the venture are equally guilty. The law is simple: *Qui facit per alium facit per se* – who does something through another, does it himself.'

Ibsen glared at him. 'Look, this is a farce. I am a gentleman and well connected. My cousin is John St Barbe, one of the

Elder Brethren of Trinity House and a prominent ship-owner. My brother-in-law is married to the daughter of an earl. You cannot treat me like some common criminal. I have influence and money. You may be a knight of the realm and a functionary of the Admiralty but you are surely not averse to some reasonable compromise? What say we settle this like worldly-wise men? Say a significant contribution to a charity of your choice – in cash of course?

'What shall we say, £1,000? No, why be mean, I am sure you have a good cause that could use £3,000? The smuggling offends nobody except prigs and the Treasury and as to the marine, I am truly sorry. Perhaps I could make a contribution to the poor man's relatives to ease their changed circumstances? My gratitude for settling this matter here and now would be considerable, what say you?'

North stepped around the desk and looked down on the shorter man with contempt. 'You damn yourself with your own words; I did not say it was a marine who had been killed. What I say, you miserable worm, is that you stand endangered of adding an attempt to bribe a king's officer to your indictment. The type of people you associate with might be as venal and immoral as you are but you have a lot to learn about those who are charged with putting a stop to your nefarious activities. In any case I am well acquainted with Mr St Barbe, who is one of the most honest and honourable men I know. If I was you I would not look to him for support.'

Ibsen sagged but the marine behind him struck him in the

small of the back and he straightened up again. 'You'll never get a conviction without the other principals in the dock.'

North nodded. 'As I see it you have to weigh up the chances of them being caught. I have the mate of the *Marigold* in custody and he has agreed to tell me how to find Rees's brother and Potter. When all the rats are in the barrel it will be a case of who turns on the others first. The courts may allow one person to turn King's Evidence. You might just save your neck by being that one person before I get to choose among the volunteers.'

Ibsen looked at him grimly. 'I have your word that I won't hang?'

'All I can do is to give you my word that I will do my best but at least you should look forward to a long sea voyage to the far side of the world for the rest of your life.'

The hardships of transportation with all its horrors could still be diluted by ready cash and Ibsen had ways of sending money to Australia through his East Indian Company connections.

'Then I suppose that is all I can hope for. Has Pascoe told you about Rees and Palmer's house in France?'

'Not in detail but I am sure he is eager to do so.' The ship lurched as the sea became more choppy and Ibsen staggered as much in fear as in the confines of his leg-irons.

Ibsen pleaded, 'Can I sit down, sir, please? A drink of water would be appreciated too.'

North nodded and gestured for water to be brought.

Ibsen thought for a moment. 'About a mile and a half north of Barfleur there is a fortified house beside the coast road with a large barn on the opposite side of the road. The house is called Marmande. The barn is where they store the goods they buy. There are only two or three people not directly employed who know about the place. There is a small bay a few hundred yards away on the coast where their luggers can anchor.'

North said, 'Well this is a good start. When we reach Shoreham you will be provided with pen and paper and you will set down a detailed account of all your activities and the identities of all who are involved. Failure to include any information will of course be held against you. Do not essay to leave anything out; I can tell you from past experience of running a ship that concealed things almost always come to light in the end. There is one other matter I want to know about now. The three slave girls on the *Marigold.* For whom were they being carried?'

Ibsen took some time marshalling his thoughts. 'Well, I suppose somebody else will tell you if I don't. He is Lord Robert Longman of West Harting.'

North was shocked, though he hid it well. Longman was the son of an earl and his country house was less than twenty miles from North's own home in Tarring. Longman had a bad reputation for loose living and outrageous behaviour but his many shortcomings were rarely brought to public notice thanks to his long-suffering parents. North had never heard of him being a slave owner, although much of what went on at Longman Hall was shrouded in secrecy. Whatever his sins he had not allowed any of them to be heard about outside of his home. His father rarely visited the house and it was unlikely he knew the full infamy of his son's activities.

'Tell me more,' said North. 'I have been told that an agent of his brought the women on board *Marigold*.'

'Joseph Cram is Longman's creature and just as debauched as his master. The main reason for secrecy is that Longman's father is dead set against slavery.'

He went on to explain that it was not the first time that slave women had been smuggled into the country for Longman, though normally it was just one at a time. The main reason they were not brought in openly was that they were so abused that several had died before they could be smuggled out again to be sold in the West Indies. While there were few people who would care enough to go against the rich reprobate, it seemed that Longman had made a bad enemy of Granville Sharp and Thomas Clarkson who had made it their life's work to fight slavery. They had agents watching every move that Longman made in London or in West Harting. This simply added to Longman's obsession for secrecy.

North asked, 'How well do you know Longman? Are there any of these unfortunate women still at his house?'

'I find the whole thing repugnant and tend to ignore it as much as possible but I believe there is at least one woman there at all times. The system is that Rees delivers a woman or women to Cram and Cram passes over a woman who has been at Longman's house. That woman is taken back out of the country and then sent on to a Portuguese slave-dealer in Oporto to be taken to Hispaniola or Brazil. The one who is taken out of the country is sold by Rees and he keeps the money. Cram pays him on the spot for the new woman or women.'

'How much?'

'Seventy or eighty pounds each.'

North sent him below and sat in thought. He was tempted to set up the exchange so that Cram could be arrested but he was fully aware that as the laws of England stood there was no crime in buying and selling slaves. However there was a moral law which he believed in, which was summed up a paper by Clarkson, *Anne liceat invitos in servitutem dare* (Is it lawful to enslave the unconsenting?) He was beginning to realise the frustration felt by William Wilberforce and his friends. He poured himself a glass of Madeira wine, picked up a pen and wrote to Lawrence Dundas, the friend with whom he had set up the Seaman's Charity.

....

Henry Addington was feeling extremely tired this morning. Although he had been dragged unwillingly into the office of First Lord of the Treasury by the resignation of his friend

William Pitt a few weeks ago, he had done his best to set to rights the situation he found the country to be in. Despite the widespread rumour that Pitt had resigned over the king's refusal to contemplate Catholic emancipation, Addington knew that Pitt's real reasons were sheer exhaustion and unwillingness to try to hold his squabbling government together any longer or to patch up the dangerously weak economy. As to the French treaty, Addington being pilloried for its egregious shortcomings was ironic. Few knew how desperate the country's financial position was – it was either peace or a rapid slide to insolvency.

He had arrived back at White Lodge just as the clock struck eleven. He was well used to late nights but the somewhat suspect meat pie that his grumpy butler had served up with pickles at midnight might have been a mistake. He belched as he pushed aside the breakfast plate with the remains of lamb cutlets and eggs and turned to his wife. 'Ursula, my dear, what was all the noise I heard as I was getting out of bed?'

'The laughter of our guest reading the *Times* leader concerning Captain North turning Bridport upside down and having nineteen men marched off in chains to the Assizes for smuggling and receiving un-customed goods. It seems that there was so much brandy concealed he had his men smash dozens of barrels as a lesson to the inhabitants and the spirits ran down the streets. Apparently it is confidently predicted that Sir Michael will turn his attention to London next! Lord Hawkesbury was laughing so loudly I thought he could be heard in Richmond. He said that now that Bridport had felt the Tiger's claw, London had better beware.'

Addington had brought his Foreign Secretary down to his home in Richmond Park to work on the Treaty with him over the weekend. Addington belched long and loud, apologised as he held his hands to his stomach and asked, 'Where is Robert now, my dear?'

'I believe he is walking in the park. A little exercise will do you good too, Henry. I love having you at home but this journey to Town and back is having a bad effect on your health – particularly your digestion!'

The country was agog at the reports of Captain North's activities. No hero, however loved by the people, is entirely received with warmth if he goes about doing unpopular things like broaching brandy casks and having tons of illicit tobacco and un-customed wine and spirits carried off to customs warehouses. However, on balance, the Tiger of the St Lawrence was given the benefit of the doubt and most of the gentry still raised a glass to him, hoping that the next knock on the door wasn't to enquire as to the provenance of the wine.

Chapter 5

The Honourable Lawrence Dundas, eldest son of Thomas, Baron Dundas, was in his mid-30s, tall and imposing in manner but kindly in demeanour. He kissed his wife Harriet on the cheek and went into the morning room to meet his visitors.

The two men were standing side by side looking out of the window into the garden. The taller of the two was the 42-year-old Thomas Clarkson and the thin, austere, sparely built man standing next to him was Granville Sharp. Sharp was in his early 60s and had the hollow-cheeked look of an invalid. He had a prominent Roman nose and piercing eyes.

Dundas picked up a letter from his writing desk and said, 'Gentlemen, the reason I have asked you to come here today concerns this letter which I received yesterday from Captain Sir Michael North, a friend and co-founder of a charity we have set up for poor and distressed seamen. In the course of his naval duties he has come across a situation which has angered him deeply but seeks my advice on dealing with it. He also mentioned your names knowing that the three of us are acquainted. He understands that the two of you have taken an interest in the activities of Lord Thomas Longman, the son of Earl Branscombe?'

It was the younger man who spoke first. 'Granville and I have good reason to believe that Longman is bringing female slaves into the country to torture and abuse them, indeed we believe at least two of these women have been murdered by him. Unfortunately, we have insufficient proof.'

Dundas waved the letter. 'I think you will find this interesting.' He read it aloud.

Sharp banged a fist on a nearby table. 'It is as we suspected! But Sir Michael is right, how can we prove it? If the man Cram is the only public go-between then Longman simply has to deny all knowledge and he will get away with it.'

Dundas said, 'I agree that there seems no legal recourse but perhaps there is another way of approaching this matter. Longman has no money of his own to speak of and depends on his father for an allowance until he is 25 when he will be able to control his own estate. I believe that the earl is far from happy with the boy and it would not take much for him to do something to drastically curtail the scoundrel's activities even if it was simply to avoid public scandal.

'The earl is in his house in Town today and I have arranged for Captain North to meet me there to speak to him. I would like you to come with us and strengthen the matter by adding your voices, what do you say?'

The two men looked at each other. 'What is there to lose?' said Sharp.

Clarkson agreed, 'We are at your disposal, Lawrence.'

'Good. We will pick up Branscombe's friend Lord Tommy

Rolle on the way. If anybody can influence Branscombe it will be him. He may be something of a country bumpkin but he has solid good sense and is actively opposed to slavery.'

....

Richard Spencer Longman, Earl Branscombe, was always at his worse in the morning. His crustiness usually mellowed after luncheon and by the evening he was a charming and cheerful man. This morning he was particularly out of sorts and his head ached after having a flaming argument with his middle son Thomas the previous evening over the boy's purchase of a phaeton which had cost the extraordinary sum of £350. He had wrecked the vehicle on the drive up to London through racing it through the Surrey village of Ripley and colliding with a haywain.

His secretary coughed to attract his attention.

'Yes, what is it Gibbons?' Branscombe said irritably.

'Lord Rolle is here with the Honourable Lawrence Dundas and three other gentlemen; your eleven o'clock appointment, your grace.'

Branscombe lowered his voice. 'Any idea what they want, John? *Five* of them, sounds like Thomas's debts catching up with him again.'

'Ah, not debts this time, your grace. Two of the other gentlemen are prominent anti-slavery campaigners and the other is Sir Michael North. Perhaps looking for some funds?'

'North? Damn fine fellow, John. Rescued Cecil Moncrieff's wife and son from the Moors, captured several Spanish 74s and half the damned French navy. Good speaker too. St Vincent praised the man to the heavens in the Lords and God knows St Vincent has few favourites. Show 'em in.'

Branscombe looked at the five men who appeared at once united in purpose but unlike each other in appearance. 'Well, well, gentlemen, what is it to be, a donation I expect? Well, it is a good cause, how does one hundred guineas sound? Don't hold with slavery myself.'

It would appear that Dundas was the spokesman. 'I am pleased that you dislike slavery, your grace, but it is not money we seek. This is a delicate matter and you may be displeased with what you hear.'

Seven or eight minutes later Branscombe sat back on a sofa, his face registering sincere shock. 'You have proof of this?'

North said, 'We have witnesses prepared to swear to the truth of the matter but I am obliged on behalf of myself and my friends to point out that as the law stands, it is unlikely that a criminal charge would be brought without direct evidence. The reason we have approached you is that there is little doubt in our minds that this alleged reprehensible conduct will at some stage be given a public airing that you would find uncomfortable.'

The bluff, somewhat dishevelled Lord Rolle added, 'Got to be sorted out, Dick, no use denying it, your son is a scoundrel.

You need to clip his wings now and even then it may be too late if somebody comes up with proof that he has killed these poor women. Sorry if that offends but it's the plain truth.'

Branscombe knew in his heart that the story he had been told was true. His first reaction was to speak angrily and curse the men who had brought this to him but he was bleakly aware that they were right. If the public came to hear of the treatment of these women and worse if the word 'murder' was mentioned he could expect endless vilification and shame. Despite his own blood running in his son's veins he had to publicly disown him if this was true. His stomach protested this latest generator of bile.

Without a word he went to ring a small bell on a side table. When Gibbons came in he asked him to find his son and bring him here.

Lord Thomas Longman walked into the room as if he hadn't a care in the world. When he saw the five men in a line staring at him he faltered slightly but recognising only Lord Rolle, it was merely a moment's hesitation. He assumed this was another attempt by his father to get him to join some masonic lodge or other.

North looked at him with interest. He had heard bad reports about the man but this was the first time he had seen him. Longman was 22 years old and put him in mind of the late Midshipman Boyle who had been murdered on *Prince Rupert*. He was tall and slim but his face was pasty-white and marred by erupting acne. He was wearing beautifully cut pantaloons, a white ruffled shirt and an open waistcoat which was embroidered with silver and gold wire and pearl buttons.

Branscombe looked at him as if he had never laid eyes on him before.

'Thomas, these gentlemen have brought me disturbing news. They believe that you have female black slaves in your West Harting house. Is this true?'

'What of it, father? There is no law against it.' His voice was languid.

'Apart from the fact that I have repeatedly and explicitly told you I will have no truck with slavery and that I believe no gentleman should be so stupid as to risk his reputation by keeping personal slaves in England, why was I not told of this?'

Longman shrugged his shoulders but said nothing. Branscombe walked to a bookshelf and, lifting a large family Bible with both hands, brought it to the table.

'Thomas, place your hands on this Bible and swear to me that no person, slave or free, has suffered abuse in your house and that no person has been wilfully murdered.'

Longman's white face coloured up and he shouted, 'Lies, who says this? I will cut out his heart!'

North came forward. *'*I say this on the evidence of two of the men who have supplied you with these women.'

His eyes set in a fierce stare, Thomas Clarkson moved to a position beside him. 'My colleague Sharp and I have it from a servant in your house that two bodies have been buried in the grounds. We have also the evidence of agents that a badly injured black woman was carried out to a carriage at your house and driven away along with your man Cram.'

Longman was incandescent with fury. 'Damn you, all of you, you have no proof. Get out of here!'

Branscombe shouted him down. 'It is I and I alone who will dismiss people from my house, not you! Now swear on this Bible that none of this is true.'

His hand trembling, Longman placed it upon the Bible and, after a moment's hesitation, said 'I know nothing of these matters. I swear that if somebody in my house has done this I know nothing about it.'

Lord Rolle said quietly, 'May your soul rot in hell, Thomas Longman.'

Longman dashed to a cupboard, throwing it open and snatching a sword, and screamed, 'I will run you through, you fucking oaf!'

As he charged forward Rolle stood firm but at the moment Longman's sword was raised, North struck it upwards with his own. Longman turned to North and struck an *en garde* pose. 'Come on then, you interfering pig, I will teach you to carry tales! I am Lord Longman, not some fucking sailor on one of your ships, I paid good money for those bitches and they belong to me to do with them whatever I please.'

'And you killed them, didn't you?' stated North bluntly.

'They are property and I do what I wish with my property, when I finish with them I get rid of them like the rubbish they are.' There was froth and spittle coming from his mouth, so great was his anger. His face was scarlet and every muscle of his body quivered with rage.

North insisted, 'You *killed* them!'

'Yes, I fucking killed them!' said Longman, then he suddenly realised what he had said. In an overwhelming fury he took a pace forward and raised his sword to strike North's head.

Before North could move forward to parry the blow, Earl Branscombe stepped between them and struck his son hard across the face once and then again. 'Enough! I wish to God duelling was not illegal or I would be tempted to have Sir Michael skewer you like the rat you are. My *son*; my *disgrace* that you were ever born!' He snatched the sword from him.

His anger still obvious, Branscombe said, 'I cannot abide the sight of you. You will remain in your rooms until tomorrow when you will be taken on board my ship the *Olympus* and carried to Calcutta where I will see to it that you are given employment as the lowest clerk in the Honourable Company's offices. You will take nothing with you except the clothes you stand up in and if you *dare* show your face to me while I live I will kill you myself.' He reached into a waistcoat pocket pulled out a half-crown and tossed it at his son's feet. ''Tis a pity this is the smallest coin in my pocket! You are disinherited and I sincerely hope that you will go to hell for your blasphemy and for murdering those unfortunate creatures. Go!'

He beckoned to his secretary. 'See that two strong men stand guard over him. They are not to let him out of their sight for one moment until he is on board the *Olympus* and the ship is away from the land. They will make sure he has nothing but the clothes he is wearing, is that clear?'

As they reached the street in St James' Square, North looked at the other four men, shock at what had occurred written large on every face.

He spoke calmly. 'Today has been one which we will never forget without loathing and horror but a form of justice has at least been done.'

Earl Branscombe had asked North to go with his secretary and two footmen to the West Harting house as soon as possible and deal with whatever they found there. He was too sickened to go there himself. The house would be sold and all the servants dismissed without pay or references. Lawrence Dundas would go down to Sussex with them to add weight to the matter but North intended to have Cluney Ryan and half a dozen of the men under his command there.

Chapter 6

The results of the Shoreham Patrol, as it had been named, were proving extremely satisfactory and those more clandestine activities had been carried out to a greatly appreciated extent by the Lords of Admiralty. But none of these events were more satisfying to Michael North than those of 14th April 1802.

The schooner *Juniper* had made landfall three miles north of Barfleur at three in the morning. North took with him Lieutenant Lang, Cluney Ryan and three dozen seamen in two 24-foot cutters and walked up the beach in silence. He had deliberately chosen a night when the moon was obscured by heavy clouds. It had rained for most of the afternoon and was set for more rain before the night was through.

The coast road was a few hundred yards inland and as they moved along the nearby beach southwards towards the distant town nothing could be heard above the sound of the surf on the beach except the eerie screaming and yapping of a pair of mating foxes. Sometimes it sounded almost like a terrified child with the excited laughter of a teasing girl echoing off the trees nearby.

Cluney Ryan gripped his cutlass tighter and pulled his pea-jacket closer against the rising wind in their faces. He was 45 years old and had begun to admit that he was no longer the spry young journeyman gardener who had volunteered to join the navy in Cork Harbour these 23 years past.

He had served as coxswain of *Prince Rupert* and as one of Michael North's personal followers had been with him now for nearly seven years. He was a thin, bald-headed man with a ready smile and a courageous heart. Ever the source of sage wisdom, despite lack of formal education, he was respected by all and envied by most.

His mother, no doubt influenced by his wicked little smile as a newborn, had him baptised Cluney. This name had been the source many years later for his nickname Rogue Ryan. It had been Michael North, himself born in County Clare, though to a Protestant baronet, who had first called him Rogue – being one of the meanings of his given name.

Today his mother would be fussing over his twin brother Ambrose and some little birthday present or a few extra slices of ham with his breakfast would be the order of the day. Ryan's mouth watered as he thought of those succulent, richly flavoured, smoky slices of ham, tucked under at least three fried eggs and sitting contentedly next to a pile of sliced tatties. Oh, and a dish of tea with real fresh cow's milk! What he would give right now … He was brought back to earth as he stumbled over a slimy, green rock and dropped his cutlass, his ears filled with the hissed abuse and admonishment of his fellow sailors.

Maison Marmande loomed out of the steadily increasing drizzle. The grey-stone house and the barn opposite were in darkness. An unhappy-looking mastiff emerged from beneath a scrap of a shelter beside the outhouse at the side of the main house and looked at the procession of men gloomily before turning round and creeping back out of the rain without a sound.

The building was in poor repair with all sorts of rubbish scattered around the outside. Cluney Ryan, Billy Leary and six other men took station at the rear with four men on each side of the house. Most of the rest of the seamen were dispersed along the road nearby.

North tested the front door carefully; it was locked and bolted on the inside. He went to a nearby shuttered window and eased the bolts, opening the shutters quietly. The window was about 20 inches square and as he lifted the inner latch with the point of a knife it swung inwards, pushed by the wind. North beckoned to John Mitchell, an agile young topman, who climbed through.

A minute passed and then North heard the sound of bolts being softly withdrawn. The door opened and North crept inside with half a dozen seamen following him.

A blanket-wrapped figure was sleeping in a chair near the embers of a fire, his musket leaning on a nearby table and an overturned pewter pot and two empty wine bottles on the floor at his feet.

Mitchell crossed quickly and threw the blanket over the man's head, swinging a line around the man's throat and continuing by winding it three or four times around him, lashing him to the chair. He completed the parcelling by clubbing him accurately through the blanket. North whispered, 'Stay here.'

After checking two empty downstairs rooms the rest of the party started up the staircase which started to groan audibly as North reached about halfway. They finished the climb in a rush.

One man ran from his room with a cutlass in his hand. North came forward, taking the slash of his cutlass on his sword. He drove his opponent back into the room where a screaming woman was against the far wall with bedclothes clutched around her.

Nothing had been said after that first shout. Both men grunted with the effort of thrust and parry. The man, walking backwards, stumbled and North struck the cutlass from his hand. 'Give it up, man! You are beaten.' He raised his hands in surrender.

There was the sound of a gun being discharged in the next room but North kept his eyes firmly fixed on the man in front him. 'Your name?'

'Abel Rees, who are you?'

'Captain North.'

'*North*! You were there when my brother John was shot!'

'Yes, Mr Rees, an unnecessary death. If he had surrendered he would have been lived – at least until he met the hangman. Come on now, in front of me.'

They came out into the short corridor outside. Corbin Potter was leaning against a wall, his left hand clutching a bloodstained right forearm. He had managed to get his trousers on under his nightshirt whereas Rees was naked except for a dirty white shirt.

The two men were bundled downstairs and allowed a blanket each. Sounds of gunfire from outside the house could be heard. North went to the window and then withdrew his head quickly as a ball smashed into the frame.

He turned to the others. 'Stay here. If they as much as draw breath, you have my permission to shoot them.'

He went to the back of the house, unlocked the door and came out. There were two men there. The older man knuckled his forehead. 'The cox'n and the rest is shooting at some men in the barn, your honour.'

'All right, Loomis, stand fast here.'

North went to the side of the house and found Ryan sheltering behind the front corner with three other men. From cover a dozen or more seamen were pouring shot into the barn. Ryan was reloading his pistol.

'Sir, two men, maybe three, in the barn. I think we got one of them.'

North called out, 'You in the barn. We have you surrounded. We have no argument with you. Throw out your weapons and we will allow you to go free.' He repeated his words in French.

There was silence in the barn for a few minutes, then a voice called out, 'All right, mister, here's our dags.'

Three pistols were thrown out of the door. A pause then a musket also tumbled through.

'Come out now, your hands on your heads.'

Three men walked out into the rain which was now driving away from the shore in fitful gusts. A quick search of the barn disclosed stacks of contraband and the corpse of a fourth man. North ordered the barn to be torched, then told the captives to get out of his sight.

Rees and Palmer were marched barefoot down to the beach and the whole party struggled through driving rain and shifting shingle the 600 yards or so north to where the boats were drawn up under the care of two seamen. The smugglers were taken off, their feet cut and bleeding, and once on board *Juniper* were put in irons below deck.

After they reached England a swift trial for murder and smuggling followed and three weeks later both men were hanged in Deptford Dockyard. Ibsen, spared the rope, was sentenced to seven years' penal servitude.

Chapter 7

February to 1st May, 1802

Apart from making a serious dent in the smuggler's trade, Michael North's patrol's activities also involved carrying secret agents and reports back and forth between France and England.

None of these vital but subtle operations produced anything more significant than the one which involved Henry Gillespie and Michael Bryan, the art dealers. There was also valuable intelligence conveyed by a nurseryman who was recruited by George Hibbert. He brought back priceless information to England following his several visits to Malmaison carrying hostas and proteas as a gift to Josephine Bonaparte.

On 1st May George Hibbert sent a note to North when he and Isobel were at the Dulwich house asking him to meet him at Magistrate Colquhoun's house in Westminster Square.

They were joined by George Hibbert and Henry Gillespie.

Hibbert opened the discussion. 'Sir Michael, the reason we asked you here today is that Gillespie here has some information that needs to be verified. Henry, why don't you explain?'

Gillespie leaned forward in his chair. 'A few weeks ago one of my contacts in Rouen, who works in Perrier's shipyard, told me that the American, Fulton, had left off testing some improvements to his underwater boat *Nautilus* for the moment and was leaving Rouen to deal with a problem concerning another project. That was all he knew and, frankly, it didn't mean much to me at the time. As you know Fulton is a man of interest to us because there is little doubt of his genius and that he is very useful to Bonaparte. He worked for the Duke of Bridgwater for some years and perfected his steamboat on his grace's canals.'

He went on to say that the information had become more significant when it was later compared with a letter that George Hibbert had received from his friend, the botanist and plant collector, James Niven. Taking advantage of the peace, he had travelled from South Africa and was at present at Malmaison. He was advising Josephine Bonaparte on additions to her rose garden. It seemed that her husband had a meeting there with a group of people including his Minister of Police Fouché, two civilians, a senior admiral and Robert Fulton.

While the conversation could not be overheard, Niven noted that one of the civilians, whose French was barely adequate, was present and was undoubtedly English. Niven's curiosity aroused, he watched and followed the Englishman and discovered that his name was Cosworth. One afternoon Niven had secretly gained access to the man's bedroom and amongst other things found that there was a British naval lieutenant's uniform coat in the armoire.

In London, enquiries were made with the Admiralty and the only person that the name and description fitted appeared to be Lieutenant Jacob Cosworth. Cosworth's parents' London house was watched and three days ago Cosworth was seen returning. He had been detained by Wickham's agents and carried off to Somerset House where he had been securely confined pending interview.

When confronted Cosworth refused to explain his presence at Malmaison. However he stated that he would speak to a senior naval officer provided he received a guarantee that he would not be tried for treason.

Gillespie said to North, 'Because we are not at war with France, the matter has to be handled delicately, Sir Michael. We believe Cosworth has important information that he might be persuaded to reveal. We cannot simply grant him immunity without knowing what he will tell us but, on the face of it, a conviction for treason without that information would be difficult. Therefore we have to accede to at least part of his condition. We would like you to speak to him.'

North agreed that he would go to Somerset House that same afternoon.

Chapter 8

2nd May, 1802

Somerset House was home to the Navy Board, the Victualling Board and most of the other offices of the Royal Navy. Some of the senior officials had quarters there in order more conveniently to work in their offices. One of these sets of rooms had been taken over by a small group of civilians and naval officers detailed to collate and disseminate intelligence, and it was here that Jacob Cosworth was to be found. He was in a small room which contained a truckle bed, a chair and a washbasin. North saw as he entered that the man seemed confident and self-assured. The interview would have to be carefully carried out if he was to shake the man's composure.

Cosworth was aware of the danger he was in but had time to rehearse his story.

He would say that about 12 weeks ago, having landed at Boulogne, he had taken a hired carriage to Paris where he took rooms at an apartment building in the parish of St Eustache opposite the bakery at La Maison Stohrer in the rue Montorgueil. Each morning he would cross the street to buy fresh bread and the speciality of the house, delicious pastries.

One day, while in conversation with the baker, he had met another regular customer, a thin, grim-faced man, whom he engaged in conversation. On his part the meeting was not by chance. He had made assiduous enquiries before he had settled in his rooms and knew that a nearby house was occupied by a senior clerk in the Police Ministry named Jules Rossignol.

He would say that he set out to impress Rossignol by spending money freely and carrying him around the town making him feel important as an adopted guide to a wide-eyed Englishman. After gaining his confidence he had engineered a meeting with Joseph Fouché himself where he had confided to the minister that he felt he was not appreciated by the Admiralty. He would be willing to resign his commission and work for Fouché in Paris. There was no question of treason, of course – how could there be with peace between their two countries? Many English people were in France now; some, like shipwrights, actively working in French shipyards.

His story would continue by saying that he let the idea sit with Fouché for a week or so and eventually received an invitation to meet Fouché at Malmaison to be introduced to a senior admiral who was being given command of an expedition to the Carribean. It was suggested that Cosworth should travel as a supernumerary and possibly as an interpreter. On his return, should the admiral give him a testimonial, Cosworth might find himself being offered a senior post in Fouché's ministry. He had gone over his story a dozen times and thought it foolproof. It had to be or it would be the firing squad or the noose.

He looked up as North entered.

'Lieutenant, I am Captain North, good afternoon.'

Cosworth stood up. 'Good afternoon, Sir Michael. I know of you, of course. Well, it seems that these fools took me seriously. It is gratifying to see that they have sent me somebody of importance.'

North looked around him at the dreary room. 'This will not do. Let us find somewhere less oppressive, Lieutenant. Come with me.'

North led him downstairs from the apartment to the ground floor of the Navy Pay Office. The clerks had been sent home for the day and the only persons present were Lieutenant James Lang and North's cox'n, Cluney Ryan. North introduced Lang who would make a note of their meeting.

North indicated a seat and sat opposite Cosworth, who seemed relaxed. Pouring tea, North sat in silence for a full minute looking at the other man. The evidence that Cosworth was involved treasonably with the French was compelling but North pushed that aside in his mind and assessed him as one would a chess opponent.

Cosworth was in his late 30s. He was old for his rank but not unusually so. There were many lieutenants with insufficient 'interest' to advance their careers. In fact, in seniority, despite being a lieutenant for 12 years, Cosworth was nowhere near the top of the list in order of seniority in the rank.

 North could see that his face and figure seemed to indicate a liking for rich food and plentiful wine but even those fond of high living could not be underestimated when gauging brainpower. His uniform was expensively cut and North noticed that his shoes were adorned with good-quality buckles. A crisp linen handkerchief was tucked into his sleeve and as he sat, returning North's scrutiny, he was taking snuff from a valuable monogrammed gold box. North had found out that Cosworth's father was a successful merchant and that the son had been educated at Winchester.

North nodded to him. 'Why do you not begin by explaining how you came to be seen in the company of First Consol Bonaparte at Malmaison?'

Cosworth leaned back confidently and folded his arms.

'Like many officers the Peace has sent me to half pay, Sir Michael, and I wanted a break from the monotony of waiting for a letter from the lordships offering a posting. So I thought if I travelled to France, I might discover information which, presented to their lordships, would improve my chances of a ship. You cannot be unaware, sir, that my years in the rank should have produced promotion to post-rank. It seems to me that it is often the case that promotion is not linked to ability but simply to influence and pressure from patrons. In my case I have not that advantage.'

North decided to appear sympathetic. He replied, 'In my view the process of promotion is also assisted by recognition of merit. If you have not caught their lordships' eye it may be that you have been unlucky during the war. However, that is not for me to say.'

Cosworth smiled and nodded, 'Well, be that as it may. It was my belief that important intelligence could be gathered at Malmaison.'

'Forgive me for interrupting again, Lieutenant, but I am curious as to how you managed to gain admittance to Malmaison.'

Cosworth spread his hands 'It came about by what may seem a curious circumstance but was the result of careful planning on my part.'

As North listened to Cosworth he could see glaring inconsistencies. Why would Fouché trust a stranger, a lieutenant in Britain's navy, to be present at what was probably a secret meeting with Robert Fulton? Even more unlikely, he thought, with Bonaparte himself present.

'Lieutenant, what authority from their lordships had you to infiltrate Fouché's offices or indeed Malmaison?'

Cosworth appeared confident but North noticed a hesitation, it was as if being asked the question had not occurred to him. 'I had no authority at all, Sir Michael. Chance favoured me with the opportunity and I grasped it boldly.'

Rubbish, thought North. 'Very, well, continue, please. What happened at Malmaison?'

'Well, sir, I was introduced to Admiral LaTouche-Tréville the commander of the fleet at Rochefort and it was agreed that I would accompany him on an expedition to Saint Domingue, where he was charged with suppressing rebellion.'

'And then?'

'I decided it would be unfair to my father to depart for the West Indies without explaining so I returned to London to take my leave of him. Imagine my surprise when I was taken up as a traitor. This country is no longer at war with the French and the expedition to Saint Domingue is merely a police action, nothing to do with this country.'

'But you intended to infiltrate the Ministry of Police to obtain information useful to this country. How would this voyage, which might take years to complete, assist you in that endeavour?'

'To establish my credibility. I could hardly say to Fouché that I wanted to dig and delve into his files and records without building trust.'

'And in all this you believed that despite a complete absence of permission and indeed of knowledge, their lordships would welcome your enterprise?'

'If I had not been dragged off the street and confined in this place, I would have proved myself and their lordships would have gained valuable information, Sir Michael.'

North stood up and walked over to Lieutenant Lang whose

pen had busily recorded the conversation.

'Mr Lang, how long have you known me?'

Lang set down his pen and looked up, his face carefully without expression. 'Nigh on seven years, Sir Michael, ever since I served as a midshipman when you were a lieutenant yourself.'

'In all those years has it been your abiding impression that I am a brainless idiot, lieutenant?'

Lang half-smiled. 'Not always, but perhaps when you choose to risk your life at the head of a boarding party, sir. Though, thankfully, the dear Lord has taken care of you in those moments of insanity.'

'Thank you for that kind testimony, James.'

He clasped his hands behind his back and returned to Cosworth, looking down at him.

'When I asked you what happened then, I would rather have thought you would mention your presence in Madame Bonaparte's rose garden when the First Consul met with Fouché and the admiral. You were there, were you not?'

Cosworth was beginning to experience a sinking feeling. 'I remember now, yes, I was there but it was merely a social opportunity to meet General Bonaparte.'

'Nobody else of importance?'

Cosworth seemed to lose his casual attitude and became much more alert. 'There was a man, an American, I don't know his name. He seemed to be an artist of some sort. I didn't really speak to him. Of course there was also this gardener chap with Madame Bonaparte, but he was merely a servant of some sort.'

'Mr Cosworth, I am going to give you time to think about your situation. That will be all for today but I suggest you think very carefully when you concoct your next story. You are teetering on the very edge of a high precipice and no hand will reach out to draw you back unless you start being truthful. When I speak to you next the name Robert Fulton should be the first words you utter. Lieutenant Lang, you and Ryan will escort Cosworth to his quarters.'

Over dinner at Rules' fish restaurant, North enlightened Hibbert and Gillespie. Hibbert was frowning heavily.

'The problem is, Michael, that Niven was unable to hear one word about the reason for Fulton's presence. Fulton is the *bête-noire*. I doubt whether many people realise how dangerous his inventions are, particularly when being commissioned by Bonaparte. Fulton has already built a steamboat and tested it on the Seine and we know that Bonaparte caused it to be armed with two heavy carronades. Thankfully it appears that the boat sank but it seems only a matter of time before there is a ship of war that does not have to rely on wind-power. The havoc that would cause would be unconscionable.

'Then there is this devil-boat, the underwater boat, an obscene instrument of war. With that and the rumour that Fulton is looking to construct a grenade or mine that can be set off at sea – he calls it a torpedo – his activities are a continuous threat to our country.'

'Perhaps he should be bribed to come and work for us again, George?'

Despite the safety of the private dining room Hibbert lowered his voice. 'The Duke of Bridgwater is already reaching out to him with just such an offer, sanctioned by William Pitt before he resigned.'

North set down his fork. 'I understand how important it is to find out what Bonaparte and Fulton are planning but our source of information is just one man and the accuracy of his testimony very, very suspect. I believe no effort should be spared to trace Fulton's present whereabouts and make him a very generous offer to switch his allegiance back to us. Is this being done?'

Hibbert said, miserably, 'Every agent we have in France, whether it be Wickham's people, a half dozen naval officers supposedly on leave or our own clandestines are searching high and low. I believe he has left France. Unfortunately France possesses or controls so many places outside France itself he could be anywhere from the toe of Italy to the polders of Holland.'

Chapter 9

The resumed interview was to have taken place the following afternoon but an urgent message was received at North's brother's house where he was staying overnight and North and Lang set out at nine in the morning. The message was written in Cluney Ryan's barely literate hand and urged him to come as quickly as he could. When they arrived they were met by a troubled Ryan.

'I am sorry, your honour, but Lieutenant Cosworth was found this morning hanging in his room. He's dead.'

North said sharply, 'Is the body still there?'

'Yes, sir. I found him myself when I took his breakfast to him. I could see he'd been dead for some time – hours anyway, so I left him hanging. I advised Mr Towry, the Victualling Commissioner who came and looked at the body. Then he told me to lock the door and make sure nothing was moved until you arrived, sir.'

Cosworth was in his nightshirt, hanging from a stout hook that had been screwed into a ceiling beam. About his neck was a rope made from strips of a torn shirt, plaited into a thin cord.

North held the other two men back. He looked carefully at the body, the beam and the floor and beckoned the two forward.

'Note this sawdust on the floor. The hook must have been

inserted just before he was hung. How did the hook get here? Ryan, there is a list of Cosworth's possessions in the desk Mr Lang was using, bring it here please. James, we will cut him down now. Climb on the chair and cut the rope. I will take the weight of his legs and we will lower him to the floor.'

Once Cosworth's body was on its back, North eased back the sleeves of his nightshirt. 'Look closely, these red marks have a regular imprint – a cord was tied about them, I believe. Now look at his face. The mouth is opened wide and here, two of his teeth are broken. There is a trace of blood and fragments of tooth on the floor near the bed. Also between his teeth, there are two broken strands of cotton. He was gagged. And here, bruises on the neck wider than those caused by the rope. Help me turn him on his face, James.'

North lifted Cosworth's mop of long hair from his neck. 'This purple bruising on his head may mean that he was struck unconscious with a blow to the base of the skull. I suspect he was dead before he was hung. I have seen two suicides by hanging and in both cases the man's bowels were opened as he hung. Not so here. There is no doubt in my mind that he was already dead. This was an inept and clumsy attempt to conceal the fact that he was murdered, James, probably strangled.'

Ryan brought the list of Cosworth's belongings to the room. North compared it to the items present including the cupboard containing the dead man's clothing.

'It says here three shirts, one of silk and two of cambric. They are all here so whoever did this must have brought with them the shirt they used as a rope – probably already made into a rope.'

Lang turned to Ryan. 'This building was completely locked, Ryan? Cosworth was alone and locked in overnight?'

Ryan answered that he was. There was no other bed in this building which was why he slept next door after seeing that the outer door of the building and the door of the room were locked.

'How many people came into the offices before you found him like this?'

Ryan thought for a moment. 'There were three, sir. The night watchman came off duty at six for a cup of tea. He opened the door for me. Then the woman, Mary, what works here cleaning and making tea, follered by Mr Thompsett, the junior clerk. He comes in early for the mail to arrive and sets it on the senior clerk's table. Mary made tea and heated up some burgoo on the stove. I took it with some bread and a can of tea upstairs to the prisoner at about fifteen minutes before seven o'clock, sir.'

Lang said, 'We need to talk to the night watchman. The woman can be safely ruled out, I believe and presumably the junior clerk.' North went to speak to Towry who could offer nothing useful, while Lang interviewed the watchman.

Charley Chesney was an old salt. His left arm lost on the Glorious First of June, he was lucky to get this job and he knew it. He stood rigidly to attention until Lang told him to stand easy.

'Tell me how you do your rounds, Chesney?'

'Well, sir, I walk the whole area at least four times in the night and the rest of the time I sit either in the porter's box by the main gate or in the hut at the far end nearer the river. I can't see the whole place at any time, of course but these big buildings hold the sounds in, so I'm sure I didn't hear anything out of the ordinary.'

'Did anybody come into the gate after ten in the evening?'

'Yes, sir, there was Mr Barrow, the second secretary over at the Admiralty, he has rooms above the Sick and Hurt Board offices. That was around eleven o'clock. He often works late and I am used to seeing him. He said goodnight and went into the building. Then there was Andrew Watts, Mr Towry's man, he was half-seas over and I had to put his key in the lock for him – that ain't unusual either.'

'Nobody else?'

'Only the wagon for the paper store, sir. That was at about 5.30. The driver and his mate. I didn't know them but they are always changing around. He had the right pass and so I left them to it.'

Lang's eyes narrowed. 'You say these men were not known to

you?'

'Well, no, sir, but I opened the store for them and watched them start unloading the wagon. They seemed to know what they were doing.'

'You were there all the time?'

'No, I had to complete my round. When I got back about twenty minutes later they was waiting at the gate to be let out.'

'Twenty minutes out of sight.'

Chesney shifted from foot to foot, 'I am sorry, sir, but all the buildings except the paper store was securely locked up. I didn't think anybody could get in.'

'Very well, Chesney, you were not to know anything would happen to Lieutenant Cosworth. Besides, this is a big place for one man to patrol.'

Lang found North talking to the junior clerk who had simply confirmed what Ryan had said.

North said, 'Well, what do we know so far?'

'Sir Michael,' said Lang. 'I suspect that there were at least two men who came in with a wagon to deliver paper. The watchman did not think it unusual, this place gets through tons of paper a week, it seems. Deliveries are frequent and it is not always the same driver and mate. They showed him a delivery note and a pass.'

'Find out the name of the paper merchant and go and see him, James. I will have to report to the Admiralty and get word to George Hibbert. This is a damned bad business!'

Fourdrinier Brothers the paper merchants had their offices in Sherborne lane in the City. Henry Fourdrinier was a handsome man with a cleft chin. Lang judged him to be in his mid-30s. After he had received Lang in his office he stood with a puzzled look on his face, toying with his square and compasses watch fob.

'Delivery? No, Lieutenant, our delivery is never on Wednesdays. We mainly receive material on that day and we need all our staff and our transport to bring it into the warehouse. We are due to deliver to Somerset House tomorrow morning and the wagon then goes to the Home Office with a consignment.'

Lang was pensive. 'I cannot see how these men could pass themselves off that easily. They had a wagon with packages of paper which they unloaded – or at least appeared to unload. They also had a pass which was shown to the watchman.'

Fourdrinier held up a hand, his expression changed. 'Wait a moment, this paper; is it still at Somerset House? If so, let us go there now. I will probably be able to tell you its origin. That might help. As for the pass, well it is on Navy Board headed paper but I should imagine it is not too difficult to obtain a sheet and forge the pass.'

They went straight to Somerset House where Lang had a clerk

open the paper store. It was about 30 feet long, solidly built and with window glass set in the roof. There were racks each side. The racks had legs set in pans of turpentine to discourage vermin.

The clerk was able to say that the piles of paper sitting directly on the stone floor could not possibly have been there the previous day since every sheet would have been stacked on the shelves. It would be remarked upon adversely if the senior clerks were to find paper stacked directly on the floor. There was also far less in the delivery than would normally be there.

Fourdrinier took up a dozen sheets of foolscap paper and carried them out to the light. He producing a large magnifying glass and proceeded to examine it carefully. He sniffed the paper and frowned.

'Well, Lieutenant, this is very interesting. This paper was made in France. It is very expensive, costing twice the average but the quality is superb. It cannot be more than two years old and was produced in Leger Didot's works by a process invented by Nicolas Robert of Essonnes three or four years ago. I know about this because Didot has asked me and my brother to finance the process.'

Lang pointed back at the piled paper. 'Assuming this is all of the same, who in this country would have a stock?'

The paper merchant smiled. 'That is a fairly easy question to answer. I know from Didot that he has only supplied three buyers of any quantity at all apart from samples. One is the private secretary's office of the Czar in Moscow, where I should think it remains. The second is to First Consol Bonaparte and I know that consignment was less than half this quantity. The third customer is the most likely for I believe the paper was sent to London. The customer was the Prussian government and they intended the consignment for their embassy in London.'

Lang asked, 'Did you say the *Prussian* embassy?'

'That is where I suggest you direct your steps, Lieutenant, though I cannot for the life of me think why the paper should end up here.'

James Lang was just as puzzled but after saying goodbye to Fourdrinier, he set off for the Prussian ambassador's residence in Pall Mall. He was admitted and a senior secretary, Herr Grasse, listened to what he had to say.

'Lieutenant, this is astonishing. Two days ago a wagon carrying a supply of paper and other materials was sent here from our warehouse in the docks at Wapping. It never arrived. The man driving it was found with a fractured skull just outside the dock gates and one of my clerks, Carl Wieck, who was with him, has disappeared. From what you tell me, he may have been involved. His older brother is serving with the French navy and Carl makes no secret of his admiration for Bonaparte and France. I have had to speak to him on several occasions about his views, which do not reflect those of my mission.'

'Is the driver dead?'

'Very badly injured and unlikely to come to his senses ever again, I am afraid. I have already sent out some of our people to try to find Wieck but without success.'

North received the news with mixed feelings. He had to believe that the Prussian embassy was not involved. They had no reason to do France's dirty work.

'Well, James, this is very frustrating but I cannot see how we can take the matter further unless this man Wieck comes to light. A wretched result Cosworth dead and his killers neither captured nor identified.'

It seemed that nothing further could be done.

Chapter 10

<u>4th May, 1802</u>

North wanted to dig deeper into the Cosworth murder but Carl Wieck seemed to have vanished and none of the various intelligence bodies in London could ferret out more information. North was convinced that although the murder itself was bungled because it failed to present a convincing suicide, the mind behind it was much more intelligent.

James Lang was entrusted with the task of trying to pull all the threads together. He spent several days going over the area of Somerset House and questioning anybody who might have been in the area at 5.30 on that fateful morning.

Three days into his efforts he was rewarded when he visited a shabby house at Number 8 Princes Street in Pimlico, a few streets away from Elliot's Brewery, the heady smell of which filled the air. The house was owned by a thin, sharp-boned woman who rented out rooms. The Prussian embassy had given this as Wieck's address.

Mrs Harriet Tolworth had come down in the world since her days as a minor actress with half a dozen beaux to pay for her company. The house had been bought for cash but had left her with a pittance to eke out her existence. At first she had tried to present the accommodation as a genteel and discreet place where discerning gentlemen might be entertained at a price. It seemed that she had been badly advised as to the location of her enterprise. In hot weather the smell of the brewery could almost knock down a sober man.

The area was well known for its market gardens to the south and its pleasure gardens. It was therefore ripe for the sort of business Harriet had in mind but the war had left its mark. Local entrepreneurs planning great things for the almost empty fields running down to the river had become cautious and Harriet's street on the northern edge near Belgravia became neglected and shunned by 'the quality'. In the end, like many others in the street, Harriet sub-divided the house's larger rooms and took in a variety of tenants, all of slender means and low expectations in life.

Lang found her to be morose and suspicious but a few silver coins and the production of two bottles of port wine brightened her wan features.

'Yes, the Prussian gentleman. He was a good tenant, always paid his rent on time and not too much funny business with female visitors and that sort of thing. I run a respectable house, Lieutenant.'

Lang smiled. 'I expect that would mean that you need to keep a close eye on things, madam?'

Harriet walked over to her cabinet and brought back two glasses as Lang pulled the cork from a bottle of port wine. She filled both glasses without asking if he wished to join her.

'You don't know the half of it, sir. Mr Wieck was one of my

better tenants. As to the others, well, comings and goings in the night, doxies, irate tradesmen looking to be paid. Things like that. And me with no man to look after me! Well, you can imagine, Lieutenant, it ain't easy but I do my best.'

Lang reached out and patted her hand. 'I'm sure you manage very well but you have to be vigilant, of course.'

It took a few glasses and some flattery but Harriet was persuaded to share some of her confidences. Wieck had been visited on a number of occasions before he disappeared. There were two men. One was an Englishman in his 40s – could be a naval gentleman but dressed in a good-quality brown coat and breeches. The other was definitely French. She knew a Frenchie when she saw one and that cocky way of tossing his head and flirting with her, well ...

'Did they come on foot?'

'Well, yes, the Frenchie lives in Mrs Harmsworth's house just along the street – Number 2. I saw him there just yesterday. Mind you, that Mrs Harmsworth ought to be ashamed; he's even younger than you, begging your pardon, Lieutenant.'

Lang asked her about the disappearance of Wieck. Apparently Harriet had been to the street market to buy fish. She always went early to get the best fish so she was back in the street at around 8 o'clock that morning. She had not quite reached the house when she saw Wieck, carrying a large leather bag, coming out on to the street where a closed carriage was waiting and the Frenchie was holding open the door. Well she didn't think he was making off or anything because his rent was paid up a month in advance.

'I don't think he was going far.'

'Why?'

'Well the carriage driver lives local, George Bates. He doesn't work outside the area – maybe Westminster or the City, sometimes as far as Hampstead village but that's it.'

'Where can I find Bates?'

'He rents a stable in the mews behind Lower Grosvenor Place.'

Lang decided to visit Bates's yard first. Lower Grosvenor Place was about ten minutes away on foot. There was parkland north of the street and a triangle of houses on the south side running down through Ranelagh Street and Upper Eaton Street. The only entrance into the mews area at the rear of the houses was in Ranelagh Street, between the houses. Walking into the area at the centre of the triangle Lang could see a dozen car-men cleaning sedan-chairs and one-horse Hackney carriages. The man he sought was sitting on a wall, a clay pipe in his mouth, reading a copy of the *Gazette*.

Lang assessed him as he came closer. The man was stocky and bewhiskered. He was in his mid-40s and despite his rough garments was straight-backed and had an air of intelligence.

'Mr George Bates?'

The man looked the uniformed Lang up and down and said, 'Not if you've got a press gang around the corner, sir.'

Lang chuckled, 'Marines, I guess?'

Bates nodded. 'Done my twenty, saved up my money and bought the carriage.'

'I believe I see before me a man loyal to his king and country, do I?'

'You do, sir, you do.'

He explained that he was seeking a German and a Frenchman who lived in Pimlico but, it seemed the German was last seen a few days ago getting into his carriage.

'Frenchman name of Marcel Mesonant, sir, regular of mine but that was the one and only time I saw the German – military type, foot soldier, ranker, probably Prussian. That any use to you, sir?'

'Excellent. This Mesonant lives at number two Princes Street near the brewery, is that right?'

'Well, there are a couple of other places. Likes women with big balconies and loose purse strings that one. I took him and the German to one of his other ladies that day. That was Stows Rents off York Street; Mrs Paget at number six.'

Lang produced a half-sovereign. 'Yours for a half-day's work, Mr Bates. Take me to Panton Street to pick up my captain and then to Stows Rents.'

It took Bates five minutes to bring a tall black horse from the nearby stables and back it into the shafts of a well-kept carriage. They set off eastwards and soon reached North's brother's house in Panton Street where Lang explained his intended course of action. Within a few minutes North and Lang were into the carriage and it was on its way eastwards towards the centre of Westminster. Past the Blewcoats school, along Chapel Street and left into Gardener's Lane the street was crowded with noisy, dirty carts and men struggling to herd a dozen shaggy cattle through the traffic.

Into York Street in the heart of Little France, they turned towards the abbey. Just before Broad Way there was a narrow alleyway leading into the rents, which Bates explained was a much less conspicuous way of reaching the houses in the interior. At the end of the short alley, Lang turned to his left and skirted round the backs of the houses on that side. There were small productive gardens here but he could not see anybody working on them. North walked along the front of the houses.

The Rents themselves were half a dozen tall grubby houses each side of narrow cobbled street, hung with lines of drying clothing. The aroma of human waste, rotten food and unwashed people struck the nose like a smack in the face.

The house marked number six stood out from the others because somebody had made an attempt to clean it up. A basket of fresh vegetables had been brought round from the surprisingly well-kept patchwork of small gardens behind the houses. A handsome woman was seated on a settle peeling potatoes into a bucket of water. She looked up with a frown and started to get to her feet to retreat into the house, her peeling knife clutched in her hand.

North raised a hand to stop her, 'Mrs Paget? Please don't be afraid, I mean you no harm but I am anxious to speak to Marcel Mesonant, is he here?'

She was a well-rounded woman and her voice was breathless, 'I don't want no trouble, captin.'

'Just tell me where he is ...'

As he spoke there was a sound of raised voices and breaking timber at the rear of the house. North dashed past Mrs Paget. The corridor was dark but an oblong of light at the end denoted the rear door. He ran out into the garden. Lang was on his knees, with a moaning man lying on the ground in front of him. The man's face was bloody and when Lang turned, North could see that he had not escaped the fracas unmarked. There was a red patch on his left cheek and forehead which was probably destined to become a shiner.

North drew his sword and rested the tip against the man's chest. 'Your name, quickly now or I will run you through.'

The man's tone was surly. 'Mesonant, Marcel Mesonant, what is going on?'

'That is something we will discuss at Somerset House.'

North caught the widening of eyes as the name was mentioned.

'Somerset House? I know nothing of this place.'

'Bad memory, eh? Well I think I will be able to jog it for you. On your feet!'

Between them North and Lang dragged the man to Bates's carriage which was barely big enough for the three inside.

On the 15-minute journey to Somerset House, North questioned the Frenchman closely in his own language. Mesonant dissembled at first but decided that he could safely give up the Prussian Wieck after being told that North was much less interested in him.

Chapter 11

North drew Lang to one side as they entered the building in which Cosworth had died. 'Keep him here, James. I will send some help from the Admiralty. Say nothing to him. Take him to the room Cosworth died in, sit with him but say nothing.'

The drive to the Admiralty took about ten minutes. Throwing Bates a guinea piece, North bid him wait in Whitehall while he went into the Admiralty building. It took North a quarter hour make some arrangements and to collect three sturdy servants and load them into the carriage. North looked up at Bates on the box.

'Back to Somerset House, Mr Bates, and unless Lieutenant Lang needs you further I bid you a good day and thank you.'

North walked down to Horseguards and had a quick conversation with the corporal of horse in the stables.

He emerged on to Green Park mounted on a borrowed horse. She was a tall bay with, at first, a mind of her own. North settled her as he crossed the park. By the time he was jogging towards the entrance near Buckingham House, she was quieter and knew who the master was. By the time North dismounted outside the courthouse in Bow Street, she was so docile that when he scratched her behind the ears, she just nudged his shoulder for more. He patted her neck and laughed as he tied her to a post.

Sir Richard Ford was in his office behind the court room. He rose to his feet with a smile and extended his hand when North was shown in. He sat down again and listened intently as North spoke, nodding occasionally.

When North mentioned the hunt for Wieck, Ford said, 'I shall send with you three of my best Brave Fellows, Sir Michael. I assume you will want them to carry pistols?'

....

The Guildable Manor of Southwark was a rabbit warren of narrow streets and market stalls that afternoon. Between St Saviour's and the Clink Prison were the dirty waters of Saviour's Dock and on the Clink Street side a looming warehouse, black and grim, its whole appearance one of abandoned despair. A sign above the wide double door, which was hanging by a single corner, declared the building to be owned by Saloman Brothers. In the sharp wind blowing in from the river, the sign swayed and groaned.

The rear of the building backed on to the river. The three red-waistcoated runners with North held his horse while he walked quickly to the riverbank and looked down. The shore here was retained by a green, slimy, stone wall. The tide was still rising a little and the longboat below, her stern pushed upriver by the tide, was secured to a ring in the wall.

North waved a hand at the midshipman seated in the stern, who lifted his hat in salute. All was prepared here.

Sending two of the runners along Clink Street to cover the far side of the building, North and the man with him drew pistols and went to the main door. They pushed against it and it resisted for a bare moment before creaking as it swung inwards.

North pointed to floor where there were numerous footprints in the dust. He whispered to the third man, 'Stay here. I will take the stairs. Watch for anybody coming down.'

The building had only been disused for a year and fortunately the stairs, though creaky, were sound enough. North reached the first level. Here was an empty warehouse spreading the full extent of the building, daylight streaming in from many windows. The room was empty. He reached another level; the same quiet almost peaceful place without a sign of a human being.

The same on the third level but as North emerged on to the top floor of the building the sound of scuffling feet was much heavier than the few lean rats that had crept away from him on the lower floors. He took the last three steps at a rush, thrusting out the pistol. Movement came from his left and a sudden shaft of bright daylight as a hatchway was opened out on to the platform of a crane derrick.

North shouted, 'Stand fast! It is no use trying to escape, the building is surrounded. *Machen Sie die tür geschlossen!* Shut the door!'

The man turned for a moment then snatched at a rope and

jumped.

North ran forward. The man was swinging from the end of the rope, out above the river. He looked down briefly then let go, falling feet-first into the river. The longboat was less than five yards away.

One of the seamen in the bows caught him by an ankle as he tried to scramble up an iron ladder to reach the top of the wall. One of the runners looked down at him, a pistol aimed at his head. He seemed to shrink into himself as he fell back into the boat.

North called down, 'Mr Truscott, carry him to Stangate Wharf by Westminster Bridge. I will meet you there.'

By the time North arrived at the wharf on the north bank near the lower side of the bridge, Wieck was standing between two beefy sailors, his clothes still shedding water. North handed the reins of his horse to one of the runners and thanked him for his assistance. He had a coach nearby and he, Wieck and his two escorts were soon being carried along the north bank the short distance to Somerset House.

Lang had been sitting for nearly two hours without a word, reading a book. Mesonant, his right wrist manacled to one of the window bars, was staring out over the river.

His heart almost jumped from his mouth as the door suddenly opened and Wieck came tumbling in, his short jacket and pantaloons sodden and stinking of river water. He reached out with pinioned hands to try to prevent his face striking the floor with no success.

Then North followed him, a grim smile on his face.

'So here we are. Two bungling killers and no doubt the shade of Lieutenant Cosworth watching you. You will pay the price for the murder of course but perhaps we can obtain some clemency for you if you tell us the names of those who paid you to kill Cosworth. Take your time.'

He brought over a bottle of claret and poured some for himself and Lang then sat down next to him. The silence dragged on for a minute or two until Wieck asked, 'If we are to hang why should we co-operate?'

North folded his arms and asked, 'Have you ever seen a man hang, Wieck?'

'No, sir, I have not.'

'It is a messy business, is it not, Mr Lang? Do you remember the man who was hanged in Halifax, Nova Scotia when we were there in the year nought?'

Lang relied, 'Indeed I do, sir. It was ghastly. Lieutenant Thomas Fry for murder, wasn't it? As I recall it took eight minutes with his feet flailing the air and the shit streaming down his legs. For a moment I thought the noose was slipping but then his neck broke and his head was almost torn off. *Damned* messy business, sir.'

North said, 'Then of course he was hanged from the yardarm with eight seamen hoisting him up and a round-shot in a net tied to his ankles. Hanging somebody from a scaffold can be much worse.'

'Why is that, sir?'

'Well, the hangman has to be very careful to measure the rope exactly or when the trapdoor opens the man's feet might strike the ground. His ankles get broken but I suppose that is nothing compared to the agony of trying to get breath into your lungs. Broken ankles, can't stand up, you see? Can't get free of that damned rope. It is instinctive of course, the body will force you to breathe – the brain has no control. Consider if you will those moments of sheer terror, the bag over your head, so powerless yet so desperate to breathe? A broken neck and a swift end would be a mercy but it is unlikely. If I had to be executed I think I would beg to be shot, at least it's quicker.'

Lang agreed. 'Much quicker and if death can be in any way painless, surely the more desirable. Then there is also the matter of shitting yourself.'

'Quite so.'

Wieck's face was twisted in horror, and he began to gasp. Mesonant dry-retched. They almost fell over each other to blame the man who had recruited them.

Of course the arrest the following day of Capitaine Roger

Vrignant a few streets away from the French legation and the ambassador disowning him were matters of huge interest to the public at large. Unusually Wieck and Mesonant, after their trial for murder, were shot rather than hanged. Vrignant was incarcerated for life in the King's Bench prison in St George's Fields.

He was fortunate: the King's Bench, though mainly filled with debtors, was considered much more comfortable than any other of London's gaols.

Chapter 12

North sat at his desk in the converted boathouse he used as a headquarters office in Shoreham harbour poring over his usual pile of paperwork.

He was in serious dispute at present with the storekeepers at Deptford. Despite the nearness of his command to Portsmouth it had been decreed that supplies of most of the needs of his ships would come under the wing of Deptford. Unfortunately that yard had a reputation for dishonesty and in the matter of supplies was at its worst.

Shortages against inventories and poor quality were the burden of many captains in the unfortunate position of being supplied by Deptford but in the case of North's squadron, these deficiencies were the battlefield in which a war was being waged between North and the storekeepers. The ground upon which the battle was fought shifted from topic to topic but nothing vexed North as much as the rotten biscuit being supplied to his men.

Supplies of fresh food were not a problem since they were obtained locally and directly by North's staff. In the matter of ship's biscuit, however, regular supplies were sent by wagon from Deptford. Captain Spicker had drawn North's attention to the diabolical quality of the biscuit six weeks ago and there had been increasingly angry exchanges of letters between North and Robert Clay, the assistant commissioner and supplies manager at Deptford and the supplying victualler himself.

Despite a series of complaints from North, it was still a frequent occurrence for bags of biscuit to be opened and condemned as unusable. The well-established custom of the masters of the squadron gathering together and examining the bread was now necessary after each delivery. At least half of the 'bread' supplied was practically inedible.

In desperation North had samples sent to the Victualling Board and in return the victualler had sent samples of the bread he said was being supplied. As a result of the victualler's samples, the board pronounced the bread suitable. North wrote to the board that it was pointless looking at samples sent by the victuallers, since they bore no resemblance to that being delivered. The only proper course was to have a Board representative present when the boxes were opened on reaching Shoreham.

This last plea was ignored so North tried a different tack. He passed the word that any ship's master in the flotilla who refused to sign for a delivery would have his backing. As a result the contractor could not receive his pay.

He then asked the port commissioners at Plymouth and Portsmouth to examine a sealed box taken at random from the next shipment and give their opinion. Since each box contained several bags of bread it was likely some of it would be the substandard article. It was a shrewd move. Neither man had a connection with Deptford Dockyard nor the particular victualler, so he believed their verdict would be impartial.

Both commissioners wrote to the Admiralty and the Victualling Board with copies to North stating that in their opinion the bread was unserviceable. Commissioner Saxton at Portsmouth opined that of the thirty pieces of bread he tested not one was fit for rats to eat, composed as it seemed by rotten flour and chalk dust in equal parts.

What happened next was unexpected.

North heard the noise of a wagon rumbling on the cobbles on the strand near the building. The noise stopped and started again. It moved away up the slipway slope. Then was a more rapid rumbling and with an almighty crash the front of the building swayed and began to sag. North jumped to his feet, his hand scrabbling to reach his sword.

The roof creaked and groaned then, shaking and heaving, it collapsed into the building. North tripped and fell back behind his oak desk, which probably saved his life.

Anxious hands tore at the debris until they found the commodore. As they pulled him to his feet a seaman screamed and fainted. North looked at the aghast faces around him. A voice shouted, 'No, no, they've killed him and left his ghost!'

He looked down at his uniform and saw that from head to toe

he was covered in white flour. He brushed off most of the flour and scooping some of it on to his finger, put it to his lips to taste.

He said to Spicker, who had just rushed up, 'Well, this proves one thing, more damned chalk than flour.'

Seeing that he was uninjured, laughter began to spread with North laughing the loudest.

Two marines came down the slipway, which in places was ankle-deep in biscuits and flour, dragging a struggling, red-faced man between them. They thrust him forward. One of them said, 'This man was with the wagon. He must have deliberately loosed the horses and let the wagon run down the slope.'

Spicker reached out and shook him by the lapels, 'What is this outrage? Who are you?'

The man was almost as furious as Spicker, 'Campbell Denton! Captain North may know me better as the victualler he has been trying to ruin. I have just personally delivered his fucking biscuit.'

North nodded, 'Well, Mr Denton, let us see how a sea voyage clears your head, shall we? Captain Spicker, you may press this man into His Majesty's frigate *Fisgard*. Let him experience what our jacks have to eat for a few weeks then you may set him on shore again. Perhaps that will improve his attitude.'

Denton shouted, 'You can't do that! I'm a businessman, not a sailor!'

North shook his head, 'My ears must be filled with chalky flour, I can't hear a word you're saying. Did you say you would rather be arrested for attempted murder, criminal damage and ruining my best uniform?'

That should have been the end of the matter but the assistant to the Deptford commissioner felt so challenged that he sent North a letter, the relevant part being:

> *Perhaps I cannot argue your treatment of Mr Denton but be assured that I will not rest until the insult to my own integrity is expunged. Accordingly I have requested an enquiry into the quality of all supplies to your command. Should it be found that your complaints are unfounded I shall expect you to refrain from further imputations of dishonesty directed against this office.*

North handed the letter to Spicker to read.

Spicker shook his head, 'Is he mad? Does he have so little grasp on reality to insist on this course? I suspect that at least four tenths of ship's victuals are substandard at all times. What world does he live upon?'

North replied, 'It will not happen. He must know that there is just as much determination on the board not to dig into these matters. I am not suggesting that all the victualling commissioners are corrupt but even those who are honest will see that sleeping dogs lie undisturbed. However this could cause a confrontation between us, the assistant commissioner and the Board itself and that may not be a bad thing.

'Perhaps it is high time such a meeting took place. I shall write to Commissioner Towry telling him I am happy to attend an enquiry. Something useful may come from this. In the meantime all supplies coming from Deptford will be randomly sampled by a quorum consisting of three lieutenants from different ships, the masters and pursers of those ships and the major of marines. See that this is done, and a careful record kept, Gustavus.'

Ten days later North examined the collated reports of the samplings. It read like a litany of shoddiness. Just one example stood out. Of a delivery of 30 barrels of salt beef three were opened by the quorum. On each barrel was painted a serial number, total weight and number of pieces of beef.

Barrel no. 273 should have contained 209 pieces but three of the pieces were found to be roughly smoothed lumps of timber and a further dozen showed signs of being chewed. There were two dead rats in the barrel.

Barrel no. 129 contained the correct number of pieces but in amongst them was a stray hoof that was not cloven. It was a horse's hoof.

Barrel no. 317 was probably the most interesting. Apart from the salt beef, the quorum found a blackened oilskin package which seemed to have fallen accidentally into the barrel. In the package was a purse with a few coins inside and a folded indenture. The indenture was between a master cooper and an apprentice called Peter Lemon and was dated 17th day of July, 1759. With it was a letter folded into the purse. It was on notepaper issued by the office of the Master of the Worshipful Company of Coopers, addressed to the apprentice and dated in 1766, congratulating him on being confirmed journeyman.

Lieutenant Brain of the *El Corso* contacted the Clerk of the Coopers' Company, who advised him that Peter Lemon had been Renter Warden in 1784 and had died the following year.

Of course it was not suggested that there was any certainty that the package had been in the barrel for 20 years but …

The meeting at Somerset House was brief but very noisy. The Deptford assistant commissioner was not supported by any of the other officials of the dockyard and none of the victuallers had attended. Three of the Victualling Board commissioners greeted Commodore North, who was accompanied by Captain Spicker and Lieutenant Lang.

The findings of the quorum were laid before the board. After the three men had shuffled through the papers, their faces becoming visibly paler, Sir George Towry cleared his throat. 'Very interesting, commodore, but of course this does not apply to each and every piece of merchandise, does it?' There seemed to be almost a plaintive plea for help in his voice.

North shrugged his shoulders, 'I suggest it does not have to, Sir George. Surely no item should be substandard. Of course the Board is free to conduct the same experiment, perhaps a visit to Shoreham? You could choose one of my ships at random and we will have all her supplies turned out on the quay, opened and examined. If not the same experiment with any naval vessel supplied by Deptford and chosen at random might prove instructive.'

'No, that is not necessary, Sir Michael. I think you have proved your point.'

The face of Dawson, the Deptford assistant commissioner, was flushed. 'Am I being accused, gentlemen? Well, speak up, I have the right to know.'

Towry looked him up and down, his contempt clear on his face. 'Look here, Dawson, you started this. What did you expect? Perhaps you thought to receive a grovelling apology from Sir Michael? I urge you to remain quiet while we try to sort out your mess. Commodore, you realise that the ramifications of this affair could spread far and wide throughout the service? I am not trying to gag you but this could prove disastrous and in the end everybody could suffer, even the seamen you seek to protect.

'The First Lord is gaining significant support for a general enquiry into naval matters and it is to be hoped that improvements will follow. Would you be content with a direction from the Board that practices at Deptford be strongly improved?'

'In the circumstances and provided the Board oversees those

improvements I would be satisfied, sir. I accept that the officials there, including Mr Dawson, are busy men and cannot overturn every rock but I am sure he will agree that a closer eye on things by his staff can do nothing but good.'

Towry smiled. It was an olive branch entirely in keeping with North's reputation for fairness and diplomacy. Unfortunately Dawson did not appear to grasp the opportunity.

'Damn it! I am traduced, sir, *traduced!* My reputation is at issue here. I will not have the contractors challenged at every turn. It is difficult enough to maintain the chain of supplies. I shall go to the First Lord myself!'

Towry slammed a hand on the table. 'Then you will take with you my letter dismissing you from your position, blast it! You must be stupid! We all know what goes on at Deptford and it is not good enough. Those involved do not even bother to conceal their peculations. Will you stand in the dock at the Old Bailey, alongside a dozen contractors or more, Dawson? Is that what you want?'

Dawson's face seemed frozen in wide-mouthed shock. He realised he had gone too far.

Towry turned to his colleagues and whispered conversation took place. Then he turned to North.

'Commodore, the Board wishes to record its thanks for bringing this matter before us. There *will* be a significant improvement in the arrangements and you may rest assured that any future difficulty you experience will be very much taken to heart. I understand there was considerable accidental damage to your office building in Shoreham recently, caused by a runaway supply wagon? Any costs incurred in repairs to the building will be covered by Deptford Dockyard's budget.

'Mr Dawson, you are removed from Deptford. Within three days you will present yourself to the Commissioner at Portsmouth dockyards, a man of impeccable probity and integrity, and he shall employ you as he sees fit. Let us hope that tuition in an honest and efficient environment will assist your future career. You may go.'

Journeying back to Shoreham, North and his officers were content with the result but determined not to relax their guard. Some shady practices had to be reluctantly accepted but the welfare of the men came first. It was bad enough that on some ships pursers pushed the boundaries too far, though thankfully one important result of this whole matter had been the realisation of the squadron's warrant officers that it did not do to try to pull the wool over the eyes of their commodore.

Chapter 13

June 1802 to March 1803

The fragile peace held and although North and his flotilla of small ships was fully employed and therefore his crews were kept in full training he sometimes wished that either a full and lasting peace came about or war started again. This uncertainty was sapping the patience of the nation and its navy.

Life was going on out in the Channel and a significant number of smugglers brought to book.

In parliament, Addington was pursuing a policy of doing precisely nothing to antagonise the French except to maintain a strong navy to discourage invasion.

Truth to tell this policy was not so much a sign of weakness as imputed to the much maligned Addington as the politics of reality. Britain had entered the Peace in state of financial instability. Addington had improved and adapted Pitt's tax regime so well that the country was producing almost twice as much income tax from one shilling in the pound as it had been from two shillings. As the months rolled by and Bonaparte's shadow still lay over the Channel, the government was becoming more and more confident that, if it had to come, war could be waged once more.

Addington's biggest problem was lack of parliamentary support. Unusually the Foxites, the Grenvilleites, and the

Pittites were united against the beleaguered small number of Addington's supporters. Even Addington knew that the days of his government could be drawing to a close.

With all the evidence such as North's experience at Shoreham, near to the end of this strange pseudo-peace, John Markham had succeeded in introducing and passing a bill to appoint commissioners to investigate abuses and frauds in the navy. The cost to the country was said to amount to more than £3 million a year. In the House of Lords, despite Nelson's assertion that the overwhelming depredations were being practised in His Majesty's dockyards and in no other part of the navy, he backed the bill.

HRH the Duke of Clarence, for once, also made a well-reasoned case for the dockyards to be subjected to a separate act for the same reason. He also introduced an amendment to delay the final passing of the bill for three months, which was defeated and the bill passed into law.

In fact North also believed that the practices of the dockyards were a far bigger cause for concern than the rest of the system. In this he was slightly at odds with his naval friend Lord Cochrane, who believed the Admiralty itself with its crop of venal officials and placemen was the more severely corrupt.

For much of the time which was beginning to be known as a phoney peace, the Norths were contentedly enjoying their life together, made even more sublime by Isobel becoming pregnant for a second time in the summer of 1802.

The first sign of grey clouds on their own horizon came at the beginning of March in 1803.

At about that time Cutter No. 4 had brought home an agent carrying a secret despatch from Lord Whitworth the Ambassador to France stating that he feared that Napoleon was about to close the country's borders and declare war. This did not come as a surprise to North nor did it to most people. Bonaparte had been flexing his muscles for almost the whole period of the Peace. Despite the treaty he had not withdrawn his army from the Low Countries. Switzerland, Northern Italy and many of the smaller German states had been annexed into the French fold.

Tens of thousands of his troops were encamped on the Atlantic coast opposite England. There were many other arrogant abuses of the treaty, showing that it was meaningless to Bonaparte. While continuing to bully his way across Europe, he had the effrontery to accuse the British of perfidy in not adhering to the agreement that they quit Malta. Addington had suggested a ten year lease but this was clearly not acceptable to Bonaparte either.

Bonaparte clearly believed that Addington was so weak that he could push him around and the British would keep backing down but he had gone too far.

At last orders went out to prepare for war. The reductions to naval strength were reversed and ships being built were to be finished with all speed.

Two days later an urgent message came to Shoreham carried on Cutter No. 3 which had been stationed off St Malo. Henry Gillespie needed urgent transportation and was apparently wounded and lying in the barracks on the Île du Large, one of the St Marcouf islands.

These islands close in to the French coast had been uninhabited but in a cheeky move the British had occupied them with a small force for the duration of the late war. Handed back into French hands, the islands were again practically deserted but it seemed that a few Royalists had secretly based themselves on the tiny islands and had smuggled Gillespie in from the nearby mainland after other men had brought him from Paris. Napoleon had ordered the islands to be fortified in case the British decided to seize them again but the work was not yet started.

North set off immediately in *Juniper*. Quietly moving around the Cotentin peninsula, *Juniper* dropped anchor three miles south of the port of St Vaast-la-Hougue in the area of the Baie de la Seine between the islands and the coast and North boarded the gig. France and England were not officially at war though North felt that would make little difference if the French decided to seize *Juniper*. Therefore the ship was kept dark and as quiet as possible.

Under muffled oars they rowed gently to the larger of the low-lying islands and drew the gig up on to the beach. Pistols drawn, North led five men to the wooden sheds. These had served as barracks for the small party of marines that had successfully held out for years against the most determined efforts of the French.

As they approached the largest shed a voice called out in a trembling whisper '*Qui va là?*' North responded with the prearranged passwords '*Arc en Ciel!*'

Inside the hut Gillespie was slumped semi-conscious in a chair near the window. He was covered in a blanket which North eased away to reveal a bloodstained shirt. 'It's not as bad as it looks, Michael,' Gillespie murmured.

'Don't worry, my friend, we'll get you out of here and I have a good surgeon's mate on *Juniper* who will patch you up.'

The three Royalists who had rescued Gillespie shook North by the hand and wished him good luck as his men carried Gillespie carefully down to the gig. They reached *Juniper* 20 minutes later and cast off.

All was well until they were just south of the Isle of Wight when the lookout noticed a sail half a league astern as the sun rose. As North stood next to Commander Fowler their glasses towards the distant ship they could see the tricolour flying from the mainmast. It was a 74-gun ship and North was sure he had seen her somewhere before. Then he realised what had triggered the thought. The ship had a large tan-coloured patch on her fore-mainsail. She was the same ship he had seen months ago after the encounter with Benedict Smythe's privateer.

While war had not been declared there had been many incidents of aggression between both nations and North was not going to take chances. He ordered all sails set and turned towards Bembridge and the safety of St Helen's Bay. The winds were light and *Juniper* was on her best point of sailing but on the French ship royals were added to give her more speed. Then studding sails were set and she closed the gap to *Juniper* significantly.

Another hail called their attention to another ship, this time fine on the port bow. North and Fowler turned quickly. Another French ship, a corvette of 20 guns, was standing between them and Bembridge Point. It was an ambush!

North's thoughts raced. Somebody must have betrayed them. Grimly he ordered the schooner's eight guns to be run out though there was little chance of surviving the power of the corvette even if the 74-gun ship did not catch up with them. He went to the tiller and leant his weight to the bar as the helmsman laid the ship far over on its starboard beam to bring her prow pointing east-north-east towards Shoreham and away from the trap. Luck was completely out. There was a *third* ship blocking their way in that direction. The lookout whooped with joy and shouted 'Deck there! The ship to starboard is the good old *Prince Rupert*, God bless 'er!'

The pursuing 74 had turned as *Juniper* had turned, cutting the corner to chase her victim. North swung his glass back to her. He could clearly see the panic sweeping through the ship as they spotted *Prince Rupert*. Their ship was in stays.

Floundering and swinging erratically the French crew managed to turn her and start tacking back the way they came. The corvette had also sped off further in towards the coast and was likely to be trapped in the Solent. With half a hundred ships at Spithead her chances of reaching the open sea again seemed slightly less than the proverbial snowball's chances in the nether regions should the British ships suspect a belligerent intrusion.

North removed his hat and waved it at *Prince Rupert* as *Juniper* came alongside her. He bellowed through the speaking trumpet to her captain, 'Hail brother, well met!'

His younger brother Captain Richard Peter North replied, 'As usual, Michael, I am here to pull your chestnuts from the fire!'

There had been a trap indeed but the canny John Markham had laid it bare and made counter-measures. He was on hand in Portsmouth with his counterpart William Wickham to meet *Juniper* and see Gillespie safely to London after sincerely thanking Michael North.

Before he left *Juniper,* Gillespie said to North, 'you remember that business with Cosworth at Somerset House? I tracked down the man who brought Wieck to London. Of course he did not know who I was but I had him to myself one evening and filled him with wine.'

He went on to say that after an evening of carousing, he had walked arm in arm with the man along the rue de Bagnolet and as they were passing the church of Saint-Germain-de-

Charonne, Gillespie managed to turn the conversation to Robert Fulton.

The man had slurred the name. 'Robert Fulton's in Holland.' He paused and drew himself straight. 'Who the fuck are you anyway? Why are you asking about Fulton?'

He snatched something from his jacket and lunged at Gillespie. At that moment all that Gillespie could feel was a hard pain in his side, like a punch, before he realised he had been stabbed. Without thinking he punched the man in the face and he fell back, banging his head on the iron gate of the cemetery.

Gillespie, realising that if the man lived he would become a hunted fugitive, took up the fallen knife and stabbed him in the heart. Then he dragged him into the cemetery and on to a mound of earth next to a newly dug grave. He rifled the dead man's pockets of cash and documents as a robber would have done and rolled the body over and into the empty grave.

It was not until he had reached the apartment lent to him by a sympathetic Royalist, an associate of the Baron de Batz, that he was overcome by loss of blood.

His journey to the coast had been a nightmare ending in being carried to the islands off the coast where North had found him.

Chapter 14

<u>18th March to 19th April, 1803</u>

The birth of his daughter Louise Isobel North on 18th March, 1803 happened on the sunniest day of the year so far. Isobel was delighted and Michael was stunned. It seemed so impossible that a tiny child could be so beautiful. His heart full of emotion, he sat beside his wife and, touching her cheek, told her of his love for her so many times that she laughingly pleaded with him to stop. Michael knew that she had never been happier than having him and her two children in her life, she had told him so many times. He knew that his love for her was the magical force that seemed to make his heart beat stronger each time she entered a room where he was.

Of course it was inevitable that their time together would be interrupted on many occasions since his promotion to captain three and a half years ago. On 27th March, North was summoned to the Admiralty.

After the glorious spring day before, he arrived on a grey miserable morning that seemed to be heralding in the gloom of war once more. His interview with John Markham was brief and to the point. He was to make the best of his way to Spithead where he would take command of the 74-gun ship HMS *Tigre*. It seemed that he was destined to command ships that had been captured from the French, this particular one having been taken at the Ile de Groix in June of 1795. More recently it had been with Sir Sidney Smith at the siege of Acre.

He would have *Juniper* as his tender and the crew of *Fisgard* would be transferred in its entirety apart from standing officers while *Fisgard* was undergoing a refit at Chatham. *Tigre* had been laid up in ordinary but it was now with its caretaker crew and a draft totalling 100 under his new 1st Lieutenant, William Birchall who had been with North in the Chagos operation commanding the 18-gun brig *Harpy*. Captain John Hodges of the Marines, late marine lieutenant of *Prince Rupert*, would command the 90 marines embarking on *Tigre* in the next few days. Finding a further 180 or more seamen would not be easy but word would go out and flyers would be distributed. There were a number of ships paying off in Portsmouth and although other captains would be vying with each other for volunteers from those ships North's reputation as the Tiger of the St Lawrence should be able to collect a few score. The Tiger was to command the *Tigre*.

Further orders would be sent to him on *Tigre* and he could expect to have his lieutenants and warrant officers sent to him speedily since his departure would not be long delayed.

After hurrying to Tarring and taking a stressful leave of Isobel and his son and the tiny daughter completely unaware of the significance of his absence, North had his coachman take him to Portsmouth with Cluney Ryan riding in the carriage with him.

As they stood waiting for a boatman to row them out to the *Tigre,* North turned to Ryan. 'You know, Cluney, you don't have to come with me. You have a place at Tarring Hall for as long as you wish.'

Ryan looked at his old friend and commander with a grin. 'Reckon you'll need me to watch your back again, sir. Besides a nice sea-trip with all that fresh air? Sure, it will be as sweet as walking through the Vale of Tralee on a summer's morning.'

When North reached the deck and removed his hat to the ensign, three calls shrilled and Lieutenant Birchall came forward, hat in hand. 'Good morning, Sir Michael, and welcome. The crew is sparse at present though I have managed to gather up around forty men who have served with you before apart from the *Fisgards* and the commissioning crew. We are just 425 seamen and 95 marines all told but Mr Hodges is on shore with Lieutenant Fowler drumming up more volunteers and Mr Lang is visiting the *St George* which is paying off. Commissioner Coffin at Chatham has promised at least 50 men in a few days.'

'Very good, William. Have the men on deck in ten minutes. I will read myself in.'

A marine with prematurely white hair watched as the bosun's mates ran through the decks whistling for all hands. Rattans were wielded against the tardy as men stumbled and ran to their divisions. The marine was standing near the wheel watching the sand running through the half-hour glass, so that he would be ready to ring the bell. He looked at the back of the new captain, Sir Michael North CB. Well, he looked the part all right, tall and broad-shouldered, smartly dressed and with a sword which by its hilt had to be a very expensive presentation sword. As he raised a hand to still the men, the marine noticed a prominent purple scar that crossed the back of his right hand and disappeared under his sleeve.

The old ritual was carried out that most on board had heard a few times at least, since they were nearly all rated able or better but they noticed that North did not read out the Articles of War. No doubt he would read them out on Sunday mornings if there was no chaplain. In fact North believed that reading out the Articles to a sceptical crew in a sonorous voice declaiming all its dreadful penalties and myriad offences was a farce. He replaced his commission in his tail-pocket and spoke for a few minutes.

'Men, there is no doubt war is coming again whether it be in a few weeks or in a few months and we must be on the sea to help watch over our country once more. With scores of ships laid up in ordinary you may rest assured their lordships have given us one of the best of them. I will not detain you long this morning. Looking around me I see familiar faces and I am sure those who know me will tell the rest of you that my rules are simple.

'Obey the Articles of War and promptly and fully implement the orders of your officers. I ask for a clean ship and a dutiful crew. I will have this ship the best that can be made. When the call comes to fight again there will be glory and prize money for all. So let us be about our duties and God save the king.'

James Lang, who on this ship was third in seniority, came on board an hour later with three boatloads of volunteers. With twelve more brought by Captain Hodges, that meant a total of 51 new faces.

The following day, 2nd April, North had the fife and drums playing through the streets of Portsmouth and flyers handed out to all and sundry. Such was his reputation that apart from six seamen who had travelled from Buckler's Hard to join *Tigre* there were 12 more that signed on that day. During the Peace the merchant ships, spoilt for choice, had signed up the best of the navy's topmen and specialists but now found themselves losing them as their ships were boarded when they approached land. Those who returned to the Royal Navy in this way had mixed feelings but on the whole were happy enough to 'volunteer' and receive the bounty as soon as they were given the chance.

North had shrewdly sent *Juniper* to cruise off the Channel Islands and intercept merchant ships in the area as one place where the press was unlikely to be hovering in full force. This yielded 21 first-class seamen in one week and filled *Tigre's* berths.

The new 4th Lieutenant, John Fellowes came on board shortly after 9am on 8th April followed by the gunner and the surgeon. North was fortunate in that the one-time surgeon of *Prince Rupert* Saul Levy was available and happy to join the ship. Most of the other warrant officers had been amongst the permanent skeleton crew including the purser, James Lister.

North up-anchored with almost a full crew and moved the ship to the Downs to await orders.

As they moved off North passed the binnacle. He looked down and frowned. After a few moments he beckoned to Birchall.

'William, take a look at the compass. Am I wrong in thinking it is not displaying a true course? Looking at the sun it seems to me that the ship is at least ten degrees off course.'

Birchall agreed. He had a small compass in his cabin and went off to fetch it. He held it in his hand as he approached the binnacle.

'Sir! The needle in my compass swings the closer I get to the binnacle. There must be something magnetic there.'

North called to the quartermaster to lend him his dirk and as both Birchall and the quartermaster looked over his shoulder, he scraped at the yellow metal ring around the compass. As a dull silvery colour was exposed, both men said as one, 'Iron!'

North said, 'Yes, gentlemen. Some scoundrel in the dockyard has replaced the brass ring with an iron one.' He levered the casing of the compass from its seat and carried it to the starboard rail. 'Now, we see that we would have been almost nine degrees off course. Such an error if relied on could have wrecked us at some time. Somebody will answer for this. Mr Birchall, have the armourer make a copper ring to place about the compass, if you please, and take this ring to your cabin for safe keeping. Enter this heinous event in your log.'

In Portsmouth *Tigre's* crew were fully employed restoring her depleted stores.

There had been one unwanted duty for North that came about purely from the fact that he was off Portsmouth at the wrong time. A court martial had been formed on 19th April to enquire into the conduct of Commander Raymond Fryston of the *Hound* sloop in absenting himself on shore without permission while 31 pressed men rose up and escaped from the sloop.

The president of the court, Captain Sir Hugh Pavier, acting third officer commanding at Portsmouth, met North on the quarterdeck of HMS *Dreadnought*.

'Sorry to drag you into this, North, I am afraid this is an open-and-shut case but I want to hear all the evidence and I needed a few captains I could rely upon to be impartial. You see, I believe there is somebody high up interested in the matter and while I must say no more at present, I do not want undue influence to be imposed upon a fair decision.'

They walked to the great cabin, which had been extended by striking the partition walls as if it were in preparation for a battle. Pavier had assembled six other captains though in Portsmouth it was not unusual to have up to 15 sitting on a board. The Admiralty's view was that at least 12 should sit for capital offences but in less weighty cases six or eight would suffice.

North knew three of the captains, Michael De Courcy, Philip Durham and William Cuming; the other three, Miles Worth, George Hurrell and Francis Collette were strangers. While De Courcey and Durham were friends of his, Cuming was a man he had little time for, being a flogging captain prone to excess in that area.

The signal gun was fired and the court convened. There were several dozen onlookers including three fashionably dressed ladies on the arms of equally elegant men. North sat in his seat to the right of the president. He could not help recalling the last time he had sat on a court martial three years ago in Halifax, Nova Scotia, in that case as president when as a result a lieutenant was reduced to the rank of seaman and hanged. At least here in home waters nobody could be hanged without the confirmation of the First Lord which took some pressure off the court.

Before the board commenced the business of the day the surgeons of HMS *Tremendous* and *Cambridge* attended to certify the inability of the captains of those two ships to attend due to illness. This was of course a formality but Pavier was shrewdly heading off a criticism as to the usual make-up of the board, nine or ten being the normal Portsmouth line-up.

After the usual formalities, the first witness was called and attested that he was Midshipman William Johns of the sloop HMS *Hound* of 16 guns, and between seven and eight o'clock on the evening of 12th March he had been lying in his cabin ill when he had heard a commotion on the deck. The officer in charge of the deck, Midshipman William Hutton, then entered his cabin to inform him that a sentinel had been overpowered. He had been posted to watch over the pressed men through a grating over the hold in which they were confined. After the pressed men rose up, the crew had been sent below and the escapees were in the process of seizing a boat.

Johns was the senior midshipman, Hutton at the age of 14 being the only other. Johns made his way to the deck where he saw the pressed men in the process of shoving off. He picked up a pistol and fired it at the escapees but the gun misfired. He then picked up a musket and fired it but the ball struck the side of the boat without injuring the occupants.

The court asked, 'Who was the commanding officer at this time?'

Answer, 'I considered myself commanding officer over the pressed men but not over the ship. Master's Mate Wylie was trussed up below deck as I later discovered and the crew battened down in the hold by the pressed men.'

The court elicited that there were 14 crewmen on the ship and four of the press gang, the remaining eight of the press and Lieutenant Crabbe being on shore.

The court, 'Where was Commander Fryston at this time?'

Answer, 'He too was on shore, I believe he was ill.'

Captain Durham, on a nod from the president, asked, 'Have many pressed men deserted from the sloop previously?'

The uncomfortable reply was 'Quite a few, sir.'

Lieutenant Crabbe gave evidence that he had been charged with recruiting as many men as possible since the sloop was commissioning and was drastically short of men. He was aware that Commander Fryston was on shore but it was not until Fryston returned, after the escape of the pressed men, that Crabbe learned that he had been ill.

Commander the Honourable Raymond Fryston followed after several witnesses had made similar statements to the court. He was a slim, well-dressed man who affected a lazy drawl, which from the start did not put most of his judges in a sympathetic mood.

His rank, name and date of commission put into the record, the court asked why he was out of his ship at the time of the incident. He stated that he was attending a physician and would have returned to the ship before midnight. The reason he gave for attending the physician was a severe stomach complaint. When it was put to him that evidence had already been elicited that he had slept out of his ship for three nights previously, he pleaded that he was incapable of rising from his sickbed for three days. He was vague as to how he had been in that sickbed and not sick on board the sloop.

Asked as to the specifics of the desertion by the pressed men, he stated that he had left clear orders to his lieutenant, John Crabbe, that a strong, armed guard should be placed over the pressed men and that he had been surprised that Crabbe had actually gone on shore. Asked as to the reliability of his senior, he answered that he had little confidence in him but 'What could you expect. Crabbe was after all the son of a market gardener and not a gentleman. Also the quality of the midshipmen leaves a lot to be desired.'

The court, 'Were you aware that Hutton was sick, suffering from the marsh fever?'

Answer, 'Well that might well be true.'

The trial went on for the rest of the morning and North could not see any mitigating circumstances so far. On the other hand he noticed that from the benches at the far side of the room, the coterie of well-dressed people who had commandeered the front-most seats was making disdainful noises during almost everybody's testimony except that of Commander Fryston. When the commander appeared the six people began to smile and mutter approving whispers as he gave evidence.

Pavier adjourned the court at 1pm and the captains retired to the wardroom for a light lunch. Philip Durham, chicken drumstick in hand, leaned towards North.

'Y'know, Michael, I am not too pleased. Captain Hurrell practically told me just now that it was a disgrace that Fryston was being tried; it should be Crabbe or Midshipman Johns. I told him I thought he should keep his thoughts to himself until the proper time.'

'Quite right, Philip. I don't want to discuss this right now but there seems to be a group of Fryston's friends in the cabin. It could be that they think we would be persuaded by some sort of display of support for Fryston. Frankly, as far as I am concerned all I want to hear is the evidence.'

There was a crush of people at the stern end of the ship so North went to the beak to relieve himself in the roundhouse. As he returned an attractive woman, one of the people from the cabin, waved a hand at him. She may have been in her 30s at first sight but closer could be seen to be a good 15 years older. She arched her back and North could see that her bows were extremely impressive over a very narrow midships.

'Sir Michael, a moment if you will. You may not remember me. Lucretia Martin. I was at Admiral Dacre's soirée when you and Lady Isobel were in London last year? I am a little embarrassed and wondered if you might advise me. You see Commander Fryston was in my house during his illness and ...'

North held up his hand. 'I must stop you there, madam. It is improper to converse with you on the subject of Commander Fryston. If you have anything to say, please speak to the defending officer.' He started to turn away.

She hissed at him, 'Find him guilty and you will be sorry, mark my words. The Duke of Clarence himself is taking an interest and it would be well for you to remember that.'

North ignored her and made his way to the cabin. Before the proceedings recommenced, he advised the president of exactly what had occurred on the deck.

Pavier nodded. 'You are not the only one, Michael; his friends have been making the rounds it seems. As a board of enquiry we will discuss our conclusions in private at the proper time and we shall air these matters then.'

Fryston seemed strangely calm and self-assured when his testimony was resumed. No doubt he was well aware of the efforts of his supporters to influence the court.

North looked at him. Fryston had folded his arms and leaned back after Francis Collette had asked him whether he had sent a message to his lieutenant regarding his indisposition. Fryston had said that he had. It was pointed out by de Courcy that Lieutenant Crabbe had stated that he had received no such a message. Fryston shrugged his shoulders and said that Crabbe was obviously mistaken.

North said, 'My colleague Captain Collette asked you about sending a note to your ship but that still does not answer the question of permission from higher authority. You are answerable to the port admiral. Did you receive the permission of Lord Gardner to sleep out of your ship?'

Fryston shrugged. 'His Lordship is a busy man. No doubt one of his clerks misfiled my request.'

'In which event, Commander, you assumed that permission had been given?'

Fryston shrugged again, 'I was laid low, any reasonable

person would have seen that I was incapable of returning to the ship. Besides, we are not at war.' There were a few chuckles and murmurs of approval at the front of the audience which North ignored.

Collette asked, 'I assume you are calling a physician to give evidence?'

'I would have thought the word of a gentleman sufficient,' replied Fryston with asperity.

The president said sharply, 'A court martial does not recognise the difference between a gentleman and any other witness, Commander. For example Lieutenant Crabbe, by virtue of his commission, is a gentleman, even if his father was not, and it would appear that his version of events is significantly different in respect of this note. I am sure that we can have word sent if your physician is not to hand?'

Fryston, somewhat less composed, replied, 'I believe he is away from home at present.'

De Courcy said, 'Your ship has seen a total of 24 deserters so far this year, in addition to the pressed men that escaped. To what do you attribute this high number of deserters? Is it lax discipline or perhaps you are far too kind and simply allow them to wander off?'

Fryston said angrily, 'All ships are susceptible to desertion, especially in a big seaport.'

De Courcy nodded. 'And especially when the commanding

officer's back is turned, right?'

The defending officer asked permission to call character witnesses.

The president folded his arms. It was fairly common practice to allow the tongue of good report from senior officers who knew a defendant but he suspected that the character witnesses in question would be from the front row of the audience.

'Very well, I shall allow any naval officer you care to call, within reasonable limits, and two civilian witnesses provided their evidence is restricted to character.'

The first witness was a man who appeared to be in his 60s, in the uniform of a vice admiral. North recalled the name Tennant. He was a superannuated officer who had never held flag command – a yellow admiral. Sidney Smith had once remarked to him of another yellow admiral, 'a showy but somewhat fragile butterfly that is never seen in stormy weather.'

Tennant was hardy fragile. He was overweight and sweating, his face red from simply walking the length of the cabin. He had been brought on board in a bosun's chair. He gave his name and glared at the array of, to him, junior officers on the other side of the long table. Before he could be asked any questions he said in a gruff voice, 'Probably save some time if I tell you that young Fryston is an honest and diligent officer, one of my best when he was a junior lieutenant. Never known him to be untruthful; ran a tight ship. What more do you need to know?'

Pavier asked, 'You have heard the evidence, sir, so please tell the court why you think he seems to have made this error in not making sure he had authority to sleep out of his ship?'

Tennant spread his pudgy hands wide, 'Come now, gentlemen, who amongst us has not spent the odd night on shore, particularly when overtaken by illness? We are not at war; surely things are not viewed so stringently in time of peace? Besides, Fryston was the guest of Lord and Lady Martin, most respectable people – ah, seated here if you want confirmation?' He lowered his voice confidentially, 'Friend of Prince William, too, you know?' He tapped the side of his nose.

North could not resist commenting, 'Being aware of his attitude to "running a tight ship" himself, I am sure that the Duke of Clarence would not be too impressed with a subordinate assuming that the matter of permission could be taken for granted, would he, Admiral?'

Knowing as well as most naval people present that as a captain the prince was a martinet of the worst kind, this brought a smile to the members of the board. Tennant bristled. 'Are you implying the opinion of a vice admiral is not to be considered, *Captain?*'

De Courcy butted in. 'I am sure Sir Michael, who is of course Deputy Adjutant of the Royal Navy, though not sitting here in that office today, is fully appreciative of your opinion, Admiral. However, we are here to reach an impartial conclusion, not to be influenced by a person's connections, impressive though they may be. I believe you have yourself sat on courts martial, sir?'

In fact amongst the many things Tennant had not done on his way to high but obscure rank was by careful avoidance to have sat in judgement at a court martial, though he was not going to share that with these blithering upstarts. 'Damned waste of time this whole business, if you ask me. His lieutenant should not have left the sloop to a couple of snivelling midshipmen!'

The president held up a hand. 'Which is a matter for the court to decide, don't you think? Thank you, Admiral; I don't think we need to detain you any longer. Are there other witnesses for the defendant?'

Lieutenant Montague Smart, despite his name at best not the cleverest counsel Fryston could have chosen, shuffled his papers and stuttered out, 'Umm … Lord, I mean Lady, Lucretia Martin, sir.'

'Which is it to be, Lord or Lady Martin?'

'Her ladyship, sir.'

Asked her name she replied in a sultry voice, 'Lucretia, wife of Baron Julian Martin of Llanidloes.'

One of the captains to North's right mumbled, 'Where's that?

Some piddling little place in Wales ain't it?' The blush this brought to her face was satisfying.

The president was impressed by her physical appearance as was every member of the board, including, it must be admitted, Michael North, who had already had the benefit of a close presentation of her superstructure.

'Well now,' said Pavier kindly, 'take your time, your ladyship. Do you know the accused, Lieutenant Fryston?'

'Yes, he is a friend of the family and often visits. We have a house in Portsmouth and my husband has interests in the supply of goods to the navy. Mr Fryston is the younger son of Lord Fryston of Brentwood; I have known him for some five years.'

The court asked, 'In your opinion is he a man of integrity?'

'He most certainly is! More so I might say than some other naval officers who have visited my home. My husband is often away and I have been embarrassed by the unwanted attentions of a number of men but never by Raymond.'

De Courcy leaned forward. 'Forgive me, Lady Martin, but it has to be asked, was your husband at home when Mr Fryston was laid low by illness?'

Her face coloured. 'Yes, he damned well was! I don't know who has been spreading rumours behind my back but my husband is no William Hamilton! I keep a respectable salon – even the Prince Regent himself has been my guest.'

More than one person present wondered if the king's womanising eldest son was more than friendly with her but nobody voiced it.

Pavier nodded, 'Well, thank you, Lady Martin; that will be all.' He turned to the defending officer, 'Unless there is anything else, Mr Smart? No? Do you not wish to address us concerning the evidence?'

'Ah. Yes, of course, sir. Umm. The court has heard that Lieutenant Fryston gave specific orders concerning the safe-keeping of the recruits, I mean the pressed men. It has been established that this was indeed the case and therefore he cannot be blamed since his officers failed in their duty.

'As regards being absent from his command I would suggest that this was a minor matter. We are men of the world, I mean, well, er.'

Pavier said, 'Is this the best you can offer, Mr Smart, are you sure you want us to take note of your comments? Very well, then the court will consider the matter, please clear the cabin.'

The captains removed their coats and passed the claret. Pavier said, 'Let us start by having a show of hands and see how close we are to agreement. All those that believe Fryston guilty of neglect of duty?'

North, Durham and de Courcy raised a hand.

'Not guilty?'

Cuming, Collette and Hurrell – the latter hesitantly – raised their hands. Worth stated he was not convinced either way. Pavier's casting vote would carry it but he decided to try to reach something approaching consensus.

'Well then, this leaves us with an alternative. We can find Fryston guilty of sleeping out of his ship without permission – deal with that as severely as possible without dismissing him from the service – but we would have to find Lieutenant Crabbe guilty of neglect of duty?'

Durham shook his head. 'Can't have that! The lieutenant left an officer in command while he carried out his duties. You would have to find the senior midshipman guilty of neglect despite being sick. That, I do not like.'

North said, 'Surely we are missing the point. The desertion of the pressed men was avoidable and ultimately the officer in command of the ship is responsible for the actions of those under him. We have all walked the deck of a ship of war and are fully aware of that responsibility. I agree junior officers, particularly Lieutenant Crabbe, could be censured in this case but Fryston commands and it was his responsibility. Sleeping out of his ship without permission may be an aggravation of the matter but in view of his illness, leniency might be extended, I suppose. But added to neglect of duty I can't see how we can avoid cashiering him.'

De Courcy blew out his cheeks. 'If indeed he was ill!'

'Well,' said Pavier, 'Let us hear from those who say not

guilty.'

Cuming said, 'Look, whether he is guilty or not, he is too damned well connected. I don't know about the rest of you but the Duke of Clarence would be a bad enemy to make.'

There was a sudden silence and Miles Worth, who had not raised his hand, said, 'I had been undecided but now I would want to be shown as believing the case proved and damn his connections!'

Pavier looked at Collette and Hurrell, 'Well, gentlemen?'

Collette said, 'Damn it, Worth is right, we can't give in to blackmail. In any case I will take it upon myself to see the Prince and make it clear that I, for one, will be very public if he tries to screw any of us down. North is right too; the commanding officer has to be responsible.'

Hurrell agreed with some reluctance since it seemed to him that he was being disloyal to his relative, Vice Admiral Tennant. On the other hand he agreed entirely with North. For all of Fryston's bluster, he was the responsible officer and in any case he did not believe his story of illness for one minute.

That left William Cuming who said, 'I want it recorded that I dissent from the majority.'

Pavier half-smiled. 'Are you sure, William? When the record is published you may be called upon to explain yourself. Frankly, it has always been an open-and-shut case, in my opinion. It is only the element of influence and pressure that have made things sticky … for some.'

'Very well, he's guilty.'

Pavier raised his eyebrows. 'Dismissal from the service?'

'Got to be, I suppose,' mumbled Cuming.

'Everybody agree? Well, let's get on with it. Damned unpleasant business but the man is not worth saving, in my opinion.'

Collette sighed. 'I have to say that for a pair of tits like that, I would probably have been tempted myself!'

They stifled their smiles as they left the wardroom.

Fryston's face was white when he saw his sword, point towards him, on the court table. His supporters were in uproar and had to be severely warned by Pavier before silence could be achieved.

Chapter 15

When Vice Admiral Tennant had recovered from the journey to the shore he wheezed as he stepped straight into his carriage and told the driver to get him out of Portsmouth – a town he loathed – and back on the road to Bath. He reached into the hamper on one side of the seat and drew a bottle of fine Burgundy from it, eased the cork and poured himself a glass to help him recover his composure. Not for the first time he hesitated as he brought it to his lips.

He was not stupid. He was well aware that his love of good wine and food were damaging his health. He was in the Yellow division because the Admiralty had chosen to promote him to rear admiral – unassigned – in preference to other captains they deemed more useful. But on rare occasions their lordships might be persuaded to re-employ him in a more active role. However, an unfit admiral would almost certainly be passed over for a decent command. Perhaps it was time to cut down on the booze. But not at this moment!

Damn them! A pack of mere captains had made him look a fool and they must suffer for it. The devil of it was that he was only too aware that his influence over naval affairs was even smaller than when he had the ear of Admiral Sir Alan (now Lord) Gardner. It was Tennant who as a senior captain had accompanied the headstrong Gardner when he tried to negotiate with the mutineers at Spithead in '97. He had witnessed Gardner losing his temper, laying hands on the mutineers' delegate and threatening that he would have the whole pack of them dancing at a yardarm. It was Tennant who had earned Gardner's gratitude by supporting the fiction that the man had tried to assault the admiral.

He was not in St Vincent's good books, how could he be? St Vincent detested his enemies and favoured few. As he fumed over his treatment by the board of captains at this damned court martial one name stood out from the rest – that grass-combing bugger North!

A sudden thought came to him and he raised his cane to hammer on the inside of the carriage roof and shouted to the driver to turn back.

An hour later he was seated in a comfortable armchair in the Keppel's Head Hotel on the Hard near Portsmouth dockyard, a bottle of port specially reserved for flag officers set before him by the proprietor, Mrs Gauntlett. He looked around him at the fading wall-hangings and the barely respectable furniture, so different than when he had stayed here 25 years ago shortly after the hotel had been built and when Sally Gauntlett was a much younger, very charming and willing woman.

The message he had sent to *Brittania* had received a speedy enough reply and here he was waiting for the man who now entered the select lounge and looked about him.

Rear Admiral Henry Downham Butler had enough influence as a supporter of the Pitt administration to be given command of one of the divisions of the Channel fleet and with peace still officially in place, the Admiralty had felt that they could take a chance on the man's lack of naval genius to have him, at present, the second most senior officer in command at Portsmouth. He was a florid man of middle years with a well extended waistcoat and sparse fair hair. He was also quite short in height and very conscious that his nickname was Half-pint Harry.

He nodded at Tennant, sat down and accepted the brimming glass that was handed to him.

Tennant smiled at him. He was still so incensed that he wanted to get into his stride at once but courtesy dictated the usual pleasantries. He asked after his sister Edith who was married to Butler, knowing well that although Butler detested the horse-faced battle-axe; he lived in more fear of her than the entire French fleet. The usual social bilge out of the way, he sat more upright in his chair and stabbed a finger in his brother-in-law's direction. 'Harry, I have just been at the court martial of young Fryston – damned unpleasant business. The buggers found him guilty and cashiered him!'

Tennant was lukewarm towards Butler but he was useful. He knew that Butler had reached his high rank more by the attrition of his fellows than any true ability and his gargantuan daily consumption of wine tended to enfeeble an already impoverished headful of grey-matter. His present posting was probably more in the vein of 'he can't do much harm unless a war breaks out' and was permanently furious at the injustice of it.

'I take it he called you as to character, brother-in-law?'

'Fuck it, Harry, they more or less told me to piss off! The shit Michael North did his best to make me look a fool!'

Butler could not be sincere if he tried. 'That's appalling, Arthur. The man's a damned upstart – barely got his second epaulette and he gets as many plums as that little bastard Nelson.'

'My thinking entirely. Now, you being more or less the highest ranking sea officer in Pompey right now apart from the port admiral ...'

Five minutes later Butler raised his only objections to Tennant's idea.

'I don't know, Arthur, he is under direct orders of the First Lord. It seems he always is. Not only that, but Pitt and His Majesty think he's the man of the hour. I am not sure exactly what authority I have over him. I can't go against whatever orders he has.'

'Pitt ain't holding the reins any more. In any case you don't have to worry, Harry. I have it on good authority North is still awaiting orders and therefore must stay in the Solent. You're the senior officer on station in the absence of the admiral. While North's ship is in port you have some control of *it* even if not of *him*. Stores slow coming on board, marines redirected to another ship. Get my drift?'

'It would need the co-operation of the commissioner but that's not a big problem, I know a few things about him. Very well, Arthur, leave it to me though I am only doing this because I heartily abhor the man myself.'

Tennant grinned at him with absolutely no warmth. 'I am sure Edie would agree with me, Harry, family should stick together, what?' He wondered what hold Butler had over the commissioner, a man renowned as incorruptible.

After Tennant had left Butler ordered another bottle before leaving the hotel. He pondered Tennant's parting remark. He had been tempted to accidentally drown dear Edie on many occasions but instead did his best to be as far away from her as physically possible rather than sticking to her. He was not pleased about being used by Tennant but on the other hand he too was jealous of North's success, though he would never admit it.

....

21st April was a hot day and ideal for drying paint, so *Tigre's* sides had swarmed with brush-wielding seamen all morning. The captain's barge had been refurbished on its strakes. Dick Wells inspected the barge with meticulous care before nodding his approval. His expertise was not just founded on his two years on *Prince Rupert* as second cox'n to Sir Michael North; he had been born the son of a boatmaker in the Kentish port of Deal where many of the navy's boats were made. The 32-foot barge was clinker-built, thereby declaring its Deal origins and giving its name – a Deal pinnace. Carvel-built boats came from elsewhere; they were rarely if ever built in Deal where such innovations were regarded as suspicious and frivolous.

She carried 14 oars, six of which Wells had brought on board this morning. He had paid one shilling and a penny for each of them, the money coming out of the captain's pocket since he could not be bothered with the reams of paperwork needed to claim back the cost from the Admiralty. In fact Wells had to buy them from one of the chandlers outside the dockyard since, it seems, there were no spare oars of the required size in stock in the naval stores.

Likewise, the bosun had complained that in the matter of canvas he had politely been told that he was at the back of the queue. In fact so far back he should not bother to come asking for at least a month.

The warrant officers were used to obstruction or corruption and shrugged their shoulders but it did seem that in the last few days *Tigre* was encountering even more problems of supply than usual. The dockyard lighter had brought out ten instead of 30 bullocks and told the purser that there would not be any more for at least a fortnight – which was nonsense, of course.

Wells stopped thinking on these things and got back to the task at hand. He had also renewed the barge's rudder lanyards and fitted them himself, using crowned double wall-knots to secure the ends and at the same time attached a new, pristine, white painter and sternfast, splicing them to thimbles in their respective ringbolts.

Her crew was stowing her lateen sails and buffing the brass-work. A chubby–faced landsman called George Benham was carefully re-gilding the modest but elegant gingerbread-work on her stern. He wiped his brow with his fingertips and used the sweat to anoint one of the cherubs. Then, gold leaf delicately lifted with a chamois pad from the pages of the Bible in which he kept it, very gently he fixed it with a soft breath of air from his pouted lips. He had a small motionless audience that pursed lips with their resident artist and exhaled gratefully after holding their breath for long seconds, just in case, like.

Wells looked round as Tubal Shepherd, the ship's armourer, joined him.

'She looks good, Dickie,' Shepherd said, his soft Wiltshire burr emanating from a huge frame. 'Her ladyship will be pleased, that's for sure.'

'Aye, Tubal, lad; that she will,' said Wells with a wide grin. 'It'll be good to see 'er again, won't it?'

'Reckon it will, Dickie, reckon it will,' agreed Wells happily.

It would be the first time Lady North had come on board *Tigre*. Most of the crew who knew her were looking forward to seeing her again, though Shepherd, along with his friend John-David Herriot, now captain's clerk, would be particularly glad to see her. They had been part of a party of seamen four years ago that had been sent up to Dulwich to form a guard of honour at her brother's funeral. It was at that time that Michael North had met her and fallen in love. Shepherd and Herriot, along with at least 30 of the Tigres, had been on *Prince Rupert* on her first voyage.

Since *Tigre* was in port there were "wives" on board, their presence evidenced by the raucous sounds that could be heard through the open hatches. Though listening enviously to the Didos being cut by their companions below, the men of the watch on deck were working with a will, since their pride in the ship and their captain was almost universal. For Lady North's visit, the barky would be spotless and would not be better presented should the king himself be coming on board.

The senior lieutenant was standing on the quarterdeck watching the work being done on the barge with the same satisfaction as the rest of the crew but something was worrying him. Where was the 2nd lieutenant? The absence of the new Second, Suetonius Astley – who for obvious reasons preferred to be called Tony by his companions in the wardroom – was unexplained but the rumour throughout the lower deck was heavily in favour of petticoat fever.

The lieutenant's full name was the result of serious parental bad judgement. Suetonius Octavius Diocletian Astley (that SOD Astley to his friends and enemies alike) was renowned for his fondness for other men's wives, a predilection that had caused him considerable problems in the past and explained the four missing teeth that were very noticeable when he smiled. Because of his absence and the resultant responsibility the ship's 6th lieutenant, Robert Kettering, was suffering from nervous exhaustion, that being just a short distance from his normal fraught state.

Lieutenant Birchall was trying to calm Kettering down as he darted from stem to stern wringing his hands together and despairing of ever having the ship up to the captain's exacting standard. In his cabin, Michael North glanced up as the yeoman of the watch rang five bells in the forenoon watch. He could hear Kettering's nervous complaints. He checked his pocket-watch against his pair of chronometers, making sure it accurately registered 10.30, and sighed as he sat down behind the elegant green-leather-covered desk he had inherited from the *Tigre's* previous captain.

Kettering's high-pitched voice was a jarring reminder that he was saddled with an almost useless favourite of the equally unwelcome senior officer at present on station, Rear Admiral Henry Downham Butler. Although North was under Admiralty orders, Butler had gone out of his way to be as unpleasant and demanding of respect as possible.

George Naylor, the captain's steward, placed his second cup of tea of the morning in front of him. The source of North's annoyance was perfectly clear to him, even without the uncharacteristic drumming of his fingers on the desk. As he turned to leave, North said, 'Naylor, have somebody pass the word for Mr Kettering.'

Five minutes later, Kettering stumbled into the cabin, his thin face almost as red as his unruly ginger hair. 'S-sorry, sir, I came as soon as I could,' he gasped.

'Sit down, Mr Kettering and catch your breath.' He called for his steward to bring Kettering a cup of coffee. 'Now, Mr Kettering, usually I do not like to involve myself in the day-to-day running of the ship, that being Lieutenant Birchall's prerogative, but I really must urge you to calm yourself as you go about your duties. It would reflect poorly upon my personal reputation if you were carried off by apoplexy. It might be thought of me that I am too severe a taskmaster. Now, taking things in their order, what is putting you in this hobble?'

Kettering took a deep breath. 'Well, sir, there's the spare suit of sails. The rats have got to them. Then there are the purser's accounts. I have spent half the night trying to make head or tail of them. I know he is trying to deceive me but I can't put my finger on it.'

North said patiently, 'Now, the sails first. Unless they are inspected in the locker at least weekly, they are bound to suffer from rats and mildew. They need to be turned out and spread upon the deck on a dry day if possible. It seems that this has not been done but I apportion no blame. This morning the weather is perfect, so detail half a dozen men to assist the sailmaker with repairs. I will ask Mr Birchall to make a standing order for the bosun to turn them out once a week, weather permitting. On the other matter, I too have formed the opinion that the purser's praetorian practices are excessive. Bring me his books, I will have my clerk look over them and deal with him myself. Is there anything else amiss?'

'Well, Sir Michael, I am worried about Lieutenant Astley. Not to have heard from him for two days is very unusual …'

'Now, Lieutenant, you know I cannot enter into this discussion, it would be most inappropriate for me to comment without the premier present. Furthermore, you should regard his absence as an opportunity to exercise your skills as a commanding officer. I appreciate that you have not held independent command but you have been well trained aboard the flagship and in any case every lieutenant at any level could at a moment's notice find himself in command in battle should his seniors fall. Do not waste this opportunity. Act decisively and be not afraid to make mistakes. There has never been an officer born who has not got things wrong on occasion. Fear of failure brings about hesitancy and that could cost lives. Think on it, Robert. Now, if there is nothing else I won't detain you any longer.'

He shook his head at Kettering's back as he scuttled away. His thoughts turned to Astley. The trouble was that Kettering was right. Astley had not obtained permission to sleep out of the ship but it would not normally be a big problem to stay on shore for one night in the event of a legitimate emergency but not for two. What was wrong was his failure to contact Birchall or North. At the least it merited a reprimand on his return. The bigger problem was that, eventually, Admiral

Butler would find out and no doubt use the misdemeanour as a weapon in his ongoing campaign to make life as difficult as possible for North. Bearing in mind the recent court martial of Raymond Fryston, obviously North could not turn a blind eye to Astley's absence.

While ordering his thoughts he walked out onto the open gallery abaft the cabin. He reached into his waistcoat pocket and fingered the locket that bore Isobel's likeness. He stood for a few minutes looking out over a line of moored frigates and the schooner anchored in a line to leeward.

Behind the leading frigate *Boadicea* 38 was *Mermaid* 32, the command of Captain Robert Dudley Oliver. He saw the tall, spare figure of Lieutenant Corbett, her acting First, leaning far out over the stern quarter to inspect a bumboat coming alongside carrying two presentable whores, both dressed in red dresses and flowery hats.

The schooner was *Tigre*'s tender the *Juniper*, under Lieutenant John Catchpole. She was busy hoisting on board a new 18-pound carronade, which, with one similar, would replace two of her 22 hundred-weight, eight-and-a-half-foot long 6-pounders. As the combined weight of the carronades was almost exactly one ton, North had recommended and authorised that *Juniper* carry extra stores and powder to make up some of the ton and a quarter weight difference.

Dragging his attention away from the harbour, he decided that he would have to take official notice of Astley's unauthorised absence. Calling for his clerk, he also summoned his second coxswain – a man in whom he reposed considerable trust.

North gave Herriot two tasks: firstly to write a letter to Astley requiring him to repair on board *Tigre* immediately upon receipt of the letter and secondly, at a later time to go through the purser's books.

'I want you to take the letter on shore with Cox'n Wells at once, Herriot. Take the gig. My best information is that Lieutenant Astley is a guest of Commissioner Saxton. If you do not find him there, I want you to make extensive enquiries. It is important that he is found.'

'Aye, sir,' replied Herriot, refraining from voicing his views.

Chapter 16

After Dick Wells had been instructed to be vigilant and to note everything that was said and done, North sent them off. Herriot reflected upon Sir Michael's annoyance, which, unusually, he had allowed to be noticed. His reluctant course of action was now irrevocable. Willy-nilly, Astley was on the slippery slope towards a court martial and North's renowned patience had finally run out. The fact that Dick Wells was to bear witness to the delivery of the letter reflected the seriousness of the situation.

'Well, Dickie,' said Herriot as the lads leaned into their oars, 'that-sod-Astley's done it this time, that's my vardy! I reckon Astley's prick is gonna get 'im well in the shit this day.'

Wells nodded thoughtfully. 'His nibs ain't blessed with much in the way of officers this time, John-David, that's for sure, 'cept Mr Birchall and Mr Lang a-course. I s'pose the Fourth ain't too bad as long as you don't cross 'im but the Fifth don't know 'is arse from 'is elbow, nor does Astley. As for that waste of space Kettering, the sooner he goes the better.'

They sat in reflective silence as the four-oared gig came alongside the quay. Making their way carefully up the weed-covered stone steps they turned towards the town and the home of the dockyard commissioner, Sir Charles Saxton. Although not actually situated in the dockyard itself, the grey-brick building was a conveniently short distance north of the high wall that marked the boundary. They approached the house by the servants' entrance at the side.

Sir Charles's daughter Philadelphia Hannah (Mary to her family) opened the door. She was the treasure and adored fiancée of the captain of the *Mermaid*, Robert Dudley Oliver. His feelings being returned in full measure by Mary, she had not been tempted to succumb to the blatantly expressed desires of Lieutenant Astley. However, she was aware that he had been so little cast down by her firm rejection that he had immediately cast his net further abroad. After skilful angling, he had snared the succulent 39-year-old Katherine Hemmingway, wife of the absent Rear Admiral Eustace Hemmingway, 16 years her senior. The admiral was with his command in Irish waters.

Pointing towards the town, Miss Saxton gave Herriot and Wells directions to the Hemmingways' house, adding with a mischievous grin, 'Be discreet now, won't you.'

A high, forbidding wall surrounded the house where Rear Admiral and Lady Hemmingway had their Portsmouth home. There were two entrances, one of which was the main carriage entrance, the other a discreet servant's door a few yards away along the side of the house. By force of custom, neither seaman would have enquired at any other but that latter entrance. The bell was answered by a fussy-looking manservant who clearly had better things to do than talk to common sailors, even if they were both smartly jacketed in dark blue with silver-gilt buttons.

'I don't 'ave time to hanswer questions from the likes of you,' he said haughtily as he started to close the door in their faces. He suffered considerable agony as Dick Wells dragged him through the narrow gap with his meaty hand gripping the crotch of the flunkey's milk-white breeches.

'What's yer name?'

'K-Kennedy.'

'See here, K-Kennedy, matey,' he said in a quiet, thoroughly terrifying voice. 'I've a mind to be answered and shall not be denied. So just you think again. Is Lieutenant Astley 'ere, yes or no?'

'You … you …'

'Well? Want me to break somma them 'andsome teef o' your'n? I ain't a patient man b'nature, am I John-David?'

'That you ain't when dealing with bruss fellers like this'n, Cox'n!'

Transferring his hand to the man's lapels, Wells shook the hapless servant like a rat being savaged by a bulldog. 'Tell me, Mister High'n fucking Mighty, is Lieutenant Astley 'ere or no? An' I'll 'ave the truth outa yer, if yer please.'

'He's … he's … gone. The admiral's … come … 'ome.'

In short, gasping phrases he managed to get the message across than Astley had departed with alacrity from this very door not more than twenty minutes since, with his master hard at his heels, a dag in each hand. Astley had been somewhat encumbered by having to drag on his breeches as he ran.

Dick Wells took Kennedy along with them by the simple expedient of tightening the grip on his collar and booting his arse repeatedly as he yelped his way down the lane to the main thoroughfare and pointed towards the east with a desperately co-operative finger.

'They went orf that way, I swear it!' he sobbed.

'I shall be back to chastise you, cully, should you be a-lying ter me, mark my words.'

'That 'e will, ho yes, that 'e will,' added Herriot with a huge grin.

The last they saw of the battered retainer was of him crawling on hands and knees through the carriage entrance.

One hundred and fifty yards away was the Crown, where it was possible for junior officers to secure a fairly clean bed for twopence a night, best to bring your own sheets though. A small gaggle of strumpets was milling about in an excited group at the mouth of the alleyway beside. The object of their interest was the supine, partly clothed body of a naval officer. As they drew closer, Wells and Herriot saw that it was none other than the lieutenant himself.

'Strewth, Dickie!' Herriot muttered. 'This is a bit of do, ain't it?'

'Too bleeding right, mate!'

'Oi, you there, Ganymede! Yes you, yer beef-witted twat! What's occurred?' Herriot demanded.

The potboy gaped from him to the huge cox'n. 'Which, this gent 'as got hisself shot, ain't 'e? This other gent were chasin' 'im an' did 'im wiv his bulldog. Gawd! You shoulda 'eard the poor bugger scream when 'e went darn!'

At that moment, three red-faced officers of marines came hastily from where they had been summoned from a nearby house of pleasure by the bosun of the *London* 98. The senior of the three, a captain, jerked a chin at Wells. 'Who are ye, man?'

Wells knuckled his forehead and explained briefly, showing him Sir Michael's orders for Astley.

'I take it this poor fellow is dead? Has anybody checked him?'

'Aye, sir, 'e's 'ad it, that's a fac',' said Herriot grimly, rising from where he had been kneeling beside the body.

'Well now, here's a pretty fix!' replied the officer, turning to the lieutenant by his side, 'see here, Drake, you had better go to the dockyard commissioner's office as fast as you can and fetch him here. Lewis, see if you can find the under-sheriff. Mr Wells, take the names of these people; they are witnesses. I'll get some men to carry Lieutenant Astley into the Crown. There is no point in leaving him here; he's dead by shooting, that cannot be gainsaid.'

An hour later North stood in the parlour of the Crown beside Sir Charles Saxton who was white-faced as he examined the black-rimmed wound in Astley's chest.

'God, Sir Michael!' he whispered fiercely, 'What to do, what to do? I suppose we will have to find Admiral Hemmingway and detain him?'

'I think you should come with me to the admiral's house and enquire further, Sir Charles; although, of course, he may not have returned there. I dread the thought of arresting him on board *Caesar*. His crew would rise up and stop us, I have no doubt.'

'But it must be done, for his sake as much as anything. Better we take him on board *Brittania* and have him put into the charge of Admiral Butler than hand him over to the civil powers. That way we may be able to contain this mess,' said Saxton, gritting his teeth.

They walked the short distance to the admiral's house, accompanied by the marine captain and Captain Jonas Fell of the *Phoebe* frigate. Marines from *Phoebe* and from Silk's ship, the *Donegal*, had surrounded the house. As the officers crossed the gravelled courtyard, a shot rang out from the upper floor of the house. They paused and a dozen armed marines rushed forward protectively to surround them, their muskets towards the upper windows. There was a crash of shattering glass and the body of a woman fell from a window, her white gown streaked scarlet with her blood.

North and the others stood transfixed as the body of Lady Hemingway smacked into the ground with such a dreadful and final thud that rushing to her aid would have been pointless.

Her white-haired husband screamed his anguish aloud as he stood framed in the wreckage of the window. 'Who is there among you who would have done less?' he sobbed in a bleakly resigned voice. 'Oh bring me death, bring me death!'

With what seemed awful deliberation he put the muzzle of a pistol to his throat, angled it upwards and pulled the trigger. His shattered face seemed to fall from his gore-spouting head as he plunged like an unhanded marionette to the gravel below. In death, his splayed fingers seemed to reach out in silent accusation to the body of his dead wife a few feet away.

Sir Charles vomited into the still waters of a nearby ornamental stone basin and even North, his sensibilities inured to violent death by many years of the conflict against the French, was horrified by the *denouement* of the sad story.

Having composed himself, Saxton stood deep in thought as North gave orders to have the dead couple carried into the house and laid out under the supervision of *Tigre's* surgeon and Lieutenant Lang.

As he walked back to his house with North, Saxton was still thinking and started as he realised North was asking him a question.

'Sorry, Sir Michael, I was miles away, what did you say?'

'I was asking whether you would have any objection to me arranging for Astley's body to be sent to his family?'

'Indeed, I would be grateful if you could take care of it. I suppose I should be relieved that the matter is in effect closed though I am not looking forward to writing the report.'

North nodded. 'I trust you will allow me to enclose a note endorsing your actions?'

Saxton said, 'Kind in you, sir.' He hesitated. 'Sir Michael, while we are here in the open air as it were and not likely to be heard, I have something to say to you.

'A few days ago Rear Admiral Butler came to me and made a strange request. He asked me to arrange matters to make things difficult for you. I was shocked and asked him why. It seems he was asking on behalf of his brother-in-law Vice Admiral Tennant who thought you should be taken down a peg. Naturally I was quite indignant but Butler reminded me that my daughter's fiancé, Captain Oliver, was dependent on him while he was with his fleet and, although he did not come out and say it, implied that he had the means to make Robert's life a misery.'

He paused, an awkward look on his face, and North gestured for him to continue.

'Now, I am not proud of the fact that I have had my people making what I hope are minor difficulties for your ship. I deeply regret agreeing in a moment of weakness and I apologise with all my heart. What concerns me equally is that Butler is casting around to make more trouble for you personally.'

North was frowning. He had been meaning to talk to Saxton about a series of obstructive incidents. Everything he had learned or knew about Saxton spoke a man of high integrity which had made the situation all the more puzzling.

'Sir Charles, I thank you for your candour and of course what you have said shall remain between us. I have an idea that may spike Butler's guns concerning Captain Oliver.'

When he had finished speaking, Saxton expressed his gratitude and shook his hand. What North had outlined was quite cunning but brilliant. Of course he would tell nobody but he was relieved on behalf of his future son-in-law and furthermore resolved to make a point of re-directing the campaign of obstructions on to Butler. From now on Butler would find it was a perilous plan to blackmail the man who controlled His Majesty's dockyard.

Chapter 17

The following afternoon a gun drew *Tigre's* attention to a hoist on the flagship directed at *Tigre* and requiring her captain to repair on board. North had been expecting it.

North mounted the side of the ship which having been moored here for almost three months seemed to be swimming in a grey pool of her own filth despite the ebb and flow of the tide. This was, of course, unavoidable and a common enough sight but to a knowing eye it spoke volumes for the rear admiral's unwillingness to sail the sea.

As he stepped on to it, the deck itself was spotless and the lieutenant greeting him stood back as the sound of three pipes died down and North removed his hat to the ensign.

The officer of the watch, Lieutenant Glazier, was uncomfortable with the fact that the flag captain had specifically told him to meet Captain North and take him to the wardroom like some visiting junior officer to await a summons. North was perfectly aware of the barely veiled insult but simply smiled.

The wardroom on the 110-gun 1st Rate *Brittania* was spacious as befitted a ship with a dozen lieutenants and a dozen wardroom and standing warrant officers. The premier, Lieutenant Peter Stride, advanced to be introduced with an expression of embarrassment on his face, painfully aware that he if not the flag captain should have been warned to receive a post captain. His frowning expression was quickly replaced by one of pleasure as he saw his distinguished visitor smiling at him.

As he took his hand North said, 'Honoured to be invited, sir.'

Relieved, Stride replied, 'The honour is ours, Sir Michael. I trust you will take a glass with us?'

North looked around him. On a ship of this size under the flag of a rear admiral there were often more than a dozen lieutenants on the muster. There were seven of them plus three red-coated marine officers at the long table in the middle of the room who had all stood as he entered. Two other officers were at small writing desks and one in a deep armchair rose at the same time.

'Well, gentlemen, please don't stand on ceremony, sit you down, sit you down, please,' said North taking a seat at one end of the table and reaching out for the proffered glass.

Glazier cleared his throat. 'Apologies, sir, if we had known we were to receive you we would have ordered something more substantial. I'm afraid the wine is not of the best either.'

'It seems very acceptable, Mr Glazier. I can remember a time when I served on a flagship that the wardroom was so impoverished we had nothing but horrible blackstrap to offer guests.'

A rotund red-haired lieutenant who had sat near him said, 'I must say, sir, that we are not really used to having post captains as guests, so we are somewhat ashamed by the lack of better wine.'

'Mr …?'

'Lessingham, sir.'

'Well, Mr Lessingham, you seem to be confusing me with somebody who has never been a wardroom officer. When they made me a captain they had me change my uniform but I trust I am still the same man when it comes to appreciating hospitality. Tell me, sir, have you been on *Brittania* very long?'

It was a relaxed and laughing wardroom that *Britannia's* captain William Whitlock entered to fetch North.

Whitlock stood in the doorway for a moment and watched. His lieutenants seemed attentive and smiling as North joked with them. It seemed the admiral's snub had misfired. *Brittania* was not a particularly happy ship and laughter rare. Butler was not an active commander except when it came to interfering with the smooth running of his flagship. Whereas Whitlock rarely had to use the gratings to ensure discipline, Butler would take it upon himself to deliberately undermine Whitlock by ordering punishments with the cat almost weekly. The flag captain Montague Gordon, a hard-nosed Scot, simply stood back and said nothing when Whitlock expressed as tactfully as possible that he was the ship's captain and discipline his concern. Butler had not even reacted with rage. He simply smiled and told him that when he became an admiral he could do as he wished on his own ship.

Whitlock looked at the man who seemed more at ease with his officers than he had been in a long time. Michael Orrick North was a legend despite having barely the three years' seniority that entitled him to a swab on each shoulder.

Conducting him to the admiral's cabin, Whitlock, who had some idea what was in Butler's mind, said quietly, 'I'm afraid the incident involving Mr Astley may provoke some harsh words from the admiral, Sir Michael. I am sure you will cope with that but keep a close eye on others present. You are not amongst friends.'

'Thank you, sir. I will do my best to keep the peace.'

'I am sorry if I seem to be speaking out of turn, Sir Michael.'

North touched his arm and said calmly, 'Not at all, sir. I appreciate the advice.'

The great cabin was well furnished; the black and white chequered carpet newly laid seemed almost too splendid for a ship of war and the red plush curtains gathered at the stern-lights were sumptuous. North had been told that *Britannia's* recent middling repairs and refit had cost the country £21,700 and it seemed her cabin had enjoyed some of this profligate spending.

There were three men present besides a man who was obviously the admiral's clerk, quill-pen dipping in inkwell and clean white paper on the small desk in a corner.

North knew Butler by sight and his flag captain he had known briefly ten years previously in the Mediterranean and was not particularly impressed by him. Both men were seated behind a beautifully made, expensive mahogany desk. North couldn't help thinking that the desk would be a swine to move if the ship ever went to action stations.

The unsmiling third man, also wearing the uniform of a rear admiral, came forward to greet him. Rear Admiral Sir Charles Cotton was an oval-faced, heavily built man whose face was reminiscent of portraits North had seen of George Washington. He had a reputation as a redoubtable captain and now had the 90-gun HMS *Duke.* His manner was cool but North detected a certain curiosity in his eyes. He smiled briefly but there was no apparent warmth of friendship in that smile.

Butler did not invite North to sit.

'This business with your lieutenant, Ashley ...'

'Astley, sir.'

'Don't interrupt. I am very displeased, North and I demand an explanation of your failure to more closely supervise your officers.'

Cotton was frowning; this was not starting off well. North was clearly calm and at ease and Butler was becoming angry. On the other hand what he heard about North seemed to be true. He obviously took a pride in his appearance and his uniform was well cut as befitted a man who had made a fortune in prize money within a year of being made post and had been given a country estate by the king.

'Ah, what I believe Admiral Butler is asking is the extent to which you were aware of Astley's activities, particularly his relationship with Mrs Hemingway?'

Butler snorted. 'I'm perfectly able to frame my own questions, Sir Charles, thank you! Well, North?'

North actually smiled at him. 'I am sure you do not intend to be insulting, sir, but since you feel able to refer to Sir Charles with the courtesy of his baronetcy, perhaps you would be so kind as to my own title. I appreciate that you are my senior but I believe Earl St Vincent has decided views on the matter.'

Butler stood, mouth open for a moment, silently enraged by the fact that this damned upstart had a knighthood and he did not. 'Very well, *Sir* Michael, if that is what you wish. My question remains unanswered, *Captain.*'

'Am I being formally investigated, Admiral? I note your clerk is making notes? If so I am quite prepared to make a statement, on the record. As Lieutenant Astley's commanding officer I take full responsibility for his actions on board my ship.

'However since I do not have the eyes of Argus Panoptes, what my young officers do on shore and out of my line of sight is as much a mystery to me as it has been to all captains through the ages.

'Until the recent tragedy I had no reason to believe that Astley's actions were in any way excessive on land, though I regret that ignorance, of course. If I had the prescience to anticipate this dreadful incident I would no doubt have done something to prevent it.'

'Have you finished, *Sir* Michael?'

'I believe I have, Admiral, but I am happy to respond to any questions you may have. For example the dispositions that Sir Charles Saxton and I saw fit to make after the incident. Since the three persons most closely involved in this matter are now dead I suggest it is not in the interests of the service to have the matter fully aired in the country as a whole, though of course the commissioner and I have both sent a detailed report in the same despatch to their lordships.'

Butler smiled slyly. 'You forget, *Sir* Michael, I am the senior officer on station and it should be through me that such a report is sent.'

'At present, sir, so you are.' North intentionally rubbed it in. It was unusual for an admiral commanding a squadron to be in port here with everything that was happening in the Channel and further afield. North was not the first one to wonder about Butler's presence for such a long period of time. 'As a courtesy, Admiral, the commissioner and I have arranged to send on board copies of those reports for your information. Since he, as commissioner of the dockyard in which the events took place, has the responsibility and since he asked me to assist his investigation, I believe that matters have been covered. As a sea officer with your own responsibilities neither of us felt it right to involve you in an incident on land that in no way involved your squadron. However there is a full list of witnesses that I am sure will be available to you, should you wish to satisfy yourself as to our actions?'

Cotton had come on board on the request of Butler and while it had not been said openly, the intention was for him to bear witness that the admiral was censuring North in the strongest possible manner without instituting a court martial. For a moment he believed that Butler was stupid enough to actually order a court martial. He had also changed his mind about North. Yes, the man was close to being insubordinate but provided the clerk had recorded his exact words, North was perfectly entitled to say what he had said. The fact that he joined the commissioner into his statement in a way made him fireproof. The mention of the commissioner also had a peculiar effect on Butler.

Cotton said smoothly, 'I am sure the admiral did not mean in any sense to impugn the rigour of Commissioner Saxton's investigation or your assistance, Sir Michael.'

Butler decided to end the matter. 'You may leave, Captain North, and I trust that you will soon receive orders to sail.' He felt like adding as far as the end of the fucking world and then drop off the fucking edge!

'Before I leave, I have something to say to you in private,

Admiral.'

'You may say what you wish in front of these gentlemen.' Butler thought that perhaps now North was going to make the fatal mistake of insulting him to his face.

'As you wish, but you may want your clerk to put down his pen. I have no objections to having my words recorded but I respectfully suggest that you may.'

Cotton tensed as he saw the red rage in Butler's eyes. Then the moment passed and Butler snapped, 'Courtney! Get out! Now!'

The clerk ran from the cabin and Butler glared at North. 'Well?'

North was staring rigidly into Butler's eyes. It was Butler who flinched first.

'In the past few days, since the court martial of Lieutenant Fryston, I have found that my ship has suffered a disruptive and unhelpful series of misfortunes at the hands of the dockyard mateys. This has resulted in delays that I believe effect my readiness to put to sea.

'A few hours ago I received orders directly from the First Lord, bearing on matters decided in the highest level of government, to proceed to sea on a mission of the utmost importance. Therefore I must insist that their lordships' orders not be impeded by lack of co-operation in *any* quarter.

'It came to my notice that a certain very senior officer has put pressure on the commissioner involving a certain frigate captain who is affianced to his daughter. This has resulted in the obstructions being visited upon my ship. I will say this to your face, Admiral. If I find that frigate captain has been victimised in any way I will consider it my duty to lodge a formal complaint with their lordships.

'In fact I have taken it upon myself to arrange for *Mermaid* to be removed from your command and sent to the Mediterranean. Until she leaves here my stricture remains.'

Cotton held his breath. North's impertinence was spectacular. He was either insane or he seriously had some power not granted to mortal captains.

Butler looked at him in disbelief. 'You have no authority; you are merely a post captain.'

Cotton suddenly realised what North was going to say next and suppressed a broad smile.

'I try to refrain from reminding people of an uncalled-for honour which was bestowed upon me but I think I should remind you that I am officially at least Deputy Adjutant General of the Royal Navy. It is a fairly meaningless title but Captain Grey, the Adjutant General, has endorsed my request to their lordships that a cruise be given to Captain Oliver under the direct orders of the Admiralty.

'Now, Admiral, I bid you good day. Please pass on my

compliments to your brother-in-law when you see him, won't you?'

He turned, raised his hat to Rear Admiral Cotton, and left the cabin without looking back.

As Butler collapsed on to a stern couch, his eyes wide, mouth open and speechless, Cotton said under his breath, 'Checkmate!'

……………………………………………………………

Rear Admiral Butler's anger had affected North little. Despite his own frustration with Astley's behaviour, he was saddened by the man's death. Butler's accusations of negligence in supervising Astley fell on deaf ears. Of course, it was preposterous that North should be held to account for the failings of the philandering Astley and both he and the admiral knew that. The diatribe and censure delivered was purely from malice and North was confidently sure that their lordships would see it the same way. In any case that same evening North left Portsmouth on the tide. He left behind him a man incandescent with rage vowing never to rest until he had destroyed Michael North.

Chapter 18

<u>18th May, 1803</u>

Tigre and *Juniper* arrived off Harwich in the late evening of 18th May and were therefore guided into the harbour by the lights provided by two fires. One was set up in the upper room of the Town Gate and the other by a square, white-painted, windmill-like wooden lighthouse to the south-east of the town near the beach. As they dropped anchor the Revenue cutter, the 130-ton *Argus* 14, dipped her ensign in passing and her commander John Saunders waved his hat. She was off to patrol in her designated area between Sledway and Lowestoft. With war in the offing she would meet and patrol with her Yarmouth counterpart, the 12-gun *Hunter* captained by Lowell Riches whose beat was from Harwich to Cromer.

North had received a simple order to proceed to the Baltic and was told that he would receive final details from a trusted courier in Harwich. He expected that despatches would be brought on board the following morning but a boat was rowed out from the quay and an energetic young man bounded up the side of the ship, to be met by Lieutenant Fellowes. He was ushered into the great cabin where North was writing reports and letters. Introducing himself as Francis Plummer, he handed a sealskin covered packet to North, who motioned him to a seat.

'Have you eaten, Mr Plummer?'

'Why, yes, sir, thank you. I had a passable meal in the King's Head an hour or so ago. I was taking a turn on the quay when I saw you arrive. Having the despatches on my person, as I always do in matters of secrecy, I thought it as well to bring them on board.'

'I'm obliged, Mr Plummer, your zeal does you credit,' said North. 'You will find a passable sherry in the decanter. Please help yourself while I read this despatch.'

There was a covering note and an official letter together with a folded chart in the cover. The note was signed by John Markham.

> *Dear Michael,*
>
> *You will see from the enclosed letter that you are to be employed on two different missions, both of them matters of some sensitivity. In the first of these matters, more than ever, I urge you to be careful to act as secretly as possible. As you are aware War has not yet been declared but any act of force you feel necessary to carry out has the full backing of this Office and of the Government.*
>
> *We are deliberately providing you with the barest minimum of resources to carry out your task but if or rather when War is declared, the Enemy may well have overwhelming force available in the Baltic. So caution is the watchword.*

You will carry Mr Plummer with you; he will advise you, act as interpreter for local languages, and has our complete confidence.

Yours, most sincerely,

JM.

The letter itself was an order from the Admiralty to proceed with all despatch to the Baltic and meet with a Russian ship off the coast of Prussia. The bearer of the letter, Francis Plummer, would explain verbally exactly what was to happen. After dealing with that matter he would then make his way to Sweden.

The chart was of the Baltic seas to the north-west of Danzig. The city itself and the estuary of the Vistula was circled by a pencil mark on the map. When Plummer had finished speaking, North was thoughtful.

'How sure are you and the Admiralty of Napoleon's plan?'

'A good question, Sir Michael. It had the signs of some fanciful tale designed by our informer to extract money from us but we have checked as far as we are able and have sent agents to Paris and Berlin who, as far as they can, have brought back information that at least indicates a very strong possibility. Prussia does not want war with France but has no love for Russia. In order to keep Bonaparte at bay, they will likely roll over or at least stand aside.'

The following morning, 19th May, Plummer came on board again with his baggage. After settling in he came back on deck and was about to approach Captain North, who was standing hands on hips on the starboard side of the quarterdeck, his brow frowning in thought as he looked up at the mainmast yards. Plummer felt a restraining hand on his arm.

'Excuse me, Mr Plummer, but not now. The captain likes to have ten minutes or so undisturbed in the morning when he first comes on deck. He'll call you over when he's ready.'

Plummer turned to Lieutenant Fellowes, who had the watch. '*Tigre* is a beautiful ship, Mr Fellowes, and I must say how impressed I am by her appearance – everything neat and clean, the crew alert to their duties and a sort of contented feeling to her. One would be forgiven for thinking that this crew had been with her for years rather than weeks.'

'Aye, Mr Plummer, things are coming together well,' he lowered his voice, 'in no small measure due to the captain. This is my first voyage with him in command and before I joined I was a little intimidated by his reputation. My godfather, Lord Keith, believes he is one of the finest sailors in the navy. I am reassured since meeting him; he is much quieter and more approachable than I would have thought.

'Over the few weeks he has been getting to know the ship in a way I found quite interesting. On his first full day aboard he took off his coat and examined almost every inch of the ship from masthead to bilges. As a result almost a quarter of the rigging was brought down and exchanged. He and the gunner poked and prodded every gun and two were struck down and sent ashore to be replaced, though I confess I saw nothing wrong with them. Since then he has stood over every tradesman watching him work but not in an oppressive manner – rather as if getting the measure of each of them as individuals and indeed enjoying watching them work their skills.'

He was interrupted by the captain who was pointing up at the topsail spar on the mainmast.

'Mr Fellowes, send a bosun's mate to the starboard maintops'l reef tackles. There is a loose jeer-block. I believe a sheet has slipped. Also have the lashings on the foredeck carronades tightened, I can hear the slides moving. Good morning, Mr Plummer. I trust you are comfortably settling in?'

Plummer walked over to him. 'Very well, thank you, Sir Michael. I was just watching that sloop-rigged ship entering the harbour; she sails very fast, does she not?'

North glanced over to the harbour mouth. 'She's the Harwich packet, in from Den Haag. You are right, she seems in a hurry, I assume she has urgent mail on board.'

As they watched, the hoy fired off a gun and North saw a man waving frantically. He snapped open his telescope. 'Something's amiss, it seems.'

The hoy quickly reefed in all her sails, and came drifting in quickly with her mast bare. She did not anchor before a 4-oared gig was lowered and six men clambered into her and cast off. By the effort they were putting into the rowing as they headed directly for *Tigre,* they clearly needed to speak urgently.

The slim young man came up the side of *Tigre* so quickly that he was gasping for breath as he removed his hat to the ensign and looked quickly around, red-faced and agitated until he saw the captain approaching.

'Captain! My name is Matthew Flynn, commander of the *Dolphin* packet. There is not a moment to lose! A French 74 lies off the coast about five miles north of here. The frigate with her has taken two Newcastle colliers. We were chased into the estuary by the frigate but the 74 and the colliers are anchored with sails taken in. If you are quick enough, you should be able to catch her!'

North said, 'Calm yourself, sir. There is nothing I can do but demand the release of the colliers, which can be done by sending my schooner.'

Flynn slapped his forehead in frustration. 'Sorry, captain, you must not have heard. London declared war yesterday morning. We were given the news by the frigate *Prompte* no more than three hours ago, which was just as well or we might have fallen foul of the Frenchies too! We were on our way to Hellevoetsluis with mail. We should have left Harwich and arrived two days ago but we had to put in to Yarmouth to pick up urgent packages and missed our tide. Three of the Harwich packets are at Hellevoetsluis – the *Lady Francis,* the *Earl of Leicester* and the *Princess Royal,* I should imagine they have been captured along with Captain Boynton's *Courier* that left Harwich just after we did.'

In a trice all had changed as North bellowed for all hands. Amidst the shrilling of pipes and rushing feet, North called to Fellowes, 'weigh anchor and have her under topsails as soon as possible, please, Mr Fellowes. Make to *Juniper* to follow us. Captain Flynn, thank you sir, your promptness and decisive action will not be forgotten but unless you want to come with us, you should return to your ship.'

'We were chased into the harbour by a frigate probably of 36 guns. She may be still in the area.' He hurried to the side. 'God speed and good hunting, sir!'

North raised his hat to him as he disappeared down the side of the ship. At that moment a midshipman bawled, 'Anchor aweigh, sir!'

North nodded in satisfaction as the ship began to move. 'Hoist mains'ls as soon as convenient, Mr Fellowes. Thanks to the excellent Captain Flynn we may make our mark by taking the first prize of the new war!'

As they cleared the mouth of the river the French frigate could be seen about a mile north of them, running before the wind; her royals and studding sails erupting from her masts like fury. She was a beautiful sight. She had the grace of a dove and the wings of a swift.

James Lang, who was standing beside North, grinned. 'Well, I expect the 74 will be ready for us now, sir?'

'Indeed, James. Mr Plummer, you might wish to descend to the orlop deck where it is safer and if you would give my compliments to the surgeon, I am sure he could use an extra pair of hands.' Turning back to Lang, he said, 'Clear for action, please, Mr Lang! Mr Birchall, join me in walking the gun decks, please. We shall give the good news to the men.'

It was a strange feeling going into action again after so many months of being on land, sharing a happy bucolic existence with his family, interspersed by the cut and thrust of parliamentary debate whenever he could drag himself away from Tarring. Polite and not-so-polite warfare on the floor of Westminster Hall may seem to vary from a pillow-fight to a bare-knuckle brawl on occasion but it held nothing like the sense of keen anticipation North now felt.

In the distance a larger ship could be seen beyond the French frigate as the lookout called, 'Deck there! Ship of the line and two small ships fine off the larboard bow!'

'Guns ready at your disposal, Sir Michael!' called Lieutenant Lang.

North rubbed his hands together. 'Mr Birchall, please have somebody fetch my sword, and my best scraper and coat from the cabin. All officers to be properly dressed out of courtesy to our opponents, if you please.'

He turned to the marine captain, 'Mr Hodges, I believe your marines have all been issued with rifles in place of their India pattern muskets? Very well, you know I don't believe in sharp-shooters in the tops, the motion of the ship makes aiming small arms useless and gives danger of accidental fire to the rigging. Have them standing by to man the decks as a defence against boarders. Mr Birchall, when we are close enough to the enemy, I would have you take in mainsails and have the pumps manned to soak topsails.'

As North passed with Birchall along the upper and lower gun decks, nodding to excited men, exchanging a word or two of encouragement with them, he was pleased with what he saw. Many of them had worked together for less than seven weeks but they were already a family; a crew of good quality, able men for the most part. The Peace had resulted in the best of the navy's seamen being available now – at least until battle and disease brought in the press-gangs and unskilled landsmen again. He stepped to one side as two powder monkeys ran past, skipping nimbly over tackles and tubs – likely that nimbleness would be sorely tested when action began. One stopped and passed his cartridge-box to the gun captain, who put the powder-filled bags into one of his salt boxes and handed the empty one back to be returned for a refill from the gunner.

North saw and greeted a familiar face here and there, mainly old Prince Ruperts with a significant sprinkle of Fisgards all grinning and tensed ready for the fight.

He emerged on the forecastle and spoke briefly to the carronade crews before making his way aft. He noticed with satisfaction that the ship's boats had been swung out and were now towing astern. They were a liability on deck, possibly exploding in a mass of lethal splinters if struck by cannon fire. Pumps were rigged and ready; the spars and booms were made more secure with chains.

The distance between *Tigre* and the enemy had by this time reduced to less than a mile and he could see that the enemy two-decker was in fact a slightly larger ship than a 74. She was similar in appearance to the *Tonnant* class ship *Guillaume Tell* originally carrying 84 guns, captured by the British off Malta in March of 1800. That ship was now renamed as the *Malta* 80.

She was in fact the *Unité* and carried thirty 36-pounders, thirty-two 24-pounders, eighteen 12-pounders and four *obusiers de vaisseau*. These latter guns were the French answer to the carronade, originally an artillery weapon designed to fire shells. However they were so dangerous to the men firing them that on most ships of the *Tonnant* class they had been replaced by carronades.

North was aware that *Tigre* had a distinct disadvantage in weight of shot. Even though *Tigre's* carronades gave her an advantage close up *Unité* could throw 2,054 lbs from her long guns while *Tigre* only had 1,578 lbs at her disposal. This was a factor he would take into consideration.

He was also aware that *Tigre's* manpower complement would be around 100 smaller than that of her opponent, though North believed he could depend on the British quality of his seamen and his gunnery to negate the difference.

Standing in towards the land was the French frigate that had led them here, the *Couronne* 40 with two of the *Unité's* boats and the two captured collier brigs.

Unité was now turning towards *Tigre,* who had the weather-gage. In the increasing wind characteristic of such variability at this time of the year, their converging speed quickened and it was *Tigre* that opened the contest with her two 16-pounder bow-chasers. Though the actual total weight difference was small when North had replaced the original two 8-pounders he had adjusted the ship's trim slightly by moving some of the shingle ballast aft in the hold.

Now Birchall ordered the large sails brailed up and the topsails doused with water, a wise precaution against fire for any ship going into battle. North noticed that his opponent was doing the same thing but was pleased to see that the French were decidedly less efficient in doing so.

The bow-chasers were laid by one of North's most experienced quarter-gunners with almost surgical skill and using his best, personally mealed powder, resulting in a direct hit on one of the *Unité's obusiers* and serious damage to her figurehead. Rapidly reloading both guns, the next pair of shots decapitated a young *aspirante,* killed two seamen and badly wounded the ship's bosun and four other men.

Now the rest of *Tigre's* guns were coming into range and *Unité's* and *Tigre's* first broadsides hammered out almost simultaneously. The number of shot from each ship striking the other was about the same but the effect on each crew was very different. The casualties on both ships may seem to that observer to be mercifully light, less than a dozen on either ship, with one fatality on *Unité.*

The reality was that there was mayhem amongst the French crew. Most had less than one month on board and more than two-thirds of them had not only never seen a gun fired at them in anger but had very little skill in firing their own guns.

Though dozens were beaten with the flats of officer's swords and the short leather whips of the warrant officers, many simply cowered in the solid shelter apparently offered by the cannons and through fear or defiance would not reload their guns.

On *Tigre* there was a remarkable fortitude of spirit which, while not ignoring the casualties, kept the gun crews working with a will. As a result *Tigre*'s impressively uniform second rolling broadside was flying between the ships at least half a minute before the ragged response. More damage this time and more casualties.

In all this mayhem men who spent many moments of their lives living in the confining hull of a ship, however huge that ship might appear, were like a family battered by a storm. A man who sat with his elbow touching his messmate's as he ate from a square wooden plate beside him; now lying, eyes wide open in death staring up at him. A man whose sleeping body swung against his neighbour in the sixteen-inch space between hammocks now lifting that neighbour's broken and bleeding body to carry him to the surgeon. Nobody commented on men crying like children as they crawled across the blood-spattered deck to reach out for a dying friend's hand.

The grim, grimy tumult of battle raged through the ship like the curse of the gods. The noise was deafening and the all-pervading smoke, blinding.

Noah Black, a shattered tub narrowly missing his head as he knelt down to take a cartridge bag from the salt box, looked round to see his gun captain doubled over, hands clutched to his stomach, blood belching from his mouth as he fell on his side. Davy Williams the Second bent over him and then looked up at Black, shaking his head. Black nodded and took over command of the gun.

On the orlop deck the surgeon calmly pointed a bloody hand, 'You next, marine.'

Private Jemmy Locke was in agony but fearful of what was coming next, held back.

Doctor Levy was impatient; there were many more wounded. 'Come along, man, I'm not going to cut off your hand if I can save it. Here, take a big swallow of rum and sit on the table.'

On the quarterdeck North's throat was burning and his eyes stinging. He peered intently through the pall of yellow-grey smoke that the wind was only dispersing with difficulty. He was weighing up his immediate strategy. Conscious that *Tigre* was needed for his urgent mission he did not want to risk her fabric too much. The obvious answer was to close with the enemy as rapidly as possible and board her. The uncanny coincidence was that *Unité's* captain had reached the same decision almost at the same time though for distinctly different reasons.

Paul-Conrad Barreaut was furious. His crew were scum and in the 49 days he had been in command 28 had deserted. He had flogged 34 but there was still virtually no difference in the quality of the crew's work since the first day. The crew had perhaps 220 skilled seamen and 400 fools. In addition the 130 soldiers she carried had been drafted into the ship *en bloc* having previously been stationed in fever-wracked Corsica and those who were not as weak as kittens were almost openly rebellious at having been taken from their families who were still in Bastia.

There was only one thing he could do. If the gun crews would not work their guns he had to come alongside the British ship to stop the murderous pounding of his ship and use his superiority of numbers to overwhelm their crew. He gave the order. He then began to harangue his crew with terrifying allegations that English sailors had been known to kill and roast their prisoners through starvation caused by their regular miserable supply of rations. He couldn't remember whether God had been rehabilitated yet in the shifting sands of French politics, but urged his men to pray that they could beat the English when they were landed on the enemy ship.

The ships were now less than 150 yards apart.

North beckoned to Birchall and Hodges and turned to Hiram McCann, the master. 'Gentlemen, to spare our ship I intend that we should board the Frenchie. Pass the word, please. Mr McCann you will support Mr Fowler and Mr Lang who will remain on board. Mr Birchall, my compliments to Mr Fellowes, he will take the forecastle boarders, you will take the waist and I will assault their quarterdeck. Major, you and your marines will defend by the waist and forecastle with all your men except twenty on the quarterdeck. You must only make your way to the upper and lower gun decks of the enemy when you are sure both ships are well locked together. I will not lose marines through them trying to jump fully equipped from one deck to another.

'Form your parties, gentlemen, you have five minutes and may God bless and keep each one of us. Mr McCann, bring me alongside that Frenchie, if you please!'

A roar of approval went up all along the decks as the boarders snatched up pistols, pikes, cutlasses and tomahawks and rushed up to light of day.

On board *Unité* the mood was very much *dis*united. They had missed their opportunity to decide which crew should board which ship. The hated English crowded the rail and the shrouds of their ship baying like the hounds of hell. Barreaut shouted commands at a crew that was deaf to anything except their own fear. There were even a half dozen acts of open mutiny as petty officers shouted the instruction to stand by to repel boarders.

Of course the majority of *Unité's* larboard guns had not been run in, unlike those on *Tigre's* fast approaching starboard side. The two great hulls crashed together with a tremendous grating explosion of breaking timbers and overturned guns. Three French seamen were crushed to death as their guns slammed backwards across the space between the two batteries.

With a sound like a thousand devils the English poured over the rail, yelling and cursing, slashing at everything in their path and as they fired their pistols, then threw them into the faces of those still standing. Realising that they either had to fight or be cut down where they stood, the Frenchmen rallied and began to fight back. They were spurred on by the captain's assurance that the English thrust a rod up their arses and out of their mouths while they were still alive before roasting them on a spit. In the short, stunned hiatus before they acted, more than half of the British boarding party were on the French decks.

On the quarterdeck North and his boarders were confronted by seven officers and about 20 men. Hand to hand they fought, growling, gasping, cursing and grunting as they hacked furiously at each other. The clamour of battle was deafening; the stench of death overwhelming.

Cluney Ryan, his teeth clenched tight, felt that his body was drowning in sweat; though whether from the heat of battle or cold fear, he was uncertain. He drove back his opponent, a stocky lieutenant, his heavy cutlass whacking the thinner blade of the Frenchman's epée so hard that the man could not use the advantage of the longer blade. Colliding with the binnacle, the lieutenant stumbled and Ryan made no mistake. His sweeping blow cut deep into the man's neck and he died instantly.

Shocked, Ryan turned and looked around him at the heaving, angry battle. Captain North was facing his opposite number, a French captain his match in height, though more heavily built. The two men could have been elegantly fencing in some gymnasium by the lifting and turning of their blades. Then feinting to the left North whipped his sword upwards under his adversary's hilt and the sword spun away from his hand.

North was just as shaky as his opponent but hid it better. He said calmly, '*Capitulez monsieur, maintenent!*'

Barreaut lifted a bloody hand and gasped, 'Yes, Captain, I am your prisoner.'

'Strike your colours, sir! This madness has gone on long enough!'

Barreaut looked around him as if suddenly aware of his surroundings. The rest of his officers who were still standing had thrown down their swords. He gave the order and calm started to move reluctantly through the ship, the lessening of noise being quite uncanny as opponents looked at each other as much in curiosity as relief.

James Lang, nursing a bloody forearm, came aft. 'Sir, the frigate is ranging alongside *Tigre's* disengaged side. She has struck her colours without a shot being fired.'

The frigate would have boarded *Tigre* from the other side but the sight of her companion's ensign being struck and the silence as fighting ceased caused her captain to change his mind and surrender.

North said, 'Thank you, Mr Lang, though I see that you saw fit to interpret my order to stay on board *Tigre* rather loosely. Pass the word for a signal to *Juniper* to send a prize crew aboard the frigate and have her officers brought on board *Tigre*. Then get below and see the surgeon about that wound!'

He turned to the other captain. 'Sir, please retain your sword. I am Captain Michael North of His Majesty's ship *Tigre*. May I ask your name?'

'Paul-Conrad Barreaut, *Capitaine de Vaisseau,* Sir Michael. Well, at least it is my privilege to be captured by the famous Captain North. No doubt the little Corsican will be even more infuriated by you now. Before your men disarrange my cabin, sir, perhaps you would get somebody to bring over my wine-cooler to your ship. I have some exquisite white wines that I believe are rarely found in England. May I respectfully ask that you assist me in drowning my sorrows?'

North laughed, 'Why not? Ryan, take a couple of men and secure Capitaine Barreaut's personal effects and have them carefully packed and brought to my cabin. You will also seal the wine-cabinet and bring that too without sampling too much. Oh, and if he happens to have left any papers lying around make sure they do not go astray, particularly any that might resemble a signal book. Now, sir, perhaps you will have the goodness to show me around the ship.'

Unité had almost 60 wounded as well as 25 dead and later North was able to ascertain that his own losses were slightly more wounded but just 18 dead – though even that number saddened him deeply. In *Unité's* sickbay North and Barreaut spoke with the French surgeon and found that he was fully in control of the situation though there would be long hours of hard work ahead of him and his assistants.

Barreaut's greatest embarrassment was that more than 40 of his gutter-dreg crew had been found cowering unwounded and drunk in the hold. He and Captain North were about to inspect some damage below the waterline which was being plugged by French and British seamen working together but seeing the drunks North turned back saying, grimly, 'I have no wish to have these men in my sight, Captain.'

'I am not excusing my failure, Sir Michael,' he said, feeling deeply mortified by the sight of the cringing offal being chivvied along by the British jacks, 'but you see the quality of my crew? More than half of them would be better employed to dredge the mouth of the Seine with their tongues.'

North smiled wanly. 'Sir, you and most of your crew acted with great bravery and I would challenge anybody who says differently. Luck was with me today, such is the fortune of war. Do not feel any shame after losing such a hard-fought battle.'

A few hours later with both capital ships now at anchor in Harwich harbour, the frigate *Couronne* was lying inshore of the *Tigre* and the crews of the two Newcastle colliers were on shore noisily celebrating their release from extremely brief captivity. North had confirmed to their captains that he would respect the rule that they had not been in the hands of the French for 24 hours and therefore not considered prizes. Their gratitude for being freed was effusive. North had time to sit for a moment alone in his cabin, a glass of a fragrant white Bordeaux wine from Barreaut's stock in his hand, and consider the situation.

Helped by doctors from the town, the wounded of both larger ships were being treated and it was clear to North that he now had a significant shortage of men on his ship.

Tigre was barely fit for sea and if they were unlucky enough to encounter another 74, they were unlikely to win such a contest. *Unité*, the subject of almost hysterical jubilation in town with church bells ringing for more than an hour, was even more wounded though being in Harwich both she and

Tigre could expect to receive the best of attention from the skilled shipbuilders of the civilian dockyard. This was a particular relief since they would not be at the mercy of the venality, thievery and laziness of some of His Majesty's dockyards.

As the sun set, a long triple line of French prisoners was being marched inland by flanking militia-men. Their officers, in carriages under guard, though they had all given their parole, were being carried to Colchester. Including the 300 unscathed crew of *Couronne*, there were almost a thousand Frenchmen and they represented a considerable sum in head money.

He looked out of the stern-lights at the pristine *Couronne*. She was beauty exemplified; one of the finest frigates that French shipbuilders could produce and not a scratch on her. Of the 40-gun class of *Consolante*, designed by Francois Pestel, and launched two years ago she carried twenty-eight 18-pounders on her upper deck, twelve 8-pounders on the quarterdeck and four 32-pounder carronades on her forecastle. As a fighting ship she was more than a match for any ship of the same class in the world. Her captain, though perhaps not as brave as he should have been, was at least diligent in maintaining a clean, smart ship.

It seemed that her captain had intended to try to board *Tigre* while most of the bigger ship's crew were boarding *Unité*. Reality set in as he realised that not only was *Unité's* pavillon tumbling to the deck but that a strong and determined line of nearly a hundred red-coated marines was standing, weapons ready along the larboard rail of his target. Lang had run out his larboard guns despite a paucity of gun crews emphasising the certain outcome such a challenge would entail.

After thinking for a few moments North made his decision and sent for Francis Plummer.

'Mr Plummer. Tomorrow we will transfer to the *Couronne* and crew her from *Tigre.* My senior will make sure that *Tigre's* repairs are carried out expeditiously. I am sending a despatch to London reporting the situation and requesting that *Tigre's* crew be brought up to strength as quickly as possible. *Couronne* will carry us to the Baltic where we will meet our Russian friends and assess the situation. If it is essential we will wait for *Tigre* to join us but *Couronne* is a fine ship and with all of *Tigre's* marines on board should serve well enough.

Plummer agreed. 'That seems like a good plan, sir. I am still amazed by the events of the day but if this is an omen for success, I could not ask for better.'

'Ah well now, many a slip twixt cup and lip, you know? Chickens not to be counted before hatching and so forth.'

The process of selecting from among over 500 junior warrants and seamen to provide 200 seamen for *Couronne* was a headache North would leave to his lieutenants. With muster book and division sheets spread on the wardroom table, each man selected was sent to collect his dunnage and then cross the gangplank where *Couronne* was drawn up alongside. Somehow a dozen not selected managed to sneak across too.

Chapter 19

<u>20th May, 1803</u>

As might be expected all Whitehall's government offices were in a tumultuous state of activity in the first few days of the war. Lord Hawkesbury, the Secretary of State for Foreign Affairs, had almost run to the Admiralty building and was closeted with Captain John Markham, Commissioner of the Admiralty, two days after *Tigre*'s action against the *Unité.*

'Damn it, Markham! Addington is cock-a-hoop about North's latest victory; he sees it as a great omen for the success of the war. Less than two days and he has twisted Boney's nose and smacked his arse! Though the bad news is that three of the Harwich packets have been interned and their officers sent off to Verdun! I am told that the blasted French have also interned our Post Office agent at Hellevoetsluis, Mr Sevright, for spying.

'It appears he was put on board one of their frigates, *La Libre,* and carried to Antwerp where he will be sent overland to Paris. We have had to send one of the Dover packets, the *Auckland,* to Harwich or the *Dolphin* would be the only boat there.'

Markham replied, 'Speaking of the *Dolphin,* it was due to the quick thinking of her captain that *Tigre* was able to seek out and capture the *Unité* and the *Couronne.* He should be commended. I am minded to grant a financial reward of say

£1,000 for him and £500 to be shared by his crew.'

'That's an excellent idea, John. Pray add a further £750 from my department.'

Markham refilled the glasses. 'After the damage that *Tigre* suffered it has meant that North has had to transfer to *Couronne* to continue his mission and it will take at least five days round the clock to carry out basic repairs to *Tigre* before she can follow him. I am having the receiving ships at Chatham scoured for a decent crew to bring *Tigre* up to strength. The Dover battalion of marines will send a company carried on *Diadem* to Harwich, they should reach there in good time.'

Hawkesbury smiled. He was fully aware that Markham himself was a hero of the first order. In command of *Centaur* four years ago he had ravaged the Catalonian coast and captured three French frigates, two brigs and several other ships on their way back to Toulon from Syria. He had previously been involved in a number of memorable victories. He also knew that North and Markham were close friends. 'Tremendous achievement for North, what an amazing man he is, John.'

'Indeed Robert, though he is going to need all his luck and skill in the Baltic without a 74 at his disposal.'

Hawkesbury lowered his voice, 'Careful John, that mission is very secret.'

Chapter 20

22nd May, 1803

North had denuded *Tigre* of most of her officers and senior warrants along with all her marines. The usual practice of masters, bosuns and other wardroom and standing warrant officers staying with their designated ship had to be weighed against the exigencies of the present mission.

It was as well the crew was experienced, the weather was so foul it tested every man's skills and temper.

Couronne was off the Dutch coast 48 hours after leaving Harwich. In sight of Flushing two French 74s were seen in towards the shore on a northerly heading, making heavy weather in the storm that was rising. North had the tricolour flown as a *ruse de guerre* and *Couronne* was ignored as she outstretched the bigger ships and disappeared in the same direction.

The storm strengthened even further and by six bells in the afternoon watch visibility was down to a few hundred yards. The crosstrees were so dangerous that the lookouts had been ordered down from aloft and were standing with the forecastle lookout in the bows, a line round their waists attached to the rail. One of them could hardly make himself heard above the sound of wind shrieking through the rigging. His call through the gathering darkness was repeated twice along the length of the barky before it reached North on the rain-drenched quarterdeck.

'Sir, lookout reports two strange sail off the larboard bow no more than a quarter mile away. Small ships, by the look of them.'

All heads on the quarterdeck turned to the left and eyes strained to see if they could see the ships. Midshipman Crowson yelled, 'There, sir! Two ships, sloop-rigged hoys, just like the Harwich packet-boat. They both fly the Union flag under a tricolour. One appears low in the water.'

North replied, 'Yes, I see them, well spotted, Mr Crowson. I believe they have seen us and are trying to come alongside. Mr Fellowes, I want everybody to keep absolutely quiet except French speakers, pass the word. We will go to action stations quickly but silently, gentlemen. Make sure everybody keeps his voice down unless he speaks French.'

McCann had been watching through a glass, water dripping from the lens. He snapped it shut and thrust it under his long coat. He said, 'They'll never be able to launch a boat, sir – perhaps they will just try to hail us.'

After struggling to come alongside the closer hoy was 50 feet away and her captain held up a speaking trumpet. He shouted in French, 'I need assistance, my ship is sinking!'

North turned to his lieutenant. 'Have a boarding net shaken out. We will bring him to larboard – under our lee; that should make it easier for his crew to jump on board.'

'*Apportez-lui aux côtés de mon bâbord; vos gens auront à sauter pour elle!*' cried North. There was a sudden squall of rain and when it cleared again the hoy was less than 30 feet away. 'Mr Fellowes, it would not be sporting to keep that French rag aloft, please run up our true colours. Be ready to fire off the quarter-gun and put the net over the side.'

Whether any of the nearest French crew noticed the Union flag being run up the mainmast halliard, it would seem that survival was the only thing that mattered to them. They scrambled up on to the hoy's rail and leapt for the netting to climb on to *Couronne*.

As they reached the deck they were seized and searched for weapons before being thrust into a sitting position around the mainmast.

As the gun was fired the second hoy, realising that their rescuer was not French, began to turn away. A second shot across her bows resulted in her colours being struck. North used his speaking trumpet to order her to come along his starboard side. As soon as she touched, Lieutenant Lang leapt aboard with a dozen men to take possession of her. She was the *Earl of Leicester*. On *Couronne's* opposite side the other ship was wallowing low in the water; she was the *Lady Francis*. With regret North ordered that the lines which had been thrown out to secure her be cut – the weight of water in her hold endangered *Couronne*.

Fellowes looked at the prisoners squatting around the mast.

There were 16 crewmen and two officers from the *Lady Francis*. He called for the officers to follow him. As he was moving away from the seated crewmen North saw something that made him point at one of the men and call out, 'You, come here!'

The man came slowly to his feet looking around him as if to find some place to run.

'You! Winslow Marshall, damn you, what are you doing here? Jackson, Harvey; seize that man and bring him aft!'

Marshall struggled for a moment but could not break free from the two hefty topmen.

There was another interruption before Marshall could be taken to the captain. A small, red-haired Dutchman tried to help a man beside him to stand up. This man had been lifted onto *Couronne's* deck with difficulty and was now semi-conscious The Dutchman called out to North in broken English. 'Sir, this man is prisoner on the *Lady Francis*, English, you help him, yes?'

Instructing the men to take Marshall to the cabin he turned to the two French officers. 'You two pick up that man and follow me. Corporal Smart, keep a pistol on these two. Bosun, take the rest of the prisoners below and have a hot drink made for them.'

There was a sudden movement amongst the English seamen who moved to the rail to watch as the *Lady Francis* capsized.

Her hull was above the towering waves for less than 20 seconds and then she was gone.

North had gone to the cabin and was peeling off his wet tarpaulin coat. His uniform beneath had not escaped the rain and he nodded a thanks to his steward and ran the proffered towel around his neck and face. The two French officers were brought in first with the Englishman, whom they laid down on the stern couch. McCann told him that Marshall was separated from the rescued men and North told him to keep him outside for a moment while he spoke to the officers.

They were an *ensigne de vaisseau* (an acting lieutenant) and an *aspirant* in command of a prize crew from the frigate *La Libre* charged with taking the prizes into Boulogne along with the *Princess Royal*, which had become separated from them by the storm. They informed North that the prisoner was known only to them as Monsieur Smith and that he had been brought on board in irons by the other Englishman, Monsieur Marshall, who was on his way to Paris to meet the Minister of Police, Joseph Fouché. The acting lieutenant sneered as he added that Marshall was one of Fouché's agents.

The man 'Smith' was rallying a little. 'Is this an English ship?' he asked weakly.

Before answering North sent the French officers to the wardroom and then turned back to Smith.

'Yes, this is a Royal Navy ship the *Couronne*,' said North. 'Who are you?'

'Howard Sitwell – I'm an art dealer.'

'A friend of Michael Bryan, perhaps?' asked North.

The man looked at him with a frown but said nothing.

'Don't worry, Mr Sitwell, you are in safe hands. Michael Bryan and I are good friends and I am perfectly aware of his other activities. I am going to have you carried to the sickbay where our surgeon can make you comfortable. We can talk later.'

After Sitwell had been carried out, North changed into dry clothes. Lang had sent over the French crew of the *Earl of Leicester*, which had been led by another *aspirant*. For the time being, North ordered Lang to stand by on the prize. He then called for Marshall to be brought to the cabin.

He looked at Marshall grimly. The man had changed little since last time he had seen him two years ago. 'Up to your old tricks again, Marshall? There will be a rope waiting for you in England this time, not some comfortable little berth in Bedlam, you treacherous dog.'

Marshall looked at him grimly. 'You have to get me there first, North, and don't think we have no idea where you're going. I give you two weeks before you are dragged through the streets of Paris in chains.'

North raised his eyebrows. 'Don't tell me. Your little white mice in the Admiralty have told you I am off to Copenhagen to take tea with the Crown Prince.'

Marshall looked uncertain. He said nothing and looked away. It was enough for North. Only one person had been told that particular lie, a strong suspect in Horseguards, Infantry Captain Simon Cornish, for whom the trap had been laid by a casual aside from his whist partner, George Hibbert. It had been expected that the word would reach Fouché somehow and a British agent in Fouché's office would get word back to London that Cornish's infamy was uncovered.

There was much more to Marshall but it would wait. North ordered him to be put in irons on the orlop deck. Writing a report for the Admiralty took North a quarter of an hour after which he called Lang back to the *Couronne* and had Midshipman Merry and Master's Mate Prentice take command of the *Earl of Leicester* with ten able seamen to make their way home.

He had gone down to the sickbay where Sitwell appeared to be revived and more animated. Speaking in low tones he told North that he had been on his way to Cuxhaven where he would have been carried over to Yarmouth and thence to London. The declaration of war had caused the frontiers to be closed against foreigners and he had been swept up as he crossed the river Ems and landed at Emden.

Fortunately he had been able to destroy the secret papers he was carrying but he had information in his head that William Wickham needed regarding the new network of informants that Sitwell had built up in Antwerp and Bruges.

He assured North that he felt well enough to continue to England on the *Earl of Leicester* and went over to her as the prize was cast off and sent on her way back to Harwich. Before he left he suggested to North that he should interrogate Marshall concerning his activities in Holland. It seemed likely that Marshall had met with an American who was working for the French in one of their shipyards. Marshall had been with one of Fouché's men and had been acting as interpreter. Sitwell knew nothing else useful to pass on concerning the reason for that meeting.

North ordered his priorities. Marshall could wait. He had already been delayed enough and it was time to sail as quickly as possible north to the Baltic Sea.

Chapter 21

<u>24th to 31st May, 1803</u>

The storm raged on.

Three days to reach the Skagerrak where there was no relief from the wild winds and driving rain. James Lang was sagging against the binnacle. None of the officers and few of the crew had slept for more than an hour or two for days. *Couronne*'s galley struggled to cope and with the continual calls for all hands, most meals were lukewarm by the time the crew could eat.

Further in towards Copenhagen the reputation of the Kattegat was dire even in less challenging weather. In the hell of the storm aching eyes scanned for shallows and reefs to no avail. The sea was thrown into such angry turmoil that there were no clear sign of the frequent hazards. Sailing a ship by luck was no way to navigate but Lang was reduced to instinct rather than information. He looked up as the fore tops'l ripped its full length. No topman would survive that climb and there was little left but prayer to preserve the ship.

He turned his head as his captain staggered towards him from the cabin, clutching at a man-rope here, waiting a moment for the roll of the ship, then almost leaping to grip the shoulder of a quartermaster's mate.

Alongside Lang, North swung on a soaking wet leather strap that hung from the side of the binnacle box to prevent himself being swept back to the wheel. For a moment all Lang could see was the soundless movement of his lips. North moved closer, his face inches from Lang's as he shouted, 'I said, you are relieved, Mr Lang. Go below and get some food inside you!'

Lang replied hoarsely, 'The watch is but half over, sir!'

North shook his head, and a cascade of water swept from his tarpaulin hood. 'Get below, James! I have the deck!'

Lang nodded and turned to make the hazardous lurching steps to the companionway. North had relieved half the officers of the watch in the past day and a half. He had probably had less sleep than anybody. It seemed to many that his strength was the strength of the ship itself. Many a crewman teetering on the edge of panic had been calmed by seeing the rock-like figure of their captain, grimly looking forward, face lashed by the tempest – immovable and reassuring in a world suddenly delivered into the hands of Satan.

A cry almost lost in the howling wind. The dim shape of a man thrown back towards the quarterdeck as something struck him on the chest.

Desperately struggling forward, North fell to his knees as he reached a hatch-cover and gripped the edge with the frozen fingers of his left hand. He stretched out with his right hand and caught the flailing pigtail of the fallen man as he tumbled towards the scuppers. Another man was there beside North;

the marine who had been crouching to ring the ship's bell. He managed to get a hold on one of the unconscious man's arms and North grabbed the other. As they dragged him into the almost non-existent shelter of the hatch coaming, North could see a bloody gash on the marine's forehead.

The body of the other man was wedged between North and the marine but all three were now sliding across the deck towards the side of the ship. Then other hands were there, frantically snatching at clothing, arms, ankles, anything they could reach.

Disorder and despair receded as the struggling victims of the storm crawled inch by inch to safety.

North gripped the marine's hand. 'Well done, Maddox, I won't forget this. Get that gash attended to.'

Eager hands carried the seaman below. He had been injured by a loose block swinging from the shrouds and breaking his ribs but at least he would live.

Five minutes after the incident Michael North was standing again, solid and unbowed at the binnacle. North understood how important it was to appear to be indomitable to keep up the spirits of the crew. His side ached where he had struck the hatch coaming and the fingers of his left hand, suffering from the strain of holding on to the full weight of the seaman's body, were still filled with pain but to outward appearance he was indestructible.

Three hours later the wind began to abate. The storm lost much of its fury but the night watches seemed unending until the sky lightened a little with the dawn.

At last a dim glow in the east resolved itself into a weak sun and the clouds scudded away to the south-east. The rain still fell but no longer in savage, face-scouring sheets. At last sails could be set again and damage repaired though it was in the hands of dead-weary men that the ship was cajoled back into some sort of order.

Every eye around the wardroom table was red with fatigue. Heads drooping, the officers lifted oatmeal porridge to their lips barely having the energy to swallow.

The 3rd lieutenant had the deck, the captain was in his day cabin receiving mumbled reports from the carpenter and bosun as to *Couronne*'s damage.

North reached across and lifted a brandy bottle to pour more into the steaming cups of coffee in front of his warrant officers. Normally North shunned coffee for which he had little liking but he felt that it was for moments like this that coffee had been invented in order to be diluted by brandy.

'Thank you, gentlemen, I am pleased that you have the repairs well in hand. Now, I must see the surgeon. Bosun, please arrange a double issue of grog to each man after supper.'

On deck Lieutenant Cryer was taking no chances with the treacherous waters of the Kattegat. The ship was headed towards the Danish shore where the currents seemed less powerful but even in mid-channel there were a number of bad sandbanks in the area.

The quartermaster looked up to the sky, 'I do believe the rain is stopping, sir!'

Cryer looked up too. 'You are right, Davidson, and dare I say it, the wind actually feels warmer. Perhaps we will soon be dry again after nearly a week.'

Davidson chuckled, 'Best not say that, sir. Tempting fate, that is.'

They looked around as Captain North joined them. 'The sun gives heat at last. A good omen, gentlemen. Mr Cryer, as soon as the deck is dry have the watch off duty lay out their wet clothing. At eight bells, clear for action and we will exercise the guns. By then the men should be rested enough.'

Cryer thought that the men would still be tired but that could be the case if they had to go into action, so it would be good experience for the crew. North was one of the most considerate commanders Cryer had ever known but he certainly was not soft.

At eight bells the drummers began the rattle of alarm, bosun's mates ran the decks, their pipes screeching, and the men went to action stations. Guns were made ready. They were run out and the starboard broadside fired. It was a rolling barrage designed to spare *Couronne's* timbers from the shock of a simultaneous blast. Then shouting officers called for the larboard guns. The crews leapt like dancers, every movement having been rehearsed a dozen or more times in the first few days after *Couronne* had sailed from Harwich.

In less than three minutes the larboard guns bellowed.

As the guns were sponged out, North looked at his watch and smiled. Weariness had barely slowed the crew's efforts. Without a word he turned to go to his cabin. Praise was not needed. Those standing near him were pleased just by seeing that smile.

There was a sudden interruption before North could leave the deck.

'Deck there!' bawled the foremast lookout, his cry immediately echoed from the mainmast crosstrees. 'Sail, fine on the larboard quarter, sir! I see two ships, one small and one large.'

North snatched up Cryer's Dolland glass and ran to the mainmast weather shrouds. Leaning forward from the wind, which was abaft the beam, he moved quickly aloft and arrived at the side of the lookout. An arm thrust through the weather halliards below the fly-block to steady him, he trained the glass on the distant ships.

'A brig of war and a little further away a frigate. I can't make out their colours. Take the glass, Dibble. Call down to the deck when you have a better sight.'

He moved to the aft end of the small platform, took hold of the mainbrace and came down hand over hand to the deck. Rubbing his tar-stained hands together he said to Cryer and Lang, 'It is as well we are at the guns. There is a frigate and brig in the offing. I think it unlikely they are friendly but they may be neutrals. We shall investigate. Put up the helm, if you please. Mr Cryer, where is the master?'

McCann answered for himself as he climbed down from the poop deck. 'Here, Sir Michael. I have the charts for the Northern Kattegat. I judge we are three leagues nor-nor-east of the island shown as Læsø Byrum with Fredrikshavn directly to the west on our starboard beam. There is a line of reefs between us and the shore but if we head directly south by west we should stay clear of them.'

North tapped the chart. 'The strange ships are about here and heading into the Baltic as we are. If we head a little more westerly than south-west and they maintain their course, we should meet them in the channel between the island and the Danish coast. Very well, make it so, please. Keep the men at the guns but allow them off in quarter-sections to eat. I will be in my cabin.'

There were things to be done. North checked that his secret papers were in the weighted bag along with the signal book. His desk had been struck below when the deck was cleared. His cabin was now open to the gun deck. His steward had brewed tea despite the status of the ship and he gratefully drank some. He changed his breeches and stockings for silk and as his steward held it for him, shrugged on his dress coat.

He eased his sword in its scabbard, held out his hand for his hat and returned to the deck. He had heard the hail from Dibble on the mainmast. The ships were flying Danish colours. While Denmark's neutrality could not be taken for granted, the tension had subsided a little.

North used his spyglass to take a long look at the two ships.

The brig was closer but the frigate was moving towards her and would likely come to her weather side. The brig seemed to float high in the water but North could count a full broadside of nine guns. The guns were run out, as indeed were those of *Couronne.* This was simply the normal precaution and meant little. As the frigate cleared the stern of the brig North could see that she too had her lids up and the black muzzles of her guns out. She carried 40 guns, a similar number to *Couronne.*

He closed his glass but stood lost in thought for a moment. James Lang, who was standing nearby, looked at him curiously, waiting for a decision. North's brain was working hard. Lang started as North snapped. 'That's no Danish frigate! The Danes don't have a 40-gun frigate in commission. Their largest frigates carry but 30 guns – and the only one of those I am sure could still be in commission is the *Stralsund.* I know the *Stralsund* and that ship is not she!'

Four spyglasses were snapped open almost as one as the officers on the quarterdeck followed North's pointing finger.

'Mr Lang, a gun and our colours, if you please. We shall put that frigate on notice!'

The quarterdeck larboard 8-pounder thumped and a ball curved high into the sky before dropping a cable's length from the strange frigate's weather quarter. *Couronne's* colours went quickly aloft.

Men could be seen running quickly along the frigate's deck. The Danish flag fell and a French flag was run up to replace it. By now all three ships were in range of each other. The brig turned towards the Danish coast and the frigate ploughed on, her topgallants and yards now sprouting royals and stuns'ls. She increased the gap between her and *Couronne*. Despite being a French-built ship and practically a twin to the French frigate, *Couronne's* red ensign had obviously been seen – perhaps belatedly and the frigate was declining battle.

Couronne chased her, her fo'c'sl 8-pounders dragged round as bow-chasers. As the quarry made off the only reply she could make was with the aftermost of her broadside guns. To do this she had to put her helm over each time she fired. North noticed that the captain ordered the helm to starboard. Each time she turned a few dozen yards were shaved off the distance between the two ships. If she continued in this manner *Couronne* would be up on her in less than an hour.

Her swerves to larboard were not being corrected and this was bringing her closer to the hazards off the Danish shore.

Lang had been watching the sea on *Couronne's* weather and

lee quarters. 'Sir, the colour of the sea is changing. I suspect there is shallow water to larboard.'

Calling for soundings to continue every two minutes, North ran forward to the bows. The sea to larboard was indeed lighter. The master shouted, 'Sandbanks shown on the chart, Sir Michael!'

North called back 'Put the helm over! We seem well clear but we must get some westing off her.'

The French frigate was a mile ahead now and showed no sign of changing course.

North watched with growing apprehension. If she did not port her helm, the enemy would ... Then it happened. Under full sail the French frigate ran aground. Her fully strained masts could not resist the shock of the impact. Her foremast and main went by the board. He could hear the horrendous crash from a mile away.

Canvas, sheets, spars all spread over her forecastle and deck. Her jib-mast had shattered into half a dozen pieces, strung like shards on what remained of her jib rigging. Her bows were deep in the sand and breached. As water filled her, the stern came down again under the weight. She sat level and still but for the screams and panic of her crew. Her spanker was snapping and banging in the wind but her mizzenmast appeared to be taking the strain.

On *Couronne* North ordered all sails taken in and her stream anchor dropped. She came to rest with two fathoms under her keel.

'Boats sir?' Birchall asked.

'Not yet, Mr Birchall the tide-race is fierce through the channel and I will not risk our crews. That ship is firmly held at present but she holds more than 300 men many of whom are in a state of terror. We will wait to see what happens. If the ship founders we will attempt to pick up survivors but for now they must take their chances. I do not intend that they capsize our boats by crowding on to them like frightened sheep.'

The wait was not spent with easy minds. Like a lurking wolf the storm began to rise again. Every man on *Couronne* was aware of the probable fate of the men on the French ship, which was slowly but surely breaking up under the force of the wind and waves. Most sailors of either navy were non-swimmers and even those who could swim would stand little chance of surviving the rage of the sea. She tried to launch her boats. Some men managed to get on board them but every one of them was swept away into the gathering storm.

On *Couronne* under bare masts the ship strained and heaved. North had the kedge anchor dropped to reinforce the stream anchor. This was the testing moment. Thankfully it held.

As the rain began to fall more heavily the French frigate's silhouette disappeared.

The storm lasted four hours and then it suddenly ceased. It abated so quickly that the sun burst out and the ship was steaming like a huge pan of water.

When the air cleared every eye searched the sea but except for a scatter of broken timber and debris no trace of the French frigate or her crew was found. Every one of the 300 souls on board was lost except for seven men who had clung to her crippled launch through the raging torrent. Without oars and her mast and sail swept away, she was driven south almost as far as Anholt. *Couronne* found them huddled on a tiny island of bare rock as the sun rose two days later.

Chapter 22

<u>31st May to 7th June, 1803</u>

Ronehamn was a tiny village on the south-east coast of Gotland, with a good anchorage sufficient for the *Evropa* 66. Her captain, Nicholas Slavin, knocked on the door of his distinguished guests' cabin and called out to them that an English ship was dropping anchor in the bay.

One of the two men whom Slavin carried on *Evropa* was Count Alexey Andreevich Arakcheev, a soldier who had never commanded in the field. He had reached the rank of Lieutenant General by the age of 29, but fell out badly with Tsar Paul. He had covered up scandalous activities by some of his officers and was demoted. Only recently was he back in favour with Tsar Alexander.

Slavin could understand why he was universally detested by his fellow generals and most of the Tsar's ministers. Slavin was aware that Arakcheev maintained his position through fear and his ability to insinuate himself into Alexander's good books.

The other man looked across at him with a neutral expression on his face but Slavin suspected that inside he was having difficulty in maintaining that calm. Prince Adam Jerzy Czartoryski was a year younger than Arakcheev. Although born a Pole he had been elevated to the rank of assistant foreign minister. Being a foreigner, that was as far as he would get but it wasn't bad. He was known as a brilliant thinker and was very close to the Tsar as a member of the 'Secret Committee' along with Arakcheev, Rumyantsev and Speransky but he had grave misgivings about his companion.

Czartoryski's reservations about Arakcheev's presence here were based on personal knowledge of the man's deviousness and unreliability. He also perceived that there might well be a problem working with the English since Arakcheev and his friend Nicholas Rumyantsev were rabid anglophobes.

Czartoryski, despite his rank felt that the perpetual atmosphere of fear and wickedness in the tsar's court was still noticeable here on a ship on the Baltic sea.

Arakcheev and Czartoryski came on deck with Slavin and looked across at the English ship. Arakcheev pointed to it and said, 'There is something fishy here, that is a French ship, the *Couronne*. I saw her in Stockholm harbour a few weeks ago.'

Slavin said, 'The ensign is English, Count. Perhaps you are aware that the English navy captures a dozen or more capital ships for every ship that the French take. It is a thing that his Imperial Highness much admires, I believe.'

'Why do they not salute us?'

Czartoryski answered, 'I am sure they would if this was a Russian port but Sweden is neutral and we probably should not even be here.' Inwardly he winced and crossed his fingers that the English captain was not one who would stand on his dignity when he met the irascible Arakcheev.

Slavin was a career sailor proud of naval tradition and a personal friend of the English captain Sir Frederic Thesiger who had been the Tsar's naval advisor. Through Thesiger he was aware of the etiquette of receiving a British post captain. Therefore he had three of his soldiers beat a tattoo of drums as the English captain came on board.

North removed his hat to the Russian ensign and came forward with a smile on his face to meet Slavin.

He addressed him in German, a language in which he was fairly proficient though by no means fluent. Most of the Russian aristocracy spoke French in preference to Russian in any case, though North had taken the trouble to find out that Nicholas Slavin was a German Jew who had taken service in the Tsar's navy through lack of opportunity in his own country.

'Good morning, sir, I am Captain Michael North of the Royal Navy.'

Slavin smiled back, and to North's relief he spoke good English. 'Your fame precedes you, Sir Michael. You are welcome on my ship. Now I must introduce you to the diplomats, if you please. They are waiting on the quarterdeck. For your information Count Arakcheev does not speak English and neither of them speaks German.' He nodded to emphasise his meaning.

Aware that it would be useful to be able to speak to Slavin without risk of being understood, North replied, 'Thank you Captain. I take it they both speak French?'

Slavin laughed again. 'That might cause a problem with the Count. He is suspicious of your ship and thinks you might be a Frenchman masquerading as an Englishman.'

'The ship is a very recent addition to our navy, sir.'

'Fine shipbuilders, the French. I wish I had one of theirs instead of this leaky old wreck.'

Czartoryski turned to Arakcheev. 'Well, judging by their smiles at least those two seem to have hit it off. Go softly on the anti-British attitude, Count, it will make life easier.'

Slavin raised a hand to indicate Czartoryski first. As far as he was concerned the assistant foreign minister was the more important of the two, apart from the fact that he admired the man for his energy and sensitivity. He addressed them in French. 'Your highness, your grace, may I present Captain Sir Michael North, Adjutant General of the British Royal Navy? Sir Michael, may I present Prince Czartoryski, His Imperial Highness' Minister for Foreign Affairs and General Count Arakcheev, advisor to the Tsar of All the Russias?'

North noted the slight exaggeration of his virtually meaningless government title and saluted both men, extending a hand to be shaken. 'Your highness, your grace, I bring you greetings from His Brittanic Majesty King George. It is an honour to meet you.'

North introduced Plummer who had followed him on board.

Czartoryski, who had also done his homework, said, 'It is characteristic of His Majesty to send to us one of his most distinguished and valiant captains and noted member of his parliament. I am sure that your presence here is a good omen of success. Will you not tell us about your ship? We were expecting the 74-gun *Tigre*?'

'My ship the *Tigre* was badly damaged a week ago when capturing the French 74 *Unité* and also this ship which is the 40-gun *Couronne*, off the east coast of England. *Tigre* is being repaired with all despatch and should arrive here in a few days. Since the mission is not completely dependent on the size of the ships of our joint enterprise, I trust it is not a problem?'

Czartoryski replied, 'Indeed it might be an advantage if you have to pose as a French ship though I believe *Tigre* is also French-built. Let us go to the captain's cabin and review the situation.'

The two Russian noblemen and Slavin sat on one side of the table with North and Plummer on the other. Having been cautioned by Plummer as to its potency, North sipped a glass of plum brandy slowly as the discussion began with a re-statement by Czartoryski of the information his intelligencers had unearthed.

His people had firm information that Bonaparte was planning to occupy the city of Hanover and an army of 30,000 was being assembled for that purpose. France was not ready to go to war again with Prussia and the King of Prussia was vacillating as to whether he should follow the advice of Graf von Haugwitz, the Prussian minister for foreign affairs, and make it clear to Bonaparte that such an occupation would not be tolerated. Haugwitz had been in secret discussions with Vienna and with St Petersburg to form an alliance against France but the King of Prussia was lukewarm.

It seemed that the French were engaged in a plan which, if brought to fruition, would further alienate the Prussian government from their counterparts in St Petersburg.

The plan involved sending into the estuary of the Vistula three French ships flying Russian colours. Prussia did not have a navy but she had a number of armed trading ships that used the port of Danzig. They would stand little chance against a well-armed flotilla.

Prussia's commercial navy – the *Preußische Seehandlung* – had two important tasks. One was the importation and

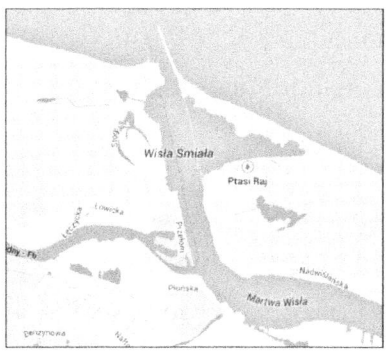

transportation of salt from France, Spain and elsewhere and the other was in connection with Prussia's monopoly of all the wax produced in an area ten miles of either bank of the river Vistula. Navigation of the

Vistula was essential to maintain Prussia's trading interests.

Czartoryski produced a chart showing the port of Danzig and the estuary.

'Here and just here in the narrows south of Wisla Smiala are old ships tied up to the quays – three on one shore and six on the other. These ships are a remnant of the old navy that was laid up forty years ago at the end of the Seven Years' War. The French plan is to tow or warp five or six of these ships out into the channel and sink them thus blocking the western river and preventing navigation.

He pointed at the chart. 'They will then proceed to the eastern arm of the estuary where they will sink more ships and block that exit to the sea. It will not just be the interruption to the cargoes of wax being collected. Gunpowder, timber and other war materials are carried downriver. In particular the timber is for the British trade.

'The French have hatched a simple plan in flying false Russian colours. The Prussians would believe it of us that we should do such a thing. Your country needs timber for shipbuilding. If Prussia cannot supply part of that trade, Sweden and Russia would benefit. If Sweden and Russia join a pact of armed neutrality, as Bonaparte urges, the consequences for Britain are severe. This is why our interests coincide.

'Now the problem is that we cannot send in a Russian ship to intercept the French since that would just play into their hands. We could warn the Prussians, of course, but instead we felt a more elegant riposte could be made by using the British navy.'

North asked, 'You want me to intercept the French ships?'

Czartoryski replied, 'Not on your own. We propose that this ship takes part flying British colours. It was supposed you would bring a 74 but even so it is not unheard of for a commanding officer to have a larger ship as his consort, I believe.'

North said, 'I take it that you do not want the French ships intercepted in the open sea but catching them in the act would be far more impressive to the Prussians?'

'We want them to know it was the French who invaded them. We hope this will inspire them to declare war on France. It will also make it easier for the Tsar to declare for the coalition too.'

'Well, that would certainly suit Britain. Very well, I will return to my ship if I may and think about the fine details. In the meantime, do we have any idea when the French will make their attack?'

'Within the next three or four days but we should have better information from our man in the French legation by tomorrow afternoon.'

Czartoryski had done most of the talking. Arakcheev sat watching with a brooding look on his face. If he hated the British it was a mild sentiment in comparison to his loathing of the upstart Bonaparte so he would give passive support for the moves that Czartoryski was proposing. He glanced down at the chart showing the layout of the Vistula estuary.

Waving a finger at the map, Arakcheev remarked, 'It seems to me that we are being too subtle. Why does our English friend not simply lie in wait for the French ships and attack them before they can tow out the hulks? Why does he need this ship? Even under false colours the Prussians may find out our identity. After all it is open war between the French and the British so no pretence is necessary.'

North said, 'I thank you for your faith that I might be able to overwhelm the French even if *Tigre* is here but I agree with his highness; this battle needs to be quietly fought on the river itself. I believe I have the resources to take care of matters in the west estuary while *Evropa* watches over the east. With respect all we need to do is to make sure that the Prussians and the French believe that the plot was foiled by the British and keep you and your country out of the picture. On the other hand *Evropa* improves the chances of success, used as a fighting reserve.'

Slavin did not feel that his thoughts would bear much weight here but he agreed with North. Too much could go wrong in a sea-battle and *Evropa* could not be seen to be in the area of such a battle out at sea where some of her crew could fall into French hands, so North would have only his own resources – inferior in strength if *Tigre* failed to arrive in time.

Czartoryski's French spy was able to give them an accurate time for the attack on the estuary the following night at midnight and North had formulated his counter-plan.

Evropa would take up position with *Couronne* several miles east from the western estuary along the coast off Stegna. *Couronne* would need *Evropa's* protection since North would land most of his crew.

A small British party would be in position at the mouth of the western arm of the estuary on the sand dunes of the eastern shore. As the French ships passed into the river they would signal to the allied ships which would sail to block the exit of the French from the estuary.

Most of *Couronne's* crew and the 80 marines on board had already been landed and secretly taken up position near the three quays where the hulks of the Prussian ships were moored. One quay was to the east and two to the west. The parties were commanded by Lieutenants Cryer and Lang and the marine lieutenant.

Plummer watched the efficiency around him and wrote in his journal:

> *No better indication of the crew's professionalism could be observed than the manner in which each man carried out his part. Capt. N. and his officers, closely watching, each warrant officer explained to his people what was required, patiently answering doubts. Well instructed and with G-d's blessing*

they shall prevail with as little loss of life and limb as possible.

The waiting was anxious and on *Couronne* North asked himself why he had not gone in with the landing party. He was confident in his officers but not used to leading from the rear.

It lacked almost 40 minutes to midnight when the signal came as the incoming tide brought in three French ships, a 64-gun ship and two frigates. They were flying Russian flags and the frigates were towing extra boats.

James Lang crouched down against a warehouse wall on the east bank. He was in a disused dockyard; a crumbling jetty reaching out into the river had a heavy but mastless ship tied up each side. Half an hour earlier Lang had sent in half a dozen French-speaking men to grab the two watchmen stationed in a small hut on the quay. They were pinioned and gagged in a corner near the dock gates, their captors making sure they heard French being spoken.

He watched the river. The French had chosen a night where the moon was new and little light was thrown on the waters. The three invaders anchored in almost perfect silence. Lang could see the shape of the nearest ship, probably the 64. There was something else. He frowned, uncertain for a minute or so. One of his men, a keen-eyed quarter-gunner, whispered, 'Boats approaching, sir.'

There were two long boats in the water and as they came

nearer Lang could see that each of them towed a thick cable which led out and back to one of the ships which were in deeper water.

Half of Lang's men were already on the hulks. As the approaching boats touched alongside the hulks, Lang raised a hand and the men concealed around him moved forward in a semi-crouch.

There was eerie silence. Lang could see men climbing the side of the nearest hulk and stepping over the rail. One of them turned and hauled up a light line attached to the heavier towing cable. Others had axes in hand to cut the cables securing the ship to the wharf.

As they started to move towards the forecastle, the French were pounced on and beaten to the deck. Lang's men from the shore entered the ships from open stern-lights and went to the rail where they aimed muskets down on the boats. The first shots rang out from the far bank where two British parties were stationed. The response came from the 64, which fired off cannon from her starboard battery.

On Lang's side the Frenchmen in the cutters stood and raised their hands above their heads. They were beckoned on to the ships. Every Frenchman was trussed up and carried below for the local authorities to find in the morning.

There was a brilliant burst of light as a rocket soared into the sky. It revealed *Couronne* entering the mouth of the river, her bow-chasers firing at the 64.

One of the Prussian hulks had been secured by the French frigate nearest the shore and her men straining at the windlasses was being slowing hauled into deeper water. On the hulk itself 20 or 30 British sailors with the marine lieutenant were fighting hand to hand with the Frenchmen who had seized the hulk.

Lang and his party, having achieved their objective, crowded back on to the quayside and ran towards the dock where the hulk had been towed from.

Shouting orders, Lang had his men in the boats tied up to the quay and away towards the slowly moving hulk. He could see other boats filled with British seamen and marines also straining to reach the hulk. He could see her name on the battered transom – *Morgenrot*.

By the time he reached her there were six boats carrying nearly 70 of *Couronne's* people nearby. There was mayhem as they all scrambled on to the hulk.

The marine lieutenant was lying dead on the quarterdeck but the French party had been subdued. *Morgenrot* was now almost in mid-channel and 40 yards from the frigate. Lang looked quickly along the deck and identified Midshipman Grant.

'Mr Grant! Is there an anchor catted?'

'No, sir, we cannot do anything except cut the French cable!'

Lang shook his head angrily. The frigate would even now be

preparing to fire on *Morgenrot* to sink her in the middle of the channel.

'Don't cut the cable! Get the boats crewed and have lines attached to the bows. Instead of trying to stop the frigate winding her in, I want to get as close as possible to the frigate before they can fire on us!'

It was a desperate plan but as long as *Morgenrot* floated it had a chance. Lang had almost 90 men with him and though the odds were against him he intended boarding and taking the frigate.

The first shots thundered from the side of the frigate and all those left on *Morgenrot's* deck ducked instinctively. There was damage but the French could not depress their guns enough to strike the hulk below the waterline. In the meantime the British cutters and pinnaces were reinforcing the efforts of the frigate's windlasses which had not stopped heaving.

It seemed that the French captain had not realised the danger. The hulk was moving faster now. She was less than 50 feet from the frigate. Timing was crucial and depended on Lang's best judgement.

Taking up the speaking trumpet he called for the rowing boats to cast off and stand by to board the frigate. He had the 30 men left on *Morgenrot* standing by at the rail.

As the hulk slammed alongside, nothing could have demonstrated the lack of flexibility of the French captain than the fact that the sight of British sailors swarming over his rail took him completely by surprise. The hand-to-hand fighting was going against the boarders but as more and more men clambered up from the boats the fight became more even. After ten minutes it became clear that the British had control of the upper areas of the ships and fighting below was diminishing in intensity. The flag tumbled and the French threw their weapons down in surrender.

Lang gave orders to herd the French below and then sent down two boat crews to tow *Morgenrot* to the nearest shore. Sails were aloft as the 40-gun frigate *La Trave* moved towards the sea as a British prize.

Meanwhile the other two French ships had cut their anchor cables and their sails were being set. The tide was against them but the wind was in their favour. There was enough room for them to pass *Couronne* and as they moved out, *Couronne* also retreated, her purpose to flush them out satisfied. All that was needed now was for the eastern estuary to be protected and that had to be left to *Evropa*.

North focused his glass on the second frigate. He could see intense activity on her deck as she seemed to be following her companions. He was about to give the order to fire on her when he noticed that she flew no colours, either Russian or French. In the moment of hesitation that followed a plain white flag was run up. The flag meant nothing except surrender and therefore stayed his hand.

A minute or so passed and there was a hoist of four signal flags. He read L.A.N.G. and laughed aloud. It seemed he could safely ignore the frigate.

North looked along his gun deck. His crew depleted by 160 seamen and 80 marines, he had barely enough to handle her sails and her guns would have to remain silent but he would manage as long as *Evropa* supported him. If he had to face the 64 alone the task would be daunting but *Evropa,* flying the red ensign, was almost the same size as the Frenchman and it would be her task to engage the 64. The objective was to beat off the French. Capturing them could bring about complications.

It was still tempting to attempt capture of at least the other frigate but North resisted the urge. With *Evropa* keeping up a rapid barrage of gunfire, that ship and *Couronne* approached the French ships. He caused another flare to be fired into the sky.

On the enemy 64, her commanding officer appeared to have decided to decline the battle. His ships were there to tow or winch out heavy hulks, not to fight an enemy of equal size. Although *La Trave*'s prize crew had their hands full with their prisoners, even her presence in British hands could tip the balance in favour of the British.

Evropa's guns were taking a toll in any case. The 64's foremast was leaning heavily to port and there was visible wreckage all along her deck. She struggled away from the fight and followed the remaining frigate westwards.

North brought *Couronne* around to support *Evropa* which had sustained some damage but was still firing efficiently. This said much for Captain Slavin's ability since the majority of the Russian fleet was indifferently handled.

The allies let the enemy go; their objective had been achieved.

The capture of *La Trave* was a brilliant bonus. The only moment of discord was when Aracheev suggested that the prize be handed over to the Russian navy as a gesture of goodwill. Fortunately Czartoryski was so outraged by the suggestion that the matter was dropped as quickly as it had been introduced.

....

The following afternoon at 3pm North, dressed in his best uniform and accompanied by Plummer and Captain Slavin, who was dressed in a British navy lieutenant's coat alongside Lieutenants Cryer and Lang, entered the council chamber in Danzig's town hall to applause from the city's councillors.

The Mayor of Danzig stood to the right of Graf von Haugwitz, who came forward to shake North by the hand.

'It was indeed fortunate that your intelligence people found about this plot and managed to get word to you, Captain. I am curious to know how you happened to be in the Baltic?'

'My mission was to carry despatches to the Tsar, your grace. It was in St Petersburg we heard of the plot and made our way here as fast as we could. Having been fortunate enough to deal with it successfully without directly involving your country, I am sending my consort on to London to report.'

'This other ship of yours, the *Ulysses*, I did not recognise her as the same ship I saw at Greenwich a few years ago, I thought she had fewer guns? But still, memory can be fallible. I wish you joy of your prize – I believe that is the correct expression. I was privileged to watch from a balcony of my hotel as she was captured.'

North, hoping to deflect interest in Slavin's ship, indicated Lang, 'May I present Lieutenant the Honourable James Lang, your grace? He was the gallant officer who took *La Trave*.'

'Well done indeed, Lieutenant! You know, gentlemen, I still can't stop thinking about *Ulysses*. Still, I seem to remember that in Greek mythology Ulysses was renowned for his cunning.'

Slavin almost winced. It was subtle but the wily count was dropping a broad hint. It would be politically as well for the Russians that they kept very quiet about any possible involvement.

Chapter 23

<u>8th to 13th June, 1803</u>

After bidding farewell to the Russians there was one matter that North wanted to deal with before he went on to complete the second part of his mission, a diplomatic visit to Sweden. He sent for Marshall. For the past week he had been too busy to deal with him and indeed had wanted him to suffer a degree of discomfort to loosen his tongue.

The young man was used to the finest of things – clothing, food, lifestyle – and it was shattering his morale to be cast down in chains to sleep on the bare boards of the cold, dark orlop of the ship and be fed on food that even the crew would avoid if possible. In some ships it had been known for men to be overcome by the noxious miasmas of the hold rising to the orlop. However in common with many enlightened captains North had made it a rule to have the shingle ballast in the hold flooded with sea-water once or twice a week and then pumped out and the air saturated with sulphur fumes. Marshall sat hunched in a chair in the cabin, his head to one side, peering at North through eyelids puffy with crying. He gave all the appearance of a broken man but North was not about to be taken in by his act.

'You know, Marshall, this traitor's life is not for you,' said North. 'You have neither sufficient fortitude, skill nor luck to carry it off. It would probably be a kindness to simply drop you over the side with a round-shot to speed you downwards.

I suppose I could see that you are more comfortable if you are prepared to see reason and abandon Bonaparte. What do you think?'

Marshall snivelled. 'It is true I am brought low, Sir Michael. With nothing but the prospect of a rope about my neck, I suppose my only hope is to tell you everything I know and hope that you will speak for me?'

North sat silently for a few moments. 'It would have to be a damned good story, Mr Marshall.'

Marshall seemed to sink lower in his chair but North detected the glint of cunning that he could not keep from his eyes.

'Before you open your mouth again, Marshall, stop and think. I know you for the devious, unprincipled little shit you are. I am not impressed by your family and connections, who I feel certain will disown you in any case, so do not think that you will have a chance of clemency in England this time. My patience is thinner than a spider's web as far as you are concerned so be warned; the truth may serve you but a lie will only ensure that you swing.'

Clearly Marshall was in a hole, it showed in his face. North could still see that Marshall was dissembling but he let him speak.

'You know, of course, that Boney is still building up his invasion army but what you may not know is that there is a secret plan to make the invasion more certain. The French do not intend to make the mistake of trying to cross the Straits of Dover hoping that the Royal Navy will be taken unawares, nor are they going to try through Ireland. Have you heard of the American Fulton and his submersible boat? Well, that is not his only invention. There is a great ship being built with 154 guns, but it is no conventional ship. Fulton has an American friend, Oliver Evans, who has perfected a type of high-pressure steam engine which can be used to pull wagons.'

North suppressed his astonishment with great difficulty. He had set aside the mystery of Fulton's whereabouts and activities and now it appeared he might learn more.

'Fulton has adapted this machine to drive a device he calls a propelling paddle which can move the ship along without the need for sails. The hull is more than fifteen inches thick and much of the inner bracing is made from pre-cast iron. I have seen it with my own eyes less than three weeks ago; the ship is irresistible.'

North asked, 'Where is this ship now?'

Marshall replied, 'In a place nobody would suspect, and that information is my insurance.'

'Not necessarily, it only needs for our agents to dig deep enough to disclose the location once they know what to look for.'

'That may be true,' said Marshall, 'but the ship is near

completion and speed may be of the essence if it is to be attacked before it is invulnerable.'

North said, 'Well, we shall see. Tell your tale when you reach England and perhaps you will simply be confined in prison for the rest of your life.'

'Will you not speak for me in the light of what I have told you? Do I get no relief of my treatment for telling you this?'

'Now this is the thing, Winslow Marshall. You choose to hold back the vital part of your information so you must see that I cannot take any chance that you might escape. Therefore you will continue to wear shackles, kept under guard and be confined below deck. However I will allow you to have one of the warrant officers' cabins and see that you eat the same food as the crew.'

After Marshall had been taken away North considered his information. Of course it could be true. As regards the shipyard where such a huge ship could be built there were limited possibilities – it was an interesting puzzle. Toulon, of course; but if Marshall had seen it less than three weeks ago, the chances were that it was being built on the Atlantic coast. In the light of what Sitwell had told him, Marshall and Fouché's man had met with an American – possibly Fulton – in *Holland*.

Marshall had been on his way southwards to Ostend and from there to Paris so it seemed unlikely that the ship was at Ostend or indeed further south. Apart from any other consideration most of the French ports were well infiltrated with informants. In any case many British tourists including a few naval officers deliberately exercising their eyes had been in and out of every regular port in the past two years during the Peace.

A ship of that size would be long in the building. First rate ships of the Royal Navy were all built in His Majesty's dockyards because of the sheer size of the facilities required and would take at least four to five years to come off the stocks. Moreover, great ships were built in dry dock and towed out when completed because it was impractical for them to be built on land.

In no other country but England were dry docks common. Techniques such as the use of caissons as dry-dock doors were probably copied by the French – who had been using similar devices for 70 years – but North could not recall any French yard where they existed.

It would be almost impossible to hide such a build in France thanks to Britain's extensive network of spies looking for just such a monster. So the ship was probably being built north of Ostend. But the same problem arose. There were very few dry docks and all of them under the eyes of British agents.

If Fulton had managed to solve the dry-dock problem and have a secret yard, it seemed likely that the shipyard was somewhere on the Dutch coast from the Hoek van Holland to Den Helder. Further south it might have been discovered by the mail packets in and out of Hellevoetsluis during the peace and even the Hook itself was less likely because of the traffic inwards to Rotterdam.

It was an intriguing puzzle but one that North was determined to solve. It had to be in an out-of-the-way place, where it was hidden from the prying eyes of foreigners but near enough to the sea to launch without difficulty.

He drew out his charts and tapped a pencil on a small village called Hoornes-Rijnsoever which sat beside a narrow channel from the Rhine behind the coastal village of Katwijk. It was practically the only place on the coast of that description which did not see many visitors. Accessible to the ocean but not actually being *on* the ocean would be useful for secrecy.

What struck North forcibly was the channel in front of the village. It was man-made and wide and the chart showed a basin which could be large enough for a ship more than 200 feet long and would not be visible from the sea. There could be heavy caissons towed in, flooded and sunk to seal off the basin; with some difficulty it could be pumped dry and an effective dry dock created.

He did not simply settle on this one option but it did seem a strong candidate. Most of the other possibilities were near or in passing distance of major cities or towns such as Amsterdam, Den Haag, Haarlem or Den Helder. Any other places capable of holding such a huge ship and indeed concealing it from sight seemed non-existent.

When his present mission was over it could be worth getting better acquainted with the tiny town of Hoornes-Rijnsoever.

As dawn broke the following morning North watched from *Couronne's* deck as the German coast receded.

North was aware that the French still had warships nearby, even if they did have bloody noses. The two French 74s that had been sent to support the Vistula operation were to the west and together they carried almost four times the number of his guns. As he was about to return to his cabin, the lookout called that a 74 was approaching from the north-west. After a few moments more he confirmed that it was *Tigre* and no fewer than four other British ships of the line in company.

An hour later North climbed the side of the 98-gun *Queen*, veteran of the Glorious First of June, and to his surprise was greeted by Rear Admiral Sir Edward Thornborough, one of the most gallant officers in the Royal Navy.

'Good morning, North and welcome on board. Lord Keith sent me to the Baltic to show the flag to the Danes – sort of discourage them to make bad friendships so as to speak. I chased a couple of French 74s into the Baltic but lost them in the fog a few days ago. Then I encountered *Tigre* as she came through the Kattegat and when your first lieutenant told me what was afoot I decided you might need some help.'

North laughed, 'Sir, I must say it is a great pleasure to see you. The first part of my mission has gone very well and your kind offer of help is not needed. However there are two French 74s in the area, possibly the ones you chased. I believe they may lie close inshore a few leagues west of here.'

Thornborough said, 'I think with the vessels at our disposal we should be able to deal with them. Why don't you rejoin *Tigre* and lead us to them.'

....

The squadron sighted the two French ships three times over the next three days. They were hull down on the horizon on the first day and on the third day close enough for North to see that they were heaving water and guns overboard to lighten themselves. By dawn on the fourth day it had to be reluctantly accepted that they had escaped during the night.

Over lunch on *Queen* Thornborough listened seriously as North told him of Marshall's information concerning the huge steam-propelled ship.

'If this is true, North, and it certainly has the ring of truth, it constitutes a serious threat to our country, 'said Thornborough. 'I like your idea of a smaller port so why don't you make your way to Katwijk after you have been to Stockholm, taking *Hotspur* with you under your command and probe between there and the Rhine estuary? The rest of the squadron will check the rest of the coast down to the French border after we have visited Copenhagen.'

This plan agreed, *Tigre* parted company with the squadron and with the *Hotspur* 74, *Couronne*, *La Trave* and *Juniper* made a fast voyage to the Swedish port of Stockholm.

Chapter 24

<u>16th to 21st June 1803</u>

Tigre, Hotspur, La Trave and *Couronne* with *Juniper* in their lee swam in an impressive line to the south of Skeppsholmen Island. North had sent a request on shore that he be received by a senior government minister. A reply had informed him that the king insisted on receiving him personally but that it would take a day or so to arrange matters.

Plummer, well briefed by the Foreign Office, advised North that the king and his government were continually at each other's throats and in any case he had a very tight rein on decision making. It was unlikely that North would be given much access to anybody but the king.

North's mission was to try to gain an impression as to the firmness of Sweden's neutrality which could not be any means be taken for granted. Plummer would act as his secretary while he was on shore and Lieutenant Lang would join them.

The Swedish court was in a chaotic state. King Gustav and his uncle Duke Karl, until a few years ago the regent, were continually feuding. Gustav had shaken free of the duke's influence and the Swedish people were hoping that at last the country might return to the 'Age of Gold' and leave this miserable period that they dubbed the 'Age of Lead' behind them. But Gustav, barely 18 when he assumed full powers as king, had been a great disappointment. For all his determination and sense of superiority, he was inept and indecisive. To make matters worse he had quarrelled violently with his nobles and firmly resolved never to call the Diet to the Riksdag again. Now, though six or seven years had passed, the political infighting was just as bad as ever.

There were many complexities to the political situation and London had warned North to tread warily. Gustav had managed to maintain an uneasy peace with the Tsar since both of them loathed the Jacobins but this was a long way from heralding an alliance with England.

North knew that there was no clear leadership apart from the army but that they would follow the king's commands albeit reluctantly. So it probably was the young king he needed to see.

It took two days of carefully phrased letters passing back and forth for the arrangements to be finalised but on the third morning after he had arrived, North was at last ushered into the royal presence. The audience chamber was long and narrow, giving North plenty of time to study the group of people in front of him as he walked the length of the floor.

The room was cool since the windows were shaded. Although hundreds of candles were lit, the length of the room allowed few clear details to be seen at the far end.

Plummer whispered to him as he walked, identifying the three men and the woman standing to the left of the king's throne.

'The woman Fossberg is the one you need to impress, Sir Michael. She is the one I mentioned. The king will listen to only two people, his chaplain and his wife. The chaplain – furthest on the left – wisely confines himself to religion and household matters. The queen holds the real power in the palace and Lolotte Fossberg strongly influences Her Majesty's opinions of matters of state.

'The taller man in the uniform of a Dragoon colonel is Carl Johan Adlercreutz. He is a supporter of the king but by no means uncritical of him. The other man is the king's old tutor Nils von Rosenstein. He is naturally inclined to liberal ideas but he is also a great admirer of Britain.'

Adlercreutz was a known quantity. He had firmly opposed the Anjala mutiny and was trusted by the king but it was said that he would always look to his own interests first. Rosenstein was a man noted for his shrewd common sense. While the king sought his advice, he did not firmly follow one path or another for very long unless the queen held him to it.

As he reached the three steps before the throne, North gave a court bow and swept off his hat.

The king was an odd creature, North thought. He had a low forehead, accented by a receding hairline. His body was slender and his head over-large. He had a prominent chin but it seemed not to signal strength, but rather to emphasise an incipient weakness. He had a ratty moustache above his thick lips and a large, hooked nose. His face was not helped by the fact that his brown eyes bulged, giving the impression that they were the windows to a vacant brain.

Naturally he addressed North in French, which he spoke with a slight lisp.

'Captain North, welcome to Stockholm. I expect that King George sent something with you?' If his eyes could show anything it was the greed beneath.

Without a word, North raised a hand and James Lang brought forward an ornate silver-chased five-foot long case. He opened it to display a pair of beautifully crafted octagonal-barrelled shotguns made by Joseph Manton and bearing his tiger mark.

'His Majesty charged me with delivering this gift and charged me to say that of all the rulers of Scandinavia, you stand most high in his affections.'

Having got this nonsense off his chest, North glanced sideways at the woman, Lolotte Fossberg. She was an attractive woman in his late thirties, said to be the daughter of a maidservant but suspected to be the natural child of King Adolf Frederick. Whatever the truth as to her birth, North had been told she was a very strong influence on the queen and through her on the king. If North was to impress anybody with England's case, it seemed it was Lolotte Fossberg.

The king, smiling as he handled one of the shotguns, said, 'Sir Michael, why do we not talk as we walk in the gardens.'

Despite his youth and notorious avoidance of intellectual matters, the king was a good conversationalist, though it seemed to North that the hovering courtiers exuded anxiety in case the royal foot entered the regal mouth. Adlercreutz particularly seemed so tense that he was virtually on tiptoes.

'I have been thinking, Sir Michael. Perhaps a state visit to England? To show support for King George?'

There was an agonised intake of breathe from Adlercreutz but before he could say anything, North replied, 'If it was not for the danger at sea, Majesty, I cannot think of anything that would delight the British people more. However, reluctantly I feel I should caution you that the loss to your people should anything happen to you would be overwhelming!'

The courtiers released so much pent-up breath that North could feel a warm blast on his neck.

The king frowned. 'From what I hear there would be nowhere safer than on your own ship, Sir Michael. It seems you are as indestructible as Britain itself!'

'Begging your pardon, Majesty, but flattering though that is, I fear that should Bonaparte hear of such a plan he would send a hundred ships against me, such is the fear you inspire in him.'

As Gustav preened himself, North winced that such grovelling shit had emerged from his own mouth. No doubt the people of his court were well used to insincere flatterers but Lolotte Fossberg looked at North quizzically. She had not expected the heroic Englishman to be so blatantly snivelling. Then she saw the look of devilment on his face.

She said, 'That is interesting, Sir Michael, of course it comes as no surprise to me.'

North nodded to her then turned again to the king. 'In fact, your Majesty, Bonaparte might even abandon his war altogether if you joined the Alliance?'

'Ah well, Sir Michael, if only I had to answer for myself but I must be realistic. My barons have little stomach for war.'

North nodded, 'A wise king judges his moment, Majesty. When the time comes I am sure Bonaparte will run from you like a terrified sheep. Thank goodness you will be on *our* side!'

'Have no doubts on that score, North! Blast it, you can count on Sweden with me in command!'

Fossberg had her hand pressed to her mouth to stifle laughter. Von Rosenstein turned and walked quickly away a few yards, his sides heaving as he too suppressed his mirth. Adlercreutz winked at North as he appreciated the Englishman's harmless leg-pulling for what it was. Plummer and Lang suddenly found a very interesting rose that they bent over to examine more closely.

Puffing himself up like a strutting pigeon, the king continued. 'You know, Sir Michael, even the Russians fear me. Every time we meet at sea our navy has trounced them like the amateurs they are. I firmly have in mind an alliance with Britain.' He glared at Adlercreutz. 'I am surrounded by blockheads and cowards of course, which is an obstacle. The dear Lord knows how many times I have tried to explain to them the elegance of my plans. It falls on deaf ears, you know. Such is the burden that a genius has to bear, as I such you are only too aware.'

'Oh, indeed, your Majesty! Mind you, I can understand how they feel when they are outshone at every moment by your abilities.'

'Just so, just so.'

By this time Lolotte Fossberg was sitting on a nearby bench, her head almost touching her knees, her shoulders rising and falling spasmodically and Plummer sitting next to her patting her hand to comfort her. A few heads turned as von Rosenstein's gales of laughter could be heard in the distance as he rushed back into the palace. The king was oblivious. It was refreshing to be in the company of somebody who appreciated his greatness.

Later that evening after the splendour of a state banquet, von Rosenstein walked arm in arm with North escorting him to his carriage.

'Sir Michael, I fear you have made such a favourable impression on His Majesty that he confided earlier to me that he was minded to offer you command of his entire navy. I had to point out to him that this would be an extremely selfish move on his part since it would deprive King George of your inestimable services.'

North sighed. 'Perhaps I did rather overdo the arse-licking, sir.'

'Not at all, His Majesty's glory can only be enhanced by such a truthful appreciation of his virtues by such a valued representative of his Brittanic Majesty.'

They stopped and looked at each other and then both burst into laughter.

'So, you do not think me guilty of *lese majesté*, Count?'

'Of course you are! But since he was the only one who did not notice it, the rest of us will have to accept it!'

The two laughing men stopped as Lieutenant Lang opened the carriage door for North and von Rosenstein lowered his voice.

'Captain, His Majesty is loved by his people of course but his advisors need to consider the consequences of some of his expressed wishes. I believe he will be advised that it would be better to have an undeclared meeting of interests with your country expressed in benevolent neutrality. We are happy to continue the mutual benefits of trade between our countries and will, so far as we are able, seek to impress our neighbours to bend their polices to the same end. As far as an alliance is concerned, my feeling is that there cannot be such a coalition at present but perhaps in a year or two, who knows?'

They shook hands and North returned to *Tigre* as satisfied as he could be that he had firmed up the best relationship with Sweden that he could under the circumstances. Bonaparte's shadow reached far over the Baltic and Sweden must, of course, steer to her destiny with caution but at least, he felt, their sympathies were positive towards Britain – at least for the present.

Before North sailed a messenger came from the king, carrying a beautifully made box containing a relic. It was an eighth-century Viking drinking horn to be presented to King George. The cow's horn, a full 16 inches long, was embellished with silver bands and filigree-work depicting a glorious battle between mounted horsemen.

Chapter 25

<u>23rd June, 1803</u>

Tigre's crew stood to as dawn broke. The night had been hot and stifling and there was little wind to cool the ship. Many men were stripped to the waist as they stood in their sections behind the great guns. The aroma of burning slow-matches competed with the smell of sweat-drenched bodies and despite all efforts of cleanliness, the miasma from the stinking gravel in the hold. Later that day the pumps would be working to flood the hold by a foot and a half and flush out the filth but just now the smells were combining in pungency.

The captain's cox'n Cluney Ryan mopped his bald head with a spotted handkerchief and belched. As an idler he had consumed a hurried breakfast after the starboard watch had eaten and then gone to the quarterdeck to stand within call in case his captain needed him. This close to shore, with all boats towing behind the barky, it was possible he might have to get the barge crew ready.

North was standing with his senior lieutenants, the master, the captain of marines and his guest the captain of the *Hotspur*, all telescopes trained on the shoreline.

The Dutch coast hereabouts was flat and featureless except for small clusters of houses that formed hamlets from Ijmuiden to Scheveningen and beyond. The channel leading from the sandy beach close to Katwijk inland towards its mother the

Rhine, was easy enough to distinguish.

North broke the silence, closing his glass and beckoning to Lieutenant Cryer.

'Very well, William. Have Lang proceed, please.'

Ryan, on hearing these words, moved quickly to the side of the ship, beckoning his waiting boat's crew. They went down first into the red cutter and at the same time the second cox'n sent his crew down into the green cutter. Within ten minutes, joined by their officers, the cutters moved off towards the Dutch shore.

An hour later James Lang in the red cutter brought back news that an armed guard boat was being rowed across the mouth of the channel and that sentries were on each bank, pitched tents and wooden huts indicating some measure of permanency.

North banged a hand on his desk in satisfaction. 'That is good, James. There would seem no need for such elaborate precautions unless there was something to be kept from prying eyes. I want you to go on board *Juniper* and give her captain my compliments. He is to take up a position off the channel at sunset and catch a fishing boat of the town returning or leaving. You will then interrogate the fishermen and find out if possible if there is a great ship being built in Hoornes-Rijnsoever. If the answer is positive you will send a small party on shore to see exactly where the ship is lying and her condition, size and so forth. Take no risks, James. If anybody is caught it is essential that they do not reveal that we are seeking this monstrous ship.'

He arranged for *Hotspur* to stand off and guard their back.

....

In the dead of the moonless night James Lang, Cluney Ryan and three of *Juniper's* seamen waded on to the beach from the waiting gig and walked inland, skirting around the cluster of small wooden houses. The fishermen had been co-operative, they had little liking for the French and none of the people of either town had been given work on the ship that was so big that it dwarfed everything around it.

It was indeed a spectacular sight. Lang rested his night-glass on a stone wall and followed the length of the huge ship as it floated in the channel. Her main gun deck he estimated to be more than 180 feet long and above the waterline she towered some 45 feet with perhaps another 15 or 20 feet below the surface of the channel which, it seemed, had now been flooded. Compared to HMS *London,* a 90-gun ship he knew well, she was as much as 15 or 20 per cent bigger and had four decks. She was bigger even than the 140-gun Spanish ship the *Santissima Trinidad,* so far the biggest warship in the world.

Santissima Trinidad was nicknamed by the Spanish sailors as *El Ponderosa* since she was such a bad sailor she was almost unfit for sea. She had narrowly avoided capture at the battle of Cape St Vincent. The main reason for the Spanish ship's uselessness was that it had originally been a 112-gun ship upgraded by closing off the upper works to form a fourth gun deck. This addition was only fit to be supplied with light guns and even then made the ship top-heavy.

It seemed that Fulton was not making the same mistake in his keel-upward design. The great ship was much longer than the Spanish ship and a little broader in the beam, creating more stability. She had straight sides and no tumblehome. Fulton, along with the great Indiaman surveyor Snodgrass, believed that there was no advantage to stability in a tumblehome. Likewise, following the example of Snodgrass there was no well-like middle-section to the upper deck. The deck ran flush fore and aft except from a pronounced camber from the centreline that would allow incoming water to run more quickly from the ship.

To anybody used to the conventional big ships she was not perhaps a thing of great beauty. That functional ugliness was even more menacing.

Under her stern, which had a prominent roundhouse, there was a cutaway under which was a massive paddle device that looked like the type of wheel which would sit in the stream of a watermill. From the upper deck a little aft of the mainmast was a black pipe with what seemed a diameter of a little under two feet. It was much bigger than the galley chimney found on a conventional ship.

Her masts had not been stepped but even in the dark of night her hull was ablaze with light from scores of lanterns as men worked, the sounds of their labour carrying to Lang's position several hundred yards away. On the quayside there were three rows of heavy cannon, 32-pounders by the look of them and, further away, rows of 24-pounders and 12-pounders. There was another long row of carronades in the area in front of a row of sheds. Lang guessed that few if any of the ship's guns had been taken on board. Closer to the ship was a mountain of pig-iron ingots ready to ballast the hold. Further away the mast sections and spars were lying in a wide mast-pond.

He had seen enough. A stealthy retreat to the gig, then to *Juniper* and back to *Tigre* was called for.

North decided that with 100 marines from *Hotspur* he had enough manpower to carry out his plan, and the following night he led 200 marines and 250 seamen ashore. The guard-posts were quickly overrun by an advance team of 30 marines and the guard boat, having been surprised by half a dozen ships' boats, surrendered immediately.

300 men had been landed on the north bank of the channel and 80 on the south side, the remainder coming into the channel in ships' boats. The shore parties marched into the two small towns and subdued the inhabitants without a shot being fired. The dockyard was only a temporary affair at present and was open on the northern bank. Pontoons had been laid on barges for the workers to move back and forth to the north bank and North led his party over the walk-way as boarders from *Tigre*'s boats climbed the opposite side of the

ship. Fifteen of North's men carried kegs of gunpowder and sixty more had with them bladders and flagons of oil and tinder-boxes.

A party on shore began the task of spiking the rows of cannon.

There was little resistance from the civilian workers but a corporal's guard fired on the boarders, wounding several before being put out of action. North found a man who seemed better dressed than the rest and grabbed him by the front of his shirt.

'Who are you?'

'I am the master shipwright here, sir.'

You will take me to where the plans for this ship are kept.'

The superintendent of works nodded in resignation and led him to what would be an admiral's cabin where several tables were piled with papers and plans. North told Cluney Ryan and one of the bosun's mates to gather up the whole lot and carry them safely back to the *Tigre*. The superintendent, who was a Brunswicker and only lukewarm in his allegiance to Bonaparte, volunteered the information that there was also a complete set of plans in a strongbox in the rope-walk on the quay and North sent off Midshipman Crowley with a small party to secure them.

It seemed another cause of discontent in the town was that the basin, which had been found to be not deep enough had been dredged without local labour. The French had brought in two regiments of infantry and put them to work on the project. The townspeople had almost every scrap of food taken from them and many were on the point of starvation. The local mayor came to North and showed his attitude by providing him with a full list of the troops camped five miles further inland.

As North inspected the ship Lieutenant Fellowes reported that two steam engines were in place inside the hold and appeared to be connected by brass shafts to a series of gears and twin 15-foot diameter, 10-foot wide paddle devices rather like a treadmill, tucked under the stern of the ship. There was a standard rudder forward of the great wheels.

North went down into the bowels of the ship with him. Like Fellowes he was fascinated by the huge gleaming copper and iron machines. They were fuelled by coal and there were great banks of coal in walled-off sections. The boiler of one engine was alight and steam hissed quietly but menacingly from apertures. He had two of the midshipmen make rapid sketches to supplement the plans.

He guessed that underway the siting of the rudder itself might be inefficient and even redundant if the paddle-wheels were activated in the same direction of turn but presumably Fulton had considered this.

Since the ship had not been completed, the top half of great paddle-wheel, in fact twin wheels, could be seen from the inside of the hull. The two wheels could be independently driven and their direction of rotation reversed to act, as it were, against each other. Possibly if the ship was relying on sail-power, which would conserve coal, the rudder would come into its own. As far as North could see the paddle-wheels were protected from shot by great wings of timber sheathed with iron plates which, while now retracted, could be lowered down into the water either side of the paddle-wheels. He still thought the ship would be vulnerable to a direct stern attack though he conceded she could be very flexible in her motions.

Not for the first time North felt he would enjoy meeting the great inventor and discussing his ideas. The smuggler Captain Tom Johnstone, himself of a scientific turn of mind, had worked closely with Fulton in the past particularly in the invention of the torpedo. Johnstone was considered by many a borderline traitor to his country but Fulton was, in effect, a neutral and therefore able to sell his services to the highest bidder. As far as North was concerned he recalled the benefits gained from using the galley-cutters Johnstone had invented.

North instructed his men to set half a dozen kegs of powder in the cross-slats of the paddles and the same number as near as possible to the each steam engine. He also put some of them to work soaking the area of decking and the coal with oil. The paddle-wheel shafts were attacked and bent out of shape by the use of armourer's sledge hammers.

As he was climbing to the quarterdeck sustained gunfire could be heard some distance away. It was time to do what needed to be done and retreat. He rapidly deployed his men with their orders to set fire to the ship.

Within 15 minutes everybody was safely on the shore except for three volunteers who would hurl lighted brands down through the ship's hatches on to each gundeck and as far down as the steam engine.

On shore everybody watched and waited, including the 120 workers and the survivors of the army guard who were marched into the nearby town hall, watching through the windows as the mighty hull began to burn. North was conscious that French troops were arriving in some numbers and that his men were exchanging fire with them. The sound of small-arms fire was now much closer. The party on the south shore had already started to move back to the beach and the boats were also moving downstream.

The sound of the powder kegs exploding around the steam engine was muffled by the hull but loud enough to testify to the engine's destruction. This moment also seemed to produce a great intensity of flame from every opening in the ship – gun ports and hatches spurted flame and there was a secondary explosion as the stern-lights blew outwards in a great roar of crimson and black. Its hull breached by the explosion, the ship started to tilt at a dangerous angle and settle on the bottom of the channel but much of it was still burning intensely above the shallow waters.

It was enough. No hand of man would be able to rescue the

ship from the consuming fire. The very cost of building the ship must have been a huge part of the navy's allocation and no doubt much thought would be given before re-starting the no-longer-secret project. North was satisfied and ordered a fighting retreat.

On the beach ships' boats and commandeered fishing boats and wherries from the vicinity were plying back and forth to the ships offshore and the marines had thrown up a perimeter 50 yards inland from the sands.

There were several hundred French infantry and a score of dismounted cavalrymen, most of them firing from a prone position a hundred yards from the British line. From the launches of *Tigre*, *Hotspur*, *La Trave* and *Couronne* their mounted carronades had commenced a fierce bombardment on the French positions and this was joined by the ships themselves, having been advised by Midshipman Crowley as soon as he was back on board.

Carrying their wounded with them, the rearguard under Lieutenant Fellowes found Captain North directing the loading of the boats. Fellowes saluted. Above the noise of the battle he shouted. 'Sir, I wish to report that we now have all but six of our remaining people on the beach. There are seventeen wounded seriously enough to need carrying and we have retrieved the bodies of twelve of our dead.'

'Thank you, John. I will return to *Tigre* now. Do not delay your departure any longer than necessary.'

None of the surviving invaders were left on shore except for six who had been captured. They had stopped to ransack a shop. There were also around 16 dead bodies that could not have been brought back. Altogether 28 men had died and 40 wounded, about half of them seriously.

In mid-channel, North and his people entrusted the bodies of their dead comrades to the sea.

North completed his report and handed it to his clerk for two fair copies to be made. *Couronne* was sent into Portsmouth with the report to be sent post-haste to the Admiralty and *Hercules* northwards to report to Admiral Thornborough and rejoin his squadron.

In many ways the last few weeks culminating in the destruction of the great ship had been probably his most significant adventure yet. The whole saga from the capture of *Unité* and *Couronne*, the foiling of the French plot in Danzig, the interlude in Stockholm and the destruction of the 150-gun behemoth had taken just five weeks – the first five weeks of a new war.

The following afternoon, in sight of the Thames Estuary, he fingered Isobel's locket in his waistcoat pocket and smiled as he thought of her and his children and the tales that Cluney Ryan would be telling them when they returned home.

Thirty minutes later North went over to *Juniper* to make the final part of his journey up to London. With him he took Lieutenant Lang, Cluney Ryan and Plummer.

Chapter 26

29th June to 9th July, 1803

North's report had been received by the First Lord personally. John Jervis, the Earl St Vincent's career had been one of considerable success. There were few people who had ever had an earldom bestowed on them from the name of a battle and before Nelson the earl was undoubtedly the most lionised admiral since Edward Hawke, the victor of Quiberon Bay.

St Vincent's abilities as an administrator and leader could scarcely be surpassed and despite being a strict disciplinarian and irascible, he was always considered to be a fair man and capable of great acts of kindness. Although he was said to have favourites to whom he was intensely loyal, none of those men were favoured by him without having first proved themselves to be outstanding officers. He was a strong supporter of Nelson despite misgivings about the man's too-public display of immorality and the jealous criticism of other admirals. That particular favouritism was not necessarily extended by the rest of the commissioners but all the while success attended Nelson, they accepted his personal shortcomings.

As First Lord, St Vincent's reforms had made him somewhat unpopular with many people in power, particularly in rooting out endemic corruption in the dockyards. Some of the changes were resented by sailors but even they for the most part were beginning to see the logic behind those reforms which had started to produce efficiencies and innovations which benefitted the navy overall. He had a deep understanding of sea-life. Born to a rich family, he had joined the navy as an ordinary seaman and lived on the same rations and regime. As Earl St Vincent he was generous in donating money to charities for those less fortunate and while he and his wife Martha had not been blessed with children he was kindly and attentive to the children of others.

As a captain thirty years ago Jervis had toured Russia, the Baltic and the Dutch coast extensively mapping the coasts and harbours and copies of some of his charts then compiled had been invaluable to North in his recent endeavours.

St Vincent stood with John Markham in the boardroom at the Admiralty and smiled at North. He could not come to like the man but he certainly admired him.

'Captain, what can I say? You certainly don't disappoint, do you? What a remarkable result to your mission to be able to destroy that dreadful ship. If it was in my power you would be given your flag this instant. If anybody deserved a rest from their labours, it is you; but the war proceeds apace and we have need of all of our best and most gifted officers.'

North smiled his thanks at the compliment.

'As you are aware I am always parsimonious in allowing captains to sleep out of their ships or indeed to be more than three miles from them, having been taught that lesson in troubled times when mutiny was a greater fear than now. I wish you to take a few weeks of well-earned rest after which you will exchange with your brother, Captain Richard North for whom I have other plans, and take command once more of *Prince Rupert*. You will of course have the customary right to take with you your followers and fifty seamen from *Tigre*. For the time being *Prince Rupert* will be stationed at Buckler's Hard which seems to be her home port, as it were.'

North nodded, such an arrangement would certainly suit him.

St Vincent reached for a glass of port. 'I intend an experiment. I want you to form a raiding squadron to be employed under direct orders of the Admiralty. Now that you have three years' seniority I am going to appoint you commodore. I have proposed on many occasions that the temporary rank of commodore should be made a substantive one but as things stand it is an unpaid appointment. The structure and methods of the raiding squadron I will leave to you to design. Within reason you may have such resources as you see fit. You will certainly be allowed several frigates and smaller craft.

'As to the operations you will undertake, I want you to once more form a close working relationship with our intelligence people and take advantage of Wickham's people and Colquhoun's network, along with tasks which may from time to time originate from the Board.'

....

Ten days later Michael and Isobel North sat in their carriage on the way from Dulwich to the City in the late afternoon.

North was thinking about the latest event in his career. There was much to do, planning, recruiting, requisitioning and training but the fact of having command of *Prince Rupert* once more was a source of considerable pleasure.

Reunited with his family he had decided he would rent a house near to Buckler's Hard so that they could have the use of it while the river was the headquarters of the squadron. The carriage drew up at the Mansion House and North helped his wife down, looking proudly at her. She was dressed in a fine gown under her cloak and carrying an exquisite Belgian fan. She in turn gently brushed away a few flecks of dust from her husband's uniform, his Star of the Order of the Bath on his left breast and the Gold Medal of the Mogador Expedition about his neck. He also wore on his breast the Star of the *Hoher Orden vom Schwarzen Adler* – the Prussian Order of the Black Eagle, the highest award for chivalry of that kingdom, presented to him a few days ago by the Prussian ambassador on behalf of the king. The motto of the Order was *Suum Cuique*, 'to each according to his merits.'

The Norths were received by John Perring, Lord Mayor of London, who came from a family of Devon wool merchants and despite considerable wealth was probably one of the most unobtrusive mayors of the city.

At table, sitting next to the mayor on his right-hand side, North was treated to a sumptuous meal. Perring was not a great conversationalist and in truth North had been reluctant to accept this invitation though since it was a great honour, he could hardly refuse.

As the plates were cleared away a trumpeter announced two footmen carrying velvet cushions. On one cushion was a presentation sword, golden hilt gleaming in the light of numerous candles, and on the other a gold box.

Taking the box from the footman, the mayor used a gavel to still all conversation amongst the 300 guests and asked North to stand. The black-gowned Chamberlain of the City approached from one side and held out a Bible, asking North to repeat after him the oath of allegiance. Opening the gold box, the mayor withdrew a rolled parchment carrying the Seal of the City.

'Sir Michael North, Knight of the Bath, Deputy Adjutant of the Royal Navy, Member of Parliament, Knight of the Prussian Order of the Black Eagle First Class, I award you the Freedom of the City of London and the Privileges thereof.' Replacing the scroll in the box he placed both in front of North, saying quietly, 'the box is yours, Sir Michael, as my particular gift.'

He raised his voice again. 'By order of the Aldermen and Councillors of the City, I present you with this sword in token of our esteem and of our gratitude for the services you have given to this city and to your king and country.'

He then launched into a long and somewhat sleep-inducing speech after which he claimed a response from Sir Michael – who no doubt received the grateful though unexpressed thanks of all present for being exceedingly economical in the length of his speech, while showing courtesy and gratitude for the honours received.

After the carriage had left Cheapside Michael and Isobel sat holding hands and talking quietly together. They believed that their happiness had reached a pinnacle on the day they had declared their love for each other but each passing day something happened which increased that happiness and love. For them and their family and friends they felt that the future held a promise of joy that could not be measured.

Chapter 27

<u>10th August, 1803</u>

For Michael North returning to *Prince Rupert* and her crew was like entering a house familiar from many years of residence after a long time of absence. The ship had changed very little; her recent captain, North's younger brother, had inherited a highly efficient, happy ship and had maintained that level of perfection.

North had brought with him his followers and his officers from *Tigre*. By custom he was also allowed 50 of *Tigre*'s seamen and had mainly selected men who had been with him for several years. Thus most of them were no strangers to *Prince Rupert*.

North's first concern was to bring together the ships that would form part of his raiding squadron. Some of the ships had already been allocated and three of them were also moored in the Beaulieu River near Buckler's Hard. The recently captured 40-gun *La Trave,* under Captain Richard Bristow Harkness, the 36-gun *Modeste,* Captain William Pyecroft, and the 14-gun sloop *El Corso* captained by Commander William Southwick. The previous nationality of these ships was no accident. The Admiralty had deliberately provided North with French- and Spanish-built ships.

He awaited the 18-gun sloop *Imogen,* formerly the French privateer *Diable á Quatre,* which with his tender the 8-gun

Juniper and the storeship *Amelia* would arrive within a few days. He had also been promised another frigate.

Bringing all the officers of the squadron together to dine on the first evening meant having bulwarks struck down to lengthen his day cabin. The evening was hot and after the Loyal Toast, North bid his guests to loosen their stocks and open their coats. As the port wine circulated he briefed them on the intended purpose of the squadron.

'Our task is simply defined. We are to do as much damage to Boney's trade and his navy as possible by conducting inshore operations and whatever else may occur to us that might serve our purpose. Naturally, I am always open to suggestions and I trust you will put your minds to thinking up annoying schemes to discommode the French.

'We start straight away. Tomorrow, *Prince Rupert*, *Modeste* and *El Corso* will set sail for the French coast off St Malo. I have information that five of the privateer captains of those ports intend to sail together for the Indian Ocean. It is my intention to make them think again. Captain Harkness in *La Trave* will sail with us at the same time but has a particular mission to undertake.

'Here's to a profitable hunting season, gentlemen, and damnation to Bonaparte!'

....

Richard Harkness was 27 years old and, he believed, well thought-of. The problem was that he was only well regarded by his immediate family and one or two people who really did not know him as well as they thought they did.

Amongst those who were by no means fond of him were the crew of *La Trave*, his new command. Most of them had recently been the crew of HMS *Oiseau* 36, now laid up in ordinary. Harkness had spent a quiet two years commanding *Oiseau* but somehow his lack of energy had not stopped the commissioners offering him *La Trave*. A straight transfer of the crew was, after all, a speedy way to get her to sea. The fact was that Harkness had stayed so far below the horizon he was considered a safe pair of hands despite lack of enterprise.

He was also a strict disciplinarian and over-fond of the lash as a way of correcting imagined laziness. It was of course a self-fulfilling proposition that the more unjustified and brutal the punishment the more the undercurrent of discontent. No crew would deny that flogging as the ultimate sanction was justified but answering for every slight misdemeanour at the gratings was too much. The crew of *Oiseau* had lived a hellish existence as their captain seemed to delight in new ways to ensure that as many as possible would be flogged.

Harkness walked on to the quarterdeck and nodded to Lieutenant James Lang as he moved to the lee side. Harkness stared silently at the forecastle seeking to find a man slow in his work or insolent in his thoughts. He thought for a moment about Lang.

Short of officers – all but his 1st lieutenant had found ways to leave *Oiseau* as soon as she had reached Chatham – Captain North had sent over Lang to act as his Second strictly on loan accompanied by his second coxswain with 25 men until officer replacements had been sent to *La Trave* from the Admiralty and more men had been pressed. He had a useless 3rd lieutenant, arrived just as *La Trave* was about to up-anchor but lacked a Fourth and was very light on midshipmen and master's mates. The master, Andrew McCall, was another newcomer. He seemed content to do his job and keep his own counsel.

Harkness was curious about Lang. He knew that apart from being the son of a lord, Lang seemed a man who particularly enjoyed North's high regard. He was also conscious that Lang, still in his early twenties had cut out and captured this very ship in the mouth of the Vistula.

He had yet to invite Lang to dinner – in any event he very rarely had his officers to dine – but perhaps it would be useful to get to know him. It certainly would not do any harm to befriend a favourite of the squadron's senior captain.

Harkness grunted to himself as he saw a new hand, a landsman, hesitating as the bosun's mate training him patiently ordered him to clap on to a stay.

'Mr Frame – start the fucker or I'll have somebody start you, you useless bastard!'

He caught a movement at the corner of his eye. Lang had spun on his heel towards him, his mouth open in amazement.

'You wanted to say something, Mr Lang?'

'No, sir!'

Harkness moved closer to him, lowering his voice but still audible to the master and quartermaster nearby. 'I make allowances for the time it will take you to get used to my ways, Lang, but be careful to keep your face in an aspect of benign support. I don't know what you are used to but I run a tight ship. Slackers and idiots receive short shrift. Bear that in mind. If a man is not up to his job I expect him to be shown that we carry no passengers, is that clear?'

'It is clear, sir. I hope you do not think me impertinent. May I ask whether allowances are to be made for training unskilled men?'

Harkness had a long face and small eyes set below a narrow forehead. When he frowned they almost disappeared under his heavy eyebrows. 'Of course they need training. However that man has been on this ship for almost three weeks. That is time enough to know his fucking arse from his elbow. Be advised, Mr Lang, I expect my officers to display enough loyalty to me to make sure that my views coincide with theirs. Speak up now; say what is on your mind.'

Lang said quietly, 'Perhaps the matter is not one that should be debated on the open deck, sir.'

Harkness was speaking louder. 'So, you decline to reply, do you?'

Lang spoke calmly, aware even if the captain was not that several dozen ears could overhear what was being said. 'Of course if I am deficient in my duties I expect to be corrected, sir, but every officer must exercise good judgement for the benefit of the ship. Since we appear to be exchanging candid remarks I believe that a ship's efficiency is measured by the way in which its crew relate to those given power over them. It may be that this power is best enforced by a strong bias towards punishment but in my limited experience, to threaten an inexperienced man or those training them can be counterproductive.'

'Oh, you do, do you? Well Mr Lang, let us see whether you can lead by example. I will thank you to run to the mainmast tops and back immediately. Perhaps that will curb your insolent tongue, sir!'

Lang actually smiled at him as he shrugged his coat off and handed it with his hat to the master. As he kicked off his shoes, several of the crew nearby tensed with anticipation. Lieutenant Lang was a newcomer, just five days on board – an unknown quantity to almost all the crew except the coxswain, who was late second coxswain of *Tigre,* and two dozen others brought over from *Prince Rupert* to help make up a very short crew. Despite a hot press, there had been few more men brought on board, amongst whom were at least 15 unskilled landsmen. The ship's establishment called for 360 seamen and marines. There were only 235 seamen and 86 marines so they were still undermanned even with the Ruperts included.

Lang ran quickly to the mainmast weather shrouds and swung outwards. The wind was strong and the ship was heeling to lee but the wind helped him by pushing him inwards towards the shrouds. Lang's progress was admired by even the most experienced topman. He reached the platform and, eschewing the lubber's hole, he leant almost horizontal as he moved. He went out, over and upwards. He came back to the deck by sliding down the backstay, ran back to quarterdeck and donned shoes, coat and hat. He saluted smartly to the captain. His stockings were ruined, his breeches stained with tar but his breathing was not noticeably heavier than it had been before his climb.

Harkness grunted something under his breath, ignoring the chuckles of the crew as he turned and went below. Perhaps Lang had learned his lesson but he was not sure. He had intended to take him down a peg in front of the crew but it may have misfired.

Lieutenant Crabtree, third luff, a smallpox-scarred 21-year-old, shook his head as he leaned in towards the 1st lieutenant and whispered, 'that looks like a troubled relationship, sir.'

Lieutenant Peter Midsummer bent his head towards the younger man and muttered, 'you would do well to keep your opinions to yourself, Crabtree. The captain may decide that you as well as Mr Lang deserve special treatment if you ally yourself to him.'

Midsummer had thought long and hard before agreeing to

follow Harkness to *La Trave*. On *Oiseau* he had found Harkness to be exceptionally difficult to serve under but had found ways, whenever he could, to mitigate Harkness's oppressive attitude by showing fairness to the crew. He admitted to himself that some of his motivation was a fear of being on the beach for months and years. He had an elderly mother and two spinster sisters who were dependent on his income and being on half pay would cause genuine hardship. He had unsuccessfully approached several captains commissioning their ships and was conscious that having spent 18 months under the much-disliked Harkness, his approaches had been negatively influenced by that fact.

Harkness was a follower of Rear Admiral Butler, now without a command and therefore unable to grant too many favours himself and *Oiseau* should have been the last favour from Butler. By some means Butler had managed to wangle Harkness command of *La Trave* and given a choice between half pay and a tyrannical captain, Midsummer was now standing on the heaving deck of the frigate bound for a special mission to the coast of France.

Chapter 28

<u>19th August, 1803</u>

Harkness's hand shook as he poured another glass of wine. He leaned back in the armchair and swore quietly. He knew that he had handled Lang's insolence badly and probably lost the chance to make an ally if not a friend of him. He was even more isolated from the crew now.

Like most tyrants, rage overwhelmed caution when he could not cope with even a minor crisis. His whole life had seemed a series of violent solutions. Brutalised by his father, rejected by his terrified mother he had suffered torment after torment. Then boarded at a school renowned for its savage discipline and finally beaten and humiliated as a 13-year-old midshipman.

As an officer, he had a tendency to avoid action against the enemy, which arose from fear of failure. His father had taught him that failure heralded punishment and punishment meant pain.

He was a solitary man by choice and with his natural tendency to avoid company it should have suited him to have most hours of the day and night alone. Perversely, being isolated by being in command simply reinforced a feeling of victimisation because of his constant feeling of injustice.

At least his misery was leavened by sufficient capital to provide a hefty stock of wine and spirits. At least he was not dependent on prize money. When his unloved father had the grace to turn up his toes Harkness had inherited the bulk of his fortune. This affluence had bought him a few lightweight friends but had not been the entrance ticket to high society that he thought it was going to be. Despite displaying his wealth and entertaining lavishly he had still not been accepted by society. Sally Jersey had even turned him away from the door of Almacks.

As he sat thinking of the injustices of his life, he sank further and further into self-pity. Now, in the deepest part of the pit rage rescued him as it had many times before. He had strength and right on his side! If Lang thought he could best him, he would find like many before that Richard Harkness could tame any beast. He was dimly aware that after his inheritance and the disappointment of Bath and London, he had changed his attitude from oppression to full-blown victimisation of his crew but convinced himself that it was the only way to make this new command an outstanding example of efficiency.

He hurled a second glass at the wall.

Outside his cabin men trembled. One man in particular felt deep fear as he realised what the sounds of breaking glass and shouted obscenities heralded.

George Crabtree had been posted to *La Trave* three weeks ago and arrived on board four days later; his posting the result of unsubtle blackmail by his mother who had a particularly close friendship with one of the commissioners of the Admiralty. That gentleman, having tired of Crabtree's mother, had looked at the lists, noticed that the swine Harkness had been given *La Trave* and had thrown his whore's son to the proverbial wolf. To be fair he had feelings of guilt afterwards.

The summons came by a trembling goggle-eyed steward. 'Captain's compliments, Mr Crabtree, and you are to go aft immediately.'

Harkness by now had been seized by such a rage that his teeth were clamped fast and his fingernails painfully dug into the palms of his hands.

Crabtree knew, almost word for word, what was coming.

'Crabtree, you snivelling piece of shit! Your division is filled with mutinous pigs set to rise up and kill every man in a bicorne hat! Go amongst them, Crabtree! Go amongst them immediately and seize the ringleaders. I will have three men at the gratings in the morning and see their ribs exposed, Find them, Crabtree, bring them to me in the morning. Find them or I will make you wish your whore of a mother had never dropped you from her filthy womb!'

Crabtree opened his mouth to protest but his power of speech had left him. Tears welled up and he turned and rushed from the cabin.

In the gloom of the spar deck men looked silently at each other waiting for the almost daily ritual of the past three weeks to be repeated. On fifteen of those days one, two or three men had been seized up to the grating and flogged. Offences such as dumb insolence, tardiness in performing duties and half a dozen minor offences covered by the most obscure of the Articles of War had been punished by flogging.

The same ritual would be performed this evening. If during his watch a man's name was taken – an angry shout a dozen times a day from the captain resulting in an entry in an officer's book – he became a candidate for selection.

Crabtree's slender shape was seen in the gloom as some men tried to crowd away from him and others more bold set their feet defiantly on the deck and stood waiting.

He brought out his book and opened it. The torrid heat of the mid-August evening seemed to rise higher. Crabtree tried unsuccessfully to put some steel into his voice. 'Er, Merriman, your name was taken for murmuring ...'

At that moment something unexpected happened. The cox'n on loan from *Prince Rupert*, Dick Wells, stepped forward and knuckled his forehead. 'Merriman was flogged last week, sir. Best you let his stripes heal, don't you think?'

There were gasps of dismay from the men around him.

Crabtree's knees were trembling. Wells was a giant who could snap his back with one hand. 'Are you offering to take his place, Mr Wells?'

'Reckon so, sir. It's nine years since I got kissed by the cat. I guess my back is healed now.' He pulled his shirt over his head to expose a back criss-crossed with deep scars. The sadist who had ordered his punishment had been as bad if not worse than Harkness. He had a left-handed bosun's mate to cross the stripes.

'I didn't deserve these scars, Mr Crabtree, sir, no more than Joe Merriman does now. I reckon if the captain wants a victim it must be my turn.'

'You know you will lose your rate?'

'Reckon I'll get it back on *Prince Rupert*, sir.'

Crabtree almost said aloud, 'At least you don't have to stay on the hell-ship.'

Tom Hardy, a prime topman before a bad fall had shattered his ankle three years past, limped forward and knuckled his forehead.

'With respect, sir, I ain't one for volunteering but I'd be honoured to take my place alongside Mr Wells. It won't be my first time either.'

Crabtree felt he was losing control of the situation. 'I am not looking for volunteers, Hardy. I am here to see that miscreants are punished.'

'In that case, sir, I guess there mus' be at least two hunerd of them missiscreants on the barky,' came an anonymous voice.

'That's enough! Wells, Hardy and you Isaac Temple, to the

orlop now! Master-at-arms, have the restraints ready.'

There were mixed feelings at the mention of Temple's name. Temple was one of the few men that were totally loyal to the captain and had followed him from ship to ship. Either Crabtree was showing a spark of genuine rebellion or subtlety. When Temple came before the captain it was unlikely he would be punished and therefore another man might be spared.

As the master-at-arms came forward to shepherd the three men away a loud voice cut across the growing murmur of rage from the crew.

'What is this all about, Mr Crabtree? What is this disturbance?'

Lieutenant Lang was not a big man but he was sturdy enough to be noticeable and he was every inch an officer. His shout made men jump.

Crabtree turned to his senior. 'Hands for punishment, sir!'

'I believe I have the deck, Mr Crabtree. Courtesy aside, it is customary to keep me informed if a man transgresses during my watch.'

'Sir, captain's orders to secure defaulters for punishment. These men are from my division.'

'Indeed? Why, pray, were these devils not secured during their watch? If their crimes be so dastardly surely they should have been seized up earlier? We cannot have the rogues wandering around the ship like swells in Pall Mall, can we?'

'The captain ordered me ...'

'Enough, Mr Crabtree. I shall seek an interview with captain. Master-at-arms, you will confine these men as you have been ordered but you will see they each have a supply of drinking water mixed with lime and sugar, it is a hot night.'

Lang made his way aft amidst the excited muttering and stares of the crew. He set his jaw. He made up his mind to confront the vicious man in his own den. He was well aware of the risks involved but was confident enough of the courts martial to expect a fair hearing if one was convened. This almost daily ritual of selecting men for punishment by what amounted to a random process was unconscionable. As he approached the captain's quarters a diffident man came up to him from one side. Leonard Preston was the captain's clerk, a man thoroughly cowed by the ogre but not entirely crushed by his miserable existence.

'Sir, please, have a care. Don't go in there.'

'I shall go in there and you will go with me. I will have you witness what occurs. Have no fear, I will protect you, you have my word.'

The sentry outside the cabin had word carried to him by a scurrying marine and was ready to either repel the 2nd lieutenant or allow him to pass. He was conflicted by his sense of duty and a feeling that perhaps, this once, he should stand aside.

His dilemma was solved by Lang himself. With Preston at his heels, he smiled at the sentry.

'It's all right, Brecht, I am giving you a direct order to admit me to the cabin, you may rely on me for that.'

Brecht saluted smartly. Like the majority of the crew he had come to respect deeply the young lieutenant during his short stay on board.

Lang entered the cabin, hat in hand, and approached the desk, carefully avoiding a slew of broken glass on the carpet. Harkness was leaning back, his eyes half closed. His jacket had been thrown on to the floor and his shirt was open to the waist. Lang had only been in the cabin a few times since he had captured the ship, but had noticed that its elegance was now dimmed. The good furnishings and expensive drapes were the legacy of its French late captain. The lights in the cabin were low but Lang could see that even in three weeks the cabin had become unkempt and grimy. It seemed that even terror could not make the steward clean the place properly and Harkness seemed oblivious to his surroundings.

'Forgive me for intruding, sir, but I believe it is time we discussed the behaviour of the officers and crew.'

Harkness sat bolt upright, his cunning eyes gleaming. 'I did not send for you, Lieutenant – how dare you enter without being announced?'

Lang raised a hand. 'I believe that every officer has a duty to his ship and his captain, sir. I wish merely to advise you that protocol has been breached and that I am requesting a court martial for the abuse and disrespect shown to me by Lieutenant Crabtree. Without consulting me he has tried to undermine my authority by having men seized up for punishment when I have command of the deck, sir.' Lang indicated Preston. 'I have asked your clerk to make a formal note of my request for your support, sir.'

Harkness's mind was in a whirl. The drink was still confusing his thoughts and this strange unexpected intrusion had thrown him off balance. 'Let me see if I understand you, Mr Lang. You want me to report Mr Crabtree to their lordships and seek a court martial for his behaviour?'

'I do, sir. I believe discipline demands it! Such a serious breach of the sanctity of command would not be countenanced on *Prince Rupert*, sir, I assure you. If I had the crassitude to embark on such a course of conduct while Crabtree himself had the watch I would expect to be punished despite the fact I am his senior. I believe it essential for good order and discipline that the officer of the watch has control unless relieved by you or by your command, sir. There are no exceptional circumstances this evening.'

Harkness wondered if he was trapped within some wild dream. 'But Crabtree was following my direct orders, Lang.'

'I appreciate that, sir. Had it not been the fact that he failed to inform me personally of your orders I would not press for a court martial. The fault is entirely his, sir, not yours.'

Harkness remained silent for long seconds, staring at the immaculately dressed lieutenant. Who would have thought him a martinet? Then doubts rose in his mind. This was a trap. If he requested a court martial Lang could turn everything on its head. The sequence of events, the record in the punishment log, the evidence of other officers, it would all come out. The unwritten rule was that all captains would be supported by a court martial except in extraordinary circumstances. The risk was that the board might be packed with captains who hated Harkness. Many men hated him; he knew that. Men of lesser ability; men of small vision. Men whose attitude to discipline was weak and neglectful.

'I decline to indulge your spite, Lang! Preston, get out and find Lieutenant Crabtree. Have him come here immediately. We'll settle this here and now. Also have the first lieutenant roused out and brought here.'

He got up and snatched his coat, pulling it on and struggling to button his shirt, giving up trying to match button with hole after a few attempts. He reached for another glass and, filling it to the brim, he tossed it down his throat and poured another. All this time Lang stood completely motionless except for the working of the ship, his eyes fixed on Harkness, his face held in a neutral expression.

Peter Midsummer and George Crabtree arrived together and

although not ordered to do so Preston followed them and went softly to the small desk where his own writing instruments were set out.

Harkness struggled to control the slur in his voice. 'I am surrounded by clowns and buffoons! Worthless officers who do not know the meaning of discipline and loyalty. You, Midsummer, have so little control over your juniors that you allow my privacy to be invaded by Mr Lang apparently without your knowledge. You need to be reminded, you fucking oaf, that it is your responsibility to settle disputes in the wardroom, not mine.'

His face was becoming dangerously suffused with blood and his voice was raised to full pitch. 'And you, Crabtree, you ... you brainless piece of pig's offal, cannot carry out a simple order without fucking up!'

He paused and his whole attitude changed. His mood swung from overwhelming anger to soft menacing stillness. He growled, 'And as for you, Mister the Honourable fucking Lang! Honourable, ha! What a damned stupid label to attach to your misbegotten name. You may be Captain North's fucking bum-boy but while you are on *my* ship you will conform to my standards. Now what do you say to that, sir? Speak up, damn you, and the words that come from your fucking mouth will need to very, very humble, mark what I say! Speak up, sir, speak up!'

Lang was completely unfazed. 'I have nothing to say in

answer to such abuse, sir, except that in front of witnesses I will say that I abhor the whole idea of duelling but I am happy to give you satisfaction for the slight I have obviously given.'

Harkness wanted to say 'Damn you! All of you will suffer for this.' What he did instead was to realise belatedly that he had gone too far. He would deal with Preston later and any note he had made would be destroyed. For now he would make a strategic withdrawal.

The swings of his mood were unnerving to watch. This was the man who held the lives of more than 250 men in his hands. His voice unbelievably mild, he said, 'Crabtree, see that the men confined are released. There will be no punishment tomorrow since you failed to follow established protocol. As far as your conduct is concerned I believe the matter should be closed. Does that satisfy you, Mr Lang?'

'It does, sir.'

'Very well, gentlemen. I apologise for losing my temper with you. In my enthusiasm to have the ship in perfect order perhaps I have driven the men too far. Mr Midsummer, tomorrow in the first dog watch you will see that the men receive a double allowance of grog with my compliments. From now on there can be a slight relaxation of discipline at appropriate times and we shall see how the crew respond. Good behaviour will bring appropriate rewards but mark my words, this ship will either be the best damned frigate in His Majesty's navy, or I will if necessary flog every man on board.

That is all, gentlemen.'

In the wardroom the three officers were joined by McCall, the master, followed by the surgeon, the bosun and the gunner. For a few minutes all of them sat in bewildered silence. McCall seemed lost in his thoughts but he was looking at Lang with profound respect. Standing over the scuttle above the cabin he had heard every word.

The grey-haired surgeon, Julius Redman, murmured, 'the man may be insane, gentlemen.'

Midsummer shook his head. 'We will have none of that talk, Redman. It is our duty to support the captain and that is what we will do. He is undoubtedly a man with a decided view on things but it is his ship and our commissions and warrants bid us to follow where he leads.'

'No man should have unquestionable power, Mr Midsummer,' said the master. 'In that direction is tyranny and repression; that is the lesson France offers us. Forgive me, but I must speak plainly. I believe our *duty* is to be a last resort against unbridled abuse if a captain becomes incapable of distinguishing discipline from punishment.'

James Lang held up a hand. 'If I may, I suggest we allow things to take their course being ever cautious to safeguard the crew and the ship. George, I apologise profusely for using you the way I did. I assure you that given the chance of a court hearing I would have done right by you. I thought it a necessary tactic to bring matters into equilibrium. Now, shall we fill our glasses and drink to *La Trave*?'

Not one person slept that night believing that sun-filled days were ahead but perhaps things would improve a little.

Chapter 29

Michael North watched and waited as the sun rose over the coast of France. It was another hot day and there was little wind. *Prince Rupert*'s decks were almost without sound. There was a soft cough from a gun captain as he bent too close to the match-tub and the abrasive smell of the burning fuses assaulted his nose.

After a few minutes North nodded to the lieutenant of the watch. 'Very well, Mr Keeley, stand the men down from stations. We will leave the guns loaded and ready for the moment but send the off-watch and idlers to their breakfast.'

North was restless. His crew were at peak efficiency and the ship finely tuned. There was no sign of the privateers expected to leave St Malo to sail to Mauritius and the only sails on the sea were those of his squadron, except *La Trave* away on her own mission.

He believed that with *Prince Rupert*, all he needed with him were *Modeste*, the brig *El Corso* and his tender *Juniper*. The smaller ships would be useful in the event that the privateers, being freshly from the port, would be able to out-sail the 74.

He returned to his cabin to eat breakfast and then turn his efforts towards reducing the size of the paper mountain that was the curse of all captains. Being blessed with the temporary title of commodore brought no real advantages. There was no extra pay – not that he needed it – but what was just as bad, he was expected to direct the activities of a squadron without being given the assistance of a flag captain. Lieutenant Keeley was an extra lieutenant as a nod in that direction but due to *La Trave*'s shortage of commissioned officers and Lang's absence there, Keeley had been drafted in to cover a watch and Lang's division.

The morning dragged on with no sign of the French. The wind was rising and it favoured the French – surely they would sail soon. In the harbour at St Malo the tide would be on the turn and if the privateers did not weigh anchor in the next half hour, they would not be leaving on this tide.

North went back to the quarterdeck just before 11 o'clock and watched as the marine tapped down the last few grains of sand in the half-hour glass and sounded six bells. The wind was now too strong for all except jib and foretopsail on *Prince Rupert* unless she wished to turn away from the shore. As if in answer to the three double taps of the bells, the foremast lookout called down, 'On the starboard beam! Three ships clearing the harbour!'

Prince Rupert, her position carefully planned, was six miles off the coast with *Modeste* and *El Corso* about two miles offshore but four miles north of the entrance to St Malo harbour. Only *Juniper* was in closer contact. She was the Judas goat.

North had painstakingly calculated that the main squadron would be over the horizon from the shore until the privateers, numbers giving them confidence, were well on their way to snatch up the impudent British schooner. It was then a question of some luck and a great deal of skill if the squadron could cut off the privateers from darting back into St Malo.

Two more ships were sighted following the first three.

Orders rang out, the mainsails were loosed and studding sails and royals sent aloft to give *Prince Rupert* every puff of wind she could capture. Even so the wind was coming off the land and favoured the privateers so they chased the nimble *Juniper*. There were now five French ships on the sea and their confidence must be high.

North went aloft to count the enemy's guns. He had every reason to believe that the largest ship was Robert Surcouf's 44-gun *Chasser de Mer*. Although Surcouf had been inactive for the past two years, British intelligence was that he was returning to his old hunting grounds to continue his significant successes. With the 44-gun ship were two carrying 36 guns and two smaller corvettes with 20 or 22 guns each.

Juniper was not just a fast schooner. She had been carefully brought back to first-class condition in Henry Adams's yard on Buckler's Hard and her eight 6-pounders changed for 12-pound carronades. She might be small but she would have a kick that could well surprise the 20-gun *La Javeline* which was now less than half a mile behind her.

The ambush of British ships was now much clearer and the hindmost 36-gun ship was seen to back her sails and turn in an ungainly curve as she made her way back to port.

Prince Rupert, being the slowest of the ships was about 800 yards west of *Juniper*. North lowered his Dolland glass. 'Quartermaster! Port your helm, NOW!'

The ship turned her starboard side towards *Juniper*. The privateer's captain appeared to have calculated that although there was no time to board and capture the impudent schooner he would at least be able to rake her before running for home but had miscalculated *Prince Rupert's* proximity.

Prince Rupert's upper-deck 12-pounders were fired well on the uproll to preserve the privateer's hull. The manoeuvre had been practiced rigorously. *La Javeline* disappeared for a long moment as huge plumes of water from the plunging shot cascaded over her. Whether by luck or design the damage to her crowded superstructure was heavy. Two dozen dead and wounded men fell to the deck.

As her captain struggled to the wheel and lent his weight to turn her towards the east, there was a massive crash of shot pounding the starboard side of his ship. Nobody had noticed that *Juniper* had almost swung around in her own length, closed the gap even as *Prince Rupert's* shot was savaging *La Javeline*, and fired off her own starboard carronades.

The first contest was over. Aghast at his ill luck, *La Javeline's* captain slashed the halliard with his own hanger and watched as his colours sagged and fell.

Meanwhile *Modeste* was up with the 44-gun ship, neither opponent showing any sign of withdrawing from the bout.

North ordered his barge to go to *Juniper* and help her commander board and accept *La Javeline*'s surrender. He could safely leave the 44-gunner to *Modeste* but there was one 36-gun privateer that had decided to set her course due south. It could be a long stern chase but with *El Corso* about to cut off the 22-gun corvette, in fact a Spanish privateer called *Santa Barbara*, there was little more for *Prince Rupert* to do.

The chase proved shorter than anticipated. The privateer was unusually poorly handled, it appeared. This was unusual since privateers' crews were, generally speaking, excellent seamen. The cause would not emerge until later. A furious argument was taking place on the *Charlemagne*'s quarterdeck between the captain, who had ordered a retreat to St Malo, and the first mate, who wanted to run south towards Lorient.

More crewmen joined in on each side of the row. Such was one of the pitfalls of democracy on ships sailing under letters of marque. The captain was elected by the crew who all had a stake in the ship's success as well as her safety. Unfortunately dissent was now rendering Captain Pierre-Claude Launey's position untenable and he threw down his hat and walked off the deck. The dispute continued with, it would seem, little regard for the consequences.

One group, set on returning to the closer safety of St Malo, rushed to the larboard falls and began to haul back on them. Another group under the urging of the first mate clapped on to the starboard ropes and the tug-of-war began. A pistol fired above the heads of the starboard group caused them all to duck down and let go of their hold. The ship, her yards now swayed to larboard, thrust dangerously into the wind. Shouts and screams were of no avail. The full stretched sails took the full force of the wind on their faces. There was a shrieking ripping sound as the foresail split her length. An explosive crack heralded the detachment of most of both of the two lower larboard mainmast spars.

Chaos and disorganised turmoil reigned. And waiting like a grinning demon less than three cables length away to the north was *Prince Rupert*, her guns like the black teeth of Satan's jaws extended from her side.

One of the crew wildly tugged at the halliard and the pavillon was down before the 74 could fire a shot.

In his cabin Captain Launey shrugged his shoulders and poured himself another glass of wine.

As North rubbed his hands and looked over the four privateers now gathered together under the squadron's guns his only regret was that Surcouf, his amazing luck continuing, had not been on board *Chasser de Mer*.

Chapter 30

<u>20th August, 1803</u>

La Trave swam less than a mile off the French coast concealed from the shore in the lee of a small island called the Île de la Comtesse.

Harkness tapped the papers on his desk, his orders. The three lieutenants waited for him to speak.

Harkness concealed the spite which wanted to unleash itself. After all there were ways to achieve his ends without opening himself to criticism by higher authority. He had thought long and hard about his next move.

'Gentlemen, Sir Michael has charged us with a particular mission which, I believe, is of paramount importance.' He shifted the papers away from the section of the chart so that they could follow his pointing finger. 'Here is our objective.'

The three lieutenants leaned forward.

Harkness's finger pointed at the town of Saint Quay-Portrieux and moved inland until he tapped a name.

'Here, the village of Plouagat. It has a manor house, the Lezhouarn, which since the revolution has been used as a prison. Sir Michael's information is that the grounds of the prison are occupied by a secret factory. In this factory the French plan to manufacture armaments on a large scale. In fact it employs fifty workers, mostly from the prison, and produces approximately fifteen cannon a week. Plans to expand make this is a significant contribution to the requirements of the French army. At the extreme end of the grounds there is a gunpowder mill. There is also a smaller workshop where experiments are being carried out into various mixtures of gunpowder. That building is probably more important potentially than the main factory or powder mill and the reason for secrecy.

'The objective is to destroy the factory, the powder mill and the workshop but to ensure, as far as possible, all of the records of experiments are also destroyed or better still captured and brought back to Woolwich.'

He pointed at Lang. 'I understand from Sir Michael that you have an efficient grasp of the French language, Mr Lang?'

'Adequate, sir.'

'A Royalist curé named Oscar Puech will be waiting for you on the beach. He will act as your guide. You will lead the mission with Lieutenant Crabtree as your second – he too is alleged to speak the damned language. You shall have twenty marines and twenty seamen. You will carry with you a dozen kegs of gunpowder against the possibility you are unable to use the powder which is on site. You will be landed as soon as it is dark. Any questions?'

Lang straightened up. 'Sir, of course I would be honoured to take Lieutenant Crabtree but, if you agree, rather than men I don't know well, I would prefer to take Cox'n Wells and the men from *Prince Rupert*. I believe the party should be as inconspicuous as possible and perhaps a smaller group without the marines will serve? These men are used to working together and there would be an economy of communication between me and them.'

Harkness almost rubbed his hands. Lang was taking with him most of the people who might just cause problems if Lang failed to be supported. 'Very well, make it so. Crabtree will second you and you may take your own men. Mr Midsummer, Mr Crabtree, you may return to the deck. I will give Mr Lang his final instructions.' A germ of an idea was in his mind. It would be as well that the other two officers were not present just now.

After leaving the cabin half an hour later Lang walked to the wardroom deep in thought and took up a pen. When Midsummer joined him he handed him a folded and sealed package. 'Peter, should I fail to return, you will oblige me by seeing that this, my will, is safely in the hands of Sir Michael, who is my executor.' He smiled ruefully. 'Indeed I would ask that you pass it to him whether I am simply delayed or missing. One never knows.'

Midsummer nodded and reached out for it. 'I assume that this is entirely a private matter, James?'

'Thank you, it is.'

La Trave's cutters landed Lang, Crabtree and the raiding party just after nine o'clock. Harkness had insisted on complete darkness and it was only at a few minutes before nine that cloud had obscured the full moon. Puech was waiting, crouched under a low sandy cliff a few yards away.

He was dressed in the black cassock of a clergyman. He was short, stout and his round face displayed what would normally be a habitual smile. At this moment he frowned. He had been waiting so long he thought that he would have to return the following evening. Now his face cleared. 'I was expecting that you might bring soldiers. I am glad there are no redcoats with you.'

Lang shook his hand. 'We were unable to arrive earlier. Now we need to move quickly.' He had a suspicion the delay to his landing had been deliberately caused by Harkness to make it difficult to return to the coast under the cover of darkness.

Puech nodded. 'At this late hour it will mean we certainly have to move very quickly, but it cannot be helped.' He led the men off the sandy beach and inland avoiding the nearby port, which was almost entirely in darkness. Plouagat was less than 20 miles, no great distance inland but even if everything went to plan it could be dawn before they were able to return to the rendezvous point. That fact also had Crabtree worried.

'Sir, forgive me. If this plan goes well the whole countryside will be heaving with French soldiers after the factory and powder mills blow. If we are forced to make slow progress, it could be broad daylight by the time we return and we will be in full sight of the port.'

Lang took his arm and bade him to keep his voice down. 'George, I cannot say I am happy that our departure from the ship was so much delayed that it is now after nine o'clock but we must do the best we can and move swiftly – we need to be there well before one o'clock. That means a fast pace. Do not voice your concerns to the men.'

'Of course not, sir.'

'You have not been in action before, have you?'

'No sir, but I believe I shall acquit myself well enough.'

'I am confident that you will, George, and it pleases me to have you by my side.'

The moon cleared the clouds and the march inland was made quite easily. At fifteen minutes before one o'clock they had reached the manor house just west of the small town. There were high walls at the front of the house but to the rear the grounds were open except for a ten-foot fence of chestnut palings that ringed the various outbuildings.

Lang whispered to Crabtree. 'Take Wells and three men with you. Investigate the powder mill and deal with any guards you may find. You can rely on Wells to set the fuses, leave him there with two men and meet me at the hut where the experiments are carried out. I intend first to look at the foundry.'

Lang led his party towards the big house with Puech at his side. There was no sign of a guard until, almost with noticing him, Lang walked past a soldier standing in a recess in the wall, his musket leaning on a nearly wheelbarrow. The man was lighting his stub of a clay pipe from the candle in a lantern. Almost blinded by the light from his candle it was only the scrape of a boot on the pathway that alerted him. Before he could act, Lang smashed the hilt of his hanger against the man's forehead and he fell on his knees and then over on to his side. He was unconscious. Giving orders for him to be gagged and tied, Lang moved nearer the foundry.

Although it was deserted inside, the furnaces were still smouldering and emitting occasional bursts of guttering flames. Red heat and light from the opened doors cast eerie, dancing shadows on the walls. Lang looked around. There were half a dozen squat, wide-mouthed mortars against one wall but the rest of the building appeared to be empty. Perhaps it was the end of the week's production and the cannon had mainly been collected and carried away but that could not be helped.

Lang beckoned to a gunner's mate. 'Wentworth, the furnaces need to be destroyed. We cannot use gunpowder on them, obviously. Get three men and climb to the rafters. Secure four of the kegs on the beams immediately above the furnaces. Then I want you to take the rest, holding just one back and place them at the end of the beams near the wall and set five-minute fuses on them. The idea is to collapse the beams on to the furnaces and the powder in the barrels falling directly on them will be exploded.

'I am going to the experiments hut but I will return before you set off the charges, is that clear?' He handed the remaining keg to one of the men he took with him.

'Aye, aye, sir,' replied Wentworth, gesturing to the other men to get started.

Lang and Puech with two seamen found the 20-foot experiments hut positioned against the east fence of the garden. The door was not locked. As they moved inside Lang heard something creak. He moved to a window and threw back the curtain. A thin, elderly man was struggling to rise from a cot against the wall opposite the window.

Lang brandished a pistol. 'Stay silent and show me empty hands if you want to live!'

The man threw his hands up, seemingly wishing they could touch the high ceiling itself.

'Robinson, gag him and tie him up.'

Lang moved to a table piled with drawings and diagrams. There was an iron-bound box on the table but through laziness or a false sense of security, the key was in the lock. He opened it. There were a dozen notebooks and a sheaf of loose papers all covered with writing and diagrams. He beckoned to Puech. Handing him a canvas bag he removed all the contents of the chest and packed them into the bag. Then he rolled up the plans and other documents on the table and thrust them in with the books.

There were shelves around the walls loaded with glass jars full of what was obviously gunpowder. Each was labelled. The contents of the jars varied in colour and texture. A second table held balances and weights, pipettes, flasks and tubes – all the paraphernalia of a laboratory.

Crabtree entered to report that the powder mill was primed with explosives.

'Very well George, here is a keg of powder. Do the same here and move that prisoner to safety. Set the charge for ten minutes, light the fuse and then get out of here. Return to the powder mill – nine-minute charges lit there and make your way quickly out of the grounds. You must take Father Oscar with you and return to the rendezvous point. Guard him and these documents with your life. You will have fifteen men with you. Wells and I will follow with the rest as soon as we have started the fuses at the foundry.

'If we are separated you will make sure you reach the rendezvous. You will not wait for the rest of us. Is that understood? Good. Now if it is too dangerous for you to join the ship, this is what you must do ...'

Lang and Wells hurried back to the foundry. Wentworth had completed his task. Lang ordered him light the fuses and the party ran back through the grounds. They were in time to see Crabtree's group disappear across a moonlit highway and into scrub-land on the far side.

Behind them there was a series of dull thuds, the echoes

overwhelmed by the ground-heaving thunder of tons of gunpowder exploding in the powder mill. Then there was a lesser series of sharp bangs as the experiment workshop exploded and collapsed in on itself.

Just as the explosions gave way to the determined roar of flames from the powder mill, the charges in the foundry brought down the roof. There was an immediate second quadruple explosion as the furnaces succumbed and then a great shower of burning embers and ashes erupted on to the great house. It took fire in a dozen places and men could be heard screaming as they were trapped in the prison cells.

Closing his ears to that unintended event, Lang led Dick Wells and his small party at a trot towards the woodland to the south-west of the road.

Chapter 31

<u>21st August, 1803</u>

George Crabtree was apprehensive but he was surprised to find that he was not afraid. With Puech crouching beside him they scanned the sea for a sight of *La Trave*. Dawn was breaking and although they had made good time they had arrived and found no boat waiting for them. It seemed for some reason La Trave had left the area.

One of the older hands, a man called Fitch who was a topman from *Prince Rupert*, crawled over to him. 'She ain't there, sir! The ship has sailed away!'

'There must be an explanation, Fitch. We cannot wait here. Mr Lang gave me orders to cover this situation.' He pulled a sheet of paper from his jacket to reveal a hand-drawn map. 'We are here, just north of the port. Along the coast is St Malo. Here, at a place called Dahouët near the town of le Val-André we can contact a fisherman who is one of our people. He will see that we are carried over to Jersey.'

Puech said. 'I should stay here and wait for Lieutenant Lang. All being well we will follow you. If not I will do my best to contact him or at least get information to Jersey as to what has happened to him. Take the documents, Lieutenant, they are too valuable to leave with me.'

They shook hands and Crabtree set off at the head of his men to walk the 25 miles to Dahouët. They would need to hide up during the day but with luck they should reach their goal by the end of the following night.

Puech found his old donkey Maximilien – named after Robespierre – where he had tied him up earlier. He scratched him affectionately behind the ears and climbed on to his back, saying, 'Come along Maxey, we need to get away from here.'

....

Richard Harkness was pleased with himself. At three in the morning there had been an unexpected event that had assisted him in his plan to abandon Lang. As *La Trave* lay anchored on the seaward side of the Ile de la Comtesse, two French 74s and a brig were sighted between the island and the coast. They were moving slowly appearing to be searching the coastline. It was a piece of luck of which Harkness took full advantage.

Ordering silence, Harkness had the best bower anchor cut and the ship allowed to drift out on the tide. Quietly setting sail, *La Trave* moved north-westward to where Harkness believed that *Prince Rupert* and the rest of the ships would be lying in wait for the privateers leaving St Malo if they had not already encountered them.

Shortly after noon topsails were seen on the horizon. An hour later and the lookouts on *La Trave* were able to clearly see *Prince Rupert*, leading a column of ships towards them.

Behind *Prince Rupert* could be seen four smaller ships. *El Corso* and *Modeste* were each side of the rearmost of the four captured privateers. Only one ship had eluded them and scuttled back into St Malo.

Peter Midsummer was furious. Seeing Harkness come on deck, he crossed to the weather side which should have been sacrosanct to the captain's use when present and stood in front of him.

'What will you report to Captain North, sir? We have abandoned the landing party and have no news of the result of their raid.'

Harkness was slightly taken aback. Ever since the explosive meeting the previous day Midsummer had seemed very quiet and withdrawn. He had not shown any signs of discontent but was now openly annoyed.

'You forget yourself, Midsummer! The report I shall make to Sir Michael will be for his ears. Shut your mouth and attend to your duty!'

Midsummer summoned up spirit that he was ashamed to realise had been well hidden these past two years. He said in a tight, low voice, 'Have a care, Captain, do not push me too far, I warn you. I have seen things these past two weeks that I do not care for, sir. There are principles it seems I must place before my own best interests and be assured I have no fear of you.'

Before Harkness could say anything, Midsummer turned on his heel and shouted to the midshipman of the signals, 'Make our number to *Prince Rupert*, Mr Turner. Mr McCall, we will rejoin the squadron.'

Harkness was conflicted. He knew he should crush Midsummer but realised it would not prevent him speaking out if he had the chance. The situation was desperate but there was one last throw. 'You will join me in my cabin, now, Mr Midsummer. Immediately, do you hear?'

He led the way. Midsummer followed him slowly under the eyes of an astonished crew.

As he entered the cabin, Midsummer stopped suddenly. Harkness was facing him with a pistol in each hand.

'Stand fast, you mutinous dog! Sentry! Sentry!'

Everything happened so quickly that the sentry, rushing into the cabin, heard two shots almost as one and narrowly avoided stumbling over the body of the 1st lieutenant.

Harkness was standing with his back against the desk, his face white and a discharged pistol smoking in his hand. Midsummer was lying on the deck, unmoving, his face bloody. A second pistol lay on the deck near the lieutenant's hand.

'My God!' cried Harkness, 'he tried to kill me! I had to shoot him! Is he dead?'

Other men were crowding into the cabin. The senior midshipman, Thomas Roland and the master were at their head. The surgeon pushed his way through them and knelt beside Midsummer. He looked up at Harkness, a thoughtful expression on his face. 'He lives, but I doubt he will last long. You men, carry Mr Midsummer to the orlop. Gently now!'

Harkness desperately wanted to make sure Midsummer was dead but he was hemmed in by concerned warrant officers. Now there were no commissioned officers on the ship apart from Harkness. But the master was a strong, stubborn man who had no liking for the captain. He too had joined the ship as a new arrival with no experience of Harkness and detested him fervently.

Harkness realised that it mattered not if Midsummer was dead or alive. He had bought himself some time in which to make his side of the story heard. There were no witnesses except the sentry and he had only seen what Harkness had meant him to see.

'That's what happened, is it, sir?' said McCall. 'Mr Midsummer produced a pistol, you managed to snatch one from your desk and as he fired at you, you fired back?'

'Yes,' said Harkness grimly. 'If the bastard lives I'll see him shot for this!'

The master held his tongue. There would be an enquiry whether Midsummer lived or not and the awkward question would be why nobody except Harkness had noticed Midsummer carrying a pistol.

He turned and went back to the quarterdeck, pulling the senior midshipman by the sleeve.

'There lies *Prince Rupert,* Mr Roland. You are now second in command of this ship. I would advise you to see that we reach her as quickly as possible. I have to make some arrangements.'

He ran down to the main deck and beckoned to his senior master's mate. John Sheridan was a man who could easily be a lieutenant in a year or two if only he was serving under a decent captain.

'John! When we reach *Prince Rupert,* the captain will repair on board her as soon as Sir Michael signals. I want you to lower the gig on the opposite side of the ship as soon as the barge is away and I want the oars double-banked with the strongest rowers you can find, do you understand?'

Sheridan reached out and shook his hand without a word. He could already hear the barge being swung out over the weather side and started selecting his own men.

Chapter 32

North came to the side to meet Harkness as he climbed on board and extended his hand. Without a word he led him to the cabin, where Harkness laid his journal and logs on the desk. North waved him towards a seat.

'Well, Captain, what news? It is good to see you here so quickly! Well met indeed. I take it the mission was a success?'

Harkness frowned. Much depended on the next few minutes. He had to be very careful how he reported – particularly the attack upon him by Midsummer. He had not gone to the orlop to see him before leaving the ship. The surgeon had assured him that in his opinion Midsummer would die before he regained consciousness.

'I am afraid before I report on the mission I must relate a horrendous incident that occurred less than an hour ago, Sir Michael.'

North listened without interrupting. His eyes opened wide as Harkness described the exchange of shots. 'He fired a pistol at you? My God, sir, this is unbelievable. The man must be out of his mind! There will need to be an enquiry, of course, but from what you tell me Midsummer may already be dead?'

There was a commotion outside the cabin and both men looked up. Lieutenant Richards, who had the watch, entered without being announced. 'Forgive me, Sir Michael, but there is a matter which cannot wait! I believe you must hear this man!' He stood back and North saw the man behind him.

North was gifted with an uncanny ability to remember names and faces of a great number of people he had met over the years. He recognised Andrew McCall, a man who had been a promising master's mate on the *Cambridge* 74, now, as he recalled, master of *La Trave.*

'Mr McCall, come in. What is the meaning of this interruption?'

North frowned as he saw Harkness's reaction. He opened his mouth to say something but choked on his words. Then he seemed to calm himself.

McCall said, 'Sir Michael, this is the first time in all my years at sea that I have wilfully disobeyed orders and deserted my post but I had to come here.' He stabbed a finger towards Harkness. 'I believe Captain Harkness shot Lieutenant Midsummer and then tried to cover it by firing a second shot and throwing the gun on the deck near Mr Midsummer's body.'

Harkness's anger spilled over. 'You fucking liar! How dare you! I am your captain. How dare you say these things?'

North held up a hand. 'This is a serious allegation, McCall. If you have no evidence for it, you are doomed, you realise that?'

'Sir, for three weeks, since I came on board *La Trave*, I have watched Captain Harkness brutalise the crew, victimise any officer that dared to contradict him and then abandon his landing party. Shooting Mr Midsummer was the final straw, Sir Michael. I cannot, I will not keep quiet any longer.'

Lieutenant Birchall had followed Lieutenant Richards into the room.

North looked at the crowd in front of him. 'Mr Richards, return to the deck. Mr Birchall, take that seat over there and make a note of Mr McCall's statement.' He held up his hand again to still Harkness. 'Captain, I have already heard your side of the story. Please have the courtesy to stay silent for the moment. I will have Mr Birchall write down your statement after we have questioned McCall.'

North watched Harkness's face as McCall spoke. The fact that a warrant officer had the temerity to leave his ship without permission and come directly to the squadron commander's cabin, risking his future, was extraordinary but it meant that the man had to be listened to with an open mind. Harkness appeared to have settled into a state of calm. He was seemingly confident that his story would be believed in the face of McCall's challenge. Which of course, North reminded himself, should be the case – the word of a holder of the king's commission should be believed above that of a ship's master.

When McCall had finished, North said, 'Your main reason for challenging Captain Harkness's version is that you, and you say other men on the quarterdeck, did not see that Lieutenant

Midsummer carried a pistol, is that correct?'

McCall did not hesitate. 'No, Sir Michael, that is not all. There is the testimony of Mr Midsummer himself.'

Harkness snorted. 'He's dead or almost so. Even if he lives it is my word against his. I don't know where he got the pistol and I don't care. The fucker fired it at me and I fired back. That's the truth.'

North shook his head. 'All of this is a matter for a board of enquiry ...'

McCall interrupted. 'Sir Michael, as I said, Mr Midsummer gives a different version. It is true he is sorely wounded and may not survive but when I spoke to him before I left *La Trave* he was conscious and I believe his mind was clear enough. He may have been very weak but he said in front of several witnesses, including the surgeon, that Captain Harkness had two pistols in his hands as he entered the cabin and that he shot him. Mr Midsummer said at least three times that he was unarmed and did not fire a gun.'

Harkness growled at him, 'You lie! You all lie, you mutinous dogs! In any case Midsummer could be dead by now. Who will believe you then?'

North said, 'Well, it seems to me that Midsummer should be heard if he is still alive. Mr Birchall, have my barge lowered. We shall go over to *La Trave* and see whether Lieutenant Midsummer lives. Captain Harkness, you will join us. I want to see Midsummer's face when he is confronted by your version of events.'

Harkness still clung to the fact that there were no witnesses. If Midsummer was alive, it would make no difference. Even if a court had doubts, it did not contradict the fact that a crime must have been committed. He was a post captain and if there was doubt, it was almost certain he would benefit.

The sea was rising and it was difficult for the barges of the two ships to reach *La Trave.* As senior officer, North mounted the side of the ship first and removed his hat to the colours. As the last echoes of shrill pipes died away he could see more than two hundred silent, tense men staring back at him. There was a low rumble of discontent and they seemed to move forward a pace or two as one body.

North raised his voice above the rising wind. 'Men of *La Trave*, I would rather we had met in better circumstances and I can only apologise if my presence offends you. I have come personally to investigate certain matters. If there is any among you who wish to speak, please be patient, you will have your chance.'

A lone voice shouted, 'It ain't you, Sir Michael, it's that whoreson Harkness!'

He was violently shushed by his companions. North turned away as if he had not heard the abuse.

The surgeon met him as he reached the orlop deck. In a

lowered voice he said, 'Good afternoon, Sir Michael. I have to report that Mr Midsummer is extremely poorly but he lives. There is a ball lodged in his skull and I am afraid that I do not have the skill to remove it without endangering him further. He is falling in and out of consciousness but at the moment, he is lucid.'

North smiled at him. 'I hope you don't mind my impertinence, Mr Redman, but I have taken the liberty of bringing over my own surgeon to give a second opinion. Normally I would not do this but these are unusual circumstances and whatever occurs may later have to be aired in court. This is Dr Levy. He is also a physician. But perhaps I should speak to Mr Midsummer as soon as possible. Stand with me, gentlemen.'

He leaned over Midsummer, who had been settled on a straw-filled mattress on the surgeon's table, his head cradled between two bloodstained pillows. Midsummer's face was grey and he was sweating heavily. His left eye was closed and his cheek on that side was slack. The surgeon gently wiped away saliva running from the corner of his mouth.

North said, 'I am Captain North, Mr Midsummer, can you hear me?'

Midsummer reached up a weak left hand and touched North's sleeve. His voice was so soft that the men surrounding him had to lean down to catch his whispered words. He spoke slurred words from the right hand side of his mouth

'I cannot see you, sir, there is a wretched grey mist between us.'

'I am sorry but I need to ask a few questions. Can you answer me?'

Midsummer gasped for breath, 'Yes, yes, sir, ask away.'

'Did you carry a pistol into Captain Harkness's cabin?'

'I did not.' He gasped for a moment and then painfully got the words out. 'Two pistols in his hands ... then bang and nothing more.'

'Why did you go to the cabin?'

'He ordered me ... he led the way ... I was slow ... I had no pistol ... no pistol, sir, I swear.'

North moved as if to stand up.

Midsummer gasped again and weakly scrabbled to catch North's wrist, 'Wait, wait ... my coat. In my coat ... for you ... from James.'

North nodded to the surgeon. 'His coat?'

'Here, sir. There is something in the tail-pocket.'

He produced a slim oilskin-covered package and handed it to North who placed it in his own pocket as he stood up.

He spoke to Redman for a few minutes a few yards away while Harkness stood unmoving staring down at Midsummer.

Levy was still kneeling next to him. He had gently removed the bandage and was examining Midsummer's skull.

Redman whispered to North, 'The ball entered the right-hand side of his skull from the side, which seems to show that Mr Midsummer was turned in that direction. His left side is paralysed probably from contact between the ball and the brain. It will be a very difficult operation to remove the ball without killing the patient, sir.'

North replied, 'I believe Dr Levy has the skill and with your able assistance and a blessing from the dear Lord, we may see a happy outcome.'

He shook Redman's hand. 'Mr Redman, Dr Levy – your patient. I will be in the cabin. Let me know immediately there is anything to report, please.'

With Harkness following him and Birchall bringing up the rear, North went to the cabin. Rain was beginning to sheet across the deck and the senior master's mate was giving orders to move as closely to *Prince Rupert* as safety would permit and also to reduce sail. On seeing Harkness abuse was shouted, though it seemed that the men shouting were hiding themselves in the crowd.

North paused and turned to Harkness as they entered the cabin. 'Captain, I want it to be clear to you. I do not sit in judgement on the way you run your ship but I am uneasy about the attitude of your crew. You would do well to stay within my sight while we are here, is that clear?'

Harkness nodded. He was still confident. Nothing Midsummer had said had any strength above his own version. It was still his word against Midsummer's.

North took the seat behind the desk and waved Harkness and Birchall to others. There were two pistols on the desk.

'Are these the weapons in question, Captain Harkness?'

'Yes, Sir Michael.'

North examined them carefully and then put them to one side. He opened the oilskin package. There were two documents folded inside. One was headed 'The Last Will & Testament of James Courtney Lang.' The second document was addressed on the outside to Sir Michael North, Bt., CB, MP. North unfolded it. As he read it he stiffened.

After he had finished he placed it carefully on the desk and stared down at it for the space of a dozen heartbeats. Then he looked up and stared at Harkness.

'This letter, Captain Harkness, is an accusation of your conduct. Mr Lang describes a reign of terror that is scarcely credible even on a ship of war. He accuses you of deliberate persecution of innocent men. *Don't you dare interrupt me!*

'He describes in detail the punishments you have meted out during the past three weeks. That is not my main concern unless it contradicts the entries in the log. He says that you have sent Lieutenant Crabtree to the spar deck on nine evenings with a requirement to select between one and three men – seemingly at random – and have them confined for punishment. If true this is a serious accusation.

'The list also describes the number of lashes ordered for each man. Among these I note two dozen for dumb insolence, *fifty lashes* for failing to salute an officer and a dozen for losing a fid overboard. These are just a few of these punishments. Now, I may have no power to curb the viciousness of your sentences but the Regulations have certainly been contravened. The maximum number of lashes is laid down and cannot be increased except by application to their lordships. Maximums have been exceeded.

'Now let us turn to the events surrounding the landing of Mr Lang and his party on the French coast. He says here that when he pointed out to you the likelihood that he would be unable to complete the mission before daybreak you ignored his suggestion that he conceal his party during that day and have you pick him up the following night. Why did you refuse to consider that suggestion?'

Harkness shrugged. 'It would have meant leaving *La Trave* exposed to passing French warships for 24 hours. In the event it was the presence of two 74s in the vicinity that persuaded me to leave the coast.'

North nodded. 'But in that case why did you not stand out to sea for the whole of today and return tonight? Instead you sailed here to meet the squadron. My orders were that you should join me at the completion of your mission. As it stands we do not know whether the mission succeeded and we have left two lieutenants and a score or more men stranded in enemy territory.'

'I am sure a resourceful man could find a way to steal a boat and make his way to the Channel Islands, Sir Michael. I repeat; I had no alternative. It was my duty to put the safety of the ship first.'

North stared at him. 'Lieutenant Lang is certainly resourceful. What you may not know is that he and I have an excellent knowledge of the coast hereabouts and the identities of French sympathisers, including fishermen and other boat owners. It is possible he will be able to reach one of them but being stranded by you in broad daylight certainly will not help. If our men are still alive and free they face 20 or 30 miles of hostile territory with hundreds of soldiers in pursuit. This may have been avoided if you had accepted Lang's suggestion to land the party earlier.'

'I made my decision based on the circumstances at the time. I was the commanding officer and I was in possession of the facts.'

North hid his anger. 'Well, we shall see if Mr Lang and his men survive and revisit this matter then.'

Harkness relaxed. Much could happen on land and the hue and cry if the foundry had been blown up would be intense. He was startled from his thoughts by North standing abruptly.

'Mr Birchall, have someone check to see if it is possible for our barge to return to *Prince Rupert*, please. Mr Harkness, I am relieving you of command of this ship for your own safety. If I leave you here I invite mutiny. Mr Birchall will take temporary command and I will have officers sent over from the squadron to support him. You will accompany me to *Prince Rupert*.' He picked up the pistols and handed them to Cluney Ryan, who had been standing unnoticed just inside the door all the while.

'Keep these safe, Ryan, and don't let them out of your sight until they are in my chest on *Prince Rupert*. Mr Birchall, you will note carefully that these pistols are a matched pair manufactured by the same gunsmith, Durs Egg of Bond Street, London. Each bears a consecutive serial number. I suspect this will identify the person to whom Mr Egg sold the weapons. Later I want you to investigate the possibility that there are other Durs Egg pistols on board. I am going to see how the surgeons are faring with Mr Midsummer.'

Horrified, Harkness suddenly realised the mistake he had made. He had used two identifiable guns that it would be almost impossible for two officers to possess separately.

Chapter 33

<u>22ⁿᵈ to 23ʳᵈ August, 1803</u>

George Crabtree and his men looked out from a stand of trees overlooking a busy road near the village of Planguenoual a mile inland from the coast. Though their objective was within an hour or so he thought that moving before nightfall would be a mistake. He hoped that Lang would come to the same conclusion, wherever he was.

Although Crabtree could not have known, James Lang, Dickie Wells and the three men with them had been captured near the beach where *La Trave*'s cutter should have been waiting. They had waited and watched as dawn broke. By an unlucky coincidence a platoon of *Guards Chaupêtres* had been searching for deserters in nearby woodland and had come upon the seamen by chance.

The day passed slowly. Crabtree and his men ate the food they had with them and filled their flasks from a tiny stream in the wood. They moved out after dark at nine in the evening. The last ten miles to the small seaside hamlet of Dahouët was completed a little after midnight. Taking one man with him, Crabtree consulted his hand-drawn map and arrived at a small cottage at the top of a sandy beach. There were half a dozen small boats drawn up and in the small inlet between the hamlet and the larger town of La Val-André, several larger vessels swung at anchor.

Tapping quietly on the door to avoid neighbours hearing, but as loudly as he dared, produced no result. The door was not locked, so Crabtree turned the handle and eased himself inside. It was a single-storey cottage with three main rooms, two of which were bedrooms. A hefty man stood in the doorway of one of the bedrooms. He was dressed in a long white nightshirt and had a bell-mouthed blunderbuss in his hands.

Crabtree hissed at him, 'M'sieur Lamourette, I am a British officer, a friend of Mr Gillespie, I need your help.'

Lamourette came forward. He was to some extent used to Englishmen making sudden and unannounced visits to his house and scrutinising the young man's uniform carefully, he asked in English, 'Which ship?'

'*La Trave* – sorry, I know it is a French ship but it was captured in the Baltic recently so you might not know it has been bought in by the Royal Navy.'

'Who is Mr Gillespie?'

'A friend of Sir Michael North.'

Lamourette lowered his weapon. 'That's good enough for me, sir. How can I help you?'

'I have with me fifteen men. We need to be carried to Jersey as soon as possible. We have blown up the foundry and powder mill at Plouagat. Soldiers are searching for us and I have vital information to carry to Sir Michael.'

Lamourette placed the blunderbuss on a table nearby. 'The tide is turning. We will need to get to my boat quickly. I will get dressed straight away. Have your men at the back of the cottage as soon as you can.'

The fishing boat was one of the larger ones anchored in the bay. With trained seamen to help, the sail was up almost as soon as the order was given and the bows of the ship turned towards the sea. With luck they should raise Jersey before dawn.

....

James Lang's wrists were red-raw under the ropes tying them together. He lost his footing again and the open cart thudded over another pot-hole in the road. Dickie Wells used his bulk to cushion Lang's falling body.

'Can you see anything, sir?' he whispered.

'We seem to be near a castle of some sort, not far from the shore. With all these soldiers around us on horses we stand no chance if we run for it.'

The cart stopped moving just then and a bewhiskered corporal leaned from the saddle of his horse and shouted at the prisoners to get down on to the road. The road was wide and led to a large pink-coloured mansion. The entrance was through an archway and two heavy doors set into a crenulated wall. They were hustled along the path and Lang could see wide water-filled ditches to each side – a moat. As the doors opened, they were shoved inside.

A man dressed in civilian clothes stood looking down at them from a mounting block. He was of average height and wore a low-crowned hat over black greasy curls. He removed a foul-smelling pipe from his mouth and used it to point at Lang.

'That one, the officer, bring him to the cellar. Take the others to my cells and make sure of their chains.'

....

It was three in the morning. Michael North was worried but he hid it carefully. His marine captain Lewis Butterworth waited for him to speak.

'Lewis, I want you to take a platoon over to *La Trave* to reinforce her marines and take command of them. I have instructed Mr Birchall to take *La Trave* and lie off Cap Fréhel in case she sees the fishing boat which should be making for Jersey. In case they have already reached St Helier, I am taking the rest of the squadron there where in any case I will leave our prizes for the time being.'

The deck of *Prince Rupert* was full of activity as the boats returned having carried the marines and a lieutenant from each of *El Corso* and *Modeste* to *La Trave*. Sails were set and sheeted home; the bow-waves rose and *Prince Rupert* speeded towards Jersey with the prizes *Modeste* and *El Corso* following her.

In the event *El Corso* signalled that she had a fishing boat off her starboard beam as the three ships came a few miles off Jersey. It took less than 20 minutes for Crabtree and his men to arrive and clamber on to *Prince Rupert*'s deck where North was waiting for them.

'What news of Mr Lang,' said North bluntly.

'He and his men have been captured, Sir Michael. As we shoved off from Dahouët the curé who had assisted us, Father Oscar, arrived and told us that soldiers seized them in the dunes near St Quay-Portrieux and carried them off to the fort at Erquy. Mr Lang entrusted these papers and books to me from the experiment hut.'

'Well, Mr Crabtree, you have acquitted yourself well and I shall make sure that is recognised. Get some rest and something to eat. I will want you to take an active part in rescuing Mr Lang.'

Crabtree felt himself grow an inch or two under such praise. He left to go to *Prince Rupert*'s wardroom hoping he might borrow a clean shirt.

Chapter 34

<u>23rd August, 1803</u>

In the gathering darkness, three cutters and *Prince Rupert*'s barge moved smoothly under muffled oars into the lee of a rocky outcrop in front of the town of Erquy.

Within half an hour a battery overlooking the harbour was overrun by invaders and the occupants suffered the indignity of being stripped of their uniforms and bound and gagged before they were carried out to sea as prisoners of war.

A short distance from the shore the pink-coloured chateau of Bienassis was surrounded on three sides by a moat but entered from an open space and a long drive. It was not easy to approach unobserved but the squad of uniformed artillerymen led by two officers brought the officer of the guard to the ramparts above the gate. To the 'Qui va là?' came a swift response.

'I am Major Ternant. Let us in. I require accommodation for the night!'

The young sous-lieutenant shrugged his shoulders. There were many soldiers on the roads of Brittany, most of them making their way northwards to join the army camped opposite the white cliffs of Dover. It was not unusual that Ternant expected shelter for the night for himself and the 30 men with him. He would have papers with him authorising the billeting so that the fort's books could show rations distributed.

Calling for the doors to be opened, he made his way down to the ground level. By the time he reached the courtyard he could see something was wrong. The artillerymen were standing in a semi-circle facing the inner chateau and the guards who had opened the gate were lying on the ground behind them. The man who called himself Major Ternant had a pistol pointed accurately at Danican's well- stretched waistline.

'No noise, now, lieutenant. I am an officer of the British navy. Hand my people over to me and we will leave without troubling you further.'

Danican replied, 'They are in the civilian prison in the inner chateau. I have no access there.'

North asked, 'Who is in charge there?'

'A commandant of the national prisons department.'

'Then you will send one of your men to fetch him here. If he is warned I shall shoot you and five of your men at random so I suggest you explain that to the man you send.'

The soldier was back in ten minutes and reported that the commandant was on his way but that he was furious about being disturbed.

A few minutes later the door opened again.

Danican could not resist looking over his shoulder. The

commandant had emerged from the inner chateau and left the door open behind him. Two of the artillerymen who had been standing either side of the door moved to block his retreat.

Pastoret's eyes were swinging this way and that trying to make sense of what he saw. He lifted off his hat and scratched at some of the fleas in his thick, black curls.

'What is going on?'

North, who was dressed in the uniform of a major of artillery said, 'Good evening, Commandant. I have come to relieve you of your English prisoners.'

'Who are you?'

'Captain Michael North of His Brittanic Majesty's ship *Prince Rupert.* Now, if you please, you will lead me to where my men are being held.'

Pastoret's mind was working furiously but he knew there was nothing he could do. That idiot Danican had been tricked into admitting the English swine. He nodded and turned towards the building. He had been minded to try to run and slam the door behind him but now he could see two men blocking his path. He was beaten.

Danican said to North, 'Captain, before you go into the inner chateau I should tell you that the prison is nothing to do with me or my men. There are in effect two prisons.' He pointed to a long barracks against the north wall.

'This is where the deserters who are seized by the Chaupêtres are held – our function is to guard them before they are sent on to St Malo. The inner chateau is Pastoret's domain. There are a dozen guards in there. They live in the building and there are another 20 living in the village.'

'And the prisoners?'

'Some are enemies of the state, thieves, swindlers and probably a few murderers but I have no details. The commandant forbids us entry unless he sends for us. I have only been in there twice in the past six months.'

'Why are you telling me this?'

Danican hesitated. 'Things happen in there. There are frequently screams to be heard and there are rumours. Some of the guards who live in the village talk. Not everybody is happy who works there.'

'And you don't want me to think you are associated with these abuses? How is that my men were taken in there rather than left here with you?'

'The officer who captured them seems to believe that Pastoret's methods of questioning might loosen their tongues about the destruction of the factory at Plouagat. He handed them over to Pastoret.'

North sent Crabtree with half of his men to subdue the garrison of twelve men of the outer courtyard in a building which stood against the south wall.

With North and fifteen men immediately at his heels, Pastoret led them to the cellars. As they moved through the chateau, warders were overwhelmed and tied up. The guard outside the door stood up as he saw the commandant. Pastoret snapped, 'Keep calm and open the door, now!'

North pushed Pastoret ahead of him.

He stood rigid for a moment, his mouth open.

James Lang was against one wall stripped to the waist, his hands shackled to rings in the wall above him. His head was lolling to one side and his chest was exensively splattered with blood.

North ran forward. Lang stirred and tried to lift his head. North could see that most of the blood was from a deep slash across his chest but his eyes were surrounded by dark bruises and his lips had been split.

Groggily Lang said, 'Thank God, sir! They have killed Frost and Robinson. Wells and Herman have been dragged off somewhere.'

'Easy, James. I am going to get these chains off you.'

With the help of his men North had Lang out of the irons and lying on a threadbare blanket on the floor. Turning to one of his men, North said, 'Take this miserable scum and have him show you where Wells and Herman have been taken. You, Lieutenant, what is your name?'

'Gaspard Danican, sous-lieutenant, sir. I swear I did not know this was happening. I and my soldiers are not allowed to enter the main house; we are quartered outside.'

North studied him. The young man could not have been more than 20 years old and was clearly terrified but he was inclined to believe him. He turned his head as the sailor returned.

'They are safe, sir, though badly beaten. Apparently Frost and Tom Robinson were hurled down a disused well in the inner courtyard. I am afraid they are both dead.'

North caught the commandant by the throat. 'You will show me this well.'

Pastoret was shaking so much he could hardly put one foot in front of the other. He pointed with a trembling finger but said nothing.

North grabbed him by the shoulder and dragged him to the side of the well. There was no sound from below. One of his men attached a lantern to a line and lowered it down. There were sharp intakes of breath as the broken bodies of the two men were seen tangled together thirty feet down floating in the water. A dozen rats were tearing at the corpses.

Overcome with fury, North literally swung the man off his feet and would have thrown him down into the well but stopped himself just in time.

'No, I have a better idea. Mr Wells, have a couple of men take the commandant to one of his own cells and lock him in.' He turned to his men. 'I know this is a lot to ask of you but I would have our comrades' bodies pulled up so that we can give them a decent funeral at sea.'

Without a word they saluted and went to the task.

The military guard were locked in their barracks, Crabtree had taken it upon himself to release the deserters and they had run out through the gates. Back inside the main prison Dickie Wells had opened one of the cramped cells where a ragged man was half asleep on a bare bench. He had beckoned for the prisoner to come out, thrust Pastoret into the cell and then handed the key to the wide-eyed prisoner who had just been released. Without a word Wells left the cells and returned to the outer courtyard. If the prisoners had been maltreated by Pastoret then no doubt he would soon receive a visit from his released victims.

Only half of North's sailors had been dressed in French uniforms, just enough to fill the front couple of ranks of the four columns as they had marched into the chateau. Carrying Lang and the canvas-wrapped bodies of Frost and Robinson on stretchers, the whole party retreated to the shore. If a larger force met them there would be trouble but they were lucky. The release of the deserters would keep the local soldiery occupied but in any case the journey took less than 20 minutes.

As the marine sentry rang six bells in the morning watch the last of the shore party came up the side of *Prince Rupert* and the boats were hoisted on board.

Dr Levy reported to North that Lieutenant Lang was comfortable and there would be no long-lasting effects. It seemed that despite Harkness's infamy in abandoning his men the operation had been drawn to a successful conclusion. On board *La Trave* Lieutenant Midsummer, recovering from a successful operation by Saul Levy, was weak but slowly improving. Under Lieutenant Birchall's temporary command *La Trave* was a much happier ship.

Chapter 35

23rd to 31st August, 1803

Captain Harkness was confined on the receiving ship *Salvador del Mundi* in Plymouth harbour awaiting trial for attempted murder and North made his way to London to report the result of his mission to the Admiralty and acquaint them with the occurrences on *La Trave*.

Despite the evidence against him Harkness was still convinced that his trial would end in his acquittal and that his actions off Brittany would be accepted as a decision made by a captain based on the situation as he found it. For that offence, at worse he would be reprimanded and perhaps lose his ship. If he went on to the half-pay list it would not be a particular hardship – his family was rich and he would lack nothing. Although he was only 27 he could wait through the years to become a flag officer which was an automatic process and perhaps by that time the events of this summer would be forgotten. Even if he was superannuated as a captain and not placed in the Yellow division, it would be better than prison.

The other charge of attempted murder was more worrying but all was not yet lost. The matter of the pistols might be difficult but all he had to do was to amend his version of events, blaming confusion caused by the horror of the situation. If necessary he would swear that Midsummer ran in and snatched up one of the pistols resting on his desk.

He was held in slightly more comfort than the hundreds of recruits and pressed men on the huge ship. As a captain he had at least the benefit of a screened-off cabin, a gunport for air and light and a shared servant. He had enough money to bribe his gaolers for privileges and to be able to send on shore to the Brown Bear in Chapel Street, which despite its shady reputation had the services of an excellent cook and some decent wine in its cellar.

The officer sent to defend him was Captain the Honourable Thomas Bladen Capel, commander of the frigate *Phoebe*.

Such an officer would be impressive in front of a board of senior officers conscious of the implied favour in which he was held by their lordships but he was his own man and needed to be sure in his mind that Harkness had a strong case.

He had been appointed to defend Harkness vigorously because their lordships wished to avoid a scandal that could rock the nation. The First Lord had no doubt in his mind that Harkness was guilty but it would not be politically expedient to have him condemned unless the result was simply dismissal; being executed was out of the question. Unofficial instructions had been received by Capel to persuade Harkness to plead guilty to neglect of duty to allow the court a way of not having him convicted of attempted murder.

Harkness was uncooperative. He remained convinced that his actions were justified and as for attempted murder, did nobody understand that he was the victim of an attack by

Midsummer – not the other way round.

In the cramped little cabin Capel was forced to sit almost knee to knee with Harkness – a situation he found almost intolerable since apart from the general stench and hell of the receiving ship, Harkness very obviously neglected his ablutions.

'Look here, Harkness, you could be executed for trying to kill Midsummer if the court turns against you. Your defence is flimsy and Captain North's evidence regarding the pistols is going to be almost impossible to deflect. If you plead guilty to abandoning your men on shore we can plead that you had intended to return as soon as you had reported to Captain North. It is a feeble excuse, frankly, but it gives the court a way to avoid having you shot.'

Harkness replied, 'Midsummer did not die. If I am found guilty a prison sentence could be passed and I have the resources to make life in prison comfortable but you don't seem to realise that Midsummer tried to kill *me*! I acted in self-defence and my word as a gentleman and a senior officer will prevail. North is lying about the pistol – Midsummer ran into the cabin like a madman, snatched it up and fired it. It was a stroke of luck that the ball struck one of the cannon and not me.'

'But having fired the gun at you how do you explain firing back at him? He had had his shot and his gun was empty.'

'I fired at almost the same time as he did – I was in fear of my life. As for abandoning my post, I have explained until I am blue in the face that I had no choice. With two 74s between me and the shore, how could I be justified in risking my ship and crew for the sake of a couple of dozen men?'

Capel shook his head and stood up. He turned to leave and then turned back and looked down at Harkness. 'You know, I did not ask to defend you – far from it. In fact I would have probably been overjoyed to prosecute you. I am bound to do my best by you and I will at least display some semblance of enthusiasm when the time comes but believe me, if it goes against you I shall not lose a moment's sleep for the rest of my life.'

Harkness hid his fury. He was realistic enough to realise that if he defended himself his temper would probably get the better of him and he needed Capel. He stood up.

'Look, Capel, in the past few days I have come to accept that perhaps I should have been less rigorous in my attitude to my crew and that perhaps I made a mistake in leaving the French coast when I did. No man is as perfect as he wishes himself to be – especially me – but I have served my country as well and as enthusiastically as I am able and I want nothing more than the chance to do so again.

'I am humble enough to admit that I need your good offices in this matter. I believe my case is strong for acquittal on all of the charges but I will be guided by you. Perhaps an admission of momentary lack of judgement at St Quay-Portrieux?'

Capel spread his hands wide, 'I would suggest you continue to think on those lines, Captain Harkness, but *please* don't insult my intelligence by trying to persuade me that you are a gem in the crown of the Royal Navy. I have said that I will defend you as well as I can.'

....

In Bath Rear Admiral Henry Butler was gloomily examining the lees in the bottom of his claret glass and still smarting over his last interview with the First Lord.

He had taken the trouble to return to London and thinking himself shrewd had decided that he would engineer a chance encounter with Earl St Vincent rather than seek an interview at the Admiralty – he was realistic enough to know that his light did not shine brilliantly in those hallowed halls. The opportunity had arisen when he had pulled a considerable number of strings to get himself invited to Amelia, Lady Castlereagh's, summer ball.

In Kensington on a hot summer evening it was oppressively hot in the ballroom, the myriad beeswax candles illuminating the room gloriously but adding their heat to the press of bodies, many of them unwashed, and it was a relief for Butler to be able to sneak out as he saw the earl leave through the veranda doors to the relative cool of the terrace outside.

'Ah, my lord! This is fortuitous; I had not expected to see you here. May I have a quiet word? It will not take a moment'

The much taller St Vincent looked down at Butler. He disliked a lot of people and particularly disliked Butler. At this moment he was the last person St Vincent would have chosen for company. On the other hand he might as well hear what the little turd had to say and then have the pleasure of telling him to go and jump in the nearest lake.

'Not really the time and place, Butler, but fire away.'

Butler said 'Perhaps a seat overlooking the garden, my lord?'

By no means by coincidence, a footmen well blessed with coin by Butler had followed them out of the ballroom and without appearing to be doing so deliberately, left a tray and glasses and two bottles of port on a table nearby.

Butler poured a glass and placed it in front of St Vincent without looking at him directly.

St Vincent, not in the least fooled by this display, said, 'Well, Butler, what is it? If you want a command you will need to present your request in the regular manner you know.' And I will damned well tell you to go to hell, he thought.

'A command would certainly be appreciated, my lord. I am able and willing to serve again. I understand Nelson's fleet may be augmented, for example. In fact I wanted to ask for a different favour.'

Despite a glowering look from St Vincent, he carried on, 'I am pressed by my family and friends to seek the presidency of the court martial to be held on the actions of Captain Richard Harkness, late of *La Trave*. I am sure that the senior officer at

Plymouth is a particularly busy man at this time and I would be only too happy to take on the responsibility. I assure you I have no bias towards Harkness. Although he has served under me I scarcely know the man. In fact it is to see that justice is done and, frankly, it is an important case.'

St Vincent set down his glass and frowned. It was of little consequence who would preside at the court martial since there would be at least ten or twelve senior officers on the board, all of whom should have independent minds. Because of the way they were chosen, Butler would have little or no say in their selection. There was a chance here that Butler, desperate as he was to avoid superannuation and a sedentary life with his harpy of a wife, would do exactly what he was told.

'Sensitive case, Butler. It needs a steady hand to make sure a storm does not arise. We may be past the time when another Spithead mutiny could happen, though we can never be complacent, but if this case was to go in a certain direction the consequences for the navy and indeed the government could be very nasty.'

Butler smiled, 'Of course I would be open to unofficial advice in this matter.'

St Vincent was silent for a few moments.

'I am minded to grant your wish, Butler, but there are a number of things I want you to think about. I may be living in the unworldly ivory tower in Whitehall but I have ears everywhere. It appears that you and your brother-in-law have set yourself on a course of antagonism towards Captain Sir Michael North over that business with Fryston. I will not tolerate underhand efforts to damage the reputation of officers I hold in high regard, Butler. North is a witness in this case against Harkness and you will curb your animosity towards him, is that clear?'

Butler protested, 'I am sure what you have been told is mistaken, my lord. I have the greatest admiration for Sir Michael – what true sailor would not? I can assure you unequivocally that I have no axe to grind. I will treat him with courtesy and an open mind as I trust I would treat all witnesses of either side.'

St Vincent stood up. 'Be sure that you do, Butler.' Before returning to the ballroom, his evening upset by this little swine, he leaned over the table and, his face a few inches from Butler, he said, 'I want you to know this. I do not like you, sir, not one bit. I believe you are shy in action and a small-minded man who is extremely lucky to have reached your present rank. I do not know how long I will be privileged to hold my office but this is the one and only favour I will ever extend to you. I do not believe you fit to command the Isle of Skye ferry-boat, Butler, and if you fuck up this court martial you will regret my anger for the rest of your miserable, selfish little life.'

He straightened and turned to leave, firing a parting shot. 'Another thing, never dare take advantage of a social situation to press for an interview with me again. Your manners are appalling and add only to my opinion that you are a worthless little worm!'

Now in Bath, Butler trembled when he thought of those last words. But he was much younger than St Vincent and as time passed there would no doubt be a different First Lord. He was not a yellow admiral; he had held command and at present was simply not in employment. He had time to think about the court martial and thought he had a way of diverting North's evidence without obviously appearing to go against St Vincent's wishes. In fact it might achieve exactly the result they both wanted. It was a question of timing.

There was also the question of prosecuting Harkness and in this Butler had a stroke of luck. He knew the prosecuting officer very well and would be able to exercise complete control over him.

Chapter 36

31ˢᵗ August to 7ᵗʰ September, 1803

Mindful that time spent with his family was a precious luxury, North had arranged for his wife and children to travel up to their house in Dulwich and he made his first priority to stop there and be with them until the following day when he would continue to Whitehall.

The garden of the house in Court Lane where Michael and Isobel North had first met was glorious. Thanks in part to gifts of rare plants from their friend George Hibbert and a few visits from the head gardener from Hibbert's Clapham home, it was one of the most sublime gardens in the village.

Isobel had taken the opportunity of returning from Tarring to invite some of the local Dulwich people and close friends from Town that she had known for some time to take tea. The rose-arbour and lawn were set with round tables laden with cakes, pastries and confections. The servants moved amongst the ladies and gentlemen with fresh tea and trays of sweetmeats. The day was sunny and the garden was beautiful.

Michael North had spent little time over the past 25 years dressed in anything but naval uniform and in fact relied on naval tailors and outfitters for his clothes. Isobel had other ideas. She thought it time her husband was dressed as a modern gentleman of means should be. She would not go as far as turning him into an imitation George Brummell, of course, that would have him mutiny for sure. So she had Mr Nayland, tailor and friend of Michael Bryan the art dealer, come to Ashworth Cottage, with tape measure, chalk, cloth samples and pattern book.

Isobel North was certainly not a domineering woman but with the subtlety of her sex was able to suggest things to her husband that he was happy to follow. Therefore it was with pleasure that she saw him emerge from the house handsomely attired in a well-cut dark green tailcoat, white pantaloon trousers and a shirt decorated with excellent lace but by no means unmanly. His cravat neck-cloth was at least the latest in fashion and the collar of his coat was high and stiff. Inwardly, as always, she regarded him as extremely edible.

She noticed the calculation in the interested glances of other women and, confident in her marriage, she was rather flattered by the envy women had for her.

One of her guests was Amelia Castlereagh whose husband was at the far end of the lawn talking to a retired admiral called Lynch, a particular friend of Michael. Isobel knew Amelia as a woman as much in love with her husband as she was with Michael. The Castlereaghs were justly known in society as the happiest of people.

Amelia came over to her and took her hand in hers. 'Isobel, dear, your garden is magnificent and your hospitality handsome but I hope you will sit with me for a moment for I have something to tell you.'

She was wearing a white summer dress decorated with tiny pink roses around the hem and on the puffed sleeves. Like all of the ladies her head was covered against the effects of the sun. She wore a pretty bonnet with a pink ribbon matching her dress.

In the shade of the arbour she removed her hat pin, lifted her hat off and put it on the small table in front of her. She ran her fingers through her hair. Smiling, she selected a delicate iced cake and bit into it.

Isobel laughed as she mumbled something, crumbs spraying from her mouth. She swallowed the cake and laughed with her. 'La, I am such a ninny, Isobel. Robert is always chiding me over my sweet tooth.'

The Castlereaghs had been married for nine years and had no children though Amelia adored other people's children and had spent a happy half hour in the nursery with the North children earlier in the day. She was in her mid-to-late 30s but looked much younger.

'Isobel, you will recall that I had my summer ball last week. With Michael not available and you in Tarring, of course I did not expect you to attend but in a way I wish you had been there. Something happened that may interest you.

'Sally Jersey was in the garden – you know how Sally is – tucked away in the rose garden with an admirer – I don't know which of the legion of ardent followers it was, mind you. Anyway, as she was sitting there she could clearly hear a heated conversation between Earl St Vincent and that dreadful Rear Admiral Butler – Half-pint Harry.

'It seems Butler badly wanted to be president of the court martial of that man Harkness and St Vincent granted it. I thought perhaps Michael would like to know in advance since it is a poorly kept secret that Butler and his wife's brother, Arthur Tennant have become enemies of Michael. I am sure that Butler can cause little harm in the court case but I thought Michael should know.'

Isobel agreed, 'Of course, Emmy, Michael is bound to find out but knowing in advance would be useful, thank you.'

Circumstances meant that North was forced to leave his family three days later and return to Shoreham. At that point there was no official confirmation that Butler would be senior on the court martial but in any case North was sanguine about the situation. It was difficult to see how Butler could turn things towards his own ends.

In Shoreham North found that *La Trave* and *Modeste* had been joined by the 38-gun *Leda* and apart from *El Corso* and the 18-gun *Imogen*, which had arrived the previous evening, the only ships missing were his promised storeship and *Prince Rupert*. *Prince Rupert* with Birchall back on board had been sailed round to the Solent to collect bullocks for the squadron and would return later that afternoon. *Juniper* was hauled up on to the shore and being careened. She had taken one ball below the waterline from the privateer she had tackled and repairs needed to be made.

Waiting in the converted boathouse that North used as his shore headquarters was an old friend, Captain Gustavus Spicker, who had been sent down to take command of *La Trave*. It was a temporary measure while Spicker's next command, the 74-gun *Montagu*, was completing her refit at Chatham. North was pleased that at last *La Trave* would have a commander who could rebuild the crew's confidence and bring her up to standard.

They walked together along the strand talking of old times and relaxed in each other's company. Although older than North, Spicker was some months junior in the rank of captain and owed his epaulettes to North, a man he had come to regard as the best of friends. Nelson may have his band of brothers and deservedly so but in the few short years that North had been a captain, many were the officers who counted themselves lucky to be one of the Tiger's followers.

The following day *Prince Rupert* eased herself from the estuary of the Beaulieu River with *La Trave*, *Modeste* and *Leda* in her wake. With *Imogen* ranging ahead, they set off to harass the shipping in Quiberon Bay.

···

Henry Butler had no say over the composition of the court martial. It was to be held on board the *Dreadnought* 98 in Plymouth harbour, and the custom was that the board would be constituted from senior officers in port at the time. The senior admiral being excused through the appointment of

Butler, he would at least send his fleet captain – another rear admiral – to be his eyes and ears. Admiral Cornwallis had recently shifted his flag from *Dreadnought* to the 112-gun *Ville de Paris* and in any case was more eager to join his fleet in the Channel than preside over the court martial of a man he had no time for and wished to perdition. He used privilege of rank to ensure that his man was on the board.

There were two dozen ships of the line and scores of frigates and other rated ships from which captains could be selected. The arrangement to ensure impartiality as far as possible was that the Plymouth Commissioner would sift through to make sure that a ship was bound to be in port for at least a week when the court martial began, then put the names of the captains or rear admirals in a hat and pull out the first eighteen at random. From that number it was believed that twelve or more officers would sit on the board.

Butler would only be given the list the day before the trial and although he had the right to reject any name it would have to be grounded on good reasons that would be open to scrutiny at a later date. He had been able, by some difficult interference, to ensure that the 74-gun *Audacious*, captained by his friend Inigo Pomeroy, would be delayed in her preparations to sail to join Admiral Rainier in the Indian Ocean. This would mean there was a strong chance that Pomeroy, a man of forceful and persuasive capabilities, would be a name that went into the hat.

Off the coast of France North scanned the horizon, the size of the ships much clearer than seeing them from the deck. *Prince Rupert* was sailing towards Ushant in a mild swell but the distant coast was clear to see apart from a slight heat haze on the land itself. He patted his lookout on the shoulder. 'Well done, Horrocks, a double tot for you this evening!'

He climbed down the shrouds to the deck, his mind filled with calculations. The ships that were making their way towards the safety of Lorient must be French or just possibly, Spanish, there being no reason why the warships of any other country would be heading there. The problem was getting near enough to them to engage them in battle before they reached safety. The old ruse of flying French flags might just work once more; at least it was worth a try.

He reached the quarterdeck. Lieutenant Birchall had the short, sometimes reckless Captain George Norris of the frigate *Leda* beside him.

'George. I want you, *Modeste* and *La Trave* to enact a little play for our enemies. I will have Gustavus Spicker and Will Pyecroft join us then I will explain further.'

Twenty minutes later all four captains were together in the cabin along with Commander Joseph Price of *Imogen.* North passed around glasses of wine and explained his plan. Spicker, Pyecroft and Norris were chuckling together half an hour later as they crossed the deck to return to their launches.

The enemy ships could be seen to be two 74s and three frigates. One of the frigates appeared to be larger than the other two. They were off the eastern end of Belle Île and the Pointe de Kerdonia. The prevailing winds were usually from the west, pinning the French in their harbours but today the wind was from the south-east. This meant that inbound ships had to tack across the wide passage between the Pointe and the tiny Île des Chevaux.

Prince Rupert's course was north by west and North's aim was to clear the western side of Belle Isle to round the northernmost end, the Pointe des Poulains near Sauzon and then swing east. She was preceded by *Imogen* who was a much faster sailor.

Meanwhile *La Trave* had set full sail and passing south-east of the island, was following the French ships towards Quiberon. More slowly *Leda* and *Modeste* were following her at a distance of three or four cables, running almost side by side.

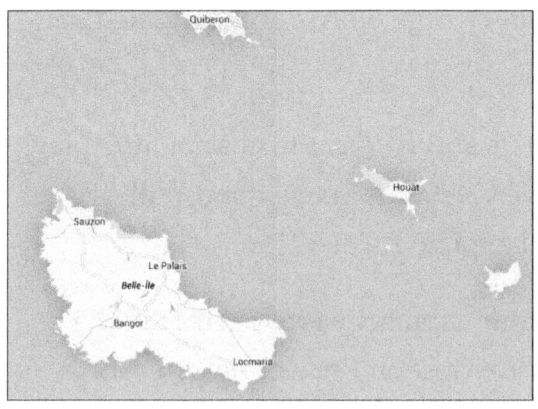

An hour later the French ships' course had altered to north by north-east and the western end of the Île d'Houat lay on their starboard beam. Behind the French ships and just in sight was *La Trave*.

La Trave began firing her bow-chasers to attract the French squadron's attention. Could the fools not see that she was being chased by two British frigates?

After some hesitation, the leading 74 came about and the rest of the French ships followed her. They were now heading back, close to the south-west shore of Île d'Houat. One of the 74s, slower in her turn, was about half a mile behind the rearmost frigate and close to the tiny island of Séniz at the north-west end of the larger island.

Meanwhile *Prince Rupert* following *Imogen* was a mere mile and a half west having cleared Belle Île. The trap was set. To the west was *Prince Rupert* and to the south-west *La Trave* was pretending to be in stays. *Leda* and *Modeste* were less than 200 yards behind her. There was a gasp of annoyance on *Dragon*'s quarterdeck as British colours erupted on all three frigates.

By the time the French commodore realised that he had three British frigates in front of him and a 74 to his starboard, with a sloop hovering near her, it was too late to retreat.

Commodore Henri-René-Paul Défourneaux shrugged his shoulders. His two 74s faced one of the same strength. He had the same number of frigates as the enemy but one, *Arianne*, had 44 guns and the other two, *Pique* and *Immortalité*, each carried 38 guns.

He turned his ship *Dragon* westwards towards the British 74, signalling to *Ville de Caen* to make more sail and join him. He gave orders to slow the ship a little so that *Ville de Caen* could catch up. The problem was that while *Dragon* was well away from land by now and had the wind, *Ville de Caen* was still close to Île d'Houat and the land was shielding her from the same wind. No matter how loudly her captain shouted at his men, it was only by keeping all his sail aloft that she gradually closed the distance of well over two-thirds of a mile.

Prince Rupert, her master taking full advantage of the northward tack, had the ship so well positioned with the wind on her starboard quarter that the gap closed quickly and North chanced a shot with three of his forward starboard guns on each gun deck. They fell short but close enough to have men on *Dragon*'s forecastle ducking out of the way.

Ten minutes more and *Prince Rupert* had furled her mainsails and turned broadside on to await *Dragon*. Défourneaux, in his agitated state, had to be reminded by his flag captain to have his own mainsails brailed up just at the moment when *Prince Rupert* sent a rolling broadside into her bowels. The main foresail caught fire as it was half furled. Men were panicking but the pumps and fire-hoses were in action and it seemed that the ship was safe even if the whole foremast canvas was in danger of being consumed. All was chaos. The gun crews, with little direction from their officers, whose attention was fixed on the dangerous conflagration, fired off their guns raggedly and reloaded them in a complete state of confusion.

Prince Rupert wasted no time. She was close enough that her second broadside, loaded with canister, swept *Dragon*'s decks with murderous efficiency. Her quarterdeck carronades demolished much of *Dragon*'s poop and quarterdeck and with an ear-splitting, ripping sound the mizzenmast came apart and, like a forest tree under the axe, fell slowly over the larboard rail.

North ordered *Prince Rupert* to steer away from *Dragon* and towards *Ville de Caen,* which was managing to come much closer.

He looked along his main deck. There was damage and he could see wounded men being carried below but his masts and yards were undamaged except for some severed sheets and shrouds. He shouted to Lieutenant Lang, barely recovered from being tortured but insistent on taking his place with the guns.

'Mr Lang, my compliments, have the larboard guns loaded with ball, double shotted. I intend to close with the other 74 and present her my larboard side. We will give her two broadsides and then try to take her stern!'

He turned to his 1st lieutenant. 'Mr Birchall. My plan is to try to damage both 74s sufficiently to allow us to avoid them joining together and having us between two fires. Have our gunners aim for masts and rudder. For once we will imitate the French!'

Birchall was smiling widely, ignoring a deep cut on his left forearm from a flying fragment of marline spike. 'Hot work, sir! But good old *Prince Rupert* is not shy, sir, no, she is not! Men! Three cheers for the ship and one more for her captain!'

North had time to look south towards the frigates. Two of

them were running side by side before the wind exchanging fire as they ran. Closer was a great pall of smoke and he could just see the other four frigates in a sinister symmetry. Each ship was circling slowly in step; their sides seemed aflame with their guns. None seemed to be yielding an inch.

The roar of the cheers from *Prince Rupert* could be heard as *Ville de Caen* waited to see which way the English ship would approach her. Technically the French had the advantage of the wind but a skilful opponent could use the wind to slow his own forward movement and swing either to starboard or port.

Capitaine de Vaisseau Marcel-Conrad Ligou was no coward and his ship was acknowledged to be better than most but he was a little unnerved by the efficient way the enemy 74 had almost crippled *Dragon*. He had expected the British captain to follow up his advantage and go in for the kill but putting himself in his opponent's shoes he conceded that it would have been unwise to board *Dragon* with an undamaged ship of equal power within half a mile.

He could see men on *Dragon* struggling to cut away the fallen mizzenmast and the fire on the foremast had broken out again. Now the flames were so high above the deck that the pumps could barely be forced to send water to quench them. He could not rely on *Dragon* to rejoin the battle for a long time.

On *Prince Rupert* the 3rd lieutenant reported that one man was dead and that seven wounded men were being treated by the surgeon. The carpenter pronounced his satisfaction that the hull was intact and the bosun advised that he would have the rigging repaired with five minutes or so.

North left the quarterdeck to go forward and encourage the men. He looked hard at Lieutenant Lang before he gave him leave to stay at his post. 'Now remember, James, if we board the enemy I forbid you to leave this ship. We did not go to all that trouble to rescue you and then see you collapse in battle. Do we understand each other?'

'Aye, aye, sir.'

North patted his shoulder and moved on. He had reached the mainmast when he stopped and looked at the second 74 again. He shook his head. It was that same damned 74 that he had now seen twice before, both occasions when picking up Henry Gillespie. The big patch on her foresail was unmistakable. Well this time he would not be running away.

By the time he had returned to the quarterdeck *Ville de Caen* had wasted her first broadside in an attempt to stop the British ship before she could come close. Two balls struck *Prince Rupert* but the remainder were wide of the mark.

One or two minutes in a battle could make all the difference and with *Ville de Caen* still loading, *Prince Rupert* had time to draw nearer and fire off all her own larboard guns in a slow measured series of 37 explosions. She fired at the peak of the uproll and the damage to *Ville de Caen's* sails and rigging was immense. She lost her main topmast and most of her jib. Her mainmast lower spars were shattered.

She slowed and the wind skewed her to larboard. She continued round the compass as it became clear that one of her rudder lines had been cut.

North seized his chance. 'Starboard your helm, quartermaster! She presents us her stern! Mr Lang, Mr Crowe, oblige me by firing every gun that bears into the Frenchman's stern, if you please.'

The continuous, horrendous hammer blows as shot after shot smashed into the stern of the French 74 striking horror and desperation into the hearts of her crew. As balls and chain-shot of unforgiving iron swept the open gun decks from end to end, men fell never to rise again. Perhaps even worse were the poor souls that witnessed but could not feel the moment an arm or a leg, a hand or a foot, was ripped away from their bodies. The loss of consciousness sent them crashing down on to the bloody remains of their shipmates. Carnage upon carnage; then merciful surcease.

In the aftermath of that terrible barrage there was almost silence on both ships as the awful truth of the slaughter spread. The silence was broken by the hateful sounds of wounded and dying men screaming, moaning and strangely, a high-pitched hysterical laugh choked off suddenly. Like a muted chorus could be heard the creak, creak, wash, wash of the ships moving and the waves kissing their sides. The choking stench of burnt powder; eyes filled with tears from the smoke were less than the tears of anguish or tears of relief.

So much was the smoke that darkness was truly upon the waters.

Lieutenant Crowe gasped and fell forward, his hands clutched to his stomach as he belatedly realised that the pain was real and that he had been shot. Eager hands lifted him and carried him below. Michael North watched, transfixed. All the many bloody battles, all the sadness and the triumphs but it never amounted to more than this. Loss upon loss, hearts filled with agony of a missed opportunity to have said goodbye to a friend. No chance to apologise for an ill-considered slight. Never again to raise a glass to a man you had known for what seemed half a lifetime.

There was an almighty crash like thunder as *Prince Rupert*'s larboard stern quarter struck and clove to *Ville de Caen*'s stern.

Then all was fury and thunder again as the battle picked up where it had stopped. Guns blasting, one overturning and trapping the legs of a shrieking powder monkey, a cut brace swinging wild but seemingly with surgical care taking the head of the captain's clerk so neatly that his body, unsure what to do, stood for long seconds before collapsing.

Then the sudden realisation that the guns of neither ship could reach around to damage the other ship and the firing ceased. Men started to steel themselves to be boarded but both crews seemed too exhausted to move.

North looked up. His quarterdeck was now wedged firmly against the enemy's stern and a man was looking down at him from a distance of ten feet, his face bloody and his mouth twisted with rage. North could hardly believe it but he could clearly see the man's left eye. It was hanging on a bloody thread from his eye socket ludicrously staring as it swung back and forth. The man raised a pistol and then seemed to lower it in resignation as he fell forward. His fall was almost graceful until he struck *Prince Rupert's* starboard rail. With a weak cry he fell into the sea leaving a golden epaulette caught in a loose coil of rope as the only evidence of his death.

North shouted for men to hack away the debris holding the ships together; he must get *Prince Rupert* clear. There was the other 74 to face. He ran to the foredeck, leaping over fallen men and broken casks, tubs and guns.

The other 74, the *Dragon*, was under way but she was leaving the fight and nearing the point at the north end of Île d'Houat. She was parallel with the shore and her bows pointed to the small channel between the islet of Séniz and the main island. As he watched he realised just before her captain did that the sunlit water between the islet and the land hid shallows. The tide was almost out. *Dragon* struck. The collision seemed smooth and slow but she was well and truly wedged on the falling tide.

North immediately changed his orders. 'Mr Birchall, bring me back alongside the *Ville de Caen*. I will give her a chance to strike or we shall board her!'

It seemed inevitable that with the extent of her casualties the

French ship could not fight on. Her colours had been cut from her halliard by a ball that had injured her mizzen mast and a new set was half hoisted. As North put his speaking trumpet to his mouth and called across to her to surrender, the hoist fell and her second captain raised his hand in acknowledgement. Her senior captain had been the man whom North had seen, horribly wounded, falling into the sea.

There was barely time for North to assess the situation. He signalled for *Juniper* to close on *Prince Rupert* and ordered her commander to send across 50 men to assist the 50 men and marines from his own ship under Lieutenant Birchall who would secure the prize. She was barely able to set enough sail to make her way out to sea but North had the satisfaction of seeing *Ville de Caen* turning before the wind and slowly making her way west as he had his ship brought about and towards the still fighting frigates.

The two frigates that had left the area were now out to the west beyond Belle Île and out of sight.

The symmetry of the dance had been broken. One frigate, the French 44, was listing badly, her colours down and *Leda* alongside her. The other French frigate was making off towards the safety of Quiberon Bay and *Modeste*, her masts at crazy angles, was sitting a few hundred yards south of *Leda*.

North was conscious that with *Juniper* excepted, all of his ships in sight had significant damage and it was essential that they should leave the area in advance of a counter-attack from

Lorient. Even if it meant abandoning *Leda*'s prize they had to get out to sea. Closer to Plymouth it was possible they could contact the Channel fleet and gain some protection.

As he came closer he saw that in fact *Leda* was less damaged than he thought. She was remarkably unscathed except for some damage to her starboard side and jib. Hailing her, he got the response that Norris would have her prize in tow in early course and could be out of the area as soon as he could.

'I wish you joy of your prize, Captain Norris! Make your way towing her south of Belle Île. I am going to take *Modeste* in tow if necessary and we shall rendezvous two leagues west of the island. I am anxious to find *La Trave*.'

Modeste had steerage but could only raise her spanker and foremast mainsail. She did not need to be towed but her progress would be slow. North shepherded her and they set off towards the setting sun.

He had dreaded going to the orlop. He knew there were at least 30 dead and many wounded. The surgeon, his assistant and helpers were standing in a field of bloody bodies. Men who had cheerfully saluted North less than an hour and a half ago were now lying on the blood-covered spare sail raising weak knuckles to their foreheads as he bent to speak to them.

One of his new midshipmen, a red-haired lad of 15, tried to rise but fell back with a sigh and died as North reached out to support him.

Saul Levy, who had served North in many a bloody battle, wiped the back of his hand over a sweat-drenched brow leaving a swath of blood from his hand reaching up into his sticky blond hair.

'Forty-seven – no, forty-six – wounded, and one more death now,' he pointed to the midshipman. 'Ten I believe I cannot save but the others should live.'

'Thank you, Doctor,' said North. He tried unsuccessfully to thrust down that sense of shame that always rose in his mind at times like this.

The ship was not whole but she was fit to sail. Her guns were reduced by five but if she had to, she could fight. Frantic efforts were being made on her repairs as indeed they were on all the ships.

The answer to *La Trave*'s whereabouts was solved. She was lying 20 miles due west of Belle Île, with the French frigate *Immortalité* 50 yards away, her colours flying under the Union flag. She had struck just half an hour ago when she had sighted the approaching squadron.

Spicker reported that this opponent had fought half-heartedly and had probably surrendered as soon as it seemed he decently could. Spicker seemed annoyed that he had been cheated out of a more significant contest.

North gathered his captains together the following day after breakfast. In the night, despite being slowed by their prizes, they had put 30 miles between themselves and Belle Île. As the watch changed at eight bells, the squadron had turned together on a more north-easterly course towards Plymouth.

On all of the bigger ships men were working hard at repairing damage or jury-rigging masts and yards. *Prince Rupert* was a cable's length from *Ville de Caen*'s larboard side, *La Trave* was towing *Modeste* and *Leda* was a little distance to the west following *Immortalité* which had *Arianne* in tow.

Having been tasked to sit at a distance to see what happened to the stricken *Dragon*, *Juniper* had reported that the 74 was far over on her starboard side. Her guns had been thrown overboard with huge amounts of stores but it seemed her demise was inevitable. So the only ship to escape was the frigate *Pique*.

Pyecroft made the feeble joke that her captain must have left the battle in a fit of pique. He was rewarded by a barrage of ship's biscuits.

North smiled. 'Gentlemen, it was a hard battle but the reward of a 74 and two frigates is a fine achievement, for which I thank you. I cannot be prouder. We should reach Plymouth tomorrow morning with luck and in the meantime, subject to essential requirements, please rest your crews as much as possible.'

At one o'clock in the afternoon, the Channel fleet was sighted in all its splendour. An hour later North was piped aboard the *Ville de Paris* and warmly welcomed by Admiral Cornwallis.

After he had received his report Cornwallis refilled North's glass and set his own down with a frown. 'I shall be honoured to release *Superb* and *Hercules* to provide a stronger escort for your squadron, Sir Michael. They are due to be rotated to Plymouth for supplies for the fleet in any case. However I have some news for you which I am afraid will slightly blunt your splendid victory.'

He went on to explain he had received a message from his fleet captain on shore that Rear Admiral Butler, who had been asked to act as president and convene Harkness's court martial, had started the proceedings the previous afternoon without several witnesses from *La Trave* and *Prince Rupert* being available. It was his opinion that this had been deliberate and intended to weaken the prosecution case.

Of course he had no wish to impose his own views but perhaps Sir Michael would feel it convenient to transfer to his tender, the *Juniper*, and return to Plymouth as swiftly as possible with any other witnesses he thought useful.

North was fuming and Cornwallis could see that it showed. He said, 'I would venture to say that whatever happens Butler will be roasted for this but since a man cannot be tried twice it would be a grave miscarriage of justice if Harkness's trial is not properly conducted.'

North thanked him and immediately left him to return to *Prince Rupert*. Once back on his ship he rattled out a series of orders and men ran and bustled to set things in motion.

At three in the afternoon *Juniper* left her squadron and the Channel fleet away to the south-west and crowded on all the sail she could carry. With North were Lieutenants Birchall, Lang and Crabtree, the master and surgeon of *La Trave* and Cluney Ryan.

Juniper entered Plymouth harbour a few minutes before the end of the second dog watch and by 8.30 that evening North and Birchall were striding along the road towards the commissioner's house.

A hasty conference was held and a little before midnight the visitors retired to *Juniper* for the night. The defending officer, Captain Capel, took breakfast with the commissioner the next morning. Captain Randolph Kitson, the prosecuting officer, was not invited.

Chapter 37

9th to 13th September, 1803

Henry Butler was feeling pleased with himself. The previous evening he had enjoyed the company of several captains whom he had not seen for a few years and who were agog to hear how he was handling the court martial. It did not occur to him that one of his so-called friends might make his way to the commissioner's house after he left the gathering.

A few minutes after 10.30 in the morning he climbed stiffly up the high side of the 98-gun *Dreadnought*, once again admiring her lines and thinking that if the rumours were true and St Vincent was on his way out, it would be wonderful to have command of such a huge ship again.

He acknowledged the whistles and salutes and went straight to the great cabin to a glass of Madeira that his steward would have made sure was ready for him. He sat back in the heavy chair and beamed a smile at the empty cabin. A few minutes later people began to drift in. There was another rear admiral – Cornwallis's creature – and eleven captains, Pomeroy amongst them. The seats set up for visitors were packed with local dignitaries and rich people from as far away as Bath, eager to enjoy the spectacle.

He believed that he could counter any criticism to rush the court martial into being before North and the other witnesses could return by pointing out that St Vincent had specifically told him the Admiralty wanted the matter solved without scandal. In his view that meant expeditiously.

Butler banged the gavel and shouted for quiet. Harkness was escorted into the cabin by his defending officer and *Dreadnought*'s senior lieutenant.

Captain Capel for the defence did not look as pleased as he should have been to defend his fellow captain. Like many present he was sure Butler had rigged the court martial so that Captain North and officers of *La Trave* would not be available but despite being the defending officer he had no difficulty hoping this strategy would backfire. In a few minutes, perhaps it would.

The Advocate General read out the charges, Harkness pleaded not guilty and then the members of the Board were sworn. The people watching, particularly the civilians, were greatly impressed by the spectacle. Thirteen formally dressed senior officers including two admirals took the bible in hand and repeated the oath to faithfully try the case.

After the formalities there was a lengthy silence, which was broken by Butler's grating voice, startling the crowd. 'I intend that this case is heard without chatter, fidgeting or disturbance. Any person offending will be taken out of the court! The defendant may be seated. In the absence of Commodore North, Captain Kitson will prosecute. Well, get on with it man!'

Kitson shuffled his papers nervously, he knew only too well

that Butler wanted him to present a weak and unconvincing case. He cleared his throat, Ah, the prisoner…'

Butler crashed the gavel down on the table. 'Don't call him the prisoner, call him the *defendant!*' He glared furiously at Kitson to remind him of the hell he would be in if Harkness was found guilty. Several of his colleagues frowned.

Since Harkness had pleaded not guilty to all charges and so many of the witnesses were absent, the prosecution had to rely on depositions from most of their witnesses except a very frail Lieutenant Midsummer.

Butler believed it was a cunning move to allow Midsummer plenty of time and quite a few breaks to allow him to regain his strength. In this way his evidence was halting and disjointed.

Captain Capel, with no alternative, forcibly put it to Midsummer that he was lying and that he had fired a pistol at Harkness. Midsummer, in a state of collapse in his chair, was almost in tears by the time two of the board members loudly objected to the distress being caused. Capel himself was well aware of the fact that he was being oppressive. In a way it was deliberate on his part to produce sympathy for Midsummer though of course he would never publicly admit it.

The court had adjourned early that day after Harkness's only two witnesses of fact, the marine guard and a seaman called Isaac Temple.

The prosecution got the sentry to admit that he had not witnessed anything except what he saw when he entered the cabin but was shouted down by Butler when he tried to get the sentry to talk about the two pistols. Since Captain Kitson was expecting the fake intervention, he said nothing.

'No evidence produced, Captain Kitson! No pistols. Where are they, that is what I want to know? Been spirited away have they? That is the sort of thing I would expect from the likes of Michael North. Found out he was wrong and buried his mistake!'

One of the captains at his side said loudly, 'Have a care, Admiral, I don't like to hear that sort of talk!'

Butler stared at him, annoyed that he had allowed himself to get carried away. The moment passed and the court was adjourned. When it reconvened, Isaac Temple was called.

Temple would probably swear to anything, such was his loyalty to Harkness. The problem was that he was so stupid that even the dullest member of the board could see the sheer improbability of Temple's insistence that every other witness was lying when they said they had not seen a pistol in Midsummer's hand. When he went on to aver that he had once cleaned Midsummer's guns for him and they were a matched pair of Durs Egg's pistols, the looks of incredulity were such that Capel cut him short and told the court he had no more questions.

Now, as he opened the court again, Butler was still pleased

with himself. Perhaps one or two character witnesses then he could close the case and closet himself with the rest of the board. He was certain that the prosecution had not proved their case beyond doubt whatever the feelings of his fellows were. Not all the depositions had been read out; Butler had found ways to limit those that were since the deponents were not available to be cross-examined and some papers had somehow disappeared.

'Is that the defence case, Captain Capel?'

'It is, sir.'

Butler raised his gavel, his eyes glinting.

In between yesterday's hearing and today's Kitson had learned things that had forced him to change direction in his unquestioning support of Butler. He held up a hand. 'Just a moment, if you please, Admiral. There is more evidence.'

Butler shook his head and smiled widely. 'No, no, Captain Kitson, you have closed your case.'

'With respect, there is legal precedence for hearing relevant testimony if it tends towards justice being served whenever it is brought before the court decides its verdict.'

'That is only true if I permit it!'

'Actually,' said a man a few feet to his right, 'It is the *court* that decides what evidence should be allowed, surely, Mr President.'

Rear Admiral John Holloway had spent four years except during the Peace as assistant port admiral at Portsmouth, where he was greatly admired. In the last few months he had been acting as Admiral Cornwallis's fleet captain and was a close friend of both Cornwallis and Admiral Keith. He was a fair man and not one to be browbeaten by anyone.

'My own view,' he continued, 'is that this is serious case where the truth is so important we should take every opportunity to hear evidence, as long as it is relevant and given in good faith.'

There was a murmured chorus of 'Hear, hear,' along the line of captains.

Captain Capel stood up. 'Admiral, if this new evidence is to be called I believe I have the right to ask for time to consider it or the defence may be unfairly damaged.'

Butler's head was spinning. If he agreed with Capel it meant an adjournment by which time North and his cronies might return. On the other hand it might just benefit Harkness. On balance, however, he thought it best if this whole farce could be wrapped up as quickly as possible. Whatever this new evidence was it could not amount to much with North several hundred miles away and those damned pistols with him. He reminded himself that Kitson was in his pocket and would not rock the boat.

'I think not, Captain Capel. Let's get this out of the way. Very well, Captain Kitson,' said Butler with a theatrical sigh, 'We shall hear your evidence but do not waste our time.'

Kitson had been spoken to forcibly by Capel and, cold sweat running down his back, realised that he would have to be seen to do his job properly and abandon Butler and Harkness to their fate.

'I have a number of witnesses to call but it may assist the court if I advise that the first witness made an early investigation of the incident in Captain Harkness's cabin and his evidence may be sufficient in itself.'

Butler sat up straight in his chair and snapped, 'Who is this person?'

Kitson half-turned to point to the forward end of the cabin. 'I call Captain Sir Michael North at present commanding HMS *Prince Rupert* under Admiralty orders.'

Captain Howlett, the elderly captain of the *Temeraire* 98, at the left end of the table, said to his neighbour, 'I thought they said he was at sea, wasn't he? Solid fellow!'

North came forward, removed his hat and bowed to the court.

'Well, well, take the oath, take the oath,' rumbled Butler. He was aghast at the man's sudden unwelcome arrival. He had trusted men posted all along the shoreline, how could they have missed him? He narrowed his eyes. North looked calm and unhurried. He was just as offensive to his eyes as the day he had made a fool of him in Portsmouth.

Having repeated the advocate general's words North handed back the Bible.

Kitson nodded to him. 'Sir Michael, will you please tell the court how you came to be on board the frigate *La Trave* on the 21st of August this year?'

'I was senior captain in a squadron under Admiralty orders to act against the enemy particularly along the French coast and honoured to command HMS *Prince Rupert*. During the course of the first of our operations I had with me several vessels including the frigate *La Trave*, commanded by Captain Richard Harkness – I identify the defendant.'

He went on to describe in detail how after Harkness had reported the incident he had received further evidence from the master of *La Trave* and had gone over to *La Trave* to interview Lieutenant Midsummer. In the course of investigating the matter he had occasion to examine the two pistols which had been left on the captain's table.

Rear Admiral Holloway interrupted at this point. 'Excuse me, just to be clear, Sir Michael, how did you confirm that these were the exact two pistols?'

'The defendant himself admitted it and the sentry, who had not left the cabin since being called in immediately after hearing the shots, indicated that the pistols were those discharged.'

'That is hearsay evidence, Captain North!' said Butler.

'Well, I assume that the sentry, who has already given evidence, could be recalled?'

'Very well but how do you know he was telling the truth?'

'I do not think he could have deceived me but I did check for myself that both pistols had been recently discharged and nobody on the ship reported that there had been any other shot. I was satisfied that they were the weapons involved and at that point the defendant confirmed this in answer to a direct question.'

He continued by saying that he had ascertained that the two pistols were a pair, made by the same gunmaker, Durs Egg of Bond Street. Since this was not a rare make of guns he had also caused the ship to be searched, particularly Lieutenant Midsummer's cabin, and was satisfied they were the only pistols of that make. He had also caused enquiries to be made at Durs Egg's place of business and was satisfied that these particular pistols had been sold to Captain Harkness three years ago. If necessary evidence could be produced to that effect.

'Could it be,' asked Captain Snow of the *Cambridge*, 'That Lieutenant Midsummer had one of those pistols in his possession, whether legitimately or not?'

'I see no reason to believe that Mr Midsummer would plan so well that he used Captain Harkness's own pistol against him. The summons to the cabin was, I believe, without any previous notice. Furthermore I ascertained by close questioning that nobody had seen a pistol on Mr Midsummer's person and indeed in his hand. I believe it stretches credibility to believe there was any other sequence of events than that described by Mr Midsummer.'

'Which,' said Butler, 'is a matter for the board to decide.'

'Of course, sir, but I am just telling you the view I formed at the time which caused me to have Captain Harkness detained.'

Captain Snow leaned forward, 'You did not accept his word as a post captain?'

'I made no judgement one way or the other. Mr Midsummer was incapacitated and the chances of his absconding were minimal in my view. On the other hand I believed it right to have Captain Harkness detained not least because I had seen for myself that his crew were in a state of serious disharmony with him and he could have been in danger himself.'

Butler folded his arms. 'Is there a history between you and Captain Harkness?'

'None whatsoever. I had never met him before he took command of *La Trave* and I entrusted him with an extremely important mission because I had no reason to believe him less than competent. Any personal views I have were formed after the incident concerned.'

Captain Darnley of the *Pompee* 80 asked, 'Was you aware of any complaints laid against Captain Harkness in respect of oppressive conduct or breach of the rules laid down as to punishment?'

'Except for the complaint of his ship's master that I have alluded to, not at the time I had him detained or before that time. I should place on record that, of course, I examined *La Trave*'s logs and journals the same day.'

Butler leaned back in his chair. He held his hand up to interrupt North before he could say what was in those records. 'Considering for a moment this pair of pistols, can you tell us what happened to them? They have not been entered into evidence and nobody seems to know where they are.'

'With your leave, sir, I have them outside the court in the care of my cox'n. Since I removed them for the cabin of *La Trave* they have been under lock and key in my chest on board *Prince Rupert* until brought here today.'

Butler jerked forward. 'You withheld them from the court. That is a serious matter, North. A matter for which you may find yourself in deep trouble.'

'Forgive me, sir. Realising how crucial the evidence was I fully intended to make sure they were securely held until this trial. As you are aware I was prevented from being here at the beginning of this trial or I would have produced them then. In fact it was only by courtesy of Admiral Cornwallis that I found that the trial was already underway. I came here as speedily as I could and the weapons are here with me. I suggest that there is no damage done to the course of justice but it would have been better, *far better*, if my presence in Plymouth had coincided with the beginning of the trial.'

'You are being dangerously impertinent to the court, Captain!'

North smiled, 'In which case I most humbly apologise for my attitude and for any offence I have given.'

Butler screwed his hands hard together under the table to prevent himself being overwhelmed with rage.

Snow had the bit between his teeth and appeared to be doing the prosecuting officer's job for him. 'What view did you form about the undisputed fact that Harkness left Lieutenants Lang and Crabtree on shore with their men and withdrew *La Trave*?'

North spread his hands, 'My only comment is the same as I made at the time. It seemed to me that Captain Harkness should have stood out to sea until the following evening and then run in again. He chose not to do so. It may well be that there were two 74s in the area but, in my view, a competent captain would have calculated that the French ships would likely be gone within hours and he could have returned.'

Butler shook his head, 'Matter of opinion, ain't it?'

North nodded, 'Sorry, I believe Captain Snow was actually asking my opinion, sir.'

Rear Admiral Holloway turned towards Butler. 'I wonder if

we might clear the court at this point. I anticipate that other witnesses will be called who would not have been available to us if Captain North had not been able to reach Plymouth until after the hearing finished. I have a suggestion that may save time but it should be discussed by the board alone. I further suggest that in the interests of transparency Captains Capel and Kitson should be present.'

Butler agreed reluctantly and the cabin was cleared.

Chapter 38

<u>13th September, 1803</u>

The members of the board helped themselves from the bottles and trays on a side table and gathered on both sides of the bench with Butler at one end.

'Well, Admiral Holloway, what did you want to say?'

'This may be embarrassing for you, Admiral, but I really would like to know why we have been wasting our time listening to the miserable amount of direct evidence brought before us until Captain North managed to get here to intervene? It seems to me that you were overhasty in convening the court martial. You admitted that Captain North was at sea but advised us that his deposition showed that his evidence was minimal. The fact that that deposition is missing meant we trusted your word. It now seems that his evidence and possibly that of others lately arrived is crucial.

'I believe that there was a serious attempt to obfuscate. I do not excuse the prosecuting officer – mark my words, Captain Kitson. Carelessness with paper statements going missing, a light touch in pressing the prosecution case?'

Captain Snow said, 'Did you not serve under Admiral Butler when he was captain of the *Juno* frigate, Mr Kitson?

Kitson's face was flushed. 'I resent the implication, sir. Papers which I believed were in my locked cabinet went missing; I have no idea where and by whom. I did not believe it problematical since witnesses could have given evidence of the contents themselves. It was not my belief that the trial would be held without them being available. I would remind you that it was the president that ruled that a deposition held little value unless the deponent could be cross-examined.'

Snow barked, 'But you did not challenge that nonsense!'

'Nor did you!' shouted Kitson.

'No,' said Snow. 'Like a fool I actually trusted the president to act honourably.'

Butler shouted, 'How dare you!'

Holloway snatched the gavel hammered furiously until the uproar died down. 'Gentlemen! Gentlemen! Enough!'

Darnley said, 'I believe Admiral Holloway is right. This trial is farcical and I for one am far from happy with your conduct, Admiral Butler – or yours, Captain Kitson. On the other hand I believe we have enough evidence now to make a judgement at least on whether Captain Harkness intended to murder Lieutenant Midsummer.'

Captain Capel raised a hand. 'As the defending officer, may I say something?'

Butler, who for the past five minutes had vacillated between exploding with anger or storming out of the cabin, nodded wearily. 'Go on, go on.'

'I was not aware of any of this alleged misconduct but I am bound to say that although I have deep regrets that I ever allowed to get myself involved in this trial I would not want Captain Harkness damned because of the actions of others. That would smack of unfairness, I believe. If the court will allow me I will see Captain Harkness and try to find a way in which justice can be satisfied.'

Snow nodded. 'Always was impressed by that brain of yours, Capel. It is a sound idea. If it can be achieved without too much embarrassment to the service, that would be preferable as long as justice is served. Speak to him, then we can continue this discussion or hear the remaining witnesses.'

....

Harkness was shaking with fury which gave way quickly to fear. Butler had assured him that North would be away at sea for weeks and depositions would disappear. Obviously his sudden return had taken Butler by surprise as much as Harkness but now that North had dropped his bombshells Harkness could see that the fat was well and truly in the fire.

His thoughts were interrupted when the cabin door was opened and Capel walked in.

He began without preamble. 'I don't know why I bother with you, Harkness, but I am going to give you a piece of advice which might just save you from the firing squad and you had better listen hard.

'This whole court martial has been a shambles and your dear

friends Butler and Kitson have just made matters worse for you. The board is teetering on the edge of finding you guilty of attempted murder. Since you have denied this you can't expect any leniency when sentenced. I have pleaded for a last chance to get you to act in at least a slightly honourable way which might make a difference to what happens to you. Do we understand each other?

Harkness sagged, 'All right, all right, what do I do?'

'That is not for me to say but if I was instructed by you that you wish to change your plea to guilty on the attempted murder case I will do my best to plead for your life – that is as far as I will go. Thank your stars that Midsummer lived or there would no hope whatsoever.'

'Yes, all right, I'll plead guilty to that charge but not the charges of oppression and deserting my men in the face of the enemy.'

'I may be able to get them set aside but it may not be the last you hear of them. You may be wise to seek to have the desertion charge adjourned *sine die* since that would certainly result in the firing squad.'

He slammed out of the door.

Forty minutes later the court reconvened and Harkness was brought forward.

'Mr President, I wish to change my plea to guilty on the specific charge of attempting to murder Lieutenant

Midsummer.'

Butler nodded wearily. 'Do you continue to deny the other charges?'

'I do, sir.'

Capel got to his feet and asked that the remaining charges could be adjourned *sine die.*

The court was cleared again and the board deliberated. It took over an hour of very intense debate before they called the court open again.

Harkness was anticipating the sight of his sword on the court table pointed towards him and he sighed deeply.

Butler, defeat clear in his expression, pronounced sentence in a monotone. 'It is the judgement of the officers sent to try you that you spend the next thirty years in a secure civilian prison and that you serve your sentence with hard labour. The other charges against you are adjourned *sine die.* Take him away.'

'Not hard labour, you bastard, you promised me, not hard labour!'

'Take him away!'

Holloway turned to Butler and in a low menacing voice said, 'See your shit of a friend Kitson and tell him that if his resignation from the service does not reach their lordships with one week I will personally destroy him. As for you, you damned scoundrel, take my advice, if you don't want to see the inside of a prison you will keep a very, very low profile and never even think of seeking a command again – not even as a storekeeper on St Helena – is that clear?'

Butler knew that his career was finished even without Holloway's threats and it was that swine North again whom he had to thank. He may well burn his uniforms and drop out of society but he had not finished with Michael North – not by any means.

Chapter 39

27th September to 1st October, 1803

Henry Butler far from being chastened by his near brush with disgrace had come to the conclusion that perhaps retirement was a splendid opportunity to live a more interesting life. Unfortunately things did not seem to be turning out that way.

His wife had tactlessly gone to visit a sister in Dumfries whom she detested almost as much as Butler did, and not even Admiral Baldwin had visited him. At this moment he knew he had lost almost everything worth living for. He would have to face the misery of spending his remaining years shunned by the only community he had ever felt part of – the Royal Navy. Would he and his harridan of a wife have to live in a cocoon of mutual loathing until one of them had the decency to die? There would be scant social life – everybody he knew was aware of his shameful story.

He had returned to London after a week spent being cut in the salons and eating-houses of Bath. On Saturday came the bitter moment when three of the oldest members of White's committee came to him in the smoking room to inform him that his membership would be rescinded unless he resigned of his own free will.

Two days later, being the second Monday of the month, the Lodge of Felicity No. 54 met at Slaughter's coffeehouse in St. Martin's lane. The Tyler of the Lodge stood with his habitual drawn sword at the top of the stairs leading to the lodge room. He stopped Butler from proceeding further.

'Brother, the secretary has asked me to send all the senior brethren down to the back room, there is a committee meeting taking place before the main meeting.'

Butler had a nasty feeling that he knew what was coming. As he entered the small private room at the rear of the coffeehouse he knew his fears were justify. One of the Wardens, Captain Sir Richard Strachan, who at present was commanding the 80-gun *Donegal*, stopped in mid-sentence as all eyes turned to Butler. There was a moment of silence before the Master of the Lodge, Commander David Lynch of the Impressment Service, said, 'Ah, there you are, Brother Butler. Brother Strachan was just informing us concerning the proceedings in Plymouth recently. Why don't you continue, Brother Richard?'

Strachan looked Butler directly in the eye. Butler was well aware that Strachan and North had been close friends when young lieutenants. No doubt revenge was in the air!

'I was just telling the committee that I felt that I believe you made a grave error of judgement in the way in which you conducted the Harkness court martial knowing full well that vital witnesses were unavailable at that time. It seems to me, Harry, that your actions were at the very least deplorable and not those one would expect from a true and proper freemason. I believe that the lodge should record a vote of censure for your un-masonic conduct, and I shall so propose at this afternoon's meeting.'

Butler knew that his face was red with embarrassment but he was at least going to have his say.

'The proceedings of His Majesty's court martial are not a matter that concerns a masonic lodge, brethren. I acted properly and with due consideration as to the exigencies of the service. Despite the scurrilous rumours being spread there has been no suggestion from higher authority that I acted improperly.'

Major Joseph Luck of the 3rd Regiment of Foot, the lodge secretary, shook his head. 'We all have a duty to truth and justice, Brother. My nephew attended the court martial so I do have a first-hand report as to what happened. If it was not for a timely intervention by witnesses you had deliberately sought to exclude, he believes that there would have been a serious miscarriage of justice. That perversion of justice was your doing, of that I am sure.

'Official disapprobation as to your behaviour may not be forthcoming but I, for one, have no wish to sit with you in lodge in a state of disharmony. I would ask you to withdraw from the lodge to consider your position.'

Butler was fuming. 'If you want me out of the lodge you will have to get the lodge to vote on it. I shall, of course, demand the right to defend myself.'

Lynch spread his hands. 'You seem determined to humiliate yourself, brother.'

Butler's temper snapped. 'Lynch! Let me remind you I am a rear admiral and you a mere commander. I hold the highest service rank in the lodge ...'

Major Luck interrupted. 'This is not the Royal Navy, *brother* – this is a masonic lodge that happens to have a predominance of army and navy officers amongst its members. As for your insulting words to Brother Lynch, you would do well to remember rank in the outside world has no significance in freemasonry even as high as royal princes. We exist in a state of harmony and equality as brothers. Brother Lynch is the Worshipful Master of this lodge and will be respected as such in relation to masonic business.'

One of the civilian members, a banker, Gerard Gough, raised a hand and all turned to him, his age and experience having dubbed him father of the lodge.

'Brother Butler is entitled to a full hearing of the lodge membership, he is right about that. However I have to say that if I was you, Butler, I would seek permission to be placed on the country list and avoid the shame of what I believe to be an almost inevitable vote to expel.'

Butler looked around him. Eight men all staring back with obvious contempt.

He nodded, moving his head as if nodding to each man

present. 'So that is what it comes to is it? Mean-minded little turds the lot of you. Do your worst. I will not even lower myself by responding to this persecution.'

He rose and left the room, mustering as much dignity as he could. As he reached the cold air of the street he drew his greatcoat closer around him. As he walked south towards the river to cross to the Surrey shore his anger was so hot that he did not feel the cold at all.

The navy and the country had spurned him, now it was his turn to injure them. There might be virtually no friends he could call upon but he had other means – people he could suborn, people like him tired of this war and who felt betrayed by their own government. There was profit to be made and when he had milked every penny he could out of a corrupt and chaotic system he would show all these swine how to live. Maybe he would move to another country, somewhere in the sun. The south of Portugal would be nice.

Chapter 40

<u>20th October, 1803</u>

Lieutenant Frederick Black took the helm of Cutter no 3 himself. It was a little before midnight. There was no moon and although each star in the black sky seemed enormous, the light the stars added gave little relief from the darkness around the crowded cutter-galley.

The other cutter-galley, commanded by Lieutenant Jan Cornelius, would have been invisible just 30 yards abeam if it were not for her luminous wake.

In a whisper Black ordered the two red sails to be taken in. As she slowed Black signalled with a quick flash from his shielded lantern for Cornelius to copy him. Nine pairs of oars were carefully slid into each boat's muffled rowlocks and with a soft 'give way together,' the galleys continued into the tiny French port.

Black's eyes were sufficiently attuned to the darkness that he could see the outlines of the row of fishing boats that was his destination. The 20 extra men carried on the galley began to stand in a half-crouch.

They stood in a soft rustle of clothing, the only audible sound being that of Midshipman Henderson's hanger sliding from its scabbard. Certainly the noise was minimal but in the careful silence it seemed like thunder. As the oars were lifted and the galley touched the side of the fishing boat at the end of the line the men rose to their full height and stepped up on to the fishing boat's rail.

An elderly mongrel lying on the tiny poop raised itself stiffly and began to growl. A fat chunk of dead rabbit was thrown at his front feet and the hungry animal, whose last meal had been a few meagre scraps of conger eel, slurped and slathered over this gift from heaven then farted and went back to sleep.

Men moved swiftly from one boat to the next until by the time they had reached the middle of the line and met with Cornelius's men, each boat had four men as a crew and the mooring lines of sixteen fishing boats were loosed. Soon red sails were rising on their masts.

The flotilla, shepherded by the cutter-galleys, left the small bay in front of the hamlet of Rostudel, cleared the Cap de la Chèvre and turned west by south-west.

....

Prince Rupert seemed to be swimming smoothly through a ghostly lit sea. It spread in her wake like green fire. It was a common sight in the Bay of Biscay further south but here, just north of Cape Finesterre, it was unusual.

The ship's master was in a reflective mood and James Lang heard him say, 'They that go down to the sea in ships, that do business in the great waters; these see the works of the Lord and his wonders in the deep.'

Lang turned to him a question on his lips that the master answered before he could utter it.

'Psalm 107, verses 23 and 24, sir.'

A voice behind him said, 'Let us not hear the next four verses, then, master – it might provoke the "stormy wind that lifteth up the waves thereof." Mr Lang, oblige me by going forward and checking the selvagee above the larboard shroud on the foremast. The runner tackle and block seems to have become detached from the luff-tackle. The selvagee appears frayed. Have somebody replace it if necessary.'

The master smiled at Lang as he started at the sound of the captain's voice. North had come on to the quarterdeck so quietly neither officer had heard him. Very little escaped his eye and the selvagee had caught it. He came forward to stand alongside the master.

'Mr McCann, it is a warm night and the sea so quiet it lulls men into an attitude of false security. In precisely five minutes I shall shout that a fire has broken out in the gunner's storeroom. I wish to time the men as they go to the pumps. You will of course make sure that no damage is caused by water. The first lieutenant, bosun and gunner are aware this is an exercise but pray do not inform anybody else – particularly the other officers.

'When I announce that the exercise is over, I will immediately go to the cabin. As soon as I am out of sight, you will shout that you see a strange sail that has closed on us while we were distracted by the exercise. Shortly afterwards my steward will inform the officer of the watch that I have had a heart attack and I am unconscious on the floor of the cabin.'

McCann shook his head, grinning widely. 'A hell of an exercise, Sir Michael!'

North smiled back. 'Try this one, Hiram – Job 6, verse 19.'

McCann nodded. 'He shall deliver thee in six troubles; yea, in seven there shall no evil touch thee.'

....

It was a scene of purposeful mayhem for a few minutes but once the pump was in place and hoses run below, the crew were going to their appointed places quickly and efficiently. As a dozen men took hold of the pump handles, the bosun blew his whistle three times and everybody stood motionless despite the huge temptation to pump water on the dreaded fire.

North shouted through a speaking trumpet, 'This was an exercise, men! Not bad except that the fire spread and took hold in the spirit store so no grog until we return to Shoreham.'

The men groaned and laughed as North went aft. A moment after he had disappeared McCann shouted loudly, 'Strange ship off the starboard quarter, sir!'

The first luff immediately yelled out, 'Action stations! To the guns! To the guns! We have been caught napping! Somebody fetch the captain!'

Whistles and shouts, running feet, gun ports crashing open,

rumbling wheels as guns were run out. The gunner, fumbling his keys, managed to get the magazine open and almost forgot to pull on his felt slippers. Then Brigss, the steward, was tugging at the first lieutenant's arm. 'Mr Birchall, sir, the captain has had a heart attack, he is lying on the cabin floor, I can't wake him!'

Birchall shouted, 'Murray, fetch the surgeon for the captain. Mr Lang, go to the cabin and find out Sir Michael's condition, I have the deck.'

The ship was ready for action in 11 minutes despite the sudden change from exercise to supposed real emergency and Lang was sitting opposite North with his head bandaged, both men chuckling and a sharing a bottle of claret. Naylor had again run to the quarterdeck to tell the 1st lieutenant that in his haste Lieutenant Lang had fallen over and knocked himself out, badly cutting his head. The bandage was part of the theatricals, of course.

By this time Birchall was almost openly laughing but of course the exercise was a taste of disaster upon disaster that just possibly could be real.

He shook his head 20 minutes later as he accepted a glass from his captain. 'You nearly had us there, sir, though I submit eleven minutes was respectable?'

'Indeed it was, William. There is of course a serious side to this.'

'Yes, sir, but don't you think the men ought to know that the spirit room was not destroyed?'

Both men laughed heartily.

'Very well, William,' spluttered North, 'And splice the mainbrace! Issue a double tot to each man, if you please, and tell them that I compliment them on their performance.'

The rest of the night passed peacefully but many a man in his hammock waited for the captain's devious mind to spring yet another damned emergency upon them.

The day dawned bright and clear and with every man at the guns; the sight of the French coast two miles off the larboard beam reminding them that all their exertions of the night were worth losing sleep over.

In the cabin, North pushed away the remains of his exceptionally early breakfast and stood up. Briggs came forward with his coat and held it open for him to push his arms into the sleeves. He then gathered up the crockery and carried it from the room. A few minutes later as he returned with another tray containing two large pots of tea and half a dozen cups, he was followed by a group of officers who had been waiting in the lobby. North gestured for them to fill cups and spread a chart on the table. The three senior lieutenants looked over his shoulder and the captain of the *Couronne* stood in front of the table next to the marine captains of both ships.

'After our cutter-galleys join us this evening, here is our destination, gentlemen. The Île de Sein, which lies here, about five miles off the Pointe du Raz. It is a truly hazardous place, with racing currents covering more than 30 miles of treacherous reefs and shallows – called locally the Chaussée de Sein. Only a madman would think of taking a frigate, not to mention a 74, to the island without the most competent of pilots. However the island boasts one peculiarity.

'It is home to less than 150 people, many of them are dedicated wreckers but every one of them rabidly opposed to Bonaparte. This is why one must question the sanity of the French minister of war who decided that since it was a place almost immune from invasion it would make a perfect place to base a squadron of 30 gunboats – chaloupe cannonière – with 60 boat-keepers.

'Each boat is more like a raft and only draws three feet and six inches. They are lugger-rigged and armed with one 24-pounder at the prow, four swivel guns and a 13-inch mortar or 18-pounder carronade on a revolving table at the stern. They have unusually wide gangways which are fortified and built over ammunition cases. They are worked by a crew of thirty men in action but more importantly they can carry up to a hundred and thirty men each.

'Having been built to form part of Boney's invasion force, needless to say these weapons are not particularly effective against a ship of war unless within range. However their lordships believe that a plan exists to have them form part of a smaller invasion force detailed to occupy Jersey and Guernsey. They would be escorted into St Helier and St Peter Port by a number of ships of the line and frigates provided, of course, that our Channel fleet is dealt with or distracted.

'Our task is not just to destroy these gunboats. We will be assisted by some of the islanders and since they will be exposed to retribution, we shall carry them off the island and to Jersey where they will resettle until the end of the war.

'A particularly interesting French general is also on the island at present, ostensibly inspecting the gunboats. His name is Louis-Alexandre Berthier, Boney's minister of war and governor of Neuchatel. In fact it is believed he is there with his brother César to indulge his favourite hobby of falconry. My intention is that we shall invite the general to be our guest and bring him back to England. He is close to Bonaparte and a very gifted chief-of-staff to him. We believe it would be quite a blow for the French to lose their minister of war.'

The meeting went on for another hour and once North was satisfied that all knew the part they had to play, they left for their various posts.

Chapter 41

Couronne was waiting as arranged 20 miles north-north-west of Île de Sein late in the evening. A stubby fishing boat rejoicing in the name *Maris Stella* offloaded four men onto *Couronne* who could have been brothers. All were stocky and dark-haired with sharp blue eyes that missed nothing. They would act as pilots through the shoals and reefs.

As the ships came to a point nine miles due west of Île de Sein the process of transferring the designated invasion force to the 16 fishing boats was completed as six bells of the middle watch announced 3am.

The cutter-galleys would escort the fishing boats through the reefs, with the schooner *Juniper* lying half a mile west of the outer reefs.

Lieutenant Birchall commanded the flotilla from one of the larger fishing boats.

An hour or so before dawn Lieutenant Birchall led 100 marines and 40 seamen on land from the boats. Their landing was in silence and they trudged through the sand, their voices hushed. The sea-front of the low-lying island was deserted. The landing point was on the west side of the island, the main harbour being at the south-east end. From the landing point it was less than 400 yards to the harbour. As they landed a group of around 50 islanders came out to meet them.

Birchall was a few yards ahead of the leading group of marines. As he came in sight of the anchored line of chaloupes, he was struck by the silence. Not even a seabird could be heard. He held up a hand to halt the march. One of the leaders of the local men came to stand next to him.

Birchall whispered, *'Il est très calme. Où sont les bateaux-gardiens?'*

The Frenchman shrugged his shoulders.

Before they could progress any further the Frenchman produced a dagger from his belt and with a quick thrust, sunk it into Birchall's chest. As he collapsed, Birchall could hear a tumultuous blast of gunfire from all sides.

Lieutenant Black was following Birchall a few paces behind alongside a marine lieutenant. He was struck in the face by a musket ball and fell dead without a sound.

The column collapsed in on itself as the local men who had joined them drew pistols and fired into their ranks. Uniformed soldiers were pouring from huts and boats advancing rapidly, firing as they came.

Lieutenant Crabtree, with the afterguard, took in the chaos in front of him and reacted quickly. Running to one side he climbed up a ladder leaning on the side of a round tower. In the half-light before dawn he could clearly see the conflict laid out in front of him. He climbed down quickly and snatched at the coat of the midshipman who was crouching with his men behind a nearby wall.

'Ellis! Get back to the boats, take the afterguard with you and cast off. We must warn the squadron. We have walked into a trap!'

Ellis was 15 years old and though shaking with fear, he was determined to do his duty. 'What will you do, sir?'

'I must join the main party. Go on now, Ellis, I am relying on you! Report to Sir Michael that we are ambushed by at least 200 soldiers. The local men are traitors, it seems.'

Ellis waved over a bosun's mate and told him to select ten men. Then they ran back to the beach where the fishing boats were drawn up under the eye of 20 seamen. As he reached the beach there was a rush of blue-coated enemy soldiers from one side.

'Quickly, men, take two of the boats and push off.' He grabbed one of the older seamen. 'Jones, get a dozen of the men in line and cover the rest of us as we get the boats off the beach, then we will cover you as you join us!'

It was a desperate fight and nine British sailors lay dead amongst half a dozen French bodies as the two boats reached deeper water and moved out of range of the muskets.

....

When Ellis reached *Juniper* he could hardly stammer out his report. Lieutenant Harris, her commander, made a decision. He gave orders for *Juniper* to join *Prince Rupert* as quickly as the wind would take her.

Taking Ellis with him, Harris rushed up the side of *Prince Rupert* and, briefly doffing his hat to the pennant, sprinted to the cabin, to the astonishment of the officer of the watch.

North was at breakfast. He looked up as the sound of raised voices penetrated from the lobby outside. The door burst open and Lieutenant Harris almost fell into the room.

'Sir Michael, my profound apologies but this will not wait. The operation on Île de Sein is betrayed. Our party was set upon by around 150 French soldiers as well as the men we thought were local sympathisers. Lieutenants Birchall and Black may have fallen and Lieutenant Crabtree sent one of his midshipmen back to *Juniper* to report.'

North jumped to his feet, his face set in an expression of anger. He shouted for Lieutenant Lang, who was just a few yards away and hurried to the cabin.

'Mr Lang, I am transferring to *Couronne*. Our landing party has been ambushed. I am going as close as I can to the island and then send in a small party to investigate. If I fail to return you will take *Prince Rupert* to Portsmouth and send word to the Admiralty.'

'You should not go yourself, Sir Michael. Let me go!'

'No, James, it is my responsibility. I am taking the master's charts with me. I believe we can find a channel that will take us in to Sphinx Bay on the west side of the island from where I can land a French speaker to see what we can discover.'

Two hours later in full daylight, *Couronne,* flying French colours, dropped her anchor a hundred yards off the coast of the island and her gig was lowered into the water.

Couronne's captain Luke Webster had protested in vain. The fact was that his French was so rudimentary that North had dismissed the possibility of him going on shore. He had brought with him five of *Prince Rupert*'s crew, all Frenchmen who had been with the ship since December of 1799. They were Royalists and North trusted each one of them implicitly but the situation needed the expert eyes and leadership of a senior officer. Dressed as they were in nondescript seaman's clothing, he took an oar with the rest. The boat was commanded by a 20-year-old midshipman called Ransome, whose mother was French. For all intents and purposes he was in command and would present himself as such.

Three soldiers came down to the beach to watch as the gig landed Ransome, with North standing respectfully behind him.

'What do you want here? Why have you not landed in the harbour?'

Ransome gave him a withering stare, 'What is that to you? Stand to attention when you speak to me!'

The man drew back. The sight of the uniform of a naval *aspirante* had the desired effect.

'Where is the officer in command? I have been sent by my captain to report to him.'

The soldiers led Ransome and North across the island to the harbour. North's eyes scanned every side. As they approached the shore he could see scores of British marines and seamen seated on the ground. Their shoes and boots had been taken from them and there was a ring of more than fifty armed soldiers guarding them.

North, who was following Ransome with a soldier alongside him, muttered, 'where did these English pigs come from, my friend?'

From the side of his mouth, the soldier replied, 'They thought they were going to destroy the gunboats. They got a nasty surprise.'

North whispered, 'Fuck me!'

The soldier chuckled. 'You should have seen their stupid faces – those we didn't shoot, I mean. Our Major and the Englishman were over the moon, I can tell you.'

'Englishman?'

'Fucking little turd, can't stand traitors myself but he certainly cooked their damned goose!'

As they approached a brick-built house on the quayside North was suddenly cautious. The shock of seeing the grey-coated man standing next to the infantry major almost made him cannon into Ransome's back. He was thunderstruck. If the man recognised him, all would be lost.

Ransome turned, 'What's wrong with you, Reubell?'

North murmured in French, 'Sorry, sir, still can't get my land legs, is it all right if I go and sit on that wall?'

Ransome nodded, 'Go on then but don't get into mischief, you damned Gascon!'

Major Jean-Baptiste Amar frowned as the *aspirante* approached. 'Who are you and where did you come from?'

Ransome removed his hat. 'Aspirant Marcel Lindet, of the frigate *Raison,* sir. We were en route for Lisbon with despatches for the ambassador but there is a large fleet of British ships a few miles west so my captain decided to bring the ship into Sphinx Bay until nightfall. He sent me on shore to report to the commanding officer and explain our presence.'

The man standing next to Amar shuffled his feet. Ransome knew that he was an Englishman but there was something else, something familiar about him though since he appeared to be deliberately keeping in the shadow thrown by the building, it was difficult to see his face. It was as the man spoke that Ransome almost jumped – he knew that voice from another time. The man would almost certainly not remember him; Ransome was a child the last time he had been near him.

'Look here, Amar,' said the Englishman, 'I have to be carried to the mainland as soon as possible. You have what you need from me; I am going to my boat.'

As the man turned and started to walk to the quayside Ransome had to resist the almost overwhelming temptation to draw his sword and strike the traitor down.

Amar held his attention, however. 'I am in command here, Lindet, and I thank your captain for keeping me informed. However as you can see I have a large number of prisoners here who will have to be carried over to the mainland this afternoon somehow or other. So, give him my compliments but I am afraid I am too busy to receive him. I would be obliged if he will keep his men on the ship, I don't want anybody wandering around just now.'

'Excuse me, sir,' said Ransome, a sudden inspiration coming to him, 'perhaps we can be of assistance in carrying your prisoners to the mainland. If I can have a local pilot I am sure we can warp the frigate around to the harbour?'

Amar stroked his chin. 'That's not a bad idea. It may take more than one trip though. I have three officers, one of them badly wounded, and 130 men – 18 of them also wounded. They will have to have an escort. Can you carry 280 men in one trip?'

'Well it will only be a short distance and in any case the

English scum can be packed down in the hold with the rest of our rats.'

Amar smiled. 'Join me for a glass of wine while I write a note for your captain. I think I will also tell him what a bright young officer he has!'

North levered himself off the wall and wandered over to a group of soldiers who were sitting at a long table drinking wine.

'Any chance of a wet, mates?'

One of the men shifted over to allow North a space.

'So, what happened with the *rosbifs*?' He asked nodding towards the red-coated marines sitting on the ground.

The man next to him reeked of garlic and sweat. He handed North a wooden cup filled with red wine. 'Thought they were going to burn the barges. We got here first thanks to that Englishman over there. Came over from Ushant and waited for them to land. They say the local people were going to help them but now they are all locked up in the church. They are going to be shot before we leave. Dirty traitors.' He spat on the ground. 'Some of our boys dressed up in civilian clothes and met the English on the beach and brought them here so that we could give them a nice welcome. We killed about thirty of them. We only lost seven – that's not bad.'

North laughed and raised his glass. 'Here's to the army! I bet the rest of the boys on Ushant wish they were here!'

'What boys? We took every man off Ushant. Fuck me, if the British found out they could burn the damned place to the ground! Be a good thing if they did it, if you ask me. It's like they say – end of the bloody world, ain't it?'

Ransome came back and beckoned to North. 'Come on you lazy arsehole! Back to the ship, now!'

North winked at his drinking companion. 'I'll stand you a glass if I see you again, brother.' He slapped the man on the back as he left the table.

As they walked back across the island Ransome repeated what he had said to the major.

North nodded enthusiastically. 'Well done, Ransome! That is a great idea.' He chuckled, 'I don't even mind you calling me a lazy arsehole.'

His face red, Ransome replied. 'The major is sending a local man he trusts to pilot us round to the harbour, sir.'

When they reached *Couronne* North unfolded the note written by the major. He sat with arms folded, thinking for a few minutes, while *Couronne's* officers sat waiting for him to speak.

'Very well, gentlemen. I believe we can do this but it is important that we don't give ourselves away as the prisoners are being loaded. We will not go alongside the quay, pleading nervousness as to the depth of water. The boats will have to come to us. That way there is less chance of an English voice being heard – though you must impress on the men the need for silence.

'All French-speaking men on board will go on shore dressed as warrant officers to organise the boats. As soon as the prisoners are on board you will take particular care to see that the prisoners do not give the game away if they recognise us.'

Webster said, 'Perhaps we can delay things sufficiently until dusk, the darkness may help?'

'Good idea. The French will send a hundred soldiers as an escort. As soon as their officers are on board, they must be taken to the wardroom and supplied with ample hospitality. It is not going to be easy but at the very worst we can always fire a few rounds into the garrison and take our people off by force, but that will be the last resort.'

....

William Birchall's breath was laboured. He looked down at the bloodstained bandages around his chest. By sheer luck the stab wound had missed his heart and the tip of the dagger had broken on his ribs. The ribs were broken and the pain was excruciating – but he was still alive.

The French army surgeon had been the soul of professionalism and Birchall owed his life and that of at least half a dozen of his men to the man's skill.

The doctor leaned over him. 'Lieutenant, we are going to have to move you. There is a frigate in the harbour which will carry you and you men to the mainland. From there you will all be taken to Quimper. I have asked Major Amar for permission to accompany you. Several of your men are in a bad way and I want to see them safely to the military hospital with you.'

'Kind of you, doctor. You are a credit to your profession, sir!'

He was lifted on to a stretcher and carried down to the quay. The sun had almost set and long shadows were thrown by the buildings. The doctor urged the stretcher-bearers to be careful where they trod in the gathering darkness.

The stretcher was lowered into one of the gunboats that had been stripped of everything except oars so that it could carry a hundred prisoners and a score of guards with three stretchers. Three boats from the frigate were plying back and forth loaded with men.

As the stretchers were tied to ropes and carefully lifted to the deck of the frigate, Birchall tried to raise himself – there was something – what was it? Then he found himself looking into the green eyes of his captain, who, with a finger to his lips, said in French to two men nearby, 'Take this officer to my cabin and be careful with him or I will flog you!'

Birchall almost gasped at the effrontery of it. North was actually kidnapping his own people from the French.

It was not until almost ten o'clock that North and Webster went to the wardroom.

Major Amar and his three officers were so filled with wine that they seemed almost cheerful when North dropped his bombshell.

Amar slurred, 'But this ship, she is French! How can this be?'

'Well, major, I will have you dine with me tomorrow and I shall tell you the story of how we came to capture this ship – her name is actually *Couronne*. Like you, she surrendered without a shot. Now, if you will excuse me, I have some boats to burn!'

The whole harbour was soon filled with flaming gunboats, the acrid smoke drifting with the easterly wind across and out to sea. The remaining French infantrymen were rounded up and thrust into the church under lock and key in place of the islanders. Four of the gunboats were spared and had been attached to towing-ropes behind *Couronne* since North never overlooked an opportunity to gather up useful items.

The people of the island were being crammed with as many of their possessions as they could carry on to the 16 fishing boats that had come back to the western shore to carry them to Jersey.

Apparently they had just missed General Berthier and his party who had left the island before dawn.

North raised his glass to the other officers. 'Gentlemen, we have carried the day! Now, we shall return to *Prince Rupert* where we will transfer our prisoners. We will then proceed to Ushant to see what mischief we can perpetrate there! I have saved four of the gunboats, they may prove useful.'

Birchall was lying back on the stern couch. He raised a weak hand. 'Sir Michael ... the traitor ... I recognised him ...'

North walked over and drew the blanket up around him. 'Don't worry, William, I saw him. If he ever returns to England we will deal with him.'

It seemed little could dampen the jubilation and even Birchall was smiling as he fell into an exhausted sleep. He was oblivious to the hefty thumping of the table and laughter as *Couronne* sailed west towards *Prince Rupert*.

Chapter 42

<u>25th October, 1803</u>

Admiral Nelson was laughing so much that tears were rolling down his face. He turned to Captain Joseph Ore Masefield. The two men were taking wine together in Falmouth harbour on the 16-gun brig *Atalante*, where Nelson was visiting his old friend.

Nelson held up the Plymouth newspaper. 'Then after North burns the gunboats he takes *Couronne* to Ushant, burns down the army barracks and several houses in Lampaul, captures fifty sheep and the commandant's pay chest and sails back to England with his rescued men and a hundred prisoners. The islanders and their families are all safely on Jersey and the king is offering each family five acres and a cow.'

Masefield smiled. 'I liked the fact that North released the army doctor and his staff on Ushant to show his appreciation for the way he treated the wounded.'

'Would that I had him serving under me, Joe. On the other hand I doubt I could keep him under control.'

'Too much like you, sir, I would suggest!'

....

There was a score to settle.

The man who had betrayed North's mission had to be found if he had returned to England. He would think himself safe – the only unexpected visitor to Île de Sein while he was there had been the *aspirant* from the French frigate. He had no doubt taken care that none of the English prisoners had seen him close up. Perhaps he thought Birchall might die in Verdun and the rest of the officers stay there for years. All the non-commissioned officers and the men would spend the rest of the war in Givet.

It took North three days in London before he was able to uncover the traitor's lair. It would have taken less time if the man had returned to his normal haunts but he had decided to lodge elsewhere for a few days until he could meet his contacts and make sure nobody suspected him.

Millman Street was a few yards from Lamb's Conduit Street. The man had taken rooms there and was in the habit of walking in the fields at the north end of Lamb's Conduit Street and a few days ago even to shoot snipe there but today he had walked to the nearby Red Lion Square and to the Dolphin tavern. Entering the low-ceilinged inn through the side entrance from the passage, he peered through the gloom and saw his friend seated with his back against the wall so that he could see both doors.

The Frenchman nodded to him. 'Good afternoon. I am sorry we meet in such circumstances. My superiors are demanding an explanation for your failure on Île de Sein. I have, of course, told them that it was not your fault but you do see how it looks, do you not? You went there to see for yourself that the execrable Captain North failed and was captured.

Instead he turned the tables on you.'

'The damned man has the devil's own luck! How was I to know that that fool of a major would be taken in by this conveniently available frigate?'

The Frenchman patted his arm. 'Well my friend, what is it that you say here, no point crying over milk that is spilt? There is something else. You know that the First Consol has decreed that all Englishmen between sixteen and sixty years of age in France when war was declared are to be imprisoned as likely to be military men?'

'Yes, stupid idea if you ask me. Your people will probably be feeding and housing them for years and most of them wouldn't know one end of a pistol from the other.'

'Just so, but there are a few exceptions. For example there is an officer of your own navy, a Rear Admiral Sir Henry Francombe Longley? We believe he is a man of particular value to your Admiralty but we don't know why. We want you to find out why he is so important.'

The man nodded. 'I have some people I can speak to, I will let you know.'

He drained his glass and left the Dolphin to return to his rooms.

Behind him Cluney Ryan detached himself from the shadowed doorway of a boarded-up shop and followed him.

....

North had taken a room at the Boodles Club in Pall Mall. When Ryan reported he pulled on a heavy black cloak and left with him. James Lang was waiting at the front door with a carriage.

The journey to Lamb's Conduit Street that evening took less than half an hour and ordering the carriage to wait, the three men turned the corner to walk through Rugby Street and then arrived outside No. 11 Millman Street. After knocking on the door North stood back in the shadows with Lang and Ryan came forward. A tall woman wearing a black dress came to the door.

Ryan produced a pistol and thrust her back into the hallway followed by Lang and North whose heads were covered by black cloth hoods. Ryan had quickly pulled up a black scarf to cover the lower part of his face. 'Bless all here! Now don't you be afeared, achushla, we just want to visit your lodger.'

She pointed fearfully up the stairs and he nodded. 'Now, you just forget the Fenians came to your house, understood?'

She nodded vigorously, crossed herself and scuttled back to her parlour.

The room they entered was disordered and stank of stale food and split wine. The man who had betrayed his country was sitting in a threadbare armchair, his hands extended to catch the warmth for a meagre brown-coal fire. He started and began to stand up.

The taller of the masked man had a pistol in each hand.

He said, 'Matched pistols. You may remember a similar pair made by Durs Egg of Bond Street. This pair was made for the Duke of Bridgwater by Joseph Manton.'

'Who are you, what do you want with me?'

'A few days ago twenty-nine British sailors were killed and sixteen badly wounded on a small island off Cape Finesterre in France. You betrayed the mission that sent them there and this country. There is only one course to take with a traitor – execution. You may spend a few moments in prayer, if you wish.'

'North, by God, it's you! I swear you are mistaken, I am not a traitor.'

'I was there. You probably did not notice a French seaman who had to sit on a wall because he had not lost his sea-legs. I saw you as clearly as I see you now. On your knees and pray that the Almighty shows mercy on your soul, for I cannot.'

'Damn you! I thought you would do your usual glory-boy thing and land with the raiding party but instead you sent that fool Birchall. That's why I went, so that I could see you dead, you bastard!'

'On your knees!'

'Don't kill me! You can't kill me, you have no right – I must be given a fair trial.'

North shook his head. 'Why waste time and public money? Besides I am doing you a kindness. One ball and it is all over – very quickly. If you hang you could die in agony, kicking and struggling for a long time.'

The traitor began to cry and wail pitifully, but it was of no use.

After North had emptied both pistols into him, James Lang stepped forward and likewise shot him twice. Ryan walked over to him, shot him in the head and turned him over with his foot. He nodded to North.

Rear Admiral Henry Butler would never betray his country again.

Author's note

Although the war at sea consumes most of our attention in the North books we should not forget the war that was being raged on land and also at home in Britain.

Intrigue and betrayal haunted both main combatants. Political assassination and spy rings are not just the product of more modern times. William Wickham, who served as an MP, is equally well known as probably the first great spymaster since Elizabethan times. The three other intelligence people I feature in these books are real-life characters – Michael Bryan the art dealer, George Hibbert the botanist and West India director and slave owner, and the Duke of Bridgwater. As far as I know they were not involved in the clandestine war against the French but with their particular backgrounds they would have been ideally placed.

The Royal Navy in war and peace was often called upon to assist the efforts of the Revenue and the Customs men against smugglers and in fact were often more effective. A few years after the period of this story the Admiralty assigned naval ships to this task regularly.

A captain's daily life was filled with tasks such as overseeing the quality of stores coming on board. The incident of the unserviceable ship's biscuit in this story is based on the true-life experience of Captain – later Admiral – Sir Graham Moore. Likewise the court martial of Lieutenant Fryston of the

Hound sloop actually happened though not in the time-frame of this book and not with my embellishments to his defence.

The Baltic is sometimes downplayed as a theatre of war during the period against the glorious battles in the Atlantic, Carribean and Mediterranean. The two major battles against Denmark were one-sided in the sense the Britain was an aggressor against a nation with whom they were not actually at war. The difficult and often quicksand relationship with Russia meant that trade in the Baltic, which was essential to the British economy, was so threatened that we just as often warred against them as alongside them.

Prussia was militarily a shadow of what she had been under Frederick the Great until the closing years of the war and Austria's army was a disaster almost all the way through the war.

The episodes in this book involving the idea of a squadron in the English Channel raiding the French coast are all fictional but in the war itself this type of operation was regularly undertaken and the officers involved, usually frigate captains, became famous in their time. Edward Pellew, Sidney Smith and Richard Strachan were amongst the most successful.

Always short of ships to make the Carribean secure, even with the rich empire of the east less well protected than it should have been and Canada undervalued, Britain prioritised those theatres of war at sea where she knew she could win with the ships available. The intriguing fact is that despite this focus, the vital commerce of the neglected parts of the world managed to survive.

In the next book North sails through the Straits of Gibraltar to continue to wreak havoc in **North to the Mediterranean Sea.**

Visit us at
https://apianus.wixsite.com/michaeloliverfiction

Made in the USA
Las Vegas, NV
22 December 2020

14664923R00236